THE
TRUANTS

THE
TRUANTS

KATE WEINBERG

G. P. PUTNAM'S SONS
New York

PUTNAM
— EST. 1838 —

G. P. PUTNAM'S SONS
Publishers Since 1838
An imprint of Penguin Random House LLC
penguinrandomhouse.com

Library of Congress Cataloging-in-Publication Data

Names: Weinberg, Kate, author.
Title: The truants / Kate Weinberg.
Description: New York: G. P. Putnam & Sons, 2020.
Identifiers: LCCN 2019021290 | ISBN 9780525541967 (hardcover) |
ISBN 9780525541981 (epub)
Subjects: | GSAFD: Suspense fiction.
Classification: LCC PR6123.E357 T78 2020 | DDC 823/.92--dc23
LC record available at https://lccn.loc.gov/2019021290

Printed in Canada
1   3   5   7   9   10   8   6   4   2

Book design by Nancy Resnick

For Dad, who read to us, night after night

THE
TRUANTS

PROLOGUE

It's hard to say who I fell in love with first. Because it was love, I think you'll agree, when I've finished telling you.

It was Alec I longed to kiss; Alec whose face I studied when no one was looking. As if there was a clue there, in the sharp dip of his upper lip, or the loose comma of hair he tucked behind one ear. Those stories he told us while driving somewhere in his preposterous car; Georgie in the passenger seat, bare feet propped up on the dashboard, one hand chasing shapes out the open window; Nick and me in the back, sharing a bottle of beer, his shoulder warm against mine as we leaned forward to catch every word. Then, later, the four of us lying stretched out under a killing blue sky, far from some lecture hall where we were supposed to be. The scent of damp earth and pine strong in my nostrils. My fingers itching to touch Alec's, a few forbidden inches from mine.

But there was longing, too, in the way I looked at Lorna. An obsessional interest, not just in her mind, which I would readily have swapped for my own, or her voice, low and vibrating at the edges with laughter. But in the form of her, the clothes she wore: long skirts over scuffed cowboy boots and the crumpled blouses that looked like they had been pulled out of the tumble-dryer last moment, so that along with her bare, freckled face she presented the rarest type of beauty, the kind that isn't strained for.

Yes, I coveted her, too, right down to the old-fashioned bicycle she rode about campus, whose basket always held some oddity: a bag of quinces, a staple gun, or a part of a garden hose—objects that always led you, in some obscure way, to want to protect her.

I've virtually all her lectures recorded on my phone. The one I listen to most is the talk she gave before the puppet show. As though buried in those twelve minutes of that gravelly voice is the answer to all the questions that, six years later, still hang over me: If I had listened and watched more carefully, if I had picked up the signs that lay scattered all around, could I have changed the ending?

I can tell you the exact moment in the recording when Lorna walks onstage. There was no heating, I remember—or perhaps it was broken—so everyone was wearing hats and gloves inside and grouching about the cold. I can hear Nick offering me his coat, Georgie noisily opening a bag of sweets. Then about twenty seconds in, the rustling ceases, the silence becomes deeper, more intent. And I know why. We are all watching the figure walk into the spotlight, run a hand through her hair, smile down at us as if she's surprised to find it's a full house.

"We're all here today because of one woman." A pause. She must have raised a copy of the book above her head to show us. "If you haven't read her, then I'd strongly recommend you bugger off now and get warm somewhere else."

An amused hum from us, her audience, a little release of tension, a settling back into seats, into the palm of her hand. *This is the campus star, we're going to get our money's worth.* And then she's off—and this time she strikes a different note. Brisk and purposeful: If you can't keep up with me, then it's not you I'm talking to.

"Who," Lorna asks, her voice suddenly a challenge, "should we call the criminal? The person who commits a crime, or the one who tricks another into doing so? Is it ever valid to take justice into one's own hands in order to prevent other, more dreadful crimes from happening? Could *you*, if the right sort of pressure was applied, kill someone?"

At this point, if I whack up the volume to the point just before the sound quality begins to break, I think I can hear it: Alec's steady breathing beside me. *In, out. In, out.* If I close my eyes, I can feel the pressure of his thigh as he shifts forward in his seat, drawn as we all are to the figure on the stage. Then he leans in to my side, his face a few inches from mine, and whispers something. "Can't hear you," I whisper back. He leans even closer, his warm breath chasing down my back. "I said . . ." And then he must have put his lips right up close to my ear, because the speaker doesn't pick up anything at all.

Lorna's voice continues—I know the words by rote—and yet I don't hear them anymore. Because although I don't remember what it was he said, I am back there—back on those unforgiving seats, amidst the strong smell of eucalyptus as someone nearby sucks a cough sweet, with Alec's smile in the dark and my heart banging with one repeated question—"*Do you feel it, do you feel it?*" And I stay there, well after the applause dies and there is just the scratchy sound of my phone as I fumble to switch it off in my pocket.

Back there, back then—a place I want to be, dancing along a line of heady, taboo possibilities. Rather than here, now, sitting amidst the rubble and debris of the whole awful thing.

I press rewind on the file and start listening again.

CHAPTER 1

Dear Dr. Clay,

Having been ill for most of Freshers' Week, I have only just made it down to the English department to open my mail. I was due to start your course "The Devil Has the Best Lines" next Tuesday, but a note from the administration office informs me that due to "oversubscription" my place has been deferred to "a future date as yet unknown."

I am writing to tell you just how crushed I am by this news. Since I first read your masterpiece The Truants *I have considered your scorching and irreverent commentary as something of a manifesto for life. I applied to this university purely so that I could be taught by you, and on receiving a place immediately requested to study in either of the modules that you offer this term. Since my place in "The Devil Has the Best Lines" was confirmed at the beginning of the summer I have completed the reading list, including a full immersion in the gin-soaked minds of Hunter S. Thompson, Zelda Fitzgerald, and John Cheever.*

I did this mainly in the back room of a pet shop in Reigate where I took a job this summer, cleaning shit out of budgerigar and hamster cages so that I could finance my studies. All of which was made bearable by the idea of being taught by you.

So this news is a blow indeed. Considering we have not yet met I can't understand what I have done . . .

Someone knocked on the door. I ignored it and carried on typing furiously.

> *. . . that makes me suddenly less desirable or eligible than another student . . .*

More knocking.

> *It feels, to paraphrase a famous poem, like someone is treading all over my dreams. I am writing this letter as a last-ditch attempt, an appeal to your humanity . . .*

The door banged open. A blond guy with lazy, knowing eyes in a handsome face. Mark, or maybe Max. Second year. Historian. Let's say Max.

For a moment he stared at me in confusion. Then his gaze moved from where I was sitting cross-legged on the bed and roved suspiciously over the contents of the room: bare, Blu Tack–scarred walls, narrow single bed, small hanging wardrobe, my half-unpacked suitcase.

"Sorry, wrong room." He had already turned to go when he twisted round, hand on the doorframe. "Hey . . . Didn't we meet in the bar last night?"

I nodded, biting back a sarcastic comment. I have lots of very curly, long dark hair, a wide mouth, and quite a slight figure: Boys notice me briefly, I think, then look elsewhere. Max had patently introduced himself—walking toward me, smiling straight into my eyes—in the hope of chatting up Georgie. A moment of deference toward the friend of the target . . . I knew the score. It had already happened a couple of times last night, enough to make me suspect that my new friend was one of those girls that men find irresistible. Something about her almost too-curvy body, her boyishly cropped blond hair, her sloping, sleepy eyes made everyone—even me— think about sex.

"So, Georgie's a good friend of yours?" Max said, sitting down on the end of my bed and pushing back a fringe of newly washed hair.

"Kind of." If it hadn't been for the letter I'd just been writing, I might have been amused by being used so transparently. Tapping out the end of my sentence, I signed off with a digital flourish: *Yours, ever-hopeful, Jessica Walker.*

"You weren't at school together or anything?"

"Why do you ask?"

"Just wondering. Girls are so tight with girls they've met at school. You seemed kind of into each other." He was one of those guys who was a lot less handsome when he smiled. More of a smirk really, showing too many teeth cluttered in his jaw.

"We met last week."

"But you're best friends already." He nodded knowingly. "Do you know where she is? She said she'd come for a coffee with me but I'm sure she said she was in Room 16B. This is 16B, isn't it?"

I nearly laughed. *Thanks for that, Georgie.* "She's gone home for a few days."

"Oh?" He hesitated for a moment. "To see her boyfriend?"

I shrugged. "I haven't checked her schedule."

He raised his hands defensively. "Right." He looked at me again, as if being forced to read instructions on a manual that he'd hoped he could bypass. "Remind me your name?"

I looked at the weak, handsome face, his shirt belted into pressed jeans. Minor public school, I hazarded. Father's a chauvinist. Lazy worldview.

"The answer is, 'I don't know.'"

"You don't know what?"

"I don't know whether Georgie has a boyfriend."

The lobes of his ears went pink, but he managed to pull himself together in time to laugh it off. "I'm sure she has. Just tell her Max stopped by, will you?"

After he left, I reread the email a couple of times, the cursor hovering over the "send" icon. It was a stupid letter, a childish, petulant letter, written on the back of four days of stomach flu and a wobbly trip to the bar that Georgie had talked me into "because there's only so much Ava Gardner you can get away with before you become Howard Hughes." I had written it for myself really, not actually to send. It was only because it was a Sunday and the administration office was closed, leaving me no place to vent my disappointment, that I had even thought of hunting through the university website to get Dr. Lorna Clay's email address. Then I looked over at my copy of *The Truants* alone on the shelf above the built-in desk—its pages so well-thumbed that it wouldn't close properly—and thought, *Fuck it, what have I got to lose?* And with a sudden rush of adrenaline, clicked the mouse.

As soon as I snapped shut my laptop, regret settled over me like an itchy blanket.

And then the itch sank deeper into my bones as I felt myself being dragged backward in time. Back to Boxing Day at home nine months before, with my sister scowling on the sofa as my father made bad jokes about her boyfriend (Dan Pike: plenty more fish in the sea), not understanding that being dumped over Christmas when you're twenty-one doesn't call for a punch line, much less a pun—my dad, who painted fantastical figures in the shed at the end of our garden but left his imagination locked up there, and my older brother, smirking as he stroked the knobby spine of our chocolate Lab, Gladstone, by the fire, and the twins not giving a shit, and my mother not really listening, much less caring, so that in the end I had stood up and walked out.

And the thing I happened to have in my hand as I walked into the kitchen, a book we had been given at Christmas by Uncle Toto, of all people. That feeling when I read the first few pages of *The Truants*, my bum warm against the stove and the smell of mince pies, like hot tar, in the air—a book that should have been cleverly irrelevant at best, a book about some drunk, dead writers. *Literary criticism*—when the hell did that change anyone's life, for God's sake? Except it did, mine. And I knew it would, almost from the first paragraph, because Lorna's voice pulled me in and down, like a riptide carrying you underwater and far out to sea so that when, about page five, I flipped to the author picture on the back and saw her clever, beautiful face and read the sentence about where she taught, I thought: *Here she is at last.* The person who will take me out of this small, airless world before the banality chokes me.

The rooms in Halls all had narrow floor-to-ceiling windows. I stood up to open mine, then remembered you couldn't. To discourage suicides, I thought, looking at the gray paving slabs below.

Under a flat morning sky, a stream of people was walking away from the zigzag-shaped residence halls, across the scrubby grass toward the gray cinder blocks that made up the back of the canteen. Without the glowing prospect of Lorna's teaching, I was confronted by the drab reality of where I would be living for the next three years: a concrete shithole in the middle of flat, windswept Norfolk on what—if you looked at a map—actually was the bulging arse of the United Kingdom.

Worse, I would now be shoved into some other, unknown module, most likely with Dr. Porter, who wore skinny black jeans and one earring and had pegged me as a Lorna groupie when I'd come for my interview. No doubt he would be teaching something pretentious and incomprehensible, like "The Phonetics of Postmodernism" or one of those other courses that made me sympathize for a moment with my mother's views on studying English Lit.

Spots appeared on the window, multiplying rapidly.

It had started to rain.

I waited until I saw Max and his carefully coiffed hair emerge down below and strike off toward the canteen in search of a consolatory bacon-and-egg roll. Then I pulled on some clothes and walked two doors down the corridor. Checking my watch, I knocked loudly and stepped in.

It was dark and slightly stuffy in Georgie's room. She jackknifed up in the bed, one hand pushing her eye mask up into her blond hair and the other pulling out one of her earplugs and scrabbling for the bedside lamp. When she saw it was me, she sagged back against her pillow with a groan.

"Are you fucking *kidding* me?"

"Sorry. But it is midday. And I'm having a crisis."

Georgie pulled out the other earplug. The mask sat across her forehead at a drunken angle, one puffy eye squinting at me. "Oh, hon. Not sick again?"

"Worse," I said. "Heartsick. Been dumped by Lorna."

My first week at college had been a catastrophe in social terms. Barely an hour after my mother had dropped me off with my suitcases, a peck on the cheek, and a brisk look around the room— "Seems clean at least!"—the cramping had begun. Followed by three days of shivering and sweating out a stomach flu in my room, looking glumly through my window at the clump of students that formed and re-formed around the bar, scribbling self-pitying notes in my journal whenever I could summon the energy.

On the third day, temperature still raging, a fuzz at the edges of my vision, I dragged myself down to the introductory English drinks. Which was when Georgie, wearing tight, faded jeans and silver sneakers, her bleached hair cropped high to the hairline on her long, fine neck, had sidled over to me. "Ugly bunch, aren't they, English students?" she muttered, talking out of the side of her mouth like a gangster as the white-haired dean of studies gave a turgid welcome speech. "Can you believe Lorna didn't show at her own party? A living legend, that woman. Rumor has it she's seeing my supervisor, Professor Steadman." Georgie pointed to a tall, bespectacled man with gray hair. "But that *can't* be right, surely . . ." She paused, looking at me more closely. "Hey, do you know your teeth are chattering?"

Next day, to my delight, she turned up at my door with armfuls of chocolates and sweets that she announced, loudly, were "munchies" ("There's a rumor going around that you've been smoking weed in your room all week. This will fan the flames nicely"); two different kinds of prescription painkiller ("Tuck in, plenty more where they came from"); and a magazine jammed full of photos of horsey-looking aristocrats at parties ("Don't knock it. I'm related to half of them and have kissed most of the rest. Look at this guy, Tristan Burton-Hill. He's so posh he can't actually close his mouth . . .").

For the next couple of days, to my surprise, she kept popping by: one day sitting at the end of my bed with a wheel of hard cheese, which she hacked at with a teaspoon until it bent, the next bringing a handful of wildflowers that looked like dirty daisies, which she had picked by the lake on campus. "They're called sneezewort, for your dribbly nose. I went through a stage of pressing wildflowers as a kid. I learned the whole wildflower encyclopedia, which is kind of weird, looking back at it. Amazing what an only child will do to pass the time. Then I got into pottery and made endless shitty bowls. I mean, endless. Got away with about five years of never buying a single Christmas present. Shall I put them in your tooth-mug? How are you feeling today? Still got the shits both ends?"

That was the thing about Georgie. She changed tone so fast that your head whirled. Mostly, she was like a slot machine flashing all its lights in constant jackpot, but there was a kindness there, and in amidst the glib, smart chatter, beguiling glimpses of something more tender.

"Ask to be put in the Christie module with me?" she suggested now, from beneath her crooked eye mask. "Wouldn't that be a laugh?"

Georgie was doing joint honors in Philosophy and English. She claimed the Philosophy part was just to make her "sound more attractive," but I already had a strong sense that, despite her air of careless hedonism, she was also whip-smart, secretly studious, and heavily invested in showing her parents—"neglectful narcissists, the pair of them"—just how fucking clever she was.

I nodded. "I did wonder. But it's bound to be full, too."

The other thing that Lorna was renowned for, apart from the cult status of *The Truants*, was "rescuing" female authors who had been lost or dismissed from the canon as irrelevant. One of these "personal revisionism" courses was on Agatha Christie, about whom, rumor had it, she was now writing a book. When I'd signed up for the modules online I'd looked at Lorna's Christie course, "Murdered by the Campus," with a flicker of longing.

In my early teens, thanks to an old lady I'd visit at an old people's home in Reigate, Stella, I'd read a lot of Agatha Christie out loud. In my later teens, I started reading them for myself—a bit of fun in between more serious books. But although I loved the cat's cradle of the plot, the way the clues and red herrings were stitched together, I knew the characters were thin at best and the themes scant: I couldn't see how even Lorna would make this into an actual undergrad course. So I hadn't hesitated long before clicking on her other module, "The Devil Has the Best Lines."

Georgie was getting out of bed now, pulling off her nightie without embarrassment, fixing the clasp of a bra under her heavy breasts.

"Situation clearly calls for a drink," she said, spinning the bra round and flicking up the arm straps with a practiced movement.

"But the bar isn't open for another four hours."

She glanced out the window. "It's only spitting, really. We could take a bottle down to one of those benches by the lake."

She picked up the tall, thin bottle of Russian vodka from her desk. The label was in Cyrillic, which impressed me.

"Shall we?"

I looked into the bottle's thick, wavy glass. "Got a much better idea actually."

CHAPTER 2

Once you turned right out of Halls, past the canteen, you left all thoughts and memories of green behind.

The center of campus was a dense, gray network of Brutalist structures and pathways. Concrete seemed to wrap itself over the ground, up the walls of the department buildings, shops, library, and even, most days, across the dull pewter skies. "The Bowl" sat in the middle of this, a ring of steps shaped like a squat amphitheater that served as a way station for student traffic (eating, scrolling, flirting) between seminars.

"If it wasn't a Sunday and I wasn't carrying a bottle of vodka, I would say you were taking me to the Ark," said Georgie.

She climbed two steps to avoid a gangly boy with an oversized Adam's apple who was sitting on his own, eating something squishy out of a cling film wrapper. His eyes darted side to side as we passed. *Unlikely pair*, I could imagine him thinking. Pale, slim girl with big hair and loose, scruffy clothes followed by a tall, voluptuous blonde with a tan that spoke of her exotic year off.

"The Ark" was the campus nickname for the vaguely boat-shaped Humanities block, the largest and most imposing of the buildings around the Bowl. To my mind, it looked more like a Soviet battleship, run aground in a sea of cement. The main doors were open. We walked past seminar rooms, doors closed, lights off. At the far end of the corridor a janitor was squeaking his way along

with a mop, trailing the stink of bleach so that the speckled linoleum shone with damp.

"How do you know where we're going anyway?" Georgie said as
we rode up in the lift to the third floor. "You've been holed up in
your room all week."

I took her down the corridor to the security doors at the far end:
NO ACCESS. EMERGENCY EXIT ONLY. Georgie's eyebrows lifted as I
pushed down the double metal bars with a clunk. Narrow stone steps
that smelled of damp and mouse shit took us up another flight.

"Showed up early on interview day. This way," I said, weaving
across a room full of insulation to the door on the far side.

"Let me get this straight," said Georgie, skipping over some
pipes. "You show up at a university that you'd never have stooped
to apply to except for the fact you've fallen in love with a—
mother*fucker* . . ." I turned to see she had tripped and just managed
to save herself from a fall.

"Ouch, you okay?" I asked.

"I'm fine, fine . . . stubbed toe."

"Never understood that term," I remarked. Then, somewhat to
my amazement, the words popped out: "I've always thought, well . . .
that a few more people *should* fuck my mother."

Georgie laughed knowingly. "Be careful what you wish for. I
rather wish fewer people had mine."

Blushing, half-laughing, I pushed open another set of doors, and
suddenly the light changed and we were under the wide, gray sky.
The fire escape clattered as we climbed the last remaining stairs to
a small, flat rooftop.

"Holy cow," said Georgie, grinning. "This is great."

It was the highest point of the Ark. From where we were standing you could see the whole of the university—the cluster of concrete buildings that extended like jointed spider's legs from the
Bowl, the pathways toward the four zigzag-shaped residences that
squatted on the edge of the green sweep of grass leading down to

the lake and the woods. Down in the Bowl, the guy with the over-sized Adam's apple, now no bigger than a Lego man, was standing and making his way up the steps.

We sat on a bulge in the asphalt. Georgie cracked open the bottle of vodka. She had a go and passed it over, then took out a crushed bag of fish-shaped cheese crackers from her pocket.

I tried to think of something halfway interesting to say, but found myself still thinking about my mother. Di Walker was an obstetrician and mother of five. Which suggests someone warm and nurturing, at ease with mess. But, despite spending her days dealing with one of the most intimate aspects of the human condition, she was a chilly, undemonstrative woman, who didn't run much to shows of affection. I'd always suspected that I, her middle child and second daughter, interested her the least. In fact, as I told Georgie, I struggled to remember a time when my mother and I had been alone together in anything other than a car for more than an hour.

"What, never?" said Georgie, taking another swig. "That *can't* be true."

"The only time I can think of was once when she took me for tea after picking me up at a police station on the coast. All of us had been on the train together, playing that card game Shithead—"

"I love Shithead!" broke in Georgie.

"—on the way to some family event. I moved rows to have a sleep. Of course, they got off at the station without me. It was a good couple of hours before someone noticed I wasn't around, by which time I had woken up at the end of the line. I had to wait with the police until my mother picked me up. She must have been feeling guilty because on the way back we stopped at a tearoom. The lemon meringue pie tasted like washing-up liquid." I paused, remembering. "But I thought I should eat it, or the tea might feel like it hadn't really happened."

Georgie shot me a glance. Her parents—aristos with a giant pile in Suffolk who held a huge, weeklong, drug-fueled music festival in the grounds every summer—had idolized her as a child.

"And I do mean idolized," she said. "Like an object. I was this pretty little sprite with long white-blond hair that my mother loved dressing up with flower crowns, then sending out into their parties with bottles of champagne for the guests. Of course, she was always having an affair with someone . . ."

I turned to look at her. "Really? Like an *affair* affair?"

"Sure. You know, extramarital sex. Or *extra* extramarital sex in her case."

I blinked. "Do you think she knows you know?"

Georgie shrugged. "My mother is technically unable to think or feel from anyone else's point of view. Actually, as far as I can tell, both my parents are at their happiest when my mother is in the upswing of an exciting new infidelity."

"Wow." I took a gulp of the vodka. "I always thought my parents were at their best when the builders were in. They used different voices. Offered to make each other tea."

Georgie laughed long and hard at this, throwing back her head so that I saw a mole—chocolate brown, startlingly large—on the underside of her chin. And I felt a wave of joy, because that's how it felt, saying bold things to make Georgie Duncan laugh.

Then she stopped suddenly, her hand on my arm. "I'm sorry, you're making it funny, but it's probably not."

I glanced down, wondering whether to ask about the faint scars on the undersides of her wrists. I leaned forward instead. "Hold still a sec." I reached toward the side of her face. "You've got a bit of your earplug caught . . ." I tugged gently to free the little scrap of wax hanging from a strand of her blond hair. "There, that's better."

Georgie, who'd held very still, grinned. "Ah, thank you. That's something you'll learn about me. I'm a slob. Another thing I've inherited from my mother."

"That's perfect, then," I replied. "I'm nosy enough to notice. I'll keep an eye out." I picked up the vodka. Unscrewing the cap, I poured a shot into it, right up to the brim, and handed over the bottle. "Let's strike a deal. I'll look out for you, make sure you don't turn into your mother. You look out for me, make sure I don't end up like mine."

We both stood up to knock back the shot. And maybe it was the sweet sweep of the vodka kicking in and the view spread out before us, or else the giddy sense of possibility we shared—a friendship that already felt different from, and more exciting than the ones I'd made in all the years back home—but suddenly the concrete world below didn't seem so much ugly and gray as forbidden and thrilling. And I thought: *Even without Lorna, even if I have to wait, this might turn out to be just the right place for me, after all.*

Then I stepped forward to get a better look at the drop from the roof to the small figures moving on the steps of the Bowl and felt a disturbing lightness spread through me. For a moment, just for a moment, I wondered how it would feel to jump.

CHAPTER 3

Late the following morning, I was sitting on my bed, spooning up sugary cereal and reading an email from a friend back at home, when a new message pinged into my inbox. It was five lines long.

> *Dear Jessica,*
>
> *I'm sorry to hear you have been ill. The office was meant to let you know that I have moved you into my other course, on Agatha Christie, "Murdered by the Campus," which starts Thursday, nine A.M.*
>
> *See you then. I look forward to it?*
>
> *Lorna*

I read it three times, milky spoon suspended midair—once with relief, once with elation, then with a sudden landslide of embarrassment.

What, oh what was that question mark doing there? Did it mean her last sentence should be decoded as "I can see by the appalling hyperbole in your email that you are obviously a raging neurotic, so I'm bracing myself for the prospect of having you in my class"? Had I just alienated the person I most wanted to impress? Or was it just a typo? Could it be a typo? How likely was it that a teacher of English Literature (and a prize-winning writer, to boot) would fail to notice such an oddly placed question mark when looking back over what she had written? Surely all writers did check over their prose, however unimportant, before pressing send?

Eventually, after far too long spent staring at my screen—excitement and paranoia playing cat and mouse in my chest—I decided I needed to go for a run.

Running is what I do when other people reach for a cigarette or a drink. Whenever something my family said—or didn't say—particularly got to me, and my chest felt too packed and tight to bear, I would pull on my sneakers and take off along the uneven verges of the steep field behind our hedge. Before long the burn in my lungs and the blur in my vision would take over, and I found I could outrun my thoughts, reaching a strange, weightless calm in the rhythm of my feet.

Not that anything very bad happened at Milton View. That was part of the problem: Everything ugly or interesting was edited out. Our home was an old Victorian schoolhouse right on the edge of Reigate Hill golf course. The drafty bay windows in the living room looked out over its deceptively tricky ninth hole (rhododendrons, heather, an undulating fairway).

For the most part, my parents seemed to me neither noticeably happy nor unhappy, but behaved with each other much as many of my friends' parents behaved: like two adults without much in common who happened to be thrown together on a long car journey. Drawn-out conversations about logistics, silences filled by the welcome distraction of other voices on the radio, and the recurrent niggle that things would be better if they had taken a slightly different route.

Despite being one of five, I often found myself on my own (my older siblings, Freddie and Stef, teamed up above me, as did the twins below). Mostly, I read. The nearby cemetery had an ancient yew tree; a knot in it like a giant gargoyle made an ideal seat. Time bent as I inhabited different bodies, flew through bigger, darker, more vivid worlds. Later, when I stripped off in the bathroom, my bum would look like one of those bark rubbings you do with a crayon.

Granted, there was never quite enough hot water in the house, nor goodwill from my mother. But life in the Home Counties was not exactly tough. Had I been born with a different nature, I might have called it happy.

But I was too thin-skinned, too alive to the psychological warfare that was rumbling at any given time between my siblings; to the disappointment and half-truths muffled by clashing cutlery and chatter; the dreams struck smartly, one by one, and lost in the rough.

Which is why, I think, even as a child, I stood back. Became something of a bystander: a witness, an observer.

It wasn't until I was outside Halls in my running clothes that I realized quite what a U-turn the weather had taken from the day before. It was unseasonably warm. The kind of cock-teasing mid-September day when summer promises to make a late comeback.

Still jangling from Lorna's email, I walked fast through the paved part of the campus until I got to the grassy slope to the parkland and then broke into a jog, heading down toward the lake that had been made so much of in the college prospectus.

I remember what I was listening to that day, of course: an old Nina Simone album that I'd copied from my father's vinyl collection at home. Not an obvious running choice, but it felt right for my mood. Her wide, rich voice against the scratchy background silence spurred me on with its languid power.

I passed a group of students sitting on a hill, whose eyes followed me with interest as I ran by; two girls bending conspiratorially over the screen of a phone; a couple walking past with linked hands, who made me feel that I had missed a whole term rather than a week. But the music buoyed me up to float a few inches above any angst or self-consciousness, like the false courage of your first vodka shot on an empty stomach.

I ran on for perhaps another ten minutes, with the heat spreading slowly through my limbs, beyond the lake and into the sparse woodland, before I saw it.

It was parked just off the track, the unmistakable shape of its rear end sticking out slightly between two trees. A black hearse, wheels spattered with mud, like you would normally see gliding into a churchyard, a glimpse of tightly bunched white roses and a coffin showing through its giant back windows.

You don't often spot hearses out of context. Even having one pull up beside you at a traffic light is enough to give you an existential lurch, a gleaming black reminder that we are, after all, only passing through. But out here on this mossy track that clearly wasn't meant for cars it looked surreal, almost contrived, like a photograph in a contemporary art gallery.

Timing is everything. The moment I rounded a bend and spotted the hearse, my favorite Nina track began to play.

You probably know it. It's based on some hundred-year-old gospel song about a guy who has been damned and is careering around on Judgment Day trying to escape the devil. It begins with some simple chords on the piano and a compulsive rattata-rattata-rattata from the hi-hat on the drums. Then the vocals come in.

That's when it starts to build, quietly at first but with an urgency that I defy anyone to listen to and remain sitting still. I had slowed to a walk, feeling a strange sense of foreboding that pushed back against my chest like a fist while at the same time urged on by the galloping refrain.

I'm not in the habit of peering into the backs of cars, let alone hearses. I don't know what I expected to see. If this had been a nightmare—and these days I'm no stranger to them—it would have been a coffin, lid open to reveal the corpse of someone I knew. But it wasn't a nightmare, although as I walked closer my legs felt gluey beneath me and the apprehensive feeling had me by the throat.

It was the clapping that did it. At a certain point in the song— it's a stroke of genius, really—the music falls away completely and we are left with the eerie sound of a pair of hands clapping, a rhythm that is slow and deliberate at first and then becomes com- pelling as more and more hands join in and it gets faster and faster.

It was right then, in the grip of the music, that I looked into the hearse. I think that's the only way to explain it. Why else would I have been so gripped by what I saw? Two naked bodies entangled on a blanket, rocking together in a private act, in a rhythm as old as time. I'd seen bits of porno movies, of course. You don't grow up with two elder siblings, one of them a boy, without being subjected to the odd grainy clip on a phone. A blonde with pneumatic boobs bent over a washing machine; people with extraordinary bodies joined at unfeasible angles. But what I was watching was of an en- tirely different order. Not gymnastic, not even spectacular, but somehow, in its private intensity, far more dramatic.

I should have turned away. If I hadn't been listening to that song I think I might have—but the urgency of the clapping coupled with the shock of what I was seeing rooted me to the spot and I didn't move. I stood there staring, even as the clapping built up frenziedly in my ears.

I could barely see her—I only knew it was a her because of a pale hand that was pinioned against the window frame in his large, much darker one. At first all I saw of him was the tousled hair hanging over his face, a long, brown muscular back, his arse taut as he drove into her.

The music made it beautiful, riveting—and that's when he looked up.

I was close enough to see every detail. The sheen of perspiration on his upper lip, the sweep of his thick eyebrows, the color of his eyes, which leaped out in contrast to his otherwise dark coloring.

But it was the strangeness of his gaze that did it: glazed, unseeing, locked inward in the intensity of the moment.

And just at that moment—exactly at that moment—the song ended. The spell broke.

Hot shame flooded my body. In horror I stepped back suddenly onto a dry branch. The crack was like a gunshot. For a moment— or did I imagine it?—his eyes seemed to focus, widening slightly in surprise. But I didn't stay long enough to be sure. Wheeling round, I started running back through the trees, heart pounding in the back of my throat, stumbling slightly on the uneven ground.

Running, not for the first time, from something I knew I shouldn't have seen.

CHAPTER 4

When I think of that day, it's the lamb I see, not the shed.

I was eight, maybe nine at the time. I know it was around Easter because the pregnant sheep had been herded into a large corrugated iron barn at the back of Farmer Roberts's land. It was a hazy, hay-fevery day, great bits of white fluff drifting through the air, when I found myself on the track that ran over the hill from Milton View, breathless and itchy-eyed, walking fast.

Even from a distance, I could hear the noises coming from the barn. I slowed my step, enough of a country child to sense something out of the ordinary was happening. Inside, it was shady and cool, a relief to my streaming eyes. I walked past several pens, some only occupied by single ewes, their bellies swollen with late pregnancy, while others stood protectively over their newborns, rolling their milky marble eyes. The smell of urine-soaked straw was strong.

It wasn't until I was halfway into the cavernous space, passing the new lambs on their tottering legs—waving their tails frantically as they tugged at their mothers' teats—that I heard low human voices. Farmer Roberts was leaning against the side of a pen, talking softly but urgently to his daughter, who was kneeling inside, next to a sheep.

I was a little scared of Farmer Roberts, for the very good reason that he only had half a face. The other half was made of what looked like—and I think probably was—badly glued-down pieces of pink plastic surrounding a glass eye. Story was, as my elder brother once gleefully related, he had tried to blow his brains out with a rifle but had missed and blown a hole through his cheek instead.

Farmer Roberts's daughter Helen was a fierce teenager of whom I was in awe—a bottle blonde with long dark roots who drove huge tractors and rarely smiled. She was not smiling now as she crouched at the back end of a ewe that was lying down and emitting low sounds. Below the animal's tail there was a large bloodstained patch in the straw.

I was approaching Farmer Roberts on his bad side, and he was so busy talking to his daughter that it took him a while to notice me. When he finally did, he lifted his head briefly and said curtly, "Stay back please," before continuing to address Helen in a soft, persuasive voice, so different from the grunt he used if he saw us about the farm.

"Okay, it's a breech, Helen, so you're going to need to give her some help. Put some more soap on your hand. Right, now slide it in very gently so you can feel what's going on . . ." I watched, rapt and a little disgusted, as Helen pushed her hand inside, her forehead shiny with effort. The ewe writhed some more, her sides lifting and falling like bellows. Then she made a sort of barking sound, and a pink sheath appeared out of her backside containing a gray filmy balloon with what looked like a tiny pair of hooves inside.

"Keep her steady now, she's almost there."

The ewe gave out a low guttural groan, which provoked another chorus from the sheep and lambs in the nearby stalls, and there was a sticky, rushing sound and the lamb's back legs began to slither out onto the straw. I felt excitement and nerves ball up into one feeling in my chest and caught the triumph in Helen's eyes.

Something, I'm not sure what, made me glance over at Farmer Roberts. The good side of his mouth was set in a grim line and I only had a half second to wonder why before Helen gave a great tug, and the sheep's sides contracted again and there was a dull popping sound.

It should have been the head of the lamb. Except there wasn't any head, just a bony stump, covered in afterbirth.

I stared at the headless lamb, too horrified to feel sick. For some reason, it didn't occur to me that the head had never grown in the first place. In that grotesque, frozen second I must have decided that it had snapped off, caught between the pulling and the contractions, because in my mind's eye, I still saw it, swilling around inside the ewe's belly.

Then the sheep struggled to her feet and moved away from her deformed stillborn.

I had time to glimpse the stunned expression on Helen's face before I was outside the barn, running, running, running.

When I got back to the house, my brothers and sister were in the middle of playing Kick the Can and I never told them. Nor did I talk to my dad, who anyway never wanted to hear anything bad, or my mother, who could take all the bad things in the world in stride but never comfort me.

I was on my own. I felt it in every pump of my arms and legs as I raced back home over the hill.

But it was years before I knew exactly what I was running from. Not just the shock of that unnatural birth. But something much worse, that had chased me away from home earlier that morning. A scene I'd witnessed in my father's garden shed.

When I think of what I saw there, that dread fills me again. And I wonder what it was, in that moment, that I lost.

CHAPTER 5

You'll think it was all about sex. But although I'll admit that sex was always there, skulking in the shadows—hands in pockets, like a rather too-obvious suspect—it wasn't the thing that drove it. Not for me.

To date (as my journal bears witness) my sexual experience had consisted of:

- A boy called Michael, whose father worked for Farmer Roberts, who took me behind a large patch of nettles and showed me his willy, then asked to see mine.
- A long, entirely unrequited crush on my sister Stef's first boyfriend, Jake, consisting of a massive attack of the thinks that stalked me day and night for a good three months and led to those first warm, sliding sensations around the groin.
- Harry Lewis, a friend of my elder brother, Freddie, who kissed me on a family holiday in Thurlestone, Devon—ironically, on the edge of a golf course. We "went out" for a week and on the last night he fingered me (in a sand bunker, unfortunately).
- On my instruction, my school friends created "the Tuesday Club," a vodka-soaked group meeting each

week to tell stories, the taller the better. I fell in love with my best male friend, Luke, and we developed an intense platonic relationship, which I obsessed about. When, finally, it was consummated on Valentine's night, in the backseat of his small hatchback, the experience was so mediocre that, despite a few repeats, after leaving school we never spoke again.

I wasn't twenty minutes back from my run in the woods when Georgie burst in without knocking. She looked over to where I was sitting at my desk, wrapped in a towel, hair still damp from the shower.

"Ah-*ha*! I've been looking for you all day." She flopped down on my bed. "Where you been?"

"Just pottering." I felt my face flush. I swiveled round to my computer to close Lorna's reading list, then swiveled back again. "What's up with you?"

"What's up, my lovely, *is* me. My mind has just been b-l-*own*. Which is not something I thought I'd be saying after my first Philosophy seminar with Professor Steadman."

"You've been to class already?"

"Eight A.M. this morning. I had to get up at seven-thirty."

"How dare they?" I said with a grin. Then, hitching my towel a little higher under my armpits, I relocated to the other end of my bed so that we were facing each other.

As soon as she started talking, my thoughts traveled back to the scene I'd just witnessed. Part of me was dying to tell Georgie. I could imagine her eyes widening with delight—"Sex and death, how *titillating*"—but a bigger part wanted to keep it to myself. Shame, yes, and a tight, cold feeling that was worse than that. But something else, too: It was *mine*, that scene I'd stumbled on in the woods. Extraordinary and mine.

"So Steady's talking about the ethics of Abraham killing his own son when the arsey journalist interrupts again and this time everyone is so quiet you can hear a pin drop . . ."

"Sorry. You lost me. What arsey journalist?"

"Christ, Jess," said Georgie impatiently. "The guy spinning his pencil. Were you listening at all?"

"Mostly."

She looked at me more closely. "What's bothering you?"

"Nothing." I blushed. "I've just . . . I've just found out I've been swapped into the Christie course with you."

"Really?" Georgie looked genuinely delighted. "For the rest of term? Are you serious?"

I nodded, grinning. Pleased that she was pleased. "I'm a bit screwed for Thursday, though. Don't know how I'm going to manage all the reading."

"I'll cover for you . . . *Oh*." She clicked her fingers. "Nearly forgot. I had it confirmed today that Steady and Lorna are *definitely* an item. Cohabiting and everything. Ha! I thought that would get your attention."

I blinked. "Gosh, I'd sort of presumed she was, well . . ."

"Above having relationships with common mortals? I know. Well, big news. She's going steady with Old Steady. Now, listen, will you, this is important . . ."

What had been so arresting about those eyes looking out at me? Not just the searing focus, but something physical, too. An anomaly in one of the irises—part of the pale blue had been brown, like a stray piece of a jigsaw found in the wrong box. Not that it would do to romanticize him. He had been shagging in a hearse, after all. What kind of guy did that? What kind of girl, for that matter? And what would be the post-coital ritual? Sparking up cigarettes while listening to Gregorian chants?

"You got that, right?" Georgie was looking at me sideways.

"Yes," I said quickly. "You said: Steady was laying out ethical frameworks . . . examining Abraham's choices . . ."

"Right." Georgie nodded suspiciously. "And he's no slouch, my supervisor, he's clever and sharp and has us all thinking. He's just brought up Sartre or some other bullshit. And that's when the South African journo stands up and *lets rip*."

"What's a South African journalist doing in an undergraduate class?"

"Oh, for fuck's sake, Jess. I *said*. He's on some sort of study leave, to write a book. He dips in and out of classes as . . . I don't know"—she waves a hand—"a fellow or something."

"Okay. So how does he let rip?"

Georgie sat up quickly, her eyes shining. "Well, here's the thing . . ." Her short hair was mussed from lying back on my pillow, her round cheeks flushed. She looked like a putto from the ceiling of the Sistine Chapel who'd gorged on too much wine and sex. Amazing really, how she could make a muffin-top look good.

"He must have met Old Steady before, because first he tells him to stop talking. Just like that, he says: 'Stop talking, Hugh.' He calls him Hugh! Everyone's mouths fall open. Then the journo goes very calm and cool. He tells this story about a photojournalist friend of his who took a picture of a starving African girl that a vulture is eyeing up from a few feet away, waiting for her to die. The picture wins lots of prizes, the friend becomes famous—and a few months later, he kills himself." Georgie paused to check I was following. "He tells us this story, all calm and quiet. Then, when we're all hooked—he's divine this guy, did I mention that?—he rounds on Steady. Takes him to the cleaners.

"Surely, says the journo, philosophy shouldn't be so academic, a cluster-fuck of linguistics and hypotheticals. It's there to help us think. And to choose. His voice is so quick and clipped—you know that accent South Africans have—but he looks Steady in the eye, too, and when he stops talking he gives him a little nod, so it feels like a challenge rather than disrespect, you know? Then he excuses himself and walks out. As he leaves he brushes against my elbow and I feel like I've been touched by some rock star. In any case, poor old Steady is left blinking in front of the whiteboard with a marker pen hanging from his hand, looking completely floored. And everyone stares at each other as if to say: Did that just happen? And if so, did anyone record it on their phone?"

"Dramatic, then," I said, smiling. I'd known Georgie Duncan for eight days now. I was pretty sure that everything that happened to her was dramatic.

"Ah, but we haven't even got to the good bit," Georgie said, leaning forward, her eyes dancing. "I didn't even notice as he passed, he must have done it so cleverly, but he slipped this on the table next to me." She held out her hand, palm flat. There was a little square of torn-off notepaper, with two seams where it had been folded into four.

I took it. The handwriting was very small and neat, forward slanting. That slanting, spiky print that left-handers often have.

Drink at the Rose at six? Alec

Looking at the piece of paper in my hand, I felt a sudden chill. As if the sunshine that Georgie had trailed into my life had clouded over and I was doomed to spend the next three years in darkness, groping after Lorna's brilliance like the intangible light of some distant star.

Then I looked back up at my new friend's face. Glowing, irresistible, insecure.

"Jess, what if he doesn't—"

"You're gonna knock him out," I said firmly.

CHAPTER 6

"Where do I find Crime?"

The librarian was a beautiful man in his thirties with a carefully trimmed beard and a baby blue T-shirt stretched over his toned chest with the words I CHEAT AT YOGA stamped on it. He didn't bother looking up to answer.

"Crime doesn't have its own section," he said, swiping books aggressively past a laser. "It's all in Fiction."

"Ah, okay." I looked down at the piece of paper I was holding. "And Autobiography?"

Beep, beep, beep, beep. He still hadn't looked up, but I had a strong hunch that his eyes would be the exact same blue as his top.

"Second floor, last stack. Unless it's by a fiction writer, in which case it's still in Fiction, under the author's surname. Up to six books for two weeks, after that it's a late fine," he said with clear relish. "Ten pence per book per day that it's overdue."

I headed into the stacks, past churning printers smelling of hot ink and warm paper, and the static hum of the computer terminals. There were a couple of familiar faces working at the desks in between. In the Geography section, a tall guy with a brace and headgear who was always hanging around outside the bar cracking jokes in a loud Welsh accent; in History of Art, a girl with short dark hair who I had last seen wrestling with a smoking toaster in one of the galley kitchens. A few pairs of eyes flicked sideways as I passed by, and I felt the thickness of the atmosphere, the strain of collective silence and its undercurrents. I thought of the man from the hearse. Was he a student here? Would I know him if I saw him? Would he know me?

Fiction took up most of the bottom floor. I walked through the shelves until I got to the *C*'s. Calvino, Carey, Carver, Carroll. The Christies jumped out at me. A long line of colorful paperbacks amidst the solemn hardbacks.

It was only seeing them here, so out of place with their jaunty, blood-spattered covers, that it really sank in: *Lorna Clay* was going to be teaching me about *Agatha Christie*. All of a sudden this felt like one of those wonderful treats that life doles out while you're not looking. Perhaps it was even no coincidence that she and I both loved Christie.

I looked down at the piece of paper I was holding. The first seminar—"Searching for Agatha"—had a reading list of four books. Three murder mysteries (which I'd read, but not for a while) and Christie's autobiography (which I had never read). I had just forty-eight hours. Georgie had disappeared and, bafflingly, I couldn't find any of the books in her room. Where had she taken them—on her date? For a moment I thought wistfully of the dog-eared Christies stashed in various bookshelves around Milton View (there were several copies of *The Murder on the Links*—more than one guest had decided that it was the ideal thank-you present).

I looked down the row of spines until I found two out of the four: *The Mysterious Affair at Styles* and *Ordeal by Innocence*.

No *And Then There Were None*, no autobiography.

Reluctantly, I headed back to the hipster.

Tickety-tap, tickety-tap on his keyboard. "We stock seven copies of *And Then There Were None*. They're all signed out."

"Ah. And then there *were* none?" I suggested.

He didn't answer. I blushed. "And her autobiography?"

"Four copies . . . all out." He looked up finally. His eyes were indeed blue, with inky lower lashes, like a girl's. "You should get here more quickly next time." He glanced at the reading list in my hand. "Same thing will happen next week unless you step on it."

"Right." I'd given up trying to smile now, but it was still stuck to my face. "Are there any libraries in town?"

"Yes, but it takes a few days to become a member. When do you need the books by?"

"Today."

"Oh dear," he said, looking positively delighted now. "Not a chance."

"Oh, so . . ."

"The bookshop's your only option. But it's not cheap."

"Okay, thanks." Masochistically, I wanted to tell him I liked his T-shirt. What is it about beautiful, mean people that makes you want to please them?

The bookshop on campus had varnished herringbone parquet floors and smelled of new shoes. Tables stacked with columns of fresh books announced "three for two" offers. I walked past a wall of books on Military History and found Crime skulking at the back of the shop.

There were half a dozen copies of *And Then There Were None*—presumably the shop was wise to the curriculum. I picked one up and headed over to the Biography section. There it was, Agatha Christie's *An Autobiography*. The cover showed a black-and-white study of Agatha as an elderly lady, her hair swept back in a dignified matronly style to show heavy jowls and hooded, rather unhappy eyes. I turned it over to look at the price and started to sweat. I hadn't budgeted for buying books. The money I'd saved up working at the pet shop was no fortune. After paying for housing, I had little to spend on food and drink, let alone items necessary to avoid becoming a pariah, like shampoo and toothpaste.

I stood with a book in each hand, weighing up my options.

Either I wasted precious reading time hunting down a public library in town (banking on the fact that the sadistic librarian had been wrong and I could join up immediately) or I shelled out half my week's allowance on books that I was probably going to read only once. Out of nowhere a dark thought snaked into my mind. I looked down at my satchel, the back of my neck prickling.

What if I nicked them? I mean, not really *stole* them, just took them for a couple of days, as if I was borrowing them, and then slipped them back on the shelves later. What harm would that really do? I'd just take extra care with the spines and avoid eating toast while reading. I was crouched down, debating whether to slip them into my bag when a voice I recognized, coming from the other side of the shelving, made me jump.

". . . you just said 'technically' for the third time. Really, Hugh, whose side are you on?"

Now a male voice, older, conciliatory, came into earshot: "Don't get me wrong. I just think that, given what happened, you should be more cautious. Play by the rules, for once; don't invite them to the house for starters, or certainly not after dark."

"Sod that," rejoined the voice I knew. Hearing her so close by, right behind the bookshelf, sent a nervous thrill shooting through me. "Do you know that when Jon the Don hands a student anything he puts it down on the table rather than passing it hand to hand? Like he thinks lawyers are cracking their knuckles the minute you look a student in the eye . . ." I heard footsteps and saw a pair of weathered cowboy boots—black with swirls of rainbow-colored stitching—stride past the gap under the shelves a couple of feet away. "So what if people think I have favorites? What's wrong with singling out someone because their ideas interest me? Just because I think someone's special, it doesn't mean that everyone else—"

"I'm suggesting you change your behavior, not your mind." The man's voice again, amused and resigned. "Christ knows that wouldn't get me anywhere."

Another pause, the sound of pages being flicked through. Then the clack of steps moving away on the wooden floor. For a while I remained crouched, my thighs starting to burn, trying to stop the pounding in my chest. It was Lorna's voice, I was sure of it.

I felt a sudden tightness in my lungs, as if all the events that had been set in motion by Uncle Toto's gift last Christmas had propelled me to this very spot, squatting behind the bookshelves on the concrete campus of an East Anglian university. Each fatal turn coalesced suddenly in my chest—the last-minute change in my college application (Oxbridge be hanged, their reading list stopped at 1920, they were a *century* behind); the subsequent arguments with my parents; the hours spent watching clips of Lorna light up late-night discussion panels with arguments I didn't quite understand; the excitement of tracking down the TV series on her book via some nut on the Internet who, sensing weakness, had charged three times the recommended price; all those stale, lonely days in the pet shop, the smell of guinea pig shit and despair. These all surged up in me to form this purpose: that I should summon the courage to put the books I was holding in my bag, stand up, and walk around the stacks.

"Excuse me, Dr. Clay?"

Lorna turned around. Having watched her in all those clips, it was a bit like bumping into a movie star in real life, that strange clash between the new and the familiar.

I *knew* those eyes, set wide in a freckle-dusted face, and the pale orange, wayward hair. In the flesh, though, she was taller than I had imagined, her strong features even bolder, so that the sum effect wobbled uncertainly between the strange and the beautiful before tipping resolutely into the latter. Behind her, I saw the man Georgie had pointed out at the English department drinks. Close up, Professor Steadman looked even older: He had a kind face with glasses under his thatch of gray hair, a pale blue shirt tucked into trousers that were rather too high-waisted. There was a pen clipped onto his top pocket with a little ink stain showing through.

I unstuck my tongue from the roof of my mouth. "I'm a new student of yours—Jess Walker."

"Hello." I thought I saw a flicker of annoyance cross her face, a sidelong oh-no glance back at her companion, but then she smiled and waited, her face a pleasant blank.

"We just traded emails about moving class? I'm in your Agatha Christie course now."

Her forehead wrinkled for a moment before she shook her head. "I'm sorry, I've got a terrible—" she broke off, her eyes widening. "Oh, hang on. You're the 'Ever-Hopeful Jessica'?"

I felt the blood rush to my face.

"Yes, I'm sorry." My eyes skittered nervously. "That's what I wanted to say . . ." I dried up and took a breath. "My email was a bit strong. I don't want you to think I'm some kind of crazy stalker."

"I see." She chewed her bottom lip thoughtfully. "So how come you were hiding behind these shelves?"

My stomach contracted. Surely she wasn't serious? I scanned her strong face for clues, but she looked to be very far from joking, her chin raised in a way I'd seen her adopt on television.

"No, I wasn't," I said. "At least I didn't mean to be." I think my face must have shown the horror I felt because Steady stepped forward with an apologetic smile.

"Oh, don't listen to her, she's a terrible tease. Hugh Steadman, by the way." His handshake was warm and dry; I could feel the bones of his fingers beneath fine, soft skin. "Lorna, please. The poor girl."

I looked from one face to the other, helpless as to who was telling the truth.

"I'm sorry about the letter," I faltered, back to Lorna. "I was a little delirious at the time I wrote it."

She laughed and laid a hand on her companion's forearm. "Hugh's right, I'm just teasing. Terrible habit, especially with people I don't know. It was a very good letter."

My cheeks burned. "I shouldn't have made such a song and dance . . ."

"I love a good song and dance." Her eyes were suddenly so full of friendly conspiracy that I felt like bursting into tears.

"Really?"

"Really. See you Thursday. Just do the reading."

"Yes."

Her eyes dropped for a fraction of a moment to the book in her hands, and I realized, a little late, that I was being dismissed. Garbling my thanks, I turned, in a hurry to leave before I said anything stupid. I had met Lorna, she knew who I was, and she'd said my letter was good. She was going to teach me. About literature, about life.

I had already left the bookshop and was crossing the Bowl when I remembered the unpaid-for Christie books still stashed in my satchel. For a moment, I considered turning back. Then I smiled and ducked my head, kept walking swiftly toward Halls.

A tiny, insignificant crime. It's only now, looking back at all the choices I was about to make, that I detect the very faintest of watermarks, the first of many lines I was about to cross.

CHAPTER 7

I overslept the day of Lorna's first seminar. I'd stayed up so late reading that I missed the alarm and had to throw on my clothes (jeans, favorite T-shirt: faded red, no slogan) and jam back wild morning curls in a ponytail before racing across campus. I was halfway up the steps to the Ark when I realized that I'd forgotten to bring my journal, in which I'd tucked the slip of paper with the room number on it.

Two girls were sitting on a nearby wall in a little pool of sunshine, drinking cups of coffee. I could tell at a glance that they weren't first years.

"Dr. Clay?" echoed the smaller of the two, a tiny, striking blonde with a pointy, confident face and slightly mocking voice. The fingernails around her coffee cup had a smart French manicure. "Sure, everybody in the department knows where Lorna teaches. Second floor, left-hand side, last door. Next to the drinks machine."

"Your first class?" asked the other girl, who had a rounder, more sympathetic face.

I nodded.

Something glimmered in the eyes of the pointy-faced girl. She leaned forward, lowering her voice a little. "Careful of the mind control, then."

I blinked. "I'm sorry?"

The freckled one shook her head. "Come on, Lara."

The one called Lara shrugged. "Just a health warning. Lorna's a piece of work. The stuff I hear about Cambridge . . ."

"Cambridge?" The word slipped out involuntarily. I hesitated, one foot still poised on the step above.

I'd read about Lorna quitting her last teaching post: There was a mystery around her moving from Cambridge to Norwich not long after *The Truants* was published. Not a backwater exactly, but Norfolk, nevertheless. A trade down, just when her academic star was rising. I'd decided—even without having met her—that this was very much *in* character, exactly the kind of perverse, anti-elitist move that Lorna would pull. But the girl's words unsettled me; so, too, did the expression on her friend's face as she put a warning hand on her companion's arm.

"Ignore her, you can tell she's a drama student. Lorna's an incredible teacher, I'd kill to be in her classes." Her smile suddenly seemed artificial. "Watch out for that drinks machine, though. It eats change."

Lorna gave no sign of recognizing me when I walked into class.

She sat perched on the front edge of her desk, flicking through some papers, her boots swinging a few inches above the floor. She looked more businesslike than usual, hair coiled up and stuck through with a pin, except for a few strands that had escaped around her face. Next to her were a pile of the Agatha Christie books that I had been reading; some notepads—the yellow lined ones—and a couple of pens; an oversized bunch of keys; and a balled-up handkerchief. Behind her, on the whiteboard, one sentence was written in bright green marker.

People disappear when they most want to be seen.

I walked past her, stomach fizzy with nerves, and took one of the dozen seats round three large, laminated tables arranged into a squared-off horseshoe. The seats were filling up. I recognized a handful of faces from the English drinks. That boy from Cornwall, Bill, with the gentle voice; Niko, the Greek with heavy sideburns; a girl with a blond ponytail and a chip on her front tooth . . . what was she called—Clare?

No Georgie. I hadn't seen her since Monday when she'd left for her date with the South African journalist, wearing a short denim shirt-dress and heavy eye makeup. On Tuesday morning I'd texted her. *So, did he show up?* The reply (*YES!!!*) meant I hadn't been surprised not to hear from her since. But if she didn't turn up to this class, our first with Lorna . . . Well. That *would* be odd.

The clock said two minutes past. Only two chairs left. Another guy came in, a Glaswegian called Graham wearing a scowl under his thick, sandy hair. Still no Georgie. I saw Lorna glance at the empty chair and felt my cheeks burn. Should I say, *My friend's been shagging a hot journalist for the past three days, no need to wait*?

One of the strip lights was emitting a staccato buzzing, like a wasp in distress. "Oh, that fucking light." Lorna jumped off her desk and crossed the classroom with a couple of long strides. She hit the switch on and off a few times until it still flickered, but not so noisily.

"Better. Right." She glanced at her watch. "Who can tell me which of Christie's mysteries is the hardest to crack? Bill?"

Bill, who was, I was beginning to think, rather attractive—despite, or maybe because of, one eye that tracked a little wrong—made a pitch for *And Then There Were None*. Someone else said *Murder on the Orient Express*. Niko began to make a bid for *Roger Ackroyd*.

I watched Lorna's face as she listened, leaning forward, eyes slightly narrowed, one hand fiddling with the loose end of her belt. God knows how she immediately knew all of our names without having done the usual round table introductions. Perhaps she'd studied our photos. But however she did it, she made you feel she knew you, that she had—in one of those searing glances—taken a read on your intelligence, sizing up not only your ability, but also your potential. As if she sensed, better than you, what you might be capable of one day.

"In other words," Niko was saying, "the island becomes a symbol of the solitary self . . ."

"Thanks, Niko," said Lorna dryly. "Do let us know when you're applying for tenure. Anyone else?"

I racked my brain, trying to work out what she was getting at. Which of Christie's mysteries was the hardest to crack? Was it related to that sentence on the whiteboard or had that just been left from the class before? Why had Lorna used the word "mystery" rather than "murder"? Was she talking about one of the novels she hadn't put on the reading list? Perhaps not even a murder mystery, but the romances that Christie had written under a pen name?

Unless . . . I put up my hand tentatively.

"Jess?"

"I just wondered. When you say 'mystery' . . . Are you talking about Christie's life or her books?"

Lorna's gaze seemed to sharpen on me. "Go on."

I bit my lip. Of all the Christies I'd read over the years, of everything I had absorbed over the last two days, why the hell had I brought up this: an incident I knew little about, that I had skimmed over in the introduction to her autobiography?

"I was thinking about that time *she* disappeared," I said slowly. "In real life, I mean. For a couple of weeks, wasn't it?"

"Eleven days," said Lorna. Her eyes slid momentarily to the empty chair next to mine—or perhaps they didn't—but suddenly Georgie's face flashed into my mind and I felt a prickle of anxiety. Three days . . . she'd been gone three days. Had I been remiss in not trying to track her down? Should I have told someone, the beaky woman in the admin office maybe, or at least tried to find her home phone number when she stopped responding to my texts?

Everyone was looking at me now. I felt the heat flood up in my face. "It's still a mystery because Christie never explained it. Even in her autobiography, which came out after she died. Her fans were hoping for an explanation, weren't they? But she just glossed over it."

Lorna nodded fractionally, but her expression didn't change. I couldn't tell if she approved of the line I was taking or thought I was busking it. I strained to remember. "Her husband had just told her about his mistress. Agatha got amnesia, I think, and ran off somewhere to a hotel. There was a big public outcry . . . it was on all the front pages, wasn't it?" I shook my head. "Sorry, that's about all I can remember."

"Anyone else?"

Clare knew bits and pieces, Niko tried to make out like he knew more than he did, but in the end it was Lorna who filled in the facts:

On a cold December's evening in 1926, just after her beloved mother had died, Agatha's husband, Archie, announced he was in love with a friend of theirs, Nancy Neele.

"What must have been so terrible," said Lorna, leaning forward, her eyes very bright, "was the *double* betrayal. Can you imagine— Agatha's husband, the dashing First World War pilot she was crazy about, and a *friend* of hers? The fact that it had been going on, right under Agatha's nose, in plain sight. They'd played golf together. Nancy had come for weekends at Styles, their family home."

Lorna broke off for a moment here, dropping her gaze, and I felt a strange itchy sensation behind my eyes. Like my hay fever was starting. Except it was the wrong season.

"The night Archie broke the news to Agatha," continued Lorna, "there was a horrible argument. He stormed out to go and spend the weekend with his mistress. Not long afterwards, Agatha went up to the room where her daughter was sleeping and kissed her good-bye, then slipped out of the house in her fur coat and drove off into the night. The following morning, her car, a Morris Cowley, was found crashed off the main road above a quarry, near a reservoir. Despite the cold night, her fur coat had been left in the backseat, the car's headlights still burning."

Lorna paused. No one moved. The itchiness behind my eyes felt like it was pressing in from behind. I had another flash of Georgie, this time running breathless through the woods, her denim dress torn. That story she'd told about the journalist turning on Steady. He was obviously volatile. Something could have happened to her . . .

"Eleven days after her car was found, Agatha was discovered in a spa hotel in Harrogate. Does anyone remember what name she used to check in?"

Clare's hand shot up. "Neele. The surname of her husband's lover."

"Correct," said Lorna, her cowboy boots beginning to swing again. "A *Mrs.* Teresa Neele from South Africa. So what was going on? The official statement was that Agatha had amnesia. Do we believe it? And if not, what was she up to?"

A few hands went up. Clare thought perhaps she'd had a breakdown after her mother's death and husband's betrayal.

"Possibly. But for someone having a breakdown she was very methodical," pointed out Lorna. "Took a train to Harrogate, bought some new clothes, checked in under her husband's lover's name. Even danced to the hotel band in the evenings. Does that sound like a woman falling to pieces?"

"Revenge?" suggested Kenny. "Framing her husband for murder to punish him for his affair?"

"Perhaps," said Lorna, fiddling with the end of her belt again. Was this a "tell" of hers? If so, what did it mean? Impatience? "What's so *striking*," she continued, "is how out of character it was with the way Christie ran the rest of her life. Private, reserved, a triumph of the rational—like the books she wrote, in which mysteries are only puzzles to be solved, all chaos neatly tidied up at the end, the murderer brought to account."

She looked up again and I thought I saw something sad flit across her face. A gray cloud had gone over the sun. Overhead, the light started to flicker and buzz again.

Lorna sighed. "Hang on a moment." She jumped off her desk and fiddled with the switch again. It kept buzzing. "Oh, what the fuck," she said, and flicked it off.

Without artificial lights, the classroom was gloomy and dark. Lorna perched on the front of her desk, almost a silhouette now. Her voice, when it came, had changed register, become more conversational.

"Who here ran away from home as a child?"

After a pause, a few hands rose tentatively.

"Okay, now try to remember what it felt like. And if you didn't actually run away, try to remember what it felt like as a child to hide away from your parents for some time. What is it that you want? Do you want them to find you?"

I closed my eyes, pushing the image of Georgie out of my mind, and thought of Milton View, of hours spent wandering around the Robertses' farm while my sisters and brothers formed into pairs. Then later, the walks turning into runs. Those feelings that I'd never really put words to. The sting of loneliness, yes, of being left out—but something else, too.

"Jess?"

Startled, I opened my eyes. Lorna was looking straight at me.

"You were shaking your head. What were you thinking?"

I blinked. "I was just thinking . . . about how that felt—running away."

Lorna nodded. A pulse was jumping in my throat. I took a breath, tried to order my thoughts.

"When you set off you don't want people to find you, at least you think you don't," I said slowly. "You want to be on your own, wallowing. But deep down you also want . . ." I heard my voice catch a little, felt the raw emotion like a pressure in my throat. "Well, you want them to be worrying about you, too."

It was like she had been waiting for this. I felt a sting of relief, finding words for a feeling I'd never quite understood.

Into the silence, Lorna smiled suddenly.

"Exactly right, Jess. You want them to be worrying about you."

She kept her gaze fastened on me. "Now, tell me. What is the first thing that happens when you fall in love? Madly in love, that is."

I blinked in surprise, feeling the heat creep back into my face. What should I say? That I didn't know? That I had absolutely no experience of falling in love? Or of real passion, for that matter. For some reason the young man in the hearse came to mind, the glazed, intent look in those eyes.

"I don't know."

"When, on December 3, 1926, Archie told Agatha he had fallen in love with another woman, she ran away from home because she wanted something. What was it?"

The class was completely silent now. No coughing or rustling of papers. No surreptitious glances at phones under the table. Everyone's attention was fixed on Lorna, faces wearing the same alert expression.

"The whole country was looking for her. Five hundred police officers and fifteen thousand volunteers. But what she wanted, desperately, was the attention of one person." Lorna looked at us, her eyes very shiny. "Agatha wasn't breaking down or seeking revenge. She wanted him to be thinking about her. All the time, just like he used to."

Lorna glanced at her watch and said, "Okay, everyone. Time's up." I saw others look around, blinking and slightly dazed, like the lights had just come up after a movie.

Even the world-weary Graham gave me a slight smile as we shuffled out of the classroom, as if we had just been through some major life event together.

"Knocked it out of the park, didn't she?"

I nodded, chest full, not trusting myself to speak.

Walking down the steps of the Ark, past the wall where the two girls had been sitting—now empty, and in shadow—I felt light-headed, euphoric. This was exactly what I'd come to this flat, color-less part of the country to learn. This glowing, brilliant teacher would crank me out of the narrow rut I'd otherwise be destined to travel down and make me strive to improve myself. *Exactly right, Jess.*

Amazing how, with three little words, she'd relieved me of the mantle of my ordinariness, made me believe that I had done something brave and true. If that was the "mind control" the girl on the wall had been talking about, I wanted to sign up for more. Georgie had missed out, it was a shame not to have shared the moment with her—but it had been silly of me, caught up in the drama of Lorna's class, to fret about her.

CHAPTER 8

———

"Sure you need me for this?"

I sat on the end of Georgie's bed, holding a mug of soup, watching her pull out different items from her closet, pause, assess, then toss them into a pile on a chair. "Sounds quite a lot like a hot date to me."

"Very sure." She held up a pair of impossibly small denim shorts with little mirrored disks all over them. "We've just spent three solid days with each other. Time to mix it up or I'll start to bore him."

"I doubt that."

Georgie leaned over and took a long swig from a plastic pint glass of double gin and tonic she'd brought up from the bar. "Besides," she said, crunching on the ice. "Gideon specifically invited you, too."

I snorted. "Only because you encouraged that rumor about me and drugs."

She had started climbing into the tiny shorts. The disks jingled madly as she balanced on one leg and then the other. "What do you have against house parties, anyway?"

I shrugged, putting down my mug to fix the loose corner of a picture stuck to her wall. A sepia headshot of a young woman with flying goggles on her forehead, eyes straining into the too-bright sun. The pilot who went missing on a trip round the world in the thirties, Georgie had told me, clicking her fingers, *you know, whatserchops* . . .

"Does anyone really like house parties unless they are seriously drunk or hooking up?" I wedged Amelia Earhart back down, my nail making a little sickle-shaped indentation on the Blu Tack. "It's only ever fun if you're in The Room. But no one knows which one that is. So everyone keeps wandering around, pretending they know where they're going." I paused. By now Georgie was lying on the floor, knees up as she tried to button the shorts.

"Keep talking," she said breathlessly. "It's helping."

I grinned. "Either you stick with whoever you go with, have a shouty conversation you could have had somewhere quieter, in more comfortable clothes, or you meet some new people when they're being least themselves and end up playing ego tennis . . ."

Georgie stood up, doing a twirl. "What do you think?"

She'd managed to do up the button of the shorts, just. The material had been stretched to such a degree that the little mirrored disks tinkled of their own accord.

I hesitated, looking for the right words. "Bit Christmassy, I think."

She sighed, dropping her arms. "I really like him, Jess."

I nodded. "I can tell. If you want me to, I'll come, but don't you think I'd be surplus to, well, the ideal outcome?"

Georgie shook her head. "I haven't explained it right, then."

She perched on the end of the bed, her expression suddenly vulnerable. "The boys I've been with so far . . . I've always felt older than them. Like I've lived more lifetimes. Like they're playing catch-up. But this guy, the places he's been, the things that he's seen . . . it feels like the other way around. Which scares me, somehow."

Her fingers moved instinctively to the marks on her wrists, scars that looked like spatters of very pale paint, almost silvery from age. They had clearly been blisters at one stage, burns possibly. I'd noticed them a few times since that day on the roof of the Ark, but kept chickening out of asking, thinking: *We're new friends, she'll tell me when she wants to, I don't want to pry.*

"Will you come?" She looked up, her smile lopsided. "Please?"

So I sighed and told her, "Yes, of course I'll come." As long as she didn't wear the tiny shorts. As long as she didn't drop me like a hot rock the minute after we walked in.

"Great." She jumped up, squeezing me. "You're a good friend, Jess."

Then, glancing back at the pile of clothes: "Though I think I will go with the shorts, actually."

"Dark and Stormy?"

"Sorry?"

"Dark and Stormy?"

"Sor—*oh* . . . Right. Thanks, yes. Please."

I took my cocktail and found myself a place to sit halfway up the stairs to the bedrooms where I could observe all the comings and goings without it looking too tragic that I was sitting on my own. The music was not loud and thumping like the kind you might get at a house party in Reigate, but low and snakey with a persistent bass beat. Since Georgie had spun off, two guys had—separately—asked me if I had any drugs they could buy and someone wearing a brown fedora had offered me a pill in return for some weed. *Perhaps this is what happens,* I thought. *You spend years trying to climb out of the role your family has you in only to be confused with someone else entirely.*

From time to time, I put my hand down behind me on the stairs without thinking and invariably someone on their way to the loo stepped on it. One of the more vicious hand-steppers crouched down to apologize.

"Oh God, I'm sorry," he said, looking like he actually meant it. "What can I get you? An ice pack? A new hand? Another drink?"

I hesitated, then smiled. "Sure," I said. "Any of the above."

Nick didn't look like the pasty, unhealthy-looking boys I'd met so far on campus. He was a tall, handsome Indian guy with broad shoulders, smiley eyes, and a little wave in his shiny dark hair. Second year, studying Geology.

"Geology," I said when we'd moved, with our drinks, to some chairs next to a giant potted plant. "That's . . . rocks?"

He winced. "I prefer 'Earth Science.'"

"I'm sorry." I couldn't tell whether he was joking, decided to chance it. "Tell me about Earth Science."

"Uh-uh. No way. I can't stamp on your hand and then tell you why I find rocks interesting." He paused, fingering one of the leaves of the plant. "Well, I *can* actually. But then I might have to stand on your foot, too. To stop you from leaving."

I laughed. "So maybe a less risky topic."

"Trout fishing," he said without hesitation.

"*Trout* fishing?"

"Brown trout, yes." And he told me about the fishing trip he and his father took every summer (English village pubs on brown trout rivers; as far as they could tell they were the only Indian father-and-son team on a father-and-son-heavy circuit). About the early evenings when the midges danced above the sunlit water and the birds were all in song, and whatever he and his dad were discussing, they just shut up and let nature do the talking.

"Sounds heavenly," I said honestly.

Nick nodded. "Actually I can't stand fishing. But it's the only way to get my father to belt up."

Both Nick's parents had come over from Jaipur before he was born and though, like me, he was one of five children, they sounded pretty much the opposite of my family—with, he said fondly, "far too much on the surface, and almost nothing going on underneath." The way he talked was so open and funny and self-deprecating and he had such a lovely way of sitting forward when he listened that I felt a pang of disappointment when a couple of his friends—boys, both clearly drunk—came to drag him off.

"Any chance you want to come?" he said as he resisted their tugs on his arm. "I'm afraid I agreed to drive these idiots to another party."

I shook my head with a smile, but when he asked if he could ring me tomorrow "to check on that hand of yours and tell you more about rocks," I gave him my number.

Georgie's dancing made no sense at all. It didn't help that she was so messed up. But I wasn't sure that, even if she were sober, she'd have had much of a sense of rhythm. She stuck her bum out and clicked her fingers above her head like she was in a Bollywood movie, mouthing the lyrics like she was telling you something really important. And yet, somehow, the way she abandoned herself to the music—honestly, unself-consciously—was deeply sexy. I moved my feet a bit next to her, not yet unbound enough by the rum to enjoy it. *Come on*, I told myself. *Live a little.*

At some particularly uncoordinated moment, I happened to look round.

And there he was, the guy from the hearse, looking straight at me.

He was standing by the wall next to some French windows, maybe a dozen feet away. It was him, I hadn't any doubt. A little taller than I'd imagined (he'd been horizontal, after all) with a few strands of dark hair falling over his eyes, his hands thrust deep in the pockets of a khaki coat and a slight forward tilt to his shoulders, as if he had just walked into the party and wasn't planning on staying. I wasn't close enough to see his expression clearly, but he was staring over at me with such attention that after my first thought—*Holy shit, there's the guy from the hearse*—came the second: *Oh fuck. So he did see me that day.*

I stopped moving my feet and just stood there, idiotically, with the bass pulsing through the floor. It was a good few seconds before it dawned on me that his gaze wasn't fixed on me at all, but on Georgie. She was swaying a couple of feet away, her tight, mirrored shorts glinting in the disco lights. Instinctively I turned, wanting to slip away before he did notice me, but in the crush someone pushed hard against me and I barreled into the wall and ended up nearly tripping over his foot.

"Whoa there," he said, putting out a hand to steady me.

"Thanks," I muttered, looking at his fingers splayed on my arm. Olive skin, the kind that tans, several shades darker than mine.

"Hey, do I know you?"

Reluctantly, I looked up.

He was even taller up close. With a jolt I remembered the thick bridge of his nose that should have been ugly, those intense blue eyes—lit up as the disco lights played over his face—with the strange discoloration in the left one. He looked a little older than everyone else in the room—his skin tougher and darker, more weathered. As the lights flashed again I could see faint lines traveling down his cheeks toward his jaw.

"No," I managed, my mouth dry. "No, I don't think so."

"Sure about that?" Those unnerving eyes were drilling into me, like I was a code he was trying to crack. Then he smiled, his face relaxing. "I'm sorry. That must sound like a terrible line. It's just you remind me of someone."

"Oh," I said, nodding. "A lot of people say that."

This was a lie. No one had ever said that.

"It's very striking." His eyes held mine for a beat too long, and I had an unnerving feeling that he was reading exactly what was scrolling through my mind: *Yes, it was me in the woods. Yes, I stayed too long. I couldn't stop looking* . . . Then his gaze slid suddenly to one side. I felt the heat of another body behind me. Georgie's voice, thick with booze, as she laid her chin on my shoulder.

"Hey, Alec. So you decided to show up?"

The back of my neck went cold.

Of course: *Alec*. Georgie's description of the journalist had been thin on detail. Somehow I'd formed the impression of someone clean-cut and suavely handsome. Except, now that I knew, it made perfect sense to me that she would find this strange, vital man, and vice versa.

"I did my best to stay away," he said, smiling.

"Not your fault." Her eyes were wide with mischief. "Jess and I were practicing our siren calls."

My heart was beating very fast, as if I'd been caught doing something wrong. I muttered words along the lines of "I'll leave you to it," but before I turned, Georgie had blown a kiss at us both and spun off to dance again—either to show him that she hadn't been lying on a platter with an apple in her mouth waiting for him to turn up, or because she was now so wasted she didn't know what she was doing.

"Think she's okay?" said Alec, watching her weave a little unsteadily around the dance floor.

"She tends to be." To my surprise my voice came out naturally. "Though she did start early tonight."

"Earlier than you think," he said, laughing. "They were a little confused in Starbucks this morning when she asked for an Irish coffee."

I smiled back nervously, my brain still scrambling to assemble a timeline. Monday morning was when I had gone for the run and seen this man—and it was this man, I had no doubt—shagging in the woods. Within the hour, Georgie had been in my room telling me about the arsey South African journalist who'd asked her out on a date earlier that morning. So either it had been Georgie in the hearse (impossible, virtually) *or*—

"So you're Georgie's clever friend. She talked a lot about you, hey."

Now that I knew, it seemed impossible I had missed that accent. The compressed vowels, the extra kick on the consonants, the slight roll of the *r*'s." *Georgie's clivver frrend*. Alec leaned back against the French windows, hands still in his pockets. "She said you noticed everything."

I looked up sharply at this. Did I imagine an emphasis on "everything"? But he wore a friendly, interested look—the look of someone talking to his new girlfriend's friend. My shoulders relaxed a little. Clearly, he hadn't pinned me as the voyeur in the woods.

"And you must be her new partner in crime," I said lightly.

He laughed again, pulling out a pouch of tobacco and some cigarette papers, then looked over at the dance floor, still smiling. "Doing my best. It's not easy keeping up with Georgie Duncan."

Something about the smile made my ears grow warm. So he *was* into her. Maybe the girl in the hearse had meant nothing. Alec was rolling a cigarette now, folding along the end of the paper before tearing it to make a square. Then he scattered on some tobacco, smoothing it out evenly, and began to turn and tighten the cigarette rapidly. A quick lick along the edge like he was testing a harmonica and he tapped it twice on the heel of his hand before popping it into the side of his mouth.

He was looking at the French windows behind him now. His coat was still on. Was he about to leave?

Alec tried the handle. A crack of cool air came in. He took out the rollie and tilted his head. "Keep me company while I smoke this?"

CHAPTER 9

As we stepped outside a sensor light clicked on, illuminating a small paved yard with a pile of junk in one corner—some crusted old paint pots, two conjoined seats with no legs that looked like they had fallen out of an airplane. Alec pulled up a couple of rusting garden chairs. The light, which must have been on a timer, snapped off and we fell into darkness again. A dog barked in the distance.

"Want my coat?" he said as I rubbed my bare arms.

"No, no, I'm fine . . ."

But he took it off and handed it over anyway. The material was heavy, very slightly scratchy. I draped it backward over my chest, the collar under my chin. It smelled of pine and wood-smoke. I stole a glance at his hand, lit by the glow of his cigarette. The music was a distant thump behind us.

Various lines went through my head. *You're a journalist, Georgie tells me?* Boring. *So, you two must have had a fun few days?* Inappropriate. *Were you born with that hazel patch in your left eye?* Definitely not.

"Nice to be out here," I said, my voice slurring slightly from my third cocktail. I moved my lips more carefully. "Away from the pack."

"I'm lucky," said Alec. "I live with my aunt on the coast, on a little outcrop of land. It's very quiet there. Apart from my aunt, that is"—I heard the smile in his voice—"who never stops talking."

"Right on the coast? A view of the sea?"

"Yes. Seals on the beach most days, too. Sometimes their barking wakes me up." Somewhere in the distance a church bell was tolling the hour. I started counting the long strokes. *Don't be too late*, I found myself thinking, when Alec said suddenly, "Have you ever wanted to stop time?"

My eyes had grown accustomed to the darkness enough to see the shine in his eyes, the shape of his lips. The long strokes were over. Three short ones followed. Quarter to midnight.

Had he just read my mind?

"No. Have you?"

"Yes," he said. "Once. When I was twelve. Lying under a tree in South Africa with my German shepherd." He paused, and I heard him smile again. "Wow, I haven't thought about that for a while . . ." he trailed off.

"Tell me," I said quickly, into the silence.

So he told me about the guard dogs they kept when he was growing up in Johannesburg. His favorite, Knight, had a gammy ear but a wonderful temperament.

"Good name," I commented, "for a guard dog."

"Useless at his job, though. Might as well have been a kitten. I used to spend hours lying next to him under the jacaranda tree at the end of the garden. Watching the sunlight playing through the leaves with my arm rising and falling on his belly as he breathed."

He hesitated again, then flicked the ash from his cigarette. A little shower of sparks, dying as soon as they hit the darkness.

"One day, about a week after I had turned twelve, I made a wish, for it to stop. The sun. Or the earth moving round it—I had a rather hazy notion of what made time. Then I must have dozed off for a while. Because when I woke up, Knight wasn't snoring. My arm wasn't moving up and down. At first I thought he was in this strangely deep sleep. So deep I couldn't actually feel him breathing. Then I looked up. The breeze seemed to have stopped. The leaves were completely still. That was when I noticed. Everything was so quiet, it was wrong."

"Wrong? You mean, unusual?"

"My father was an architect. Like most so-called liberals, we lived in a gated white community in Jo'burg. But the highway was pretty close. If you listened, you could always hear the rumble of cars and lorries passing. So I listened carefully . . . but there was nothing. Nothing at all. I thought maybe it was because there was no breeze that afternoon. That was when I noticed the fish in the pond weren't moving." Alec paused. "This is a longer story than you bargained for. Am I boring you?" He looked over at me. In the darkness, I could see the glitter of his eyes. "You could have fallen asleep for all I know."

"Tell me about the fish."

Alec smiled; I could see the white of his teeth. "So my dad had these giant spotted catfish. Really ugly fuckers. He'd bought them a couple of years before when he saw an ornamental pond in a magazine. For the last few months, they'd been neglected. Ever since my mother had to stay for long stretches in the hospital."

"What was wrong with her?"

"Cancer. The worst kind. When all the grown-ups stop asking you if she's okay." Alec didn't pause. "Anyway, the point is, they weren't moving. But they weren't dead, either. Just suspended in the water. Like fish you'd find vacuum-packed in your freezer. That was when I realized my wish had come true."

"Your wish?"

"Time had stopped."

I started to laugh, but he said this with such matter-of-factness that I stopped. "You mean, that's what your twelve-year-old self *thought*."

"No, I mean it had stopped. I ran into the house and looked at the wall clock. I had to stand there for quite a while because it didn't have a second hand—just Roman numerals with big spaces in between. It was hard to tell whether the minute hand was moving. It seemed to be saying just after five past six for much too long. But that didn't seem enough proof. A lot of things had gone on the blink since Mum had been ill. Then I ran over and turned on the TV. And there was the newsreader frozen mid-sentence on the six o'clock news, eyes slightly to the right as he glanced at the Autocue."

"Come on . . ." I was starting to laugh again. "But how can that be?"

"No idea," said Alec, his voice deadpan. "I told you it was a strange story."

"But, really."

"Now you're thinking: Who is this weirdo who's started dating my friend?"

"Maybe a bit." I laughed. "But let's say I'm with you. What happened next? Was no one else in the house?"

"No. My dad said he and my brother were popping to the mall to get him some sports shoes. But actually I knew they'd gone to see my mother in the hospital because I heard Dad whispering to Brown the gardener that it was better I didn't see her like that. Brown was supposed to be babysitting. But he had run out of smokes. He'd popped out to get some in the shop at the end of the road."

"You must have been scared."

"Actually, I was thrilled. It suddenly occurred to me that if time had stopped—if I had stopped it—I could do anything I wanted. No one to stop me borrowing my neighbor's new skateboard and practicing flips without my helmet for as long as I liked. Or taking a walk around Hillbrow, the next-door township which I was burning with curiosity to see. Better still, I could go into my father's study and forge a memo in his handwriting, saying how he really felt Alec deserved a one-off lump sum of pocket money so that he could get one of those watches with a luminous dial that you can use as a light to read with at night."

I laughed. "So what did you do?"

"Absolutely nothing. It crossed my mind that perhaps it wouldn't be much fun doing any of those things if you didn't have anyone to do them with. Or even my father asking me what the fuck I was doing using his ink-pen." He paused. "Instead I went to the end of the garden and just lay back down with my dog, looking up through the leaves at a tiny plane that was frozen, mid-flight. And in the end I wasn't even disappointed when I realized my arm had started moving up and down on Knight. That the leaves had begun to whisper and the vapor trail behind the plane was growing." Alec's voice was low now. "For a moment I felt better than okay. Then I heard my father's car pulling up in the driveway. And I realized that I hadn't been able to stop time. There was no stopping time. Tomorrow would happen. However much I tried to wish it away."

He fell silent then. And I knew. I thought of his father walking toward him in the garden, back from the hospital, his shoulders braced to tell a twelve-year-old boy the worst news in the world.

"God, Alec, I'm sorry."

"Yeah," he said. "Me, too."

For a few moments he smoked in silence. Then the clock started tolling again.

Alec laughed out loud. "You've got to admit, I have great timing."

"Would be better if it was still quarter to twelve."

We both stopped to count, as if it might be.

Twelve strokes.

"Now your turn, Cinderella," he said, laughing.

"Oh, no."

"Yes. What about you? I feel like you gave me some truth serum. Your go now."

I paused for a moment, thinking. "Well, I've never wanted to stop time. In fact, I've always wanted to wind it forward." And perhaps it was because of the darkness, or the cocktails, or a sense somehow that since he'd told me about losing his mother, I knew I could trust him, I found myself talking.

About all the stale, lonely days in Milton View. The hours dragging by. The golf course, with the same well-heeled people with their diamond-patterned sweaters, measuring out their weekends by whether they went round with one stroke more, one stroke less. Then my school days, a sluggish creep toward weekends, when not much happened, either. Feeling like a stranger in my own home.

"It's funny, though, the last thing I want to do is really belong there. I've been looking for the exit sign as long as I can remember. I guess I'm scared that if I don't get out soon, I'll just turn into them. One day, I'll look down and I'll be wearing those sweaters and fretting about that difficult bunker on the ninth hole."

I saw Alec smile as he stubbed out his cigarette against the side of an upturned terra-cotta pot.

"Which is why you're drawn to people like Georgie," he said softly. "You hope some of that wildness will rub off on you. Make you more exotic." Then he turned to me, and attuned to the dark now, I saw the full outline of him, the glitter of his eyes inches away. His voice, when it came, was low and serious. "Which is a shame, Jess . . . because you're something all your own."

I breathed in, feeling that drag toward him again, as if to a cliff edge. The silence prickled between us. I could see his chest rising and falling—more quickly than before, surely? For a wild moment I felt the blood rushing through my head and I thought I wouldn't be able to stop myself from leaning just a little closer, lifting my face to find his lips in the darkness.

Just then, something—a cat, a falling leaf—disturbed the sensor. The light clicked back on. I blinked at him, wide eyed, my heart crashing in my chest.

Alec smiled and stood up casually, as if nothing had happened. "Let's go in, shall we? I should check on Georgie."

I'd told Georgie that no one knew which one "The Room" was, in a party. But of course, when we found her, she was bang in the middle of it.

The booze must have run dry because the crowd in the kitchen had thinned out and half a dozen people were gathered in a little glass extension just beyond it. There was a long, low pinkish sofa and chairs, a shaggy rug that a couple of people were sitting on. I didn't recognize any of the students except Georgie, but somehow they all seemed a little older, better-looking, and more switched on than most of the people I'd seen milling around. And in the middle of the sofa, like a great lamp shedding light on all the upturned faces, was Lorna.

She was leaning forward as she spoke, wearing a dark green shot-silk dress that caught the light as she moved, her hair loose and her hands and face animated. The story must have been good because no one looked at us, not even Georgie, who was perched on one of the sofa arms beside her. Only Lorna herself glanced around when we walked in.

For a moment, she hesitated. I saw her clock both Alec and me—a tiny dip of the head, a smile around the corner of her eyes—but in that split second I felt she had seen everything. Me, him, the space between us.

Then she turned back to the group. "So, no one notices anything unusual at the dinner," she continued. "Except perhaps, in hindsight, it's strange that Monica—who is famous only as the famous playwright's wife—gets up from the table several times to go to the loo. But then she's the highly strung, much-too-thin type who probably has a tiny bladder."

"Like me," interrupted Georgie, her sleepy eyes more heavy-lidded than ever. "That's how everyone tends to describe me." A couple of the students grinned at this. Alec laughed and leaned back against the wall, crossing his arms. Georgie looked up and, seeing us, put out her arms, reflexively, like a child—"There you are!"—at which point she teetered and, laughing, nearly fell onto the cushions next to Lorna.

I hovered behind Alec, not wanting to join the others, not able to leave, still dazed by what I had felt in the yard, still feeling it, with him only a few feet away. But now it was mixed with a guilty paranoia that Georgie might pick up on it. (Though what was "it" exactly? Was there an "it"?) And over and above all this, I registered that strange effect Lorna had on a room.

I had felt it in the seminar, of course, but here, there was more of an edge to it—with the alcohol and the low light and the oddness of finding her at a student party. (Did she know Gideon? Did other faculty members come to parties? Wasn't there a rule about it?) Some kind of current transmitted from her—not just from her blazing mind and the words that she chose, but from the very energy around her, the fact that she was wearing gold earrings that flashed when she moved her head and a little makeup that made her look younger and more beautiful.

I stole a glance at Alec's face. I thought he would be watching Georgie, sprawling in her tiny shorts. But he, too, was looking at Lorna, a little smile hovering on his lips, like he was settling in to watch a show he'd been looking forward to.

"The day after the dinner, my friend Allie calls me," Lorna continued. "She's beside herself. Two rings have vanished from the jewelry box in her bedroom. The rings are priceless, they belonged to her beloved, dead grandmother."

She paused here, and a thought popped into my head. Before I could stop myself I said, "Don't all lost rings belong to beloved, dead grandmothers?"

Lorna looked over. When she saw it was me, her smile widened. "Jess Walker. Yes, they always do. But wait." She looked round at everyone, her dress reshaped by light and shadow as she moved. "Later that day, around teatime, the famous playwright calls round."

"Are we allowed a name?" asked a girl with an elegant, short haircut, who was sitting on the rug, arms looped gracefully around her knees.

To my surprise, Alec spoke up at this. "Never ask a source for a name. You might end up losing the story."

Lorna glanced at him with a slight frown, then laughed. "Sounds like we have a hack in the room. But okay, let's give the playwright a name. How about Janus? So Janus drops by with a card and some flowers to say thank you for dinner. And while he's there he pops to the loo. Later that evening, Allie decides, finally, that she *is* going to call the police and report the loss. She checks her jewelry box one more time—"

Here Lorna paused and a confident-looking guy in round glasses suggested, "The rings are back?"

"Right. The rings are back in her jewelry box. So." Lorna looked around at us all again, her face alive with challenge. "What happened?"

There was a short pause.

"Well, that's easy," said the girl on the rug. "She's obviously a klepto. The playwright's wife."

"Okay," said Lorna, nodding. "But what do we think is Janus's motive for sneaking them back? Social embarrassment? Or an act of love? Love so unconditional he'd far rather take the blame for the theft himself? In which case, should we judge him? Are white lies, even elaborate acts of deception, sometimes justified?"

Beside me Alec straightened up, uncrossing his arms. "Aren't you making some assumptions?"

Lorna turned, flashing her eyes, a little incredulous smile twitching. "*Am* I?"

"Well . . ." His voice was harder now. "The cliché, for a start: That she is thin and nervous, the wife of a famous playwright, unseen in her own right. *Therefore* she is a kleptomaniac. Some fucked-up plea for attention, something to set her apart." He glanced at the rest of the group, including them in the conversation. "But the playwright is the one who had the rings. Who's to say he didn't do it himself? Or perhaps it was his wife who did it, but entirely at his behest. Perhaps he controls her, enjoys humiliating her. Then gets an extra kick out of getting away with it."

The group's gaze had switched to Alec, registering him as a contender. I saw a few smiles, a couple of nods.

Lorna shrugged. "I think that's even more of a cliché, isn't it? The brilliant playwright pulling the strings . . ." She cocked her head at Alec. "Though it occurs to me, thanks to you"—she touched a finger to her forehead—"that perhaps they were in it together. Perhaps it is a game they're playing, to relieve the monotony of monogamy. The deadening pulse. A thrilling, ultimately harmless game . . ."

Everyone looked at Alec, as if it was his turn in a bidding war. He stared back at Lorna for a few moments. The atmosphere seemed to thicken. I remembered what Georgie had said about him taking apart Steady in class and thought, *Oh shit, he's going to say something vicious.*

But then Georgie, who had been tilting sideways on the sofa arm like a second hand on a clock, fell entirely into the space on the cushions behind Lorna's back and collapsed into giggles.

And Alec was across the room, helping her up—"Time for your ride home, I think"—and Lorna was feeling around the back of the sofa for Georgie's cigarettes and phone, and laughing, telling her it had been nice to meet her finally, and maybe she should think about not skipping the next class, however great the temptation (here she gave Alec a sweet, ironic smile).

Georgie waved at me as she left the room, but Alec paused. "Want a lift back?"

I hesitated. "Well, if you don't mind . . ."

"Not at all. God knows there's room in my car." Alec shook his head, held my gaze for a beat. Then he smiled suddenly.

"But you know that, of course."

CHAPTER 10

W ho's Nick, then?"
    The sound of the blind snapping open. Dazzling sunshine pouring in. I clamped my forearm over my eyes, blinking, and then peered at my alarm clock from underneath: 1:13 P.M. My nightie was drenched in sweat, my mouth so dry I had to work up some saliva before I could speak.

"Nick who?"

"That's what I'm asking you," said Georgie, bouncing on the end of the bed, her eyes sparkling like she hadn't touched a single toxin the night before. She was wearing a short denim skirt, her blond hair combed back, damp from the shower. "A handsome Indian boy came up to us in the canteen. Seemed worried about your hand."

"Oh," I said, glancing at my phone, which lay turned off on the bedside table.

She bounced again, smiling. "Is there something I should know?"

I sat up. I could feel my curls sticking out at crazy angles. *Now's the time to tell her what I saw in the woods.*

Of course, I'd refused the lift back from the party with them—the idea of sitting in between a hammered Georgie and Alec while trying to process that he *had* seen me spying on him in the woods was too much. I'd invented a second wind on the spot. But then I'd been stuck for a ride and too broke for a cab, so ended up walking back through the cold night, alone with the paranoid thunder of my thoughts.

"Anyway, I hope you *do* know him because he's waiting downstairs. I told him he could come with us."

"Come with us where?" My body felt stiff, like it had held on to its tension in sleep. Last night it had felt obvious I should tell Georgie. But now, looking at her excitement, it felt mean-spirited. Unnecessary. So what if her new boyfriend had been shagging someone else? It had been before they'd really hooked up, after all.

"Jon the Don is giving some deadly 'Safety on the Internet' lecture in the main theater which is completely compulsory. Meaning we have a free afternoon." She gave me an innocent look. "This way, it makes us a foursome."

"Foursome with who?" I said. "I mean, with whom?" For a hopeful moment I thought it might be one of the other boys I'd seen her flirting with last night.

"Who do you think?" she said, pulling out some shorts and a T-shirt from my closet and tossing them onto my bed. "Alec, of course. He's in the car park. By the way, have I told you what he drives yet? You're going to *die*."

Alec was standing in front of the hearse, smoking a rollie, squinting in the sunshine, his dark hair lifting slightly in the breeze. Behind him the hearse took up nearly two of the parking bays, sun striking off its paintwork. I felt my stomach pitch and looked away before we were close enough to lock eyes. *If I don't meet his gaze, I'll be fine.*

Nick stopped in his tracks when he realized which car it was. "You've got to be shitting me," he said, laughing.

"Actually they're very reliable," said Alec, pulling the keys from his pocket with a smile. "No one wants to break down on the way to a funeral. Tricky for parking, it's true, but I find the trunk space comes in handy."

I felt my face grow hotter and peered into the rear windows, half-expecting to see some rumpled blankets. But the backseats had been flipped up so that it looked more like a limo with an extra-large trunk. I saw my reflection in the bulge of a door panel. White face, big eyes, that pinch I get between my eyebrows when I'm anxious.

"Nick, Jess, meet Alec," said Georgie. "Or did you already meet at Gideon's? Obviously I don't remember a damn thing," she added, giving a throaty laugh that suggested gallons of wine and drugs, no sleep, and lots of sex.

"Hey, Nick. Yes. I met Jess," said Alec, turning to me with a smile. "But let's meet again. Hi." He stuck out his hand. I took it automatically. It was warm and dry. I found myself looking down at the sneakers he was wearing. They were gray canvas with a white stripe and scuffed at the toes, the same ones he'd worn to the party.

"Hey, again," I managed lamely.

Nick opened the back door and stood aside to let me in first. I slid in, my heart thumping.

Georgie climbed into the passenger seat next to Alec without hesitation, as if she rode around shotgun in hearses all the time. Perhaps, I realized with a twist of envy, she'd been doing just that over these last few days. Finding scenic spots, lowering the rear seats, reaching for each other . . . I flashed on that first scene in the woods. Had I been right not to tell her? But this was all wrong. A hearse should be making me think about death, not sex. *Come on, Jess.* Death. Focus on death.

"Don't you find it a bit creepy driving this?" Nick was asking, as if he'd read my mind. He was peering around the black leather interior cautiously as if expecting to find a body part stuffed in some side compartment. "Doesn't it feel full of ghosts?"

Alec hooked his arm behind Georgie's headrest, twisting round to see out of the rear window as he reversed. "Definitely a downside," he agreed. "They're all over the place."

"Oh, don't get Alec started on death," drawled Georgie. "He's from South Africa. They're all murdering each other at traffic lights or being left to rot in townships. Too cushy over here, living with his aunt in a village where no one locks their front doors. He wants to keep reminding himself."

Alec laughed out loud and then rattled the stick, the gearbox grinding as he searched for first. "I didn't put it quite like that," he said with a sideways grin at Georgie. "But as usual, you say it better."

From my peripheral vision I could tell that Nick was pretending not to look at me. I pretended not to see. Oh God. Why the hell had I agreed to come? What was wrong with saying *no*? We came to the end of University Drive and stopped at the junction, the blinker ticking.

"Where are we going this time, *chéri*?" asked Georgie, reaching down into her bag to fish out her shades.

Alec adjusted his rearview mirror, feeding the wheel through his hands as the car swung out onto the road, and for a moment his eyes met mine and I saw them crinkle at the corners. I thought of sitting in the back garden at the party, his face inches away from mine.

"Who's up for playing truant?" he asked.

On the drive to the pub, Alec told us why he had left South Africa.

The truth is, when you really like someone, it can be hard to concentrate on the details of what they're saying. It's easy to lose the thread. You're too busy zooming in and out, trying to work out what they feel about you, distracted by the story going on in your head. But not with Alec. Not ever with Alec. There was something about the way he would focus a story on one person, bring them to life, make you step into their skin and see through their eyes, that made you just want to listen.

"Stevie was a soccer prodigy," Alec told us as we bombed along country lanes banked with hedgerows. "One of the many kids who played on the dustbowl that served as a soccer field in the shadows of the mines in Marikana. At six years old he could curl in a corner, at nine he could beat the goalie from the fifty-yard mark. By eleven, he, like too many other kids, hoped the Bafana Bafana coaches would find him. Instead AIDS found his family. First his father, then his mother and sister."

Georgie, whose hand was trailing out the open window, shifted round to look at us.

"I should warn you. Alec doesn't tell stories with happy endings."

"So now Stevie becomes another underage miner, one of many," Alec continued. "But he's still exceptional. He learns faster, works harder. By seventeen, he's leading the team underground, on the rock drill. And he's on the miners' soccer team, of course. The captain there, too, right up until the strike."

Alec paused, changing gears. His words felt sharp-edged. I felt them lodge in the air, take hold. *He's doing what he did at the party*, I thought dimly. *This is what he does. He makes stories into weapons.*

"When the miners began to picket, Stevie was torn. He stood with his team, but he knew how the game was played. They didn't own the mine, the management did. And below the ground, as on the field, the first rule is: Don't fuck with the management, because they'll fuck with you. Still, he was never going to be a strike-breaker. He went along, one of the three thousand miners that sat on the Wonderkop hill demanding a rise in their measly pay. But when the police opened fire with their R5s, Stevie got his team to the Small Koppie—the rocky clearing of raised ground which was where they normally took a crap, which stank of piss and shit—and where they seemed safe, where it was clear for all to see that they meant no harm."

Tiny prickles traveled up my arms.

"That was when the police moved in. Thirteen unarmed miners—a full soccer squad, plus two subs—already on their knees, begging for their lives, gunned down in the beautiful light of a

Transkei evening. Stevie saw it all from behind a rock, remembered it as clearly as his sister's face when he'd watched her cough up blood one morning. He knew the risks of talking to a journalist like me, but he wanted to tell it all."

For a few moments, no one spoke. Fields, knitted together by hedges, spread out to either side of the road and I was suddenly conscious of the curvature of the earth beneath them.

"I did try and warn you," Georgie said quietly.

I watched Alec's hands as the hearse swung round the corners. There was something lethal about his matter-of-fact tone, how composed he was, but I could tell he wanted a cigarette. His hands kept shifting position on the steering wheel and when we paused at junctions his trigger fingers would drum an impatient rhythm on the leather. *This isn't a show*, I thought. *This is costing you, telling us this.*

"So you saw the actual massacre?" Nick said, sounding awed.

Alec shook his head. "No. I was way out in the sticks when my paper called, told me to get my arse there. By the time I arrived, the ambulances were already coming out, everything was blocked. I swung round my jeep and followed them. Managed to slip into a hospital, ended up between the beds of two miners. The one on the left was a total mess. There were about five or six nurses and doctors working on him. Someone was cutting off one of his jean legs, which didn't seem to have much in it, while someone else was hoovering up bits of shit and whatever the fuck it was from round the bed. The miner—he must have been twenty or so, I never did find out his name—was trying to talk, but you couldn't hear what he was saying. His throat was making these gurgling noises like he was drowning in his own blood. In the bed on the other side was Stevie. And he told me everything about what happened, up in the Koppie. The best story I ever had. A story that my paper never ran."

I felt the back of my neck chill. The needle on the speedometer flickered past sixty. We overtook a couple of cars and I saw the passengers stare at us as we barreled past, their eyes sharp with curiosity. A hearse speeding down country roads, not such a common sight. Nick was leaning forward to ask questions now, good ones, about why the paper hadn't run the story. And if not them, why not others? Right, Georgie echoed, chiming in. Had they not believed him, thought it sounded too good to be true?

"If only," Alec replied dryly. "But all the ballistics backed up Stevie's story. No. The worst bit was that they said . . ." He paused for a moment, as if the words, finally, stuck in his throat. "They said it wasn't *fair*. It wasn't, in their fucked-up bloodless notion of impartiality, balanced enough. Kevin, the editor who spiked it, said that in the telling of it *I'd chosen sides*. That I hadn't, in his unfor-fucking-ettable phrase, given the mine owners *a fair crack of the whip*. That I was disrespecting the reader, leading them by the nose. Thirty-four dead and seventy-eight injured. And I was being one-fucking-sided. Of course, once my paper turned it down, no one else would touch it. Jo'burg is a small place. My byline had been on its most liberal paper for the last four years. I tried eight more publications, ended up posting the story online myself. Don't suppose more than a couple hundred people read it at the time . . . So yeah, that's why I left. Because I gave Stevie my word. While he lay shaking in that bed with his dead friends in his eyes, and the stink of guts on the floor, I gave him my word. And I couldn't fucking deliver on it. *That's* why I left South Africa."

He pressed the accelerator and the engine kicked forward.

"Jesus," said Nick.

"Fuck," said Georgie.

I said nothing, looking out the window at the blur of hedgerows.

For some reason, I found myself thinking about the view of the golf course out of the bay windows at Milton View. How I'd stared at it for eighteen years, yearning for a bigger world to live in, thinking I could find it through books, clawing at make-believe in the hope I'd draw blood. *Dear God*, I thought with a sudden shiver. *Was this the "real world" I'd been trying to find?*

"Wow," said Nick. "I'm so sorry. Do you think you'll ever go back?"

Alec met his eyes in the rearview mirror. "Thanks," he said, his voice hard. "But that's not even a question for me. The only question, really, is when."

Georgie's hand came up then and touched the back of his neck.

I stared at her fingers playing with the dark whorls of his hairline, saw him glance at her troubled face with a brief, absent smile. And I knew, even then, with a sick certainty, that I wouldn't have him for long.

Not that he was mine, of course.

Not that he was anyone's, I was beginning to see.

CHAPTER 11

The beer garden at the Half-Hitch spilled down onto the banks of the River Yare. Apart from the gentle whine of the ring road, it gave a decent performance as a country pub—trestle tables with bottle-green parasols, a medium-sized vegetable patch that appeared to be in use, and even a small chicken house with a wire mesh run. Despite it being lunchtime on a weekday, there was that carnival atmosphere that accompanies sunshine in England: people smiling recklessly at strangers, caught in that sweet spot of heightened possibility before things tip over and get ugly.

Georgie was leaning forward against our table, her folded arms accentuating her cleavage above the low neckline of her polka-dot top. "Do you think you can be *born* that way?" she said in a low voice. "Or do you think it just suddenly happened when he turned thirty?"

She shot another surreptitious glance at a family at a nearby table. The father, straight-backed in a stripy shirt with the unmistakable air of an ex–army officer, had already been over once to tell us to keep the noise down. "If you throw any more peas," he was saying now to two small, miserable-looking blond boys, "you can jolly well sit in the car."

"Maybe it wasn't his fault," murmured Alec, taking out his tobacco pouch. "Maybe he was only a shy kid, until cool, sexy girls mistook his awkwardness for being square. Teachers suggested conventional career paths. Before he knew it, he'd become monstrously uptight, paranoid about vegetable missiles."

"Stop! That's *awful*," said Georgie, looking horrified. She rummaged in the bottom of her bag of chips. "Do you really think that can happen? People can pick up personalities by mistake, like being handed back the wrong coat from the cloakroom?"

We were sitting under a copper beech tree on the trestle table farthest away from the pub. Alec had bought a bottle of white wine, which sat—rather to my awe—in its own ice bucket, frosted with condensation. I was still finding it hard to meet his eyes for long, but less so. I was halfway through my second glass, and the outlines of things had begun to soften. The sunlight, filtering through the leaves, was dappling everyone's skin, matching Georgie's top. I kept thinking about how different it had felt to sit with my friends outside the Sandcastle Pub in Reigate. This wasn't "killing time," like it was there. In fact, it felt like the opposite. As if, in every exchange, something was growing between us, something that crackled with life.

"I'm a great believer in reinvention," said Nick. "I was the class fatty until I was fifteen. Geeky, too, with glasses."

We all turned to look at him. He was wearing a marled gray T-shirt. You could tell by the way it fell over his chest, and by the shape of his strong, dark-skinned arms, that he had a lean, hard athlete's body.

"You *were*?" said Georgie in disbelief. "How fat?"

"Plenty," said Nick. "Had to have my trousers made specially."

"*No!*"

"Then one summer, I got into mountain biking and started wearing contacts. After that everyone treated me differently."

"Differently, better?" I asked curiously. I liked the way he chose his words. Like he was enjoying running them through his mind first, picking the right ones.

"Varied. Some people started talking to me for the first time. A couple of friends started behaving strangely, resentfully, as if I'd broken some kind of contract."

Alec, who'd been rolling a cigarette, listening, looked up at this. The patch in his iris was bright hazel in the sunshine.

I felt Nick's eyes on me as he continued.

"Speaking of broken contracts, I heard something at breakfast. About your favorite lecturer." He broke a bag of chips wide open, laid it out on the table to share, his hands steady. "Rumors about why she left Cambridge in such a hurry. Something hushed up. About one of her students. A girl. Sybil."

"You mean, sexual?" said Georgie, her eyes wide. "*Gripping* . . . I'll have to ask my parents. Apparently, she *did* once come for a weekend party at ours. I thought they'd made it up."

"Maybe Lorna started it," interrupted Alec. "The rumor, I mean. Maybe she preferred the whiff of some affair that never happened because the reality was more mundane. Like underperforming with grades, or . . . I don't know . . . plagiarism."

"No way," I said quickly. "Lorna's far too brilliant to plagiarize anyone."

Alec shrugged. "Even brilliant people cut corners sometimes. So, listen, I was wondering . . ." He half stood to take something out of the back pocket of his jeans. With a casual glance over his shoulder, he presented his cupped palm just below table height. "Anyone feeling peckish?"

For a moment I blinked, not understanding. There must have been around fifty mushrooms in all: long, spindly stems, their pointy cream caps fringed with black gills.

"'Shrooms—you genius," breathed Georgie. She looked up, her eyes wickedly aglow. "But where . . . here?"

Alec snapped his hand closed, eyes laughing. "Why not?"

To date, my involvement in the underworld of drugs had consisted of:

- A dozen—maybe two dozen—joints behind the Sand-castle with my brother Freddie.
- A very expensive line of white powder in a pub in West London which, due to the fizzy feeling in my nostrils, the banging headache that ensued, and not much else besides, I suspect was mostly washing powder or baby milk formula.
- An "herbal" ecstasy tablet at a music festival which smelled of silage and may/may not have improved the high I got from several cans of cider.

The idea of uppers and downers didn't scare me much. Halluci-nogens, I was much more wary of, mainly due to a slew of stories revolving around my cousin Tom, who had taken a tab of acid in his year off and then spent six months in a mental institution, eating baby food. But mushrooms were *plants*. How bad could plants be?

Georgie and Alec walked off toward the riverbank to count them. Nick looked at me. Some strands of black hair had fallen over his eyes. His looks were very classical, I thought, the long straight line of his nose, his full symmetrical lips.

"What do you think?" he asked. "Fun? Terrible idea?"

"Both, probably."

Over on the riverbank Alec's and Georgie's heads were bent together, her happy laughter floating over to us.

"She's great, Georgie," Nick said. "Much more to her than meets the eye. On campus she seems kind of . . . brash. But there's a lot going on, isn't there?"

"Yes, there is." I fingered a groove on the table. "And what do you think of Alec? He seems like he's really into Georgie, don't you think?" I felt an irresistible urge to talk about them, like picking a new scab off a wound.

"Alec? Compelling as all hell. I was worried when I saw the

hearse, but he's the real deal. That story about what happened at the mine, the risks he takes in his job—" Nick broke off. He had a wonderful smile, too, I thought, his teeth very white. "Look, I'm just a geek who likes rocks. When you meet a real-life hero like that . . . Ah, looks like you're up next."

He glanced over my shoulder to where Georgie was walking back toward us, without Alec. "Sure you want to?" said Nick, kicking at a chestnut on the grass. "We can just potter about drinking wine, you know."

I hesitated. For a moment I thought of cousin Tom and the baby food. Perhaps I was trying to choke down the disappointment of seeing how well Alec and Georgie worked together—rejection and rebellion make good bedfellows. Perhaps it was the sun and the wine, and the sense that something was blossoming between the four of us. But the spirit of misrule was now in me. I took a breath.

"If you look out for me, I'll do the same for you."

Nick's eyes crinkled. "You're right. Let's. We can be idiots together."

"You okay?" asked Alec as I chased a handful of mushrooms with a long swig of wine.

"I think so," I said, my voice sounding tight.

As soon as I'd sat down with him on the riverbank, my newfound laissez-faire deserted me. It was our first time alone together since the party. My whole body jammed straight into high alert. I was glad I had something to blame my nerves on.

"Where did you get them?" I asked, chewing a few more, then taking another sip of wine. Georgie was right. They tasted like someone had made marshmallows out of your spare change. Over at the table, I could see she had slipped Nick a handful, saw him grimace as he knocked them back.

"A field near my aunt's," said Alec. "I went on a run this morning and spotted a few in some long grass. When I started looking,
there were hundreds. She makes a mean scrambled egg, my aunt
Zanny. I nearly suggested we fry them up with garlic and chili. We
have this ritual of a cold dip in the sea, followed by hot breakfast.
She's incredibly hardy for someone the size of a pepper shaker." He
smiled. "But she's a strange mix, too. Utterly nuts, but also very
moralistic. I couldn't be sure whether she would eat them all at
once or call the police."

"So you knew they were magic?"

He laughed. "You sound like a little girl asking about fairies.
Yes, I knew they were magic. Although we don't have many in
South Africa, apart from the ones people grow in nurseries. My
brother used to chew a lot of khat, though. Not as trippy, but still
gets you hooked."

He lobbed a stone. It dropped into the water, the ripples spreading outwards.

"So you and your brother—you're close?"

"'Close' is a funny word. You can be close and still not like
someone."

"Um, did you just dodge the question?"

Alec sighed. "All right, he's called Basti, and no, we don't like
each other. I have a sister, too, she's a lot nicer."

I looked ahead at the river, keeping as still as possible. This was
a trick I had learned from being in a big family where everyone
talks a lot but no one says much. If people start to confide, don't
probe, lose eye contact. Squeeze yourself into as small a space as
possible. Eventually, like wild animals creeping out from cover,
their souls will inch a little closer to yours.

"My parents tried for years to have a child," Alec said eventually.
"After a while, they lost heart. Tried to adopt. When my mother
turned forty, they were given Basti, who was two and a half. He was

a crack baby, at least that's what they called him, from addict parents. Been neglected. Left alone in the house for hours on end. Had to rummage in bins to get his own food."

"And you?" I asked, trying not to sound shocked. "From the same place?" *Maybe that's it*, I thought. That charge around him, like a force field. Survival.

He shook his head. "Two years after my parents adopted Basti, the impossible happened. My mother became pregnant."

"With you?"

"Yes. Then a couple of years later, my sister."

A silence fell. My breathing sounded too fast. I tried to slow it.

"You feel something?" he asked suddenly, leaning in and fixing me with his eyes.

"Feel something?" My chest wound up tighter. I thought I'd been doing well at masking it, but maybe it was obvious.

"From the mushrooms."

"Oh." I wanted to eat my fist. "No. I mean, not yet."

"Takes a while," said Alec, glancing at his watch. He looked back at Nick and Georgie and brushed some grass off his jeans as if preparing to get up. I realized how fiercely I wanted him to stay here on the riverbank in the sunshine, away from the others.

"Must have been tough on your brother," I said.

Alec looked over, his eyes narrowing. "Why do you say that?"

"Well, you were the miracle child. And you're"—I wanted to say gorgeous and clever—"well, probably he felt you were the favorite."

Alec's face suddenly become very watchful. I had no idea what he was thinking, only that I had his attention again.

"You may be right," he said. "But it still doesn't explain why he is such a cunt."

I lifted my eyebrows but said nothing.

"Hard to explain. He has a way of twisting the truth." Alec paused, flicked a little piece of grass into the river. "The first time it happened, I was very young. Five, I think. We were in my parents' bedroom in Jo'burg."

"Hey!" We both turned at Georgie's voice. She walked over with Nick behind her. "What are you two so secret squirrel?" She dropped down next to us, lowered her voice. "Anything happening?"

I was just about to shake my head when I noticed that the surface of the river, which I had previously thought of as a pale, rather dirty brown, had begun to shimmer as if it was made from beaten bronze. I was busy marveling at its texture when I realized that the shimmering was actually something much more rhythmical and deliberate. The river—slowly, heavily, like it was deep in slumber—had started to breathe.

"It's alive," I whispered, half to myself.

"Sure is." Nick nodded and pointed up the river. "You see all those winding curves along the bank? We rock geeks call them *meandering*. When water flows it moves a little bit faster on the outer edge than the inner, which makes those *S*-shapes. There's nothing I love watching more than a river—one of the few places where you actually get to see time carving itself into the landscape. The past flowing into the future."

We all looked at the water. The edges of the river seemed to pulse.

"The past flowing into the future," said Georgie. She looked at me. "This guy's a genius."

I nodded, mostly to acknowledge my own body to myself. My limbs had started to sink down into the bank, and I felt the rest of my senses spin out of the husk of me, as if attached by an elastic cord. The ground beneath me seemed to be sliding toward the water, so I scrambled backward. "I think we should all sit further up the bank," I said quickly.

"Don't worry," Alec said, putting a hand on my arm. "It's just kicking in. You need to adjust a bit."

He moved his hand away but I still saw the print of it against my arm and then tracking outwards, like my brain had taken thousands of sequential photos.

"The past flowing into the future," repeated Georgie in wonder. "We're all just rivers twisting along, trying to find the sea . . ." She was puffing cigarettes madly, using the glowing ends to light one from the next.

"Would you mind taking that cigarette downwind, please?"

We all looked up guiltily. The man with the stripy shirt and military bearing was standing over us with the uneasy bravado of a middle-class person psyching themselves up for confrontation. Without actually using the words "heavily pregnant," he looked pointedly over his shoulder at his wife, who was resting her hands on her swollen belly, like she was in a commercial for a mortgage.

Georgie shrugged carelessly. "My mother smoked like a crematorium when she was knocked up. Ashes all over my baby head. Your boys are very beautiful," she added, taking another drag on her cigarette and making no attempt to stub it out. "They look like angels with those halos."

The two boys looked at us, their mouths open in identical O's, excited by the drama. I started to giggle. Georgie was right. Their blond hair shone like spun white gold and seemed to be radiating outwards.

"Look," said the man uncomfortably. "I'm the first to enjoy a party. But this is a family place."

"Really?" drawled Georgie. "I thought this was a place that sold alcohol. Steady drinking is the real problem, you know." She looked at the empty pint glasses on his table. "You should watch out for that. It creeps up on you and before you know it, you're losing your temper with the kids, taking a swing at your wife—"

"Time for a walk," interrupted Alec firmly. He stood up, half-lifting Georgie by the elbow. "Why don't we go and take a look at those chickens?" He steered her off toward the henhouse.

I looked back at Stripy Shirt, feeling a pang of sorrow for him.

Suddenly I understood. His uptight collar was strangling him. "Perhaps if you undid that top button—"

"Jess," Nick broke in quickly. "Chickens?"

Alec took a seat on a tree stump and rolled himself another cigarette while Georgie and I sat in front of the wire mesh, mesmerized as the rooster picked his way round the coop, his fleshy red comb jostling over beady eyes. Three hens pecked at the ground.

"Look at that rooster," said Georgie in awe. "The way he controls everything." We followed him as he moved around with his slow, jerky tread for what might have been hours.

"Water. We all need water," said Alec eventually, standing up. He glanced down. "Think you should get out of the sun, too." He put the back of his hand briefly to one of my hot cheeks and I felt my heart drum wildly. "You're burning up with that pale skin," he said softly. "Why don't you go and sit under the trees?"

Georgie gave me a shrewd look as he walked off. "Burning or blushing?"

I blinked in consternation, my mind blank.

Then she rose to her knees suddenly, her eyes glowing. "Let's go for a swim."

"What?"

"Let's go for a swim." And before I had time to answer, she had run behind the copper beech. Still giggling, I ran after her. Nick called my name, but by now Georgie was wriggling out of her skirt and he didn't follow.

The dark purple canopy of leaves overhead looked so lustrous that I wanted to lie down and just stare at them.

"You can't just strip off here," I whispered, peering round the trunk. Quite a few tables in the garden had emptied, including that of the family with the two boys, but there were still a handful of people finishing their lunches. "And you can't swim, either. You're tripping." I looked round a little wildly for Alec, but there was no sign of him. "What are you going to do, leap in the river?"

Georgie snapped open her bra strap and I couldn't help staring at her large breasts with their upward-pointing brown nipples. She started peeling off her underwear. There was a small strip of pale brown hair down the middle.

"The river is Time," intoned Georgie, giggling hysterically, and stepping out from behind the trunk, she ran toward the water, shouting "Wakey, wakey!" as she streaked past the tables. I put my hand over my mouth, feeling the laughter bubbling up inside me, and ran over to the bank in time to see Georgie fling herself in. A large splash broke into a shower of gems as she hit the surface. Nick was standing beside me.

"Oh shit," he said, but with some admiration. "I hope she can swim."

"It's amazing!" screamed Georgie. "Like swimming in silk." Then her blond cap of wet hair was bobbing up and down under the water again, and I heard a posh voice from one of the tables say in some disgust, "She'll drown herself," and the next thing I knew, Alec was beside us kicking off his shoes and wading in to get her.

"Come here, you nutter." He reached her in a few steps and put his arms around her, pushing her hair gently off her face, smiling into her eyes. "You absolute nutter."

After that, things got a bit blurry. Perhaps Stripy Shirt had said something to the pub owner because it seemed like the moment Alec pulled Georgie out of the water, there were two police officers in the garden: a man with a jowly face and a woman with a mannish haircut and a disapproving mouth. The woman threw a gray blanket around Georgie as the man pulled the bag of mushrooms out of her bag and said grimly, "Right. You can all come with us down to the station," which sounded so much like a movie that it was another reason for us to fall about with laughter.

Things were much less funny after that. I dimly remember a humming noise in the police station and having to fill out a form, but the print was crawling all around the page and it took me hours to write my name. And then the policeman who had found the mushrooms was giving us a lecture in a small, brightly lit office, but his jowly cheeks were melting down onto his white collar while he spoke. I started to laugh again, though this time it threatened to turn into tears.

They let us go with slapped wrists and a warning. Mainly, I think, because Alec did the talking. I don't know how he managed to appear so completely sober, but I heard him explaining calmly to one of the officers about "a difficult time" and "death in the family," and the next minute we were back out on the street. It was evening and gray light had wrapped itself round the buildings, softening their edges.

"Everyone okay?" said Alec, clicking his lighter and drawing in deeply from his cigarette.

Nick and Georgie both looked as shaken and slightly stunned as I felt. We nodded dumbly. Then Georgie got the giggles, and Alec had to frog-march her quickly round the corner, out of sight of the police station.

"That was fun," she gasped, wiping her eyes, "really fun. Where are we going next?"

Alec laughed. "You don't scare easy, do you, beauty?"

He tossed up the lighter and caught it again, once, twice. I watched it spin through the air, leaving tracks, though much fainter this time. *He never stops moving*, I thought. *Part of his body is always in motion, like there's so much energy in him that it can't be contained. I want that.*

I looked at him and saw the flame of life.

People kill for less, you know.

A few days later, the four of us went drinking—to a tequila bar this time, where a roving barmaid poured salt onto the crook of your hand before you slammed a shot. We ended up back at the university, playing music in an empty common room, heady and elated. At some point Alec and Georgie sloped off together.

I lay on a sofa, resting on Nick's chest, staring at the ceiling, listening to the lyrics of some song he wanted me to hear.

"I've never had friends like this, have you?" I said. "Back at home, I mean. There were lots of people at school I *liked*."

"But nowhere near as much as you like us," said Nick with a smile in his voice. "It's your Tuesday Club, but open for business seven days a week."

"With better stories. Real ones."

We fell into silence, listening to the music, and at some point I heard Nick's breathing quicken and felt a hot wave go through my body. The next moment he was kissing me, his breath warm on my neck, his lips tasting of salt and tequila.

An hour or so later we were in my room, and he was pulling a condom out of his wallet, his thick eyebrows knitted with concentration, fiddling with the easy-tear edge. I tried not to think about Georgie and Alec two rooms down, their bodies twisted together, hers pale under his. I tried not to think about his hands pulling her long legs around him, that tangle of hair on his forehead that would by now be damp with sweat.

CHAPTER 12

By November, we'd forgotten what it was like to feel warm. Most mornings campus was woolly with fog and it seemed you barely had time to finish lunch before the evening rolled in. I still went on runs, but my ears would throb with pain and I had to hive back to my room in the middle of the day to take a hot shower. Nick gave me a pair of fingerless gloves—black, very soft, they must have nearly bankrupted him—which I kept on as I read in the library, wondering what on earth possessed anyone to stick radiators beneath windows.

That term, the four of us spent almost all our time together, Georgie and I peeling away from the rest of our year to take off on trips in the hearse.

It was Alec who came up with most of the ideas. The Holkham estate, where we parked on the wide, wild beach, then broke into the grounds through the salt marsh, with its haze of purple sea lavender. Another day, driving through the blasted heathland they called "the Brecks" and right into the heart of Thetford Forest, bottles of Suffolk cider rattling in a cooler in the back. We went to Thetford several times after that, taking picnics we would eat sitting on top of the hearse, in among the huge silhouettes of the pines.

I remember those moments best, Georgie laughing so much the vodka came out of her nose, me leaning back into the warm loop of Nick's arms, achingly aware of Alec's hand resting next to my leg (why was it so close, did he know it was so close?), with the sunlight filtering through the trees and throwing shadows like giant prison bars across the bracken. And on the way back, Alec just sober enough at the wheel, all of us singing songs so loud that we drowned out the music on the stereo and frightened off watching deer, who paused in astonishment to watch a hearse careening by, before taking off back into the woods.

It was around this time—when the bracken had turned to rust, the days had grown shorter—that I received a summons to Lorna's house.

The email was so brusque in tone (*Jess, come to mine. Tomorrow, three P.M.*—then just the street address, no sign-off) that I had an immediate sinking feeling it was to do with one of the earlier essays I had handed in. One that she—pointedly, it seemed to me—had never returned. An essay about Christie and poisons that I'd clambered through while sweating out toxins ("Ironic, that," Georgie had said, laughing) in the couple of days following our near-arrest.

By now I'd had five seminars with Lorna, and attended three of her lectures, one of which ("Miss Marple's Revenge: Feminism in the Rose Garden") Alec and Nick had come to, as well. Afterward, the four of us had a lengthy debate in the bar about what exactly it was that constituted Lorna's particularly addictive brand of charisma. I'd made a case for the intellectual highs she doled out, making epiphany-chasing, boundary-smoking, crusade-snorting junkies of us all.

In other words, I was no less starstruck.

Outside our group, too, it was clear that she was a bigger celebrity than I had really understood. She was always referred to by her first name, and seemed to stoke admiration, suspicion, and resentment in equal parts.

Dr. Porter, in his skinny jeans, regularly dropped snide comments about his "showbiz colleague." (I later heard that they had both been short-listed for the same highly sought-after academic prize; Porter believed she had won it because the judge had a huge crush on her, while Lorna's story was that the crush was an "and," not a "because.") While she had a firm base of acolytes among her English students, rumors, like persistent swarms of bees, seemed to accompany her whenever she crossed campus: *Have you heard Steady and Lorna are going to get married? Have you heard they are splitting up? Lorna is moving to Harvard. Lorna is going to be made the next vice chancellor.*

Georgie and I discussed Lorna ad nauseam, her dry jokes, the variety of clashing yet somehow wonderful outfits she wore, her devastating put-downs to any whiff of pretention in a student. We had a running joke about which of us was her favorite, but after a while this fell flat, as it became too clear who was winning.

"Oh, you're *that* Duncan," Lorna had exclaimed in delight after Georgie's first class, "Lindy and Roby's kid. Now, that's a riveting story." And partly, due to a strand of humor they shared and I never quite understood—in which dark things could be said in a careless, lighthearted way, which I decided, with a pang of exclusion, must be a class thing—it was Georgie who seemed to amuse her the most. In defense, I became much more punchy in seminars, diving in with left-field comments that I hadn't quite thought through but that I knew would provoke a raised eyebrow—*Interesting idea, Jess, keep going with that.*

So when I was the one who got the call-up to her house (Georgie had only visited her office in the Ark once), I wasn't sure which one of us was more surprised, or disheartened. "Gosh," said Georgie, glancing at the email for a beat too long, "better hope you aren't about to be dumped."

These combined factors—insecurity, anxiety, guilt at having handed in what I knew to be shoddy work—meant that, instead of being excited to be standing outside the orange door of Lorna's red-brick house on a cold autumnal day, I was nervous and ill at

ease, twitching with imposter syndrome. Scared of not being understood; more scared that I would be.

I rang the doorbell for a second time and had just started to hop
from one foot to the other in the cold when I heard the rattle of a
lock from somewhere to my left and a side gate I hadn't noticed
juddered and swung open. Professor Steadman popped his head
out, fluffy gray hair standing up on end as if he'd just been hanging
upside down. "Sorry," he said with a sweet smile. "I can hardly hear
the bell from out back."

Although I knew in theory that Lorna and Steady were together,
it was still a bit of a shock to see him there. For a start he *looked* very
different. He was always dressed the same when I saw him around
campus, in loose corduroy trousers and a checked shirt, a leather
satchel at his hip. But the man at the gate was wearing a mustard-
colored fleece and rain boots, his cheeks pink from the cold, hands
covered with soil. The fact that he was living with Lorna seemed
even more far-fetched, like a grizzly bear shacking up with a fla-
mingo.

When I told him why I was there, his face closed momentarily.
Something else chased across his expression, I couldn't tell what.
Then his smile reasserted itself.

"Lorna's just finishing up a phone interview. What shoes are
you wearing? Oh dear, you'll need to watch where you're going. It's
part mud bath, part ice rink out back."

He led me down a narrow passage along the side of the house,
moving in that fastidious way some big men do, as if to compensate
for their size. "Out back" was revealed to be more patio than garden, a small walled space with a table and chairs and a wide strip of
flowerbed, in which a large garden fork stood wedged in the soil. I
asked him what he was doing.

"Digging up my dahlia tubers. There was a killing frost last night. You have to get them up before the ground turns too hard. Trouble is, I think I've left it a bit late already." He opened the back door and pulled off his boots, blowing hard. "Come in and have a cup of tea. You look frozen," he said, cheerfully batting off my protests that I was interrupting him at work. "Nonsense! Good excuse for a break."

Lorna's kitchen was disappointingly normal, with a small square wooden table, an island with hanging pots, even a mug tree like the one we had by the stove in Milton View.

I found myself scrutinizing every detail, looking for evidence of her flair and originality as Steady turned on the kettle and put some tea bags in mugs. (A professor of Philosophy making me tea! Adding milk! Offering sugar!) He shook some ginger-nut cookies onto a plate.

"Is it my imagination or have I seen you at one of my lectures? Oh good, really? I never imagine students come unless they have to, let alone enjoy it . . . No, no, do call me Hugh. Or Steady, as all my students seem to refer to me. Just not 'Professor,' it does make me feel very old. So," he said, offering me a cookie, "tell me about yourself. No, not your studies. *You.*"

It was rather like talking to your best friend's mother. He was so warm and interested that I soon forgot how bizarre it seemed for Lorna to have chosen him, soon forgot to boggle at how they could possibly be lovers. Somewhere toward the end of my second ginger-nut, the kitchen door was pushed open and Steady swung round in his chair.

"I've hijacked your meeting," he said as Lorna walked in, wearing a pair of high-waisted, flared seventies jeans that only she could have pulled off. "Jess here told me you asked her to come over," he said with the slightest edge to his voice. Then he smiled. "But I can see why. Your students are so much nicer than mine. I guess that's my fault for teaching Philosophy. Grandiose nitpickers, the lot of us."

Lorna leaned on the chair next to me. "Sorry," she said, eating

half a cookie and then putting it back on the plate. "My damn publishers released the title of my next book without telling me. Which
means I'm doing interviews for a book I've only half written."

"Making you a fraud," said Hugh, handing her a mug of tea.

"Which you knew already," she agreed, blowing on the surface
before taking a sip.

As she turned, gesturing for me to follow, I caught him looking
after her with a private kind of smile and it crossed my mind, *Ah,
so that's how grown-ups look when they're in love.*

I followed Lorna upstairs to a small room at the back of the house.
Her study was a surprise. I'd not yet been inside her office, but I
had once passed the door when another student was going in and
had been struck by the sight of her messy desk: a sea of books and
wonky piles of manuscripts, a pin-board crowded with flyers. This,
by contrast, was monastic. Bare white walls, one window overlook-
ing the garden. A slim laptop on an otherwise empty desk.

The only picture on the walls was a surprisingly cliché color
photo of a wave crashing against a rugged cliff face. If it weren't for
its size, it could have been a holiday postcard, something grabbed
hastily from a revolving stand in a souvenir shop.

"Sorry about the chairs," she said, dropping into one and pulling her calves up around her like a cat. "I find a little discomfort
good for the concentration."

I perched on mine nervously, not quite knowing what to do with
my hands. I clasped them, then let them hang, clasped them again.

Lorna sat, watching me fidget. "So, Jess Walker. Did you know
I was your supervisor?"

I shook my head, surprised.

"Me, neither," she said briskly. "A terrible word. I tend to ignore
it." She opened the top drawer of her desk and brought out a small
stack of printed papers, which she straightened with a little tat-tat.

"But in your case I got curious." She held the papers out to me. "So what happened here, exactly?"

It took me a moment to register that it wasn't one essay she was holding out, but two. The shoddy one I'd written after the Half-Hitch sitting below a copy of the one I'd handed in right at the beginning of term, which she had returned with just a simple tick at the bottom, no comments. At the time I'd been confused not to get more feedback, but after asking around I'd learned from a couple of her students that this wasn't uncommon. Essays would disappear for weeks and then reappear in batches of two or three at once, or even never at all (though when she sat you down she would seem to know them verbatim).

I took the pages like they were an uncorked grenade. "Which one?"

Lorna cocked her head. "Which one do you think?"

I flicked through the first one, my face burning. "I'm sorry, I wasn't really myself when I wrote it."

"I'm not talking about that."

I looked up, surprised. This was, in its way, much worse news. I'd been pleased, no, quite smug about the first essay, written over a few hours, in the burn of having just had the first seminar with Lorna.

If she hadn't liked that one, I was really in trouble.

She shook her head as if I'd said this out loud. "No . . . What I mean is, what happened *between* those two essays? The first one is superb. You didn't exactly answer the question, but it was brilliant in its way. And maybe even *because* you didn't answer the question." She added with half a smile, "What you said about Christie's ability 'to read the reader'—it really made me think." I waited. Surely there was something more coming, but she lingered on this last word with a slight frown. "Then the next one, about poisons. Pedestrian. Lumbering. Entirely lacking in imagination. Not to mince words, it's a piece of shit. So what happened in between?"

An image flashed across my mind of Alec leaning down beside

me at the Half-Hitch, his finger brushing my cheek—*you're burning up.*

"I wasn't quite myself," I mumbled again.

"Too vague, I'm afraid," said Lorna briskly. "You're better off telling me you were unwell or hungover. Looking at those two pieces of work, the freshness of the first one, the staleness of the last, the way you are in class, sometimes alive and kicking, other times—lost, somehow, at least that's how it seems. I wondered . . . Are you okay? What makes you turn on and off? Did you get your heart broken?"

I must have looked as taken aback as I felt because she burst out laughing. "Don't mind me, I'm incredibly nosy. Hugh is always giving me lectures about boundaries. Such a boring way to live, though, don't you think? Like we're all playing a giant game of cricket. I tend to think most of the magic in life happens just outside the lines, anyway."

Looking at her, curled up and red-gold in a shaft of winter sun, I had a sudden urge to confess the whole disastrous predicament. My feelings for Nick, warm, real but tainted by my attraction to Alec. My love for Georgie, stained with guilt. And then worst (and best) of all, a creeping hope that Alec might feel something for me, too, a hunch that would never have stood up in a classroom, let alone a court of law, gleaned as it was from a few words here and there, a touch on the arm, a gaze held for a couple of beats too long.

I opened my mouth, made a strangled sound, and then shut it again. Lorna was looking out the window now. Down below we could see Hugh toiling away in the garden, a little heap of soil next to him, as if he was digging a tiny grave. The closed window cutting out the sound like a TV on mute.

"You were so interesting in that class on Agatha's disappearance," said Lorna thoughtfully. "I'd like you to think some more about it. Maybe keep it in mind for your dissertation."

I blinked, confused by this change of direction, not sure whether to be disappointed or flattered. Hadn't she just been asking about my broken heart?

"About the disappearance?"

"Yes, what lay behind it. Why, for example, did Agatha sign the hotel register with her husband's lover's name?"

"I guess . . . she was trying to make a point."

Lorna smiled. "A point. Yes, but what? The third point, perhaps."

I frowned. "I don't understand."

"The triangle. A couple and then the third point, the disruptive force. Christie's books are full of triangles, of secret loves, of betrayals among friends, among family, often among the sisterhood. Am I right, Jess?"

The use of my name brought color flooding to my cheeks. I stared at her, trying to work out if what she was saying to me was loaded, or if it was just some dreadful coincidence. It was as if she knew my thoughts, had read and understood every one of my darkest desires.

Lorna was staring out the window again. "Look at that dear man," she said, watching Hugh. "This is the fifth year I've watched him do this. When he's taken all the tubers out, he'll put them in Tupperware boxes and cover them in cotton wool, putting them in the larder for winter. It makes almost no sense to do it, time-wise, new bulbs are so cheap these days. But he likes to nurture the mature ones, in the hope that they'll re-flower." She smiled. "It's a rare thing, being a romantic. Especially in an academic."

I swallowed and nodded, pressing my knuckles to the corners of my eyes, thankful that I'd had time to compose myself again. "Can I ask a weird question?"

Lorna smiled. "I only like weird questions."

"Okay." I took breath. "Do you think that if you want something you can't have that feeling is real? Or is it just because you can't have it?"

Lorna looked at me for the longest time before answering. I had the strange feeling that something was happening between us. Some subtle shift in the hierarchy in which, despite the differences in age and authority, a door had opened and we were in another space. A warmer space, with different reference points, except I didn't know what they were. For some reason, I found myself thinking of what Nick had said about Lorna and Cambridge. And then she blinked and lowered her gaze. "You know, that's a brilliant question. I only wish I knew the answer."

After that, we talked for another half an hour or so. Perhaps because I was already feeling so exposed I found myself being very open. We said little more about my work. The only thing I didn't mention was Alec. We briefly discussed me doing her seminar on "Breaking the Rules" the following year ("Yes," said Lorna, cocking her head, "I can see you in that class, now"). But mainly we just talked, in a way I never really had with someone older than myself, maybe not really with anyone before. And in that way that makes what you see, what you feel, so raw and right and fragile that you worry if you shift too much in your seat or go to the bathroom you'll break it, whatever *it* is.

At one point I found my eyes straying to the picture of the rock-face behind her shoulder.

"Oh, that's Beccafumo," said Lorna, turning her head to follow my gaze.

"The cliff?"

"The house," she said and pointed at a tiny clay-colored cube sitting in shrubs high above the rocks. "I built it ten years ago, on the royalties from *The Truants*. Whenever I get writer's block, I just look at that photo."

"For inspiration?"

"Mostly to remind myself of the bills."

I smiled. "Do you go there to write?"

"Sometimes," said Lorna. "But mostly I do nothing. Cook. Walk. Swim. It's my place to hide away from the world."

I nodded even though what I was actually thinking was, *If I were you, I wouldn't want to hide from the world, I'd want to keep gorging myself on life.* She seemed to read my mind because she looked at me thoughtfully and said, "My life is a wonderful privilege, you know, but sometimes the air here feels a bit thin. Finding meaning through ideas . . ." For a moment her face became still, losing its light. Then she smiled, stretching her arms above her as she issued a feline yawn and glanced at her watch.

"Oh, look. I've kept you here for much too long. You're probably dying to get away."

I wasn't, and we both knew it. But that was Lorna's elegant way of saying, *This session is over.* There was a bit of me that was relieved to go before the spell was broken. There was so much to process, my mind cluttered and jumbled, excited and disturbed. I pulled on my coat hurriedly, thanking her, anxious to go before I was unwanted.

I was halfway to the gate outside before she called out, "Jess?"

I turned.

I think of her there, framed by the doorway, the burned orange paintwork almost the same color as her hair, with that wonderful face, that timeless smile.

Then, suddenly—and did this bit happen? Or did I dream it?— the smile switches off, and without it, her face becomes cold, accusing even.

"Think about triangles," she says. And the door shuts.

CHAPTER 13

About a week before we broke for Christmas, we went to the puppet show.

As soon as we walked into the church—Nick ducking his head to fit under the low Gothic arches, Alec asking if there were programs, Georgie already looking restless, her nose pink with cold—I felt a strange sense of foreboding, as if I knew deep down that the situation couldn't hold.

The pews were narrow and hard with those footrests that don't have enough room for your feet. I sat between Nick and Alec, wishing I'd worn something warmer than my sleeveless jacket and inhaling the smell of candle wax and floor polish peculiar to churches. Georgie was on Alec's far side, still in hat and gloves, crunching her way through a bag of boiled sweets. I recognized a smattering of Lorna's students in the sea of woolly hats, but still we must have brought down the average age of the audience by a couple of decades.

A woman in a long gown who looked like she was on bad terms with her hairbrush came onto the stage, thanking everyone for their "loyal support of Shadowlands Puppet Company, which has never been more in need of your help."

"Remind me why we are here?" said Georgie, not bothering to lower her voice as she sat forward, offering round her bag of sweets. "This woman's a friend of Lorna's? With hair like that?"

"Just shush," I said, angling my phone toward the stage, then sitting back. "Listen."

I felt Alec's thigh against mine, his breath coming steadily beside me. Nick picked up my other hand and gave it an encouraging squeeze.

Even if my eyes had been closed, I would have known when Lorna walked on. The sound of flapping programs and people grumbling about the lack of heating ceased. Unusually she was wearing trousers, and no color—black, with a black turtleneck—and under the theater lighting her face looked very pale, her hair a deeper shade of rust. There were damp little curls framing her forehead and I wondered if she had cycled in the drizzle.

"We're all here today because of one woman."

And then she was off, galloping into a challenge, pulling us all into her orbit.

"Could *you*, if the right sort of pressure was applied . . ."

Alec leaned in and whispered something. I moved closer, giddy from the spell of Lorna's words, the warmth of his breath in my ear. "Can't hear you," I murmured, and he leaned even closer so that his lips brushed my hair.

"When my friend Jane told me that Shadowlands was in danger of closing down, I was sympathetic," Lorna was saying. "When she asked for my help in adapting an Agatha Christie, I was less so. After two years of championing an author often panned for her two-dimensional characters, the idea that they would literally be made from wood was something of a toe-curler . . ."

"Anyone for a downer?" whispered Georgie loudly, pulling a blister pack out of her handbag. "These pews are awfully hard."

"Then I realized I was missing a trick," continued Lorna. "Because out of all Christie's novels this one might have been devised especially for a puppet show. Its standout idea is the fact that the villain is not the murderer but the person who applies psychological pressure, teasing out murderous intent. A puppet-master, in other words, pulling deadly strings."

Silence rolled up the stone walls and filled the vaulted room. I felt the tension in my shoulders ease. Lorna was so *good*, it made sense of this evening, it trumped the mild panic of being sandwiched so firmly between Alec and Nick.

"This is Poirot's final case, a novel Agatha kept locked up in a safe, to be released only after her death. It is her most morally ambiguous work, her most ethically challenging. Who is more deeply in the wrong—the killer? Or the arch-manipulator who works on people already burning with repressed fury? Who never pulls the trigger, but releases the poison in us all, the potential we all have to kill."

She looked round the small converted church, eyes glittering, red hair ablaze.

"The biggest question in this book is not 'Whodunit?' but 'Could you?' Could you be driven to kill someone? Someone who feeds a deep anger inside you."

An image of my mother, mouth tight with distaste, flashed into my mind. God, how she'd resist this, resist Lorna, how skeptical she'd be of any attempt to use art as a lens through which to view life. For my mother it was all about the doing. Thinking was a luxury for when you had time on your hands. And I got that, I did, I understood the value of being busy, of being effective. But still, sitting here, feeling the pull of Lorna's words, the new space they made in my brain, I felt like a cuckoo's child. Hatched in the wrong nest.

Then Lorna was walking offstage to a storm of applause.

I had to stop myself from turning straight to Alec.

"God," said Nick with a slightly stunned expression. "She really is hypnotic."

The lights dimmed around us. I reached for my phone, which had been recording, and pressed stop.

—

Music began in the darkness. A single violin string plucked over and over, the same, persistent, nerve-racking note, like someone tiptoeing into a haunted house. Then an orchestra stirring behind it, harmonious, hopeful, before the violin crashed back in with its discordant shriek, making us all jump a little. I saw the white flash of Alec's teeth as he smiled.

The curtains peeled back. A spotlight was trained on a single puppet, an old man sitting in a train carriage reading a letter. The voice of an elderly Englishman rose above the chuff-chuff of the steam engine.

"Who is there who has not felt a sudden, startled pang at reliving an old experience or feeling an old emotion? 'I have done this before . . .' Why do those words always move one so profoundly?"

It was strange how quickly I forgot they were puppets. The actors' voices were so believable, the puppeteers so masterful in creating all their tiny human gestures, that—despite the cold church air and the pressure of Alec's thigh against mine—within minutes I'd been sucked into the drama, feeling the tension mount as we drew slowly but inexorably toward a murder.

Poirot's voice, measured and deliberate. "You and I, Hastings, are going hunting once again."

The good-looking Nurse Craven, whose hands were too long and white for a nurse: "The—the atmosphere of the place. Don't you feel it? I do. Something *wrong*, if you know what I mean?"

It was around this time that I began to feel light-headed. I tried to breathe deeply, bright spots dancing before my eyes. I put my hand out in front of me, saw that it was trembling in the half-light. Low blood sugar, perhaps. I had forgotten to eat since before midday.

"It is a question, *mon vieux*, not of you playing a guessing game, but of preventing a human from dying."

Next to me Alec sat very still, watching the stage intently. I sneaked a glance sideways. He must have noticed me looking because he turned, and I had to pretend I was concerned about Georgie, who had obviously taken a couple of the tranquilizers she was pimping because she had passed out, her neck cricked in an impossible position on the back of the pew.

"Is she okay?" I whispered.

Alec laid a hand on her cheek. "Yes, she's okay," he said.

"All good?" whispered Nick from my other side. I nodded, forcing my eyes back on the stage. A quiet nausea coiled round my stomach. The scene had changed, and we were out in the garden. There were painted trees, the sound of birds. Colonel Luttrel, the henpecked husband, was holding a rifle.

"Been trying to get some of these cursed wood pigeons. Do a lot of damage, you know."

That violin began again, a light plucking of strings. "Look," Alec said, nudging me. At the back of the stage a pale board had been erected so we could watch the play of shadows as they jiggled and merged. Now a new one danced onto the board, above the heads of the others. You couldn't see the puppet itself, just the shadow, but it appeared to be holding the colonel's strings.

Colonel Luttrell's voice called: "There's a rabbit nibbling the bark of those young fruit trees . . ." and then a shot, a scream that ended on a horrible gurgle, and the stage lights began to flash. The rifle fell from the colonel's hand and his body sagged with horror. "My God . . . It's Daisy."

And that's when it happened. The flashing lights, the violin, Lorna's speech, my empty stomach all combined to create a vision. Except it wasn't, it wasn't something that I was looking *at*, because I myself was in it. Seven years old, in Greece, standing poolside in my bikini with its redundant top half, my feet on hot granite, a tiny breeze stirring the tops of the olive trees, the sawing of crickets. I was staring at my sister, Stef, poised to dive from a high wall into a pale-blue swimming pool. As she lifted up onto her toes, I willed her to misjudge the distance over the stretch of stone, crack her head open on the side of the pool. And then she was flying through the air, fingers pointed to slice into the water except they didn't reach quite far enough and suddenly there was a thump and her body landed on the stone, grotesquely twisted. As she tipped into the pool, a rag doll, ribbons of blood spooled like red smoke through the water. *Could* you, *if the right sort of pressure was applied, kill someone?*

"No!" I shouted, bursting to my feet.

I don't know exactly what happened after that. I remember pushing my way past startled faces in the dark and dimly hearing someone say, "It's fine, I'll go," and then the next moment I was hunched over a white ceramic toilet bowl, knees on the cold flagstones, heaving with dry retches.

"Shhh, you're fine." It was Alec's voice. I felt his hand stroking my hair, pulling it away from my face, which was covered with snot and tears. "You're okay, my lovely."

"So sorry, so sorry. I just . . . I was feeling faint and then the lights . . ." I rocked back on my heels, half-laughing, half-crying, skin crawling with embarrassment, and through it all ecstatic: He was holding me, he was stroking my hair, he had called me "my lovely."

Alec dropped a kiss on the top of my head and stood up. "You need water. I'll be two seconds." And he walked off quickly, the rubber soles of his sneakers squeaking on the stone.

I took a couple of shuddering breaths and blinked, feeling the imprint of Alec's lips on my scalp and trying to dispel the image of my sister, who hadn't died, of course, had just ended up with a few bruises, a mouthful of blood, and a chipped tooth, but who I had willed with every fiber of my being to crash headfirst into the stone.

The cubicle door opened again and there was Alec holding a glass of water. "Better now?" he asked.

I took a sip of water and nodded. "I'm not sure I can go back in, though."

"Makes two of us," he said.

We went to the bar, a little sunken room that might once have been a vestry. Mahogany paneling on the walls, the same large flagstones. Puppets from other shows hung from nails, heads slumped, slack limbs dangling—three round-eyed Pinocchios with noses of different lengths, Little Red Riding Hood in her cape. The barman—an old, bald guy with a gray mustache, who, if strung up on the wall with the puppets, would have passed for a Geppetto— was unloading stock from the back room.

Alec ordered a bag of peanuts and two shots of whisky and water. He watched me approvingly while I polished off mine.

"Good," he said. "There's a little color back in your cheeks at least."

"Only because I'm feeling like a Class A idiot." I sucked on some ice, unable to meet his eye. "Everyone must think I'm desperately weird."

"Actually, I think everyone will assume you were a plant."

"A plant?"

"Yes, you know. To add to the atmosphere. The timing was just too perfect. Right after the gunshot, a bloodcurdling shout. Like immersive theater. It was clear you'd been put up to it. Probably by that brilliant teacher of yours."

I couldn't stop smiling. "You're much too nice."

There was a pause. I looked up. He looked back, saying nothing.

Then he did something that I know I will remember when I am an old woman. I will look down at my hands when the skin on them is wrinkled and slack and liver-spotted, and I will remember what he did. He reached across the table and he picked up my right hand, which was resting by my drink. He picked it up, and without break-

ing his gaze, began to stroke his thumb, very softly, along the
length of my index finger.

I felt my body go into free-fall. My legs felt like running water,
my stomach gripped painfully, my breathing became shallow and
too quick. I tried to concentrate on this, on controlling it, but the
air between us was so thick that I could feel the muscles tense in
my jaw.

His thumb kept tracing the length of my index finger, and then
it moved round and started probing the soft pouch of flesh between
my finger and thumb. Tiny circles now, incredibly gentle, like he
was stroking the dust off a butterfly's wings.

I stared into his mismatched irises. Every fantasy that I had
tried to box away over the past two months seemed to bloom in the
space between my ribs so that there was an exquisite kind of
pleasure-pain pushing up against my lungs. I willed my hand not
to dampen with the sweat I could feel prickling under my arms and
along the back of my neck.

So this *is desire*. The feeling of currents flowing through your
body, switching on all the circuits until every pore is prickling with
life. This feeling: *I want to fucking eat him*.

My hands had begun to do the same as his, my fingers joining
the dance, running along the length of his tanned fingers, which
were dry and warm, feeling the toughness of the pads at their ends,
and stroking the blunt, square nails.

Behind us, a glass chinked. As if in a dream, I remembered the
barman, who was washing pint glasses. The outside world. I
thought of Georgie's pale neck slumped back against the pew in the
darkness, the fire in Lorna's gaze in her study, "a couple and then
the third point, the disruptive force."

My fingers stopped.

"I know," said Alec gently. His hand stilled, too, holding mine
loosely. "Don't you think I know all that?"

I nodded and opened my mouth with only half an idea of what

I was going to say when there was an explosion of applause in the next room, the drumming of feet on footrests—and I had just snatched my hand back like it had been caught on a hot stove when Nick burst into the bar, wearing a worried expression.

"God, Jess, I'm sorry, the stupid woman at the end of the pew wouldn't let me through till the end. Are you okay?"

He looked at me and then at Alec, and his eyes dropped to the drinks on the table between us. There was a moment of stillness, the temperature plummeted: You could have cut the atmosphere with an ice pick. Then Nick said, "Thanks for looking after her, man," in a brusque voice and pulled up a chair to sit beside me, angling his back so that it blocked off Alec.

All the rest of the theatergoers were filtering in with a low buzz of opinions and drink orders. Georgie and Lorna were heading toward our table, talking animatedly. Georgie seemed miraculously revived, bearing no resemblance to the zombie who had been slumped in our pew through the show.

I tried to concentrate on what Nick was asking me—was I feeling any better now? I looked very flushed, did I want to go home?—while every nerve end was still screaming from what had just happened. What *had* just happened?

I tried to focus on Nick's face, not to look over his shoulder to where Alec's shape hovered in the periphery of my vision. My eyes felt like they were being drawn by a magnet but I knew that if I looked now, I'd give myself away.

Then, mercifully, Lorna and Georgie arrived, and soon we were all standing up.

"Jess, *there* you are. I wondered if . . ." She paused, her face a question, and I shook my head slightly. "You angel, bringing your team along. I knew I could rely on you." She looked round with that smile of hers. "Hey, Alec, good of you to come. You must be Nick," she added, looking up the length of him. "Jesus wept, you're tall. Jess didn't mention that," and she might as well have said "sexy" because Nick was blushing madly and smiling despite himself, although I could see that there was still something angry buried in his face. Then Alec was suggesting getting drinks and because everyone was turning toward him, I finally had an excuse to look at him, too. And although he was smiling his jaw looked tense.

Lorna flashed her eyes wide and clicked her fingers. "They owe me a bottle of champagne at the bar," she said. "Let's tuck into that."

Georgie collapsed into a chair, flopping her arms out.

Alec gave her shoulders a squeeze and then glanced at me briefly, but long enough to make my stomach contract, before offering to help Lorna. As they walked off I heard him say, "Great speech, other than the incitement to murder," and she laughed and I was left with Georgie, who was looking at me curiously, and Nick, who was staring after Alec, his expression strange.

"Did I miss something?" said Georgie.

"Jess just had what is known as a funny turn," said Nick darkly.

"Or making an arse of yourself," I said, forcing a smile.

Over at the bar I could see Alec standing opposite Lorna, his hands in his pockets, his shoulders back in a way that I knew meant he was about to take on whatever she was saying, and she was talking casually, one hand resting on his arm, the other twisting up her hair into a messy knot on the top of her head.

Oh, to be that confident of who you are.

My hands clasped under the table, and without even thinking about it, one started to draw circles on the other, just as Alec's had.

CHAPTER 14

On the rare weekends that all seven members of the Walker family are gathered under one roof, there's a lot to be said for the early afternoon bath. Between the rush hour of the morning (slippery floors, steamy mirrors, wet towels, air choked with deodorant) and the lottery of who gets the hot water in the evening, there's a sneaky slot just around two-thirty P.M. that I often try for. This yields the double bonus of a hot, peaceful soak while escaping the communal tyranny of the dishes. Of course, this only works if your absence goes unnoticed, but my hunch is I'm not the only middle child who's perfected the art of disappearing in plain sight.

A lot has happened since last Christmas, I thought, sitting on the loo seat cover (the hot-water pressure in Milton View is very low—you need to wait a good twelve minutes with the hot tap on full trickle before adding in the cold). And all because of Lorna's book. Or rather, all because of Uncle Toto, my mother's flaky, hedonistic younger brother, who had, in an accidental stroke of genius, given it jointly to the "Walker Juniors" as a Christmas present (no surprise there—one book for five kids, the stingy fucker).

It was almost a year to the day since I had first read it. In this very same bathroom, the one on the second floor that we referred to as "the green bathroom," though it's rather odd, that. The cracked tiles that cover most of the walls are a sludgy fawn color, and the only thing that's a definite green is a slatted blind that hangs over the window, next to the sink.

The temperature was just about right. I stripped off quickly and sank back into the bath, my legs thin and winter-white where they emerged from the purple bathwater, my pale breasts floating, my nipples scrunching in the cold air. I'd lost quite a bit of weight last term, I thought. A combination of trying to impress Lorna and disguising my longing for Alec had exhausted my adrenal glands. Then there were the runs, which, despite the weather, had become longer and more frequent and begun to contain—though perhaps they always had—an element of self-punishment.

Since I'd got home for the holiday, Nick and I had spoken or messaged every few days, but I felt increasingly guilty. Without the magic of the four of us as a bind, I knew increasingly that my heart wasn't in it.

Where was Alec right now? I wondered, for perhaps the tenth time that day. Still at Georgie's house, where he had gone to stay before Christmas? Had he been thinking about me even a fraction of the amount I'd been thinking about him? Some days I was absolutely sure that he had. Like on Christmas Day when he sent me a message: *Happy Christmas. I'm not a believer, but it's a good excuse.*

Then I would allow myself to replay the moments when our eyes had met over the heads of our lovers. The tiny hesitations in his voice, which I had filled with romantic subtexts, the brief moments of casual intimacy, little kindnesses when he'd picked up my phone or passed me his coat as if we were together, he and I, and Georgie and Nick didn't exist.

And then—the place these thoughts always led, in the three weeks since the puppet show—I went back to *that* memory, in the bar. Was it possible that he had felt it all along—that we *were* having an affair?

Stop that, Jess.

I dried my hand on the towel that I had placed within reach and picked up *The Truants*. Probably Uncle Toto had just liked the cover: a desk with a manuscript on it, a glass of whisky, and a brimming ashtray with a cigarette that's just set light to the pages so that the edges have started to curl up in the blue flame. Or perhaps he'd thought the title sounded more like a novel about rebellion than the funny hybrid that it was.

The introduction to Lorna's book posed its central argument: that writers needed to break the rules to be brilliant. The author was *not* dead, just blind drunk, very high, or having sex with anyone they could get their hands on—living life dangerously and selfishly in the pursuit of extreme insight. And the collateral damage that they left in their wake—from heartbroken partners to neglected children and even bloody corpses—all that dissolute, sometimes deranged behavior was vindicated through their art. Thank God, in other words, that they were arseholes or liars. Because what was forged in their destructive fires, in their escape from obligation, their dismissal of the rule-book and playing truant from their lives was an understanding of the very deepest drives in humanity. It was *because* of these moments that the devil became divine.

Each chapter was a short biography of a debauched but brilliant life, mingled with some incisive analysis linking their foulest behavior with their most sublime output: Kit Marlowe (a bisexual drunk); Thomas De Quincy (opium addict and tramp); and Patricia Highsmith (so addled with drink and misanthropy that she once went to a cocktail party with a hundred snails in her handbag "for company").

Knowing Lorna as I now did, I found myself smiling as I reread certain turns of phrase. I thought of her in front of the class, the light in her face and the laughter in her voice that seemed always to be saying, *Come, let's not do what all those other tossers are doing. Let's rip it up and have some fun.* And I realized with a sudden pang that part of the reason I was reading Lorna's book again was because I missed her, too. It was the lack of her, also, that made this holiday feel interminable.

I was in the middle of this thought when my mother's crisp voice came floating up from downstairs.

"Has someone moved the rooster jugs off the landing shelves? And the shaggy red lamp? Or there won't be a big enough turning circle. It's a super-king."

Her voice was getting closer—she was clearly coming up the stairs toward me—and I shrank down automatically in the bath-water.

"Phil, Freddie," I heard her calling up. "*Please* get a move on. If the mattress arrives before the other one comes down, it's going to be impossible to maneuver them both in one room." A brief pause, then, impatiently, "Well, just strip them off and dump them on the floor. It's not hard."

There was another pause and then suddenly the doorknob rat-tled loudly.

"Who's in there?"

I sat up sharply, sending a little tsunami of water rocking round the bathtub.

"Me."

"Oh," said my mother. "Jess. I thought I just saw you downstairs. What are you doing in there? You're not having a bath, are you?" she said with an edge to her voice.

I closed my eyes briefly, imagining her mouth doing that thing that looks like it is being tightened with a drawstring.

"A quick wash."

"Oh, right. And when do you think you'll be available to help?"

"Just finishing up."

She had started a sarcastic reply when there was the bump,

bump, bump of what could only be the mattress coming down the stairs from the top floor.

"Left a bit, left a bit. No, the other way. Oh, for fuck's sake, that was my thumb." My father's voice, normally so good-natured, now strained and irritable as it always became under physical stress. I imagined Freddie at the top of the stairs, his floppy brown hair falling over his pink face as he shoved the mattress a little too fast down the stairwell from my parents' room.

How stained and old would the mattress look? How long had they had it? Had any of us been conceived on it? Certainly I couldn't remember it arriving.

I had just looked back down at Hunter S. Thompson's suicide note—*No more games. No more bombs. No more walking. No more fun . . .*—when the doorbell rang.

My mother's voice exploding, exasperated. "That's them. I *knew* you'd left it too late."

"It's fine, Mum. It can just sit on the landing while the new one comes up."

Then the crash of china, and a wail from my mother: "I *said* to move the rooster jugs. That's not the one with the big comb, is it?" And Freddie, in a high camp voice, saying, "Oh no, I've broken Mum's favorite cock."

Then down below, my father, pretending not to have heard, cheerful and charming again as he greeted the deliverymen.

The water was cold, the light had changed where it leaked through a large, lopsided gap in the slatted blind. That blind must have broken recently; it used not to have a hole. But then again, this was my first time home since I'd gone to university. Funny that, to imagine anything happening at Milton View when I wasn't there.

The house had gone quiet since the mattress was installed—*well*, that was a *palaver*—and the deliverymen, who'd refused the proffered cup of tea, had left. A hush like this was rare. They were probably all in the living room watching a movie, the kind that gets rerun at this time of year. I closed Lorna's book and put it on the ledge by the bath, noting my pruned fingers, thinking it was time to get out, when a baa-ing floated up from outside together with the chug of the tractor in the field. I wondered if it was Helen driving the sheep from one field to another. She had taken over most of the running of the farm from Farmer Roberts, who was getting older. Except that it sounded like just one sheep, its bleats faster and louder than usual, so perhaps one had got itself stuck to the barbed wire on the other side of the hedge.

And it must have been this: The combination of the broken blind and the noise of the sheep and that falling light in which ghosts wake up, because suddenly I felt like I was eight or nine years old again, walking toward the studio at the end of the garden where Dad does his illustrations.

"Leave your father. He's in the Plotting Shed," my mother would tell us, which meant my father was working on some new storyboard—watercolor pages covered in scrawled inks and delicate washes of color pinned up in a line on the corkboard.

"What do you think is happening in that one, Jess?" he would say, eyes smiling as he pointed to one of his pictures. A winged horse with a little girl on its back, a ladder going up into the clouds. And I would think: *How lucky we are that our father makes stories that children want to read, that he is not like other grown-ups.*

When the blinds were down in the Plotting Shed, that meant: Absolutely No Disturbance.

But this time I want to tell him that Stef, in one of her rages, has scratched my face, which is now bleeding—you see that, Dad, *blood*—and Freddie laughed and the twins are eating the dog biscuits again and as my mother is out on a visit, he, Dad, will have to stop working and tell everyone off.

As I walk closer to the Plotting Shed I can hear laughter. My father's low, infectious rumble together with someone else's, who can't have been my mother, because my mother doesn't laugh like that, ever.

And as I get closer still, my legs light with dread and my chest fizzy—or am I superimposing these feelings now? I must be—I rub my eyes furiously: hay fever. And then I am standing a foot or so away from the glazed door, which has its own door-length blind, except it is broken, offering a long, thin, triangular glimpse of what is going on inside.

The slice of the scene is both familiar and strange. Two people I know well, my father and Ellen, a friend of my mother's, who is often over at our house, sitting in the kitchen with a cup of tea, or picking up my mother for a round of golf. And although Ellen is usually smiling and laughing—she has a little birdlike face with big eyes and short, glossy hair—this is different. She is sitting on his lap, and he is moving her back and forth quickly. And it's a game I don't understand, whose rules I don't know. Except her skirt is hitched up so that I see the tan color of her tights rolled halfway down her pale thighs, like a snake in the throes of shedding its skin.

Some sixth sense makes him turn and look at me, his middle child, staring in through the broken slat. He sees me, I can see that he sees me. But he doesn't stop, he just moves her faster, so that the muscles flex in his arms and his face is ugly—a terrible face, full of blood, with his mouth open, like a bad version of my father has climbed into his body.

After that there is a sudden movement; perhaps he is just standing up, pushing her off his lap, but I only catch it out of the corner of my eye because I have turned now and I'm walking way. Walking away, fast—no need to run, *walk sensibly and quickly when crossing a road*—through the garden gate and the gap in the hedge into Farmer Roberts's land. Up and over to the barn, where the sheep have been gathered for lambing, where Helen is already crouched by the ewe's side.

And it will be years before I find words for what I saw that day. Because in my nightmares—from which I still wake sobbing—it is the headless lamb I see, not what happened just before, in my father's shed.

CHAPTER 15

At some point just after New Year's, Freddie stuck his head around the door to my room. In the same voice he might have used to tell me an alien spaceship had landed on the golf course, he announced that "Georgie someone" was calling on the landline. This was one of Georgie's idiosyncrasies. Landlines, she said, made you feel more grounded.

I practically threw myself down the stairs. And then came Georgie's languorous and decadent voice, asking if I wanted to come and "knock about the house" with her for a couple of days while her parents were in Mustique. I almost wept with relief.

"Is Alec there?" I asked as casually as I could manage.

"Nope, he left before Christmas," she replied. Then she hesitated, as if she was going to say something, before continuing, "Do you ride? Excellent. Do you have boots? Rain boots are fine. I would say you could borrow my mother's, but she's got feet to make a Chinese empress weep."

Having grown up in a big, if ramshackle, house, and begun my education in the local village school, I thought I was pretty au fait with the sliding scale of wealth. But Georgie's house threw me for a loop. As instructed, I'd picked up a taxi from the train station. The driveway was a good three-quarters of a mile long and lined with chestnut trees. By the time we had rumbled over the second cattle grid, the driver was getting interested.

"Bloody Nora," he said, echoing my feelings, as a vast limestone house emerged through the trees and we pulled up on a crescent of snowy white gravel. "This where your friend lives, then?"

This comment came back to me a few times over the following days. Because it became increasingly clear to me that Georgie wasn't quite the same person I'd said good-bye to at the end of last term. At first she looked the same: trailing around the house with her heavy-lidded eyes and mussed hair, wearing looser clothes, which hid her curves, but still managing to ooze her delightfully dirty promise. And to begin with she even sounded the same: her laughter ringing off the high ceilings and wood-paneled walls, seemingly oblivious to the pale, somber Victorians who glared down at her from oil paintings, or the disapproval of Mr. and Mrs. Embling, the starchy West Country couple who ran the estate (which turned out, to my stupefaction, to have been an occasional hunting lodge of Henry VIII, complete with formal gardens, riding stables, and several acres of fields running down to a river). But the bruise-colored smudges under Georgie's eyes were deeper than ever and she was clearly on something all the time. Her voice was faster and more garbled and her eyes, glassy and unfocused, cut away whenever I tried to meet her gaze. It felt like a kind of loss.

The evening I arrived I asked "how much" and "what" she was taking. Georgie laughed, and in response took me to the heavy chest in her parents' bathroom and opened the top drawer. It was rammed full of different-colored uppers and downers supplied by her mother's private doctor, "a better pusher than anyone you'll find on campus."

Friday afternoons in this bathroom were the only regular time she'd spent with her mother as a kid, before the weekend houseguests would pour in. She acted out how her mother, in hair curlers and underwear, would do her makeup in front of the mirror, talking distractedly, a flute of champagne by the sink and a cigarette burning on the soap dish, before rummaging in the top drawer among the pills, selecting a pile as "ammunition for the evening." An evening in which, Georgie explained, left-wing politicians were dazzled by actors and actors were dazzled by writers, and the aim was "to intimidate the whole lot, so that they were all high on their own fear."

"But what do *you* need the pills for?" I asked, fascinated as usual by these revelations about Georgie's parents, but also suspicious I was being sent on a conversational diversion.

"I don't say I need them." She pushed shut the drawer roughly. "It's just sometimes it helps."

About to leave, she paused.

"Did I ever tell you about the psychic in Kerala who predicted I would 'stand by the grave of my mother with dry eyes'?"

"You didn't."

"I worried at the time that it meant I was destined to be a heartless bitch. I wonder now if it's something to aspire to."

And there was something so bleak about the way she said this, so bereft of even her darkest shards of humor, that I should have pressed her about it. But I didn't.

The following morning it was cold but crisp, and we went riding down by the river. Georgie was casually at home on a rather manic bright bay, while I followed nervously on a flea-bitten gray, both of whom clearly had more breeding in their left hoof than any of the woolly farmers' nags that I'd cantered through stubbly fields around Milton View. A thin skin of ice lay over the puddles.

As Georgie leaned over the shoulder of her horse to shoot open the bolt on a gate, her jacket sleeve ruched up, revealing a trail of angry red blisters across the inside of her wrist, clearly much newer than the silvery scars I'd noticed there before.

"Ouch, what's that?" I asked too quickly to check myself.

"Oh, nothing," she said, sitting up so abruptly that the gate clanged back shut. "Spilled some hot water making a cup of tea."

Unbidden, an image rose up of her deliberately pouring scalding water from a kettle onto her arms. I was horrified, of course, at even entertaining the thought that she was so unhappy she could be hurting herself. But deep down, part of me I wasn't proud of wondered what this said about the state of her relationship with Alec.

Apart from our quick conversation soon after I arrived, she hadn't mentioned him, fanning the flames of my theory that something was wrong. Feeling guilty about my own mixed motives, I'd decided not to bring up the subject again. But seeing the new burns rattled me.

"Alec's visit," I asked, kicking my horse into a trot to catch up with her. "How was that?"

Georgie made a face. "Pretty awful. My mother was smitten—obviously—she thinks that personality and looks are the same thing. My father and he instantly disliked each other."

"Why?"

"Two more opposite people you will never meet. By the end of dinner on the first night, Alec had told him—with only a thin pretense at a joke—that he was a 'bastion of the hypocritical liberal elite' and Dad had called him 'a cowboy crusader.'" Georgie pulled at the reins as her horse stopped to grab a mouthful of grass. "Then there was the fact that Alec had a fit of the sneezes every time Dad walked into the room. Turns out he's allergic to horses. Can't come near you if you've touched one. Dad is permanently covered in horsehair—he makes Catherine the Great seem positively frigid—so that was the last straw. Or at least I thought it was until I saw Alec's entry in the visitors book, apologizing for his allergy to the upper classes." Georgie gave a faint smile. "When I told Lorna she was crying with laughter."

I stared at her. "You've spoken to Lorna?"

"Yeah, she popped in on her way down to a book festival. Dad and I were out riding. By the time we got back she'd raided my mother's first editions of Anaïs Nin and taken Alec to the cleaners at backgammon."

I hoped I didn't look as jealous as I felt. I'd written an email to Lorna almost as soon as I arrived home for the holidays, a heartfelt one, thanking her for all she'd done for me that term, using words (I'm afraid I can recall) like "lighthouse" and "oracle." The automated response, *Gone Fishing. Will only be checking emails reluctantly and intermittently*, had not been followed up by anything. She probably made it a rule not to be in touch with students over holidays, I'd told myself.

"Probably a good thing she didn't stay the night," said Georgie, coming to a halt at the corner of a new field. "Both my parents were so taken by her that I think they would have bumped into each other corridor creeping."

"But Alec," I persisted, forcing myself to think about her wrist. "You two are okay?"

"Oh yes," Georgie said. "We're fine."

And she told me about a lunch they'd had when her father was banging on about some exotic ducks he wanted to import for the moat. He'd found just the ones in a catalog, only it was annoying because the climate here wasn't quite right for them. Alec had turned to Georgie and said, "It must be nice to worry about ducks."

That was why she'd fallen for him so hard, she said, her face opening up in that rare way of hers. There was always this pressure in her family to be *extraordinary*, to be special, to be different at all costs. Never, God forbid, to be normal. "Normal" was a dirty word. But with Alec, she didn't feel that. Perhaps it was the nature of his life, back in South Africa, the things he'd seen, but he made her feel that she *could* be ordinary.

Funny, I thought, looking away, *how he makes me feel just the opposite.*

Georgie looked across the empty field, the grass sparkling with frost. "Well?" she said. "Come *on*, then."

The grin she gave me as she kicked her horse into a canter was the most natural-looking one since I'd arrived. As my gray horse took off after hers, hooves thudding on the frozen ground, I decided she really must have burned herself by mistake. It was just my own guilty conscience, taking things to dramatic extremes.

Georgie could be careless and evasive. At times, she was selfish. But she was always honest, when it mattered. That's what made it so much worse.

Later that day, we walked down into the gardens, where the raves had been held every year when she was a girl (the press called them "music and ideas festivals"), crossing the moat where black swans glided, their necks delicate and arched ("Don't be fooled," said Georgie, "those bastards will come after you and break your legs"), and into a walled garden where there was a huge greenhouse with a domed roof of glass supported by rusting iron struts.

Georgie pushed open the tall glass doors. Inside, it was tropically warm, the air heady with citrus and jasmine. I passed plants with fruits I'd never seen before, spilling from cast-iron pots and giant earthenware urns.

We sat on little wicker sofas, Georgie with a novel, me with my journal which I was a few days behind on. For a while we chatted intermittently, but we were both sleepy from the ride and a large lunch cooked by Mrs. Embling (roast beef, potatoes, *and* parsnips, a bottle of heavy red wine with a delicious, slightly musty taste). When I looked up after a long peaceful stretch of my pen scratching across the paper, I saw that Georgie had fallen asleep.

I wrote for a bit longer, then flicked to the next page and idly started a pen sketch of her.

She had her elbow folded under one side of her face, like a pillow, and her legs in their muddy jeans were pulled up into a fetal position on the short sofa. The late afternoon sun coming through the glass panes colored her skin honey, and her eyelashes, devoid of their usual makeup, rested pale and still on her cheeks.

I sketched her for a while—rather badly, I couldn't get the shape of her face—and then let the pen rest, watching my friend instead.

The hot rush behind my eyes took me by surprise. What had I been doing these months, fantasizing about Alec? Making a hypocrisy of a friendship that was better and more intimate than any I had ever made before—turning my relationship with Nick, which was good and true, into an alibi for something that didn't even exist.

I gazed at Georgie, the plump curve of her chin hiding that long, elegant neck, the ugly mole, and vowed as I sat there, in among the warm heady scent of flowers too delicate for the cold, that I would give up Alec, give up the story in my head.

I picked up the pen again. This time, I found the curve of her cheek immediately.

It wasn't until I got back to the house that I turned a page to see that I had pressed too hard. Ink from the sketch had soaked through, ruining all the words in my previous entry.

CHAPTER 16

O ne of the many strange realizations I've had while telling this
story is that time remembered does not flow smoothly at all.

If you are going to imagine sand seeping through an hourglass,
then you'd do better to think of it as having grown damp, somehow.
Instead of memories trickling through in an orderly fashion, there
are long, sticky periods when nothing happens at all, followed by a
sudden whoosh in which certain events burst forth in vivid, granu-
lar detail. Closing my eyes, it's as if I am walking through campus
again, feeling the bump of my book-bag against my hip, the smell
of bad soup coming from the canteen, that flip in my stomach when
Alec's hand grazes (accidentally or not?) against mine. Followed by
days, no, weeks on end that I can barely account for.

Which is basically the story of that spring term. A few things
stick. I had my hair cut short for the first time in my life, not
Georgie-short, but to just below my chin. I'd hoped it would prove
to be a chic French look but my curls made it rather more chaotic.
I joined Walt, the student activist in our corridor, on a protest
march through campus and sprained my ankle trying to hang a
banner across the main doors to the Ark.

Most memorably (and with a bit of persuasion from Lorna, who
was in cahoots with the Drama department), I played the part of
Cleopatra's maid Charmian in a rather ambitious production of
Antony and Cleopatra set in French colonial Haiti. At the climax,

Charmian is supposed to smuggle a deadly asp to her suicidal mistress. Instead of using a rubber snake from a toy shop, our resourceful set designer had managed to source Albie, a pet grass-snake owned by a second year. Albie proved a fantastic asset to box office sales—"Have you heard there's a real snake in it?"—until the night I stumbled at a critical moment while walking onstage. Cue the snake wriggling off into the audience, lights up, lots of laughter and shrieking.

I still have a photo from that term, one of the rare ones I ever printed out.

All four of us—Alec, Georgie, Nick, and I—are sunbathing on the roof of the hearse. Although I don't remember exactly where we were parked, I can recall disconnected impressions: the feeling of the warm metal roof under my back, and the taste of that sweet cheap white wine we were drinking from plastic cups, even the startled, slightly intimidated expression of the guy who happened to be passing until he was stopped by Georgie (bare legs dangling down from frayed denim cutoffs, see-through white T-shirt over black bra, waving her phone) and asked to take our photo.

I look at that photo now. I look at each individual face and amidst the bitter backwash of sadness I am struck also by the irony of the figure I myself cut that term: an enviably confident undergrad, secure in her clique of edgy, glamorous friends with her handsome second-year boyfriend.

No hint of the landscape of my mind, which was dark and obsessive. No hint of the weather to come.

Alec was by some margin the least present that term. In fact, he would disappear suddenly for days in a row, making no contact, even with Georgie. She would hang around with Nick and me gloomily, checking her phone and seeming more skittish and unbalanced than ever, her eyes suspiciously bright or glazed, referencing him when given the slightest opportunity, and even when not. Once Nick and I had to carry her up the stairs—no mean feat—after she collapsed drunk after a bender with some Classics students. I remembered Alec once having told her he liked *The Iliad*.

When Alec did re-emerge, it was a lottery which version of him we would get. Sometimes he would seem even more alive than ever, buzzing with energy and that quick, dry humor. Other times he would be red-eyed with exhaustion and wearing an unreachable expression. He made no attempt to explain his absences, though from time to time things would filter through that partially explained these gaps: a brilliant seminar that he had held on war-zone journalism, a presentation on South African politics, or an article he had written about foreign policy for an international paper. Events he never told us about until it was too late for us to go. "It doesn't add up," Nick said once, "the amount he's away." But I had shut him down, aware of his jealousy since that night at the bar, terrified of betraying myself.

Since coming back from the Christmas holidays I'd been determined to make good on the vow I made to myself at Georgie's house. I'd thrown myself back into my relationship with Nick, who, delighted, stole a double bed from one of his housemates and made space for me to stay over most nights. But I still felt guilty almost all of the time. Not just toward Nick, who—sensing a deeper unavailability—wanted me all the more. But toward Georgie, who drifted farther from me every day, whirling off into a cloud of drugs and parties, either to provoke or to compensate herself for Alec's absences. I tried several times to sit her down, mostly on my own and once, after the episode with the Classics students, with Nick, which backfired terribly.

But passion trumps guilt in any game of the heart. Every morning I woke up wondering whether I would see Alec that day. And filled with questions. Always the wrong questions: What could I read into the way he had lingered in my room after the other two had left? What did it mean that when we said good-bye, he looked me in the eye but never smiled?

I worked hard that term, partly to try and subsume my feelings and partly because I wanted to impress Lorna. Inspired by our conversation before Christmas and daring to believe that I could be a muse to my own heroine, I threw myself into the course reading and sweated over every paragraph of my essays. To the obvious annoyance of the rest of the students in our seminar, it became evident that I had now surpassed Georgie as Lorna's favorite. Initially, Georgie spoke the most as we walked with Lorna after seminar, back across campus to the bike park. But since Christmas, Georgie had been skipping more classes, and I knew even Lorna had had trouble pinning her down for a chat ("like trying to keep hold of a goldfish with soapy hands"). I became the one who spent time with Lorna after her class, biking back with her to her house, initially on the pretext of needing to go into town to pick something up, but then increasingly just *because*. We'd stop for a pastry at the little Italian deli at the end of her street or chat in her kitchen, occasions that increasingly took the place of time I spent with Georgie.

"Between five P.M. and six P.M. is what I think of as the Loafing Hour," Lorna said once as she put the key in her front door and stepped into the hallway, kicking away that day's post. "When caffeine is no longer a good investment but alcohol not yet a wise one. When anything you're going to achieve that day has probably already happened and the only sensible thing to do is to sit around, shooting the shit and eating cake." Then dropping down on a kitchen chair, flicking off her shoes, hand through her hair, smiling up at me: "The important thing is who you choose to do that with."

Was this odd? If she'd been a man, or gay, it would have smelled funny, for sure. But Lorna was known as a rule-breaker who had her favorites. And although the conversations always felt personal, we didn't talk much about my love life, at least not directly. From time to time she'd ask me how it was going with Nick (to which my answer was always: "Fine, fine . . .") but mainly we talked about the wider world in a way that, somehow, always felt relevant to things happening in my life. She had this trick of being able to switch tone and key like a musician, so that one moment you were breaking ground and the next you were gossiping and you never felt bogged down, not for one second.

I'd learned how to anticipate when she wanted to finish one of these chats—it was often just a slight shift in stance or a silence left a beat too long—but I always walked away feeling that she was getting something out of our time together, too. Increasingly, she would let her guard down about what was on her mind—a colleague who was pissing her off, or an idea for her book she was trying to lasso. Over the weeks, this made me bolder, and more surefooted about things I would, with other people, usually leave unsaid.

And although it probably only happened twice, my strongest memory of those times back at her house is of when she would take my hand by the door as we said good-bye—a quick squeeze of the fingers that was somewhere between a handshake and an embrace. Then she'd hold them for a beat, as if she wanted me to remember her next words, as if she knew something I didn't, as if she could read the future. "Here if you need me. Anytime."

The blossom came and went early that year. For a couple of weeks it looked like nature was having a party and the trees were strung full of confetti. But the petals had already begun to fall and lie in muddy snowdrifts across the ground the morning that Alec came to my room.

I was sitting on my bed, wearing an ancient nightie, a hand-me-down once-white garment from my sister, Stef. On the advice of the pharmacist on campus I had combed in some "hair relaxant" to stop my recently chopped curls from sticking out quite so wildly and they sat, larded and slack round my cheeks, while I wrote in my journal.

There was a knock and before I had time to answer, Alec strode in. My first thought was: *Oh great, just when I'm looking particularly shit.* Then my vanity dissolved. Something wasn't right. He was breathing hard, as if he'd been walking fast or running—droplets of rain on his hair, two high points of color on his cheeks.

"What's wrong?"

He shut the door behind him. I thought I'd seen his every expression, but I hadn't seen this one: There was a kind of rawness to it, like a layer of skin had been flayed off. I closed my journal and stood up, feeling the pulse thudding in my ears.

This is it, I thought. *This is it. He's come to tell me how he feels.*

I looked into his face, that wonderful face, the mismatched eyes spilling with emotion, and my heart leaped.

"They've killed Stevie," said Alec.

The shock of disappointment made me sit down again.

"Who's Stevie?" I said mechanically.

"The miner, the one I interviewed. They've killed him."

I blinked. His eyes—I'd been so sure. My brain scrambled to catch up, to arrange my face appropriately, but it took me a while to grasp what he was saying.

"He was supposed to give evidence. Next week."

"Evidence?" I mumbled. "I didn't know there was a court case."

"Not a court case, an inquiry about the massacre. But they gunned him down, outside his house. Four men in a car."

I stared out the window. Raindrops speckled the glass.

"So what will you do? Go back?" I asked, a sudden knot of anxiety closing my throat. "But what can you do?"

I was still processing my mistake and so it was only as I asked this question that it occurred to me it was strange he had rushed to tell me his news. Me, not Georgie. I looked round just as Alec sat down on the bed beside me, putting both hands on my shoulders. I could smell him, the sweet scent of tobacco on his fingertips. My heart began to trip wildly again.

"I don't know," he said. "I just knew I couldn't leave before I saw you."

"Why?" I whispered.

A brief hesitation, then he looked me straight in the eye. "Because as soon as I heard, the first thing I wanted to do was to talk to you. About us. Was I wrong?"

It was too much. I closed my eyes, trying to stop the fearful surge of joy in my chest. Then his voice came, quiet against the hissing of the rain.

"Come away with me, Jess. Just for a couple of days." And words that have haunted me ever since: "Maybe this is it."

CHAPTER 17

I t rained like it knew we were doing something wrong.

Despite the weather, which grew worse with every mile we cycled, I was relieved that we'd ditched the car at the bike rental place. Any longer in the hearse—with the ghost of Georgie riding shotgun, Nick in the back—would have been excruciating.

Instead, hunched over handlebars for the better part of two hours, I was glad of the face-numbing rain, the ache in my pumping legs, the excuse not to talk. Alec hadn't told me anything about where we were staying, just that we were going for two nights and that I needed a change of clothes, which we'd put in the waterproof paniers strapped to the sides of the bikes.

We passed a road sign, children crossing. *"Think about triangles,"* Lorna had warned. But wasn't *The Truants* the very reason I was here? Hadn't she inspired me to break out of my stale, rule-abiding life? Which was worse: to follow your heart's desire and risk pain, or to live carefully, considerately, within the rules, telling yourself it was for the best? Was going away with Alec a statement of everything I believed in? Or was "belief" irrelevant, because I was going to do it anyway?

I don't know how Alec came up with that particular pub, stranded in the deer-park of some run-down stately home, but the rain-swept setting felt strangely apt. By the time we finally cycled down the drive, I was semi-delirious with tiredness, so that the sight of a herd of deer—spectacularly antlered, heads raised as we passed—was both surreal and unsurprising.

The Old Swan, gabled, with low flint walls and beams, looked like something from a Gothic fairy tale. Walking into the warmth, cheeks ruddy, lashes spiked with rain, we were explorers coming in from the cold.

The receptionist was middle-aged with crepey skin and glasses hanging on a red chain. Alec filled in the check-in slip while I hung back, afraid that at any moment she would ask for my ID, tell me I was too young for a dirty weekend, that she would call my parents and ask them to take me home. But she just smiled over her glasses and welcomed us, handing Alec a giant iron key for the room.

"That's quite a ride. You may want to get a drink at the bar to warm yourselves up."

"Do you?" Alec asked me.

"Sure." I nodded, relieved not to be going straight upstairs. "Good idea."

We ordered two huge whiskies and went to sit in front of the fire. Glassy-eyed, we sipped our drinks in giant chairs with scrolled arms. A grandfather clock ticked, the fire hissed. I looked at Alec's hand resting on the arm of his chair, the little lines that criss-crossed his knuckles, the milky half-moons on his nails—hands that I had studied furtively for the past six months, hands that would soon be on me—and my stomach jerked.

He looked up suddenly. "Shall we go upstairs?"

I followed him up the narrow, creaking staircase. Our door was small and crooked, with a low lintel. Alec used the huge key, the metal rasping as he jiggled it inside the keyhole, trying to find the catch.

The room was small and pretty, like a guest room in a dowager aunt's house. Sprigged wallpaper, a double bed with a pristine white-lace bedspread. *Oh God*, I thought, looking down at my feet in the doorway, where the carpet started. *This is it. Here's the line. If I cross it, I'm screwing everyone.*

Alec looked at my face for a moment, then smiled. "That first time we met, you told me how, when you were feeling weird and out of place at home, you would go down to the cemetery to read?" He paused. "Shall we read?"

I nodded, caught between laughing and crying.

Alec touched my arm. Then he picked up one of the books sitting on the dresser and, lying down on the bed, fully clothed, he started leafing through it. I lay beside him, making sure no part of me touched him, taking in a cluster of little pictures hung nearby: tiny sepia portraits in oval frames of straight-backed Victorian women and infants with frilled dresses above fat knees. The sound of page after page turning, Alec's breath slow and even beside me. Despite everything, I felt my shoulders relax, my limbs gather weight. Before I knew it, my eyes grew too heavy to keep open.

Darkness, then a click as a door opened, a slit of light.

Alec stepped out from the steamy bathroom, his hair wet, a towel hitched round his waist. It was pitch black outside now, the small latticed windowpanes showing darkness, just a side lamp throwing shadows across his bare chest. He flicked off his towel. My legs still felt heavy, fused to the bed, but my heart began to race.

"Oy, sleepyhead. Let's go down or we'll miss supper," Alec said and, turning casually, pulled on a pair of boxer shorts and some jeans.

The pub's restaurant had giant flagstones, a huge open fire. Big venison steaks were being cooked on a grill by a pot-bellied man in an apron. Above the fire, a deer skull with huge antlers was nailed to the brick wall. I dimly registered that there were other people at tables, that the room was quite full.

We sat beside a window and I stared at the menus until a waitress came over. She was a couple of years younger than me, with braces and a round face, a sprinkle of pimples on her forehead. We both ordered venison steaks—mine cooked medium, Alec's rare—and a bottle of red wine. I smoothed my napkin on my lap, straightened my cutlery, made a bad joke about the deer's head on the wall.

It wasn't just that I was nervous. It felt like my brain had frozen. *Maybe now that I finally have him to myself, I'll sit here with nothing to say.* Maybe that would be my punishment—guilt would turn me into a waxwork, I'd end up losing two friends *and* Alec. I had a vision of Georgie laughing and laughing, throwing back her head so you could see the big brown mole on her white neck. *Oh darling,* she would say, wiping her eyes, *you have fucked up.*

"Give yourself a break."

I looked up, startled. Alec was watching me with such a gentle smile that I felt the tears spring to my eyes and I had to tense my jaw to stop them from falling.

"Having feelings is not a crime," he said.

"But acting on them?" I replied quickly.

"I tried very hard not to," Alec said wryly. "I worried that she was too unstable, that I shouldn't break up with her, let alone tell you what I felt. So I just stayed away as much as I could, hoping she would lose interest, find someone else. Which she will." He paused, drew in a breath. "But I couldn't stay away, Jess. And no one needs to know about this happening."

I felt my scalp go hot then cold as the words sunk in. What was he saying? That this *was,* in fact, just a dirty weekend, that the feelings between us were just a bottleneck of sexual passion, which, once uncorked, we should leave behind and pretend had never happened? I stared at his hand resting on the tabletop, long brown fingers curled casually round his wineglass. Would I have to drag around the guilt for the rest of time, like a dead body I'd lug, wherever I went?

"Jesus, Jess. You've gone as white as a sheet. What rabbit hole did you just go down?" He leaned forward and the hand that I'd been watching was next to my face, his trigger finger touching my left cheek. "I just meant, we don't have to tell the other two about us for a while. Not when I'm about to go away. That would be unnecessarily cruel, don't you think?"

I nodded. The relief was so sharp it stung.

Alec smiled and broke open his bread roll, pulling out its soft white innards.

The waitress brought our food, and for a while we ate and drank, talking nonsense, grinning at each other. Now that he had spoken about Nick and Georgie, I felt a sudden release of tension, a rush of the euphoria I had felt when he'd come to my room. What we were doing was not such a massive deal. No one was married, or had kids, no one was even living together. The only real life-or-death situation was the one that had played out in South Africa, which had prompted us to be honest about our feelings. That was all.

"Tell me something I don't know about you," I asked, feeling a smile wind itself round my face. "Something important."

Alec smiled. "Wow, okay. Let me see . . ." He looked down, twisting the stem of his wineglass so that it winked in the light. A moment or two passed. Then he said, "If I tell you, you won't judge me?"

"Of course I'll judge you," I said, a bubble of laughter in my voice.

Alec looked up. His expression was so serious that I felt my smile fade immediately. "Sorry, I was just teasing." And when he hesitated still, a flash of something raw—I couldn't tell what—crossing his face, I said, "Go ahead, please. I'd love to hear."

Alec looked at me for another long moment, pushing his hair back with one hand so that I could see the width of his forehead, the blunt bridge of his nose, those strange eyes with their missing blue piece.

You're beautiful, I thought. *Just beautiful.*

"How would you feel if I told you I'd killed someone?"

For a moment, I stopped breathing. Felt my eyes widen so much that they stung. *Killed someone.* Fuck, what did he mean? In South Africa? On a story? In self-defense?

Alec dragged his fork gently across the tablecloth, making grooves with the prongs. "Maybe it's the news about Stevie, but I keep seeing it in my head, like it was yesterday, only it wasn't. I was your age. Maybe a year older. What are you, nineteen? Christ. So, yes. Six years ago. I was twenty. She was a year older than me."

"*She?*"

"One of those girls you meet and everything changes. The world tilts on its axis."

"A girlfriend . . ." I tried not to let the shock creep into my voice. *Killed someone.*

"We went out for a term. She was beautiful, but that wasn't it. She could be quiet for the longest time, then she'd come out with something insightful or wickedly funny that made you see everything differently. And the odd thing was, she didn't know it. She just thought she was ordinary."

I felt my cheeks flush then and looked away.

Alec laughed. "Yes. You do remind me of her. A lot. Maybe that's why I'm telling you."

I watched him press the fork harder into the cloth, the muscles in his forearm tensing. For a moment, I felt a real pulse of fear.

"When you say you *killed* her . . ."

He looked up quickly. "In a manner of speaking, obviously." He looked at my face. "Christ, Jess. What did you think? That I was some weird psycho who's now brought you to a remote pub in the countryside?"

"No. Yes. Maybe a bit."

I laughed. He didn't.

I took a long swig of wine, then put my glass down, suddenly dizzy.

"We went away for a few days," he said. "Some weeks before her finals. She was a clever girl. Much cleverer than me. She'd been headhunted by a top firm, an advertising company in New York, and was going to take the job. One night, at a bar, it was late—we'd been drinking a lot, those terrible shots that taste of aniseed—we argued."

"Because you didn't want her to go?"

"Because I didn't want her to throw it all away. Not *me*," Alec said. "I was just a twenty-year-old kid, I didn't really believe our relationship would last forever. But her spirit. That *truth* in her. That thing she was bursting with, had been blessed with. I couldn't stand the thought of her whoring herself to the corporate world in return for thirty pieces of silver. That seemed to me the worst kind of crime. I said . . . fuck, I don't even remember the words, but they were bad. I was drunk, it was the middle of the night, I believed so fiercely, I still do . . ."

He looked up, his eyes bright, though with tears, passion, or both, I couldn't tell.

"We'd rented these mopeds. She had a red one with black stripes that *delighted* her—things like that did. The plan was, once we started drinking a lot, to get a cab back. When she stood up and stormed out, I knew what she'd do. She was full of fuck-you rage. I'd been telling her she had no guts, no sense of risk or adventure. I ran out of the bar after her, of course. But by the time I was out there, she was already on it. She didn't put on her helmet—she was making a point—just tore off, into the darkness."

"Oh shit," I said. "Alec."

"It gets worse," he said with a funny half smile. "I gave chase. Thinking I was some kind of hero. Caught up with her on a corner, took it too fast—" He looked at me and the horror in his eyes froze my blood.

"They said she died instantly. But I wonder how they knew that. By the time I got to her, she was dead, but that was a few minutes after. She'd hit a wall on the side of the road. The moped was on its side, wheels still spinning, headlights trained on the wall, a terrible burn from the engine. She was just this heap in the dark. All that life . . . then nothing. Just a heap, her white arm caught in the beam."

He breathed in deeply; I could see his shoulders lifting slightly with pain.

"You know when you're in a room, and music comes on— something good—and everyone changes? She was like that. That thing music does to people. And I switched that off." He shook his head, turning away. "I'm sorry, maybe I shouldn't have told you that now. But I needed to tell you. What I did, what I've done."

"But you didn't . . ." I began and then stopped. Because what was the point in saying what everyone must have said to him, what he couldn't let himself believe? So I put a hand out to him, and he took it without speaking, and for a while we just sat there, looking at each other, and I got that strange sensation in the pit of my stomach, like when you're falling in a dream.

Apart from that once, we didn't talk about Nick and Georgie that night. But they were there, showing up from time to time, wraiths that slipped into the pauses in conversation and then disappeared like cigarette smoke twisting out of a car window. When I made a passing reference to the university, when a tall girl with short hair walked past our table, when we stood under the stars as he rolled a cigarette. But they felt slighter, somehow, after he'd told me about the accident, and they left us altogether when, flushed after our wine and steaks, we ordered brandies in glasses like upturned cowbells. And I thought, *Come on, then. I'm ready.*

"Shall we drink these in the bar?" asked Alec.

I must have looked crestfallen because he burst out laughing and said, "Just trying to be a gentleman."

Upstairs, one bedside lamp was still burning, Alec's book lay facedown on the bedspread. Only three hours had passed but I was a different person from the one who had lain down gingerly beside him before dinner. Charged now with wine and intimacy, with the new sense of closeness between us, I reached for him as soon as we walked into the room, my breath short.

I wonder how long it was—maybe only a few seconds, it felt like minutes—that we stood with our bodies against each other, my face pressed into the hardness of his chest, his lips in my hair. I inhaled his smell, trying to ground myself. Heat ran through me.

This is actually happening, I told myself. This moment I had thought and dreamed about for six months. I tried to close my eyes but as soon as I did, I saw Nick and Georgie sitting on top of the hearse, staring accusingly at me. So I kept them open as he pushed up my T-shirt and kissed between my ribs, and I watched my white fingers grip his dark hair.

The only time I stopped him, it wasn't from guilt. Burying my face into his shoulder to hide my embarrassment, I started to ask about protection.

But he turned my face and kissed me with such heat that my mind was wiped clean and felt light and white. My whole body tightened, like tiny threads had been pulled through me.

With difficulty, I pulled away again.

"What shall we do?" I whispered.

He looked into my eyes, the hazel patch in his iris seeming to dance. "Nothing."

"Nothing?"

"I'll be careful."

"Will you?"

"Maybe." He moved on top of me, put his mouth to my ear. "Take a chance, Jess. We're breaking all the other rules."

His warm breath sent ripples through me. In that split second he pushed inside me I felt a sudden resistance, a beat of fear. I saw his body through the windows of the hearse, the hand pressed up against the glass. Then he started to move above me. The beat turned into a pulse, the pulse became a drum. For a few moments, I was clinging to a rock, being tugged by a fast-moving current.

Then consciously, willingly, I let go.

When I woke up, the room was very warm and bright. Sun streamed under the short, pleated curtains and soaked the bed. Alec lay beside me, one brown arm thrown outside the sheets, his breath deep and even.

I knew that I should be worried about the fact that he had come twice inside me. I knew that I ought to be agonizing over Georgie and Nick. Whenever I'd imagined this moment—*and boy, had I spent some time imagining it*—it had been tainted by my own sense of guilt and treachery. What did it mean that I felt no anxiety at all? Instead I felt both light and replete, filled with certainty that this was exactly where I should be.

"Jess?"

I turned my head on the pillow.

"Let's go explore, shall we?" He smiled, tugging at one of my curls.

My chest was so full of words that I couldn't find any. "Okay."

"Okay?" He pulled me toward him hard so that our faces were a few inches apart. "Our first real day together. The world is ours. Can't you do any better than that?"

I grinned. "Fucking great, then?"

The rain had cleared up overnight, but it was still foggy, the mist lending everything a pale glow. We lifted our bikes over a chain with a sign that read NO PUBLIC ACCESS to go for a ride through the estate. Eventually the drive petered out into shaggy grassland. We abandoned our bikes by a tree and walked through a small copse until we came into the forecourt of the main house, so neglected and overgrown it was barely recognizable as a garden. From a distance the house had looked intact, but close up you could see it was completely derelict, huge clumps of ivy hiding great tears in the walls, blackened from what must have been a fire, long ago.

We sat on a crumbling wall, sharing a tube of wine gums. It was, I realized, exactly the kind of thing the four of us would have done together, and for a moment I had to blink to dispel the image of Georgie and Nick clambering around in the ruin, poking their heads through the gaps in the walls.

"I wonder who last lived here," said Alec.

"A bunch of inbred aristos," I suggested, "with lots of children in bonnets."

"Boys in frilly nighties," Alec agreed, "with terrifying matrons who spanked them with paddle brushes."

In the fields beyond, stags picked their way through the bracken, little more than silhouettes in the mist.

"It must have been magical, though, growing up here. Like being in a fairy tale." He offered me the top sweet in the tube. "Check you, it's a black one."

I chewed it slowly, drinking in his profile as he looked down, feet gently kicking, pulling at strands of moss that were growing between the rocks. Only a few hours since I had crossed that line, but now it all seemed possible. Perhaps he would ask me to go with him to South Africa, introduce me to his world. From this side, shot through by light, his eyes looked like smoked glass.

"You remember that day we took mushrooms?" I asked.

"Of course."

"You started telling me about something your brother did when you were very young. In your parents' bedroom."

He looked away but not before his face had shuttered. A silence fell. Then he gave me a sideways glance.

"Persistent, aren't you? Okay. So I grew up in this beautiful glass-and-steel house, stacked around a courtyard. The kind of place—a security nightmare, let's face it—that only a wealthy white architect would think of building for his family in Jo'burg. My parents' bedroom was at the top of the house, second story. My mother had this yellow dressing table in front of the window, which overlooked the garden, with a slate terrace below.

"There were the usual things on it, hairbrushes and pots of makeup and her jewelry box. Also this little china statuette of a horse rearing up on its back legs. It was very delicate, made of pale china. You know the kind—so fine, it looks blue—with gold leaf on the mane and eyes that I thought made it worth a million rand. I don't exactly know the significance of it, but I knew her father had given it to her, and he'd died when she was a little girl. I knew it was a very important treasure that we weren't allowed to touch."

He paused, looking out at the misty field.

"I'm not sure why Basti and I were in the bedroom alone that day. Both my parents were downstairs in the living room. Anyway, Basti slid open the window behind the dressing table. I remember catching his expression in the mirror. It was set in this cold, mean way. The next moment he leaned over"—Alec sat forward slightly as if to demonstrate—"and used the length of his arm to sweep everything off the table and out the window. All the little brushes and pots and the jewelry box went crashing down onto the paving. And the china horse, of course. I ran over to the window and looked down. There were streaks of red and pink on the slate from all the powders and lipsticks, bits of broken jewelry rolling around everywhere. The horse must have been in smithereens."

"God, so what happened?"

"What happened was, I was in deep shit. The next minute my parents rushed out onto the terrace and looked up at the open window where I was standing. Quite literally, in the frame."

"Where was Basti?"

"He'd gone to the back of the bedroom, so he couldn't be seen from below. When I looked round at him he was smiling at me in this peculiar way. Later that day, after I'd been told off by my mother and left to cry in my room, he came in and told me not to worry, that he knew I hadn't been thinking straight when I did it, and that made it a kind of accident."

Mice with tiny, cold feet scuttled down my spine.

"Mind games, then? Only ever with you?"

"No, but I think I was the only person who completely saw it. Apart from maybe my aunt Zanny, who has a great radar for people in her own way, and then my sister, to a degree. There was this one time Celia was in the school play, a proper production—our school was big on drama—and she had the lead part. Anyway, she rehearsed all term, was excused her exams, it was a big frigging deal. And then on the opening night, Basti went missing."

"Missing?"

"Yes, you know, disappeared completely for a whole day. There was a manhunt, police got involved. The opening night was canceled. And the following night, Celia, who'd been word perfect, forgot half her lines. Refused to do the next two nights."

I thought of Agatha Christie. Lorna's marker pen on the board. *People disappear when they most want to be seen.*

"But didn't everyone know he was a shit?"

Alec's smile was almost wistful. "No. Because he was—is—the very best. If he were here with us now, he'd be charming the pants off you. You'd be over me."

He turned to me suddenly, his smile fading. "Speaking of which, I want to tell you something. You're not going to like it."

I felt my stomach tighten. What was he going to say? *He still had feelings for Georgie. He didn't see us having a future.*

"Don't trust Lorna."

A pigeon exploded from behind the ruins with a wheeze of flapping wings, and we both whirled round, startled.

I was so surprised I let out a bark of laughter. "Lorna? But you barely know her."

"That's true. And I know you love her. But the way she plays favorites . . . I wouldn't trust her. Not as you do."

I blinked, feeling the heat in my face. Partly because of what he seemed to be implying, partly because I was trying not to show how delighted I was that he felt the need to be protective.

Then he reached forward and took my hand. Turning my palm over in his, he traced the lines with his thumb. I felt warmth spread up my arm, and my throat tightened. "You know why people fall for you, don't you, Jess?" His thumb moved along to follow the veins on my wrist. "There's something in you that makes people forget about their shitty sides. That makes them feel that with you, it could be different. Something open and pure. And this"—he looked up at me with sudden intensity—"this is pure." For a moment I thought he would kiss me but then he stood up, dropping my hand and raising his head to look at the sky. "I think the sun's burning through. Shall we go to the beach? I love your angry English beaches. Especially in winter."

It did burn through. By the time we cycled, the sky was a lofty blue and a fierce white sun cut through the chilly air. And Alec was right about the sea too, it was wild and angry. "How do you know about this place?" I asked as we stood on high tussocks looking down the deserted stretch of sand, broken only by a couple of luminous tents where fishermen had set up shelter.

"It's two miles away from where my aunt lives. Just beyond that spit of land. My window looks out over the sea . . . But don't worry"—he grinned—"we won't pop by."

In a little beach hut by the car park we bought cups of hot chocolate, watery and oversweet but deliciously warming, and a cheap red kite with little bows on the string. We walked along the water's edge, cradling our polystyrene cups, with the little kite bobbing and dancing above us. It was almost perfect. Only the sense that the clock was ticking, that at some point he would go, nagged at me. But I willed myself not to think about it, to drink in every moment.

"You must be very close to your aunt," I remarked, "to have chosen this part of the world."

Alec smiled. "Yes. In a way, we are. She's always been there for me when it counted. When my mother got very sick, right at the end, Zanny flew over from England and moved in with us for a while. My father was in no state for childcare, so she just took over. I remember lots of terrible chicken soup. Scary movies we were far too young for. She's endlessly kind, amazingly vain, and has no filter at all."

"The kind of person who tells you there's a booger hanging out your nose?"

"The kind of person who tells you your nose is very big."

I laughed. My fingers were getting cold from holding the kite. Alec took the string so that I could put my hands in my pockets.

"I'm intrigued by your brother, too."

"Everyone is," said Alec wryly. "One day you'll meet him."

We had neared the end of the beach when suddenly, without warning, Alec opened the hand that was holding the kite string. The wind picked it up immediately and it streamed out over the sea. Far away we watched it do a little jerky jig before plunging into the waves.

"Why did you do that?" I asked, disappointed.

Alec looked at me with laughing eyes, his hair blowing about his cheeks. "Because you asked me to."

"No, I didn't," I protested.

He smiled. "Jess. Darling Jess. You know I'll do anything you ask me to."

I felt a leap of joy as he threaded his fingers between my icy ones, and we carried on along the shingle, until the bottoms of our jeans were soaked with spray.

At some point, I don't remember when, Alec stooped to pick up a shell, pale pink and as delicate as a mouse's ear. He held it up to the sun so that light bled through it, before slipping it in my pocket and kissing me lightly on my cheek, as if we'd been lovers for years.

That night I slept badly. It was stuffy in the room, the old ribbed radiators throwing out too much heat. I pushed the covers down carefully on my side, flipping over the pillow so I could press my cheek to its cool side. It was as if the anesthetic of being with Alec wore off when he was unconscious. Lying next to him, I brooded on our future, turning images over and over in my head like worry beads. How long would he be in South Africa this time? Was he planning on splitting up with Georgie before he left? What happened if he wanted to stay? And if he didn't, how would we face the other two next term? The little Victorian daguerreotypes stared at me accusingly from the walls. Would guilt keep surfacing in our relationship, like blood seeping through a bandage?

Eventually I got up to open the latticed window.

Cool air rushed in, and with it new sanity.

It felt like I had just closed my eyes when I opened them again and saw Alec sitting propped up against his pillow in the darkness, frowning into his mobile phone.

"What is it?"

His face, lit up by the ghostly glow of the screen, looked grim. Scrambled by sleep, my brain took a while to grasp what he was saying.

His old paper in Jo'burg had been getting threats. Death threats. Warning him to stay away on Tuesday, the day the committee on

the massacre inquiry had planned to interview Stevie. Whoever
had killed him wanted to make sure that Alec didn't speak out on
his behalf. Which was ironic because he was all the way over here,
doing fuck-all except having the time of his life with me.

I was so distracted by this—*having the time of his life with me*—
that it took a few moments to register. Tuesday. Today was Sunday.

A sudden fear closed my throat. "You're planning to go tomorrow, aren't you? But I thought you said they wouldn't let you give
evidence. What's the point?"

Alec got up and closed the window, pushing down the stiff little
latch. "Maybe they won't. But at least I won't feel like I'm running
away. At least I'll be able to look Stevie's family in the eye."

"But if they did kill him, if they know you want to write the
story . . ." I tried to sound calm, rational. "Surely that's just court-
ing danger."

Alec shook his head. "The only person who really frightens
me in my country is my brother. Forget the mine owners and the
politicians and their nefarious schemes." He shivered and jumped
back into bed, pulling the sheets up around us like a tent, smiling
into my eyes. "Not that I'll be able to stay away from you very
long." His body was much warmer than mine, his palm moving up
and down my side like a lathe. For a while we lay there in silence.
Then he said, in a soft voice: "What do you think? That it's crazy
to go? If you tell me to stay, I will, you know."

I had a choice then. That was the moment. But the truth was, I
was too caught up in the story of being the girl he wanted, of not
being the type who worried and clung. So I swallowed the pain that
had balled up in my throat. The fear for his safety. The anxiety that
he might never come back. I was proud of myself as I took his face
in my hands.

And I told him. *I* told him. I told him he should go.

CHAPTER 18

The strange thing was, the first thing I wanted to do when I got back to campus was to return the books I'd stolen from the bookshop.

I'd meant to slip them back into the shop after I'd read them, had taken care not to break the spines as I'd leafed through the pages—no mean feat in books of several hundred pages. But somehow the weeks had passed and still they sat on the shelf above my desk, halfway between a reproach and a high five, depending on my mood.

Of course, there were plenty more important things I needed to do to put my affairs in order after I walked back into my room with a bag of dirty laundry and a pressure headache behind my eyes. *I'm crazy about you, you know that*, Alec had said, in the car park—before driving off with my guts in his passenger seat.

Break up with Nick, for starters. I had to do that before Easter holiday, which was about to begin. A god-awful task made worse by the fact that I was only going to be able to tell him part of the story, as Alec and I had agreed. Then work out what, and how the hell, I was going to tell Georgie, who had already left for the holidays (Alec wanted to talk to her face-to-face on his return, which left me awkwardly stranded between half-truths). Faced with these murky prospects, it suddenly seemed crucial to me to put the Christie books back.

Barely an hour after I returned to Halls I walked into the

bookshop with my unbuckled satchel, headed straight to the back shelves, and with the blood bumping in my ears, slipped the contraband back on the shelf.

How ironic would it be if I got caught un-shoplifting?

I was barely out of the shop, mission accomplished—a tiny drop of satisfaction in the deep, echoey well of guilt—when I spotted Nick.

He was on the other side of the Bowl. He saw me, too, just after I spotted him. He was walking fast, but when he saw me he hesitated, and instead of his usual wide, contagious smile, gave me the briefest of nods. My stomach, already tight, dropped like someone had just cut the cables on a lift.

Oh God, I thought. *How the hell does he know?* My mind whirred through a dozen possibilities, all improbable.

We descended the steps of our respective sides toward the sunken piazza, like gladiators entering the arena.

"Hey," I said nervously, when we were only a few steps apart.

He was looking particularly handsome, tall and broad against the morning light, wearing the faded olive green sweatshirt that he'd had on when we first kissed, his black hair wet from the shower and soaking into the neckline of his white T-shirt. Two spots of color burned high on his cheekbones.

"Hi," he said. "We need to talk."

I took a breath. "I know."

"No, you don't," he said. "Sit down."

I blinked. We were standing next to the dried-up fountain whose rim acted as a kind of circular bench, the tiled base within a carpet of dried leaves and cigarette butts. No one was sitting on it, but a few people straggled around the steps within earshot.

"Shall we take a walk maybe?"

He shook his head and sat down on the little wall.

Oh God, I thought again, looking at the residue on the aquamarine tiles. *He does know.* Halfway up the steps was a small group

I recognized—med students, from my year. One had lank, longish hair and greedy, watchful eyes, and was always at the bar, cracking tired jokes.

"Look," I said, shaking my head. "I don't know what you know—"

"It's much worse than that," Nick broke in. Then he looked away.

I stared at him, bewildered. I realized his voice, like his face, wasn't angry. His eyes, with shadows under them, had a strained, shocked look. Then I noticed his hands, which were resting on his knees. They were trembling.

"What's wrong?"

"It's Georgie," he said.

And he told me.

As he spoke the word "overdose," a scarlet flower of horror bloomed in my chest.

No, I thought. *No, no, no.* I could hear my pulse thudding in my ears.

"But she's alive? Where is she now?" I wasn't even aware of thinking the words, they dropped like stones from my mouth.

"In a private hospital. They found her in the stable, lying next to her horse, the one she always talks about . . . Ginger, is it?"

"Amber," I said mechanically. I had a flash of Georgie curled up like a fetus in the straw.

"Right." Nick ran his trembling hand through his hair and I felt my stomach tighten with fear. "They had to pump her stomach. It was a close-run thing. At least, that's what I think her mother said, I couldn't hear her very well."

I stared down at the withered leaves in the fountain, thinking of Alec sitting in an airplane on the way to Johannesburg, and tried to suppress a monstrously selfish fear. Now that she had been close to death, would he realize he still loved her, after all?

"But she's conscious? We can see her?" I felt my limbs starting to move as if someone was controlling them with a remote device, standing, picking up my satchel.

"She won't see you . . . she won't see any of us."

"How do you know all this?" I whispered. "Why did her mother call you?"

"She didn't." Nick swallowed and looked down. I could see that the knee under his hand was bouncing. "I was calling Georgie. She just picked up the phone." He exhaled, looked away. I saw the muscle flickering in his cheek. "It was my fault, you see. I told her."

I shook my head. "Of course it wasn't . . . you're not making sense."

He leaned in, gripping me by the arm. "I saw you and Alec," he said and, at last, almost to my relief, I saw anger fire up in his eyes. "I saw you leaving in the hearse on Saturday. In the rain. It was obvious. It had always been obvious. I knew how you felt, I just chose to look the other way. Many times."

Oh God. No. "Nick," I said, my lips numb, "nothing had ever—"

"So I called her," he continued, his grip tightening. "It was a stupid, selfish thing to do. The thing was, she was very calm. Thanked me for telling her. Just said, 'Shit happens, Nick. Weren't we the dumb ones.' Then she gave this brittle laugh and put down the phone. Something about that laugh made me call back today. I tried your phone a couple of times, but couldn't get through. Couldn't bring myself to call *him*." He spat out the word. "But that laugh . . . So I called her again, this morning. Her mother picked up. Georgie's always said she was a nutcase. But I could hear the terror."

I stared at him. The prickling horror had set into a cold slick of sweat on my back.

I thought of the trail of red blisters down Georgie's wrist.

"Listen to me, Nick," I said urgently. "This is important. I don't know how much of this is my fault or Alec's." I saw him flinch as I used his name. "But no one does that because of one thing. It takes a lifetime . . ." Even as I said it, I was scared, I didn't believe it myself.

Nick closed his eyes. *"Don't,"* he said. "I spent most of this weekend thinking about how much I wanted to rip his head off. He's an imposter, Jess. And worse. I wish I could . . ." He looked at my face, shook his head helplessly. "But I'm not going to waste my breath. You won't hear it, I know. Not from me. Probably not from anyone."

Then he glanced up at the group of med students, who, to their credit, were looking the other way and at least pretending not to be listening. His fingers traced the mortar between the uneven stone steps. *Rocks and water*, I thought, remembering the river at the Half-Hitch.

"I know nothing about poetry, as you know," Nick said suddenly. "But I came across this poem the other day. This guy talking about loving someone through the ages. From when we would have been fish or tadpoles in the ocean, and then as life forms evolved and human beings emerged, right through to the moment when it's just his girl and him sitting here . . . *shit*."

He scuffed his sneaker hard against the edge of the step.

"Nick," I said, "I don't think—"

"No, please. Shut up. Just let me, won't you? I know it's all wrong to say it now, because you think you're in love with that phony shit, and probably Georgie is, too, and she's lying in a bed somewhere swapping one bunch of pills for another, and it's all *fucked*." He pushed his hand through his wet hair. "When I saw you two together, I hated you both. And I do still now, don't think it's stopped. But I also . . . I did some thinking and I realized"—he gave a helpless little gesture with his hand—"you've probably been feeling a little like I do. In which case, there's nothing much sadder in the world than not saying it."

"Nick," I said, my heart squeezing. "Please. Don't."

He looked at me then. A shrug, a faint, crooked smile. "I can't help it. You must know. Love's just too painful a secret to keep."

CHAPTER 19

I had thought I would find Milton View a welcome escape in our weeks off for Easter. The familiarity of it—the smell of wet dog hair and the squeak of the landing floorboards outside my room—might have been reassuring. Instead it was heavy and oppressive. My father's laugh seemed more honking and phony than ever, the chat at the table more inane and limited.

I felt the lack of Alec constantly, as if someone was following me around pinching the back of my neck. He'd told me he was unlikely to be in touch before he got back from Johannesburg, which I also understood meant that I wasn't to try him, either. But as soon as Nick told me about Georgie, I threw pride to the winds and tried his mobile. A mechanical voice told me that it could not "connect with this caller." I thought this meant that he was still in transit, and so tried again, the next two days, from Milton View, both times with the same result. This made me think he had ditched his UK mobile. And perhaps, I told myself, he wasn't checking his email, either.

But it didn't stop me, in the long, slow days that followed, from checking my messages constantly, and hunting through the news for any stories on the murder of the miner. But the news just made Alec seem farther away, and I worried for his safety even more.

When I wasn't doing that I was beating myself up about Georgie. I called and left a message twice a day until finally her mother's coolly impersonal personal assistant told me that Georgie was now fully recovered and there was "no need to call anymore."

"I just wondered if I could help at all. Maybe I should tell Professor Steadman, her supervisor . . . ?"

"The college has been notified."

"Or if there was anyone else?"

"She's been in touch with her friends," said the cool voice—I thought pointedly—and hung up.

I sat there, looking at the handset for a while, and for the first time it occurred to me that maybe Alec *did* know, that maybe I was the one who was behind on the story. I was so freaked out by this thought that for a moment I considered confiding in one of my older siblings. But they were both so wrapped up in different things (Stef, a newfound gluten-intolerance; Freddie, a speeding-awareness course), we might as well have been speaking different languages.

Three days after getting back to Milton View, I called Gav to sign up for some shifts at Pet Projects.

My plan was to read behind the cash register for two weeks, then plot out my next essay in the last couple of weeks of the long break. It seemed like a good idea, especially because I was broke. I hadn't reckoned on the fact that, trapped in a Groundhog Day of guilt, anxiety, and longing, every aspect of a shitty, provincial pet shop seemed designed to amplify despair.

It's been six years since I've walked into that shop, but it's easy to recall its air of squalid disappointment, that musty smell of piss-soaked sawdust and animal fear. And even worse, the noises: the whir of the wheel in the hamster's cage and the scratch-scratch of the small tortoise, its shell the size of a coffee cup, trying to claw its way out of its heated glass vivarium. Every day, at least a handful of times, I thought of sending Alec a message. Every day I remembered who I wanted to be—that girl who didn't cling—and sat on my hands.

I'd just made it into my second week when a woman came for one of the lovebirds. Gav was next door at the bookies (which was where Gav always was if he wasn't in the shop) and I was reading *Evil Under the Sun*, one of Lorna's favorites, with a wonderful trompe l'oeil denouement, when the bell above the door tinkled.

A middle-aged woman with a pinched face and an expensive-looking silk headscarf walked in holding an empty birdcage. I'd seen her before; she'd come in previously and spent a few minutes studying the peach-faced lovebirds, Lambert and Butler. Now she glanced at their cage, where they were chirruping tunelessly, before walking over to the till with a purposeful look.

"I've come for the male," she said with a little shake of the empty cage.

I felt a twinge of alarm. The lovebirds were the most valuable creatures in the shop. They'd been around since long before I had worked there last summer and were there more for PR purposes than anything else, something to lure in the mothers with small kids on a rainy day, who might then end up forking out for a squeaky dog toy they didn't really need.

"You mean the lovebirds? I'm afraid they're £170 for the pair."

"I only want the male," she said briskly. "I've had a couple for five years. The male died a week ago. Papagena is sick from the loss, so the situation is critical. I've brought cash. We'll need to be swift because I've parked on a double yellow line. I don't know what your clients are expected to do round here without a car park."

She put down the birdcage to open her handbag.

I looked over at the lovebirds, who were scratching each other's necks with their beaks, and felt a sudden rise of bile.

"I'm afraid they only sell as a pair."

"That's funny." The haughty voice grew cooler still. "The man with the beard told me that they were £90 each, £170 for the pair."

There were quite a few animals in the shop that I was fond of and would have been sorry to see go. I had become attached to a ginger guinea pig with funny frilly ears like rose petals who always fell to snoring in my arms. But Lambert and Butler were my favorites, with their bright apple-green wings and faces that shaded from red through to orange. They were the last ones I tended to at night, when I jammed a new wedge of cuttlefish between the wires and threw a towel over the cage. When I took it off every morning they were often still asleep on their perch, their heads turned toward each other so that their beaks were resting together, like an old couple snoozing on a park bench.

"I'm sorry, but you must be mistaken," I said firmly. "You can't separate the lovebirds."

"But the owner—"

"Is not here," I said, feeling heat creep up my neck. My voice, I realized, was louder than it should have been. It was an effort to prevent it from wobbling. "You've just pointed out that separating lovebirds can cause great emotional distress."

The eyes beneath the headscarf narrowed.

"Are you telling me I can't buy the bird?"

I took a breath, squared my shoulders. "That's right. You can't buy the bird."

Her mouth tightened. "Well." She put the cage down. "I am not leaving without it."

I'm not sure what would have happened if Gav hadn't walked back into the shop at that moment. I was ready to come to blows to stop this arch-villainess. But having just lost the week's profits next door, Gav wasn't the least bit concerned about the emotional well-being of the lovebirds. Ten minutes later, the woman swept out of the shop with a loaded cage, shooting me a vindictive smile as she passed.

Butler cheeped frantically as they left, and I thought the abandoned Lambert would do the same. Instead, much worse, she went very quiet and still. For the next couple of days she remained silent and unmoving. From time to time she shifted along her perch as if she expected at any moment to come into contact with Butler's warm feathered body. The next morning Gav walked in to find me wedging a new piece of cuttlefish in between the wires, tears streaming down my face.

"Oh, for God's sake," he said in disgust. "Is it your time of the month or something?"

I spat out a denial, but secretly wondered the same. That morning, pulling on some shoes on the back step of Milton View, I'd shaken out a small stream of sand that must have collected in them from the walk on the beach. The sudden sharpness in my chest had felt like heartburn. *Just one word*, I silently messaged Alec in my mind. *Just one word, to let me know that you're okay, that you feel the same.* That the scorching guilt of betraying Georgie had its roots, at least, in something solid and pure.

Over the next couple of days, Lambert remained silent. I fussed over her like you might tend to a wounded soldier—freshening up her water bottle daily and refilling her seed bowl at the slightest dip. The sight of her standing solitary and mute on her perch filled me with an overwhelming sense of sadness that I might have questioned. But I didn't. Then one day I opened the shop and she greeted me with her cheerful treble, bouncing over to the side of her cage and rattling the wires with her beak. But instead of feeling relieved at Lambert's change of heart, this sunk me into a deeper, bleaker place, and I found myself averting my eyes as I tended to her.

The following week I was watching a frozen mouse uncurl in a bowl of warm water like a fetus on time-lapse. The urge to throw up was so sudden that I only just made it to the sink in time.

During my lunch break, I went to the pharmacy.

In the ladies' room of the café next door I peed on a stick, watching with terror as a little blue cross crept into the window.

———

CHAPTER 20

Was it strange, under these circumstances, to turn to Lorna? She'd only been my supervisor for two terms. There were those dozen or so times we'd spent together after class (fifteen, if we're counting). But she was now the adult I most respected and admired—and who had told me, quite clearly, that she had my back. Even if I'd had more choices, it would have felt quite natural to seek out her advice.

As it happened, she felt like just about the only person I *could* tell. There was Alec, who I couldn't get hold of. I tried his mobile once more, but when the call failed altogether, without even a mechanical voice, I took it as a sign and rang off, hands shaking, but feeling oddly relieved, too, suddenly very sure that I didn't want him to know. Nick and Georgie were obviously out of the question, as were the old friends I'd hooked up with for a drink or two a couple of times after my shifts. In my current state of mind, I felt they were orbiting a different planet. It's also a stark fact that it barely crossed my mind to talk to my mother, an obstetrician.

Instead, in what would have been under different circumstances a glorious moment, I quit Pet Projects without notice, made an excuse to my parents about going back to campus for some extra course work, and left for Norwich the following day.

My plan was to dump my bag in Halls, go into town, then knock on Lorna's door. An email I'd sent came sailing back with an

automatic reply saying she was *Still off fishing*, which I thought
meant she was probably at home, in her office, finishing writing her
Christie book. But on my way back from my room I happened to
glance up at the Ark and notice that her office window—third floor,
fourth along—was open.

I walked down the speckled linoleum with that shaky feeling
that often comes, having held yourself together, with the prospect
of imminent relief. It had been barely twenty-four hours since
I'd found out, during which time every symptom of early pregnancy had made itself known to me (I'd drunk a pint of chocolate milk for breakfast, then thrown up; the train from Reigate to
Norfolk seemed to be full of babies glaring at me; walking past a
fish shop was a hideous ordeal). Not having told anyone yet made
it feel more intense, like I was carrying around a stolen item in my
pocket.

So at Lorna's door I barely paused. The indicator on her name-
board was showing IN. I knocked and walked in, almost in one
movement.

The person standing at the desk looked startled, guilty even. He
stood bent over an open filing drawer, a bunch of papers in one
hand, reading glasses on his nose, hair askew as it had been when
he was bent over digging up dahlias. Professor Steadman.

"Oh, hullo," he said. "Jess, isn't it? If you're looking for Lorna,
I'm afraid she's away. I'm just checking through her post."

"Away?"

"Yes, in London, I'm afraid. She's been there this last week.
Looking after her mother. Then she's planning on going back to
Italy for the rest of the break."

Visions of sitting in her kitchen drinking wine as I talked it all
through with her crumbled, and I felt a plunging disappointment.

"Oh. I see." *Don't cry*, I thought. *Just don't cry.*

"She has a place there . . . she may have told you about it?"

I thought of the picture of the cliff face hanging on the wall of her study and nodded.

Steady slipped the papers back into the filing drawer and closed it with a little key, which he pocketed. On the desk was a pile of brown envelopes, the kind bills come in. Unopened.

"It's where she goes when she wants to be on her own. I'm very rarely invited these days."

Looking back, there was a definite edge to his voice as he said this, *these days*, but I was too wrapped up in how I was feeling to pay much attention.

"And she's not coming back in between?"

I tried to control my voice, but there must have been some note of desperation that came through because he took off his glasses and his face lost its distracted look.

"I'm afraid not. I can give you her mobile number if it helps?"

I nodded. The sudden kindness brought a lump to my throat.

Steady picked up a pen and, putting his glasses back on, wrote a mobile number on a Post-it. I looked at the crowded corkboard next to her desk, saw the flyer from the puppet theater.

"There you are," he said, handing me the note. Then hesitated. "Look, I know I'm no replacement for Lorna, but can I help at all? I was just going to catch some fresh air by the lake if you want to join me. The canteen is closed, but there is that little vending machine next to it that does passable coffee, depending on your standards."

Steady thought I was upset about Georgie. This made sense, of course. He knew we were close friends and naturally, as her supervisor, he'd heard about what had happened.

As soon as we had got our Styrofoam cups of coffee, he started asking me how she was, which was a problem because in fact Georgie still wasn't taking my calls. Steady must have misread my awkwardness because he started talking about how it was all too easy to blame yourself in this sort of situation and think you should have picked up on the signs. But the truth was the writing never *was* on the wall, and we all struggled when it came to not seeing things we didn't want to see.

I nodded a lot and sipped at the awful coffee. I couldn't exactly say: *I'm upset not only because my friend nearly killed herself, but because there is a small bundle of cells sitting inside me, fifty percent of which belongs to her boyfriend.*

"Of course, I did wonder if it was anything to do with Alec," said Steady suddenly. So suddenly I nearly spilled my coffee. We were still walking, partway round the lake now. I felt the color rush to my face. "I know they were stepping out," he continued. "And he's . . . well, unreliable. You're all pretty close, Lorna told me."

"Yes," I said. Then, as casually as I could manage, "What do you mean by 'unreliable'?"

"Well . . ." He hesitated. "I don't know, really. I met him a few times at the beginning of the year, and he rather impressed me. But there was something unstable about him, too. He's been through a lot, I know. But, of course, you're much closer to him."

I wanted to hear what exactly led him to think this, but my heart was beating so wildly now that I couldn't quite bring myself to ask. Instead I kept walking, casting around for something neutral to say.

"My point is," continued Steady, "that even if something had happened . . . in that department . . . Well, it doesn't mean that that was *the cause.* These things are never linear."

"Right," I said. "No."

But the word "unreliable" was still making its way through me and for a moment I had a flashback to the room with the sprigged wallpaper in the Old Swan, Alec's breath hot in my ear. *Take a chance, Jess. We're breaking all the other rules.* For a moment the ground beneath me seemed to pitch wildly. I stumbled over a stick, spilling my coffee.

"Goodness," said Steady, putting out a hand quickly. "Are you all right?"

"Fine," I said breathlessly. "Bit dizzy. Forgot breakfast."

There wasn't a bench nearby, so I sat on a tussock instead.

Steady stood in front of me, legs planted, hands in pockets, frowning. "I'm sorry," he said ruefully. "I was trying to make you feel better, but I've done the opposite, haven't I? Blathering on."

I shook my head. "You haven't."

Steady thought Alec wasn't reliable. But if anyone was to blame, it was me. After seeing him at Gideon's party, I should have kept my distance. Both from Georgie and Alec. Probably from Nick, too. And now I was in this pathetic, clichéd mess. Suddenly, I felt a crushing sense of self-disgust and my vision blurred. I blinked quickly but it was too late, Steady was taking something out of his pocket—oh God, it was a handkerchief, how humiliating—and muttering to himself how much he wished Lorna were here.

"The problem with Lorna Clay," he said, sitting down next to me on the grass and passing over the handkerchief without looking, giving me time to collect myself, "is that one minute she's here, and everyone knows about it. And no one can get quite enough of her because she has this *thing* that everyone wants a bit of. But the next minute, you've turned round, and she's vanished." He continued, "Do you know Mowbry?"

I shook my head, pressing my lips together, willing the tears to stop. "Teacher or student?"

"A town a few miles over there." He gestured to the tree line on the other side of the lake. "It has a good farmer's market in the main square on the first Thursday of every month. Great cheese."

"Oh," I said, nonplussed. Was he trying to distract me? If so, he wasn't being very subtle about it—he seemed to have plucked the subject from thin air. Perhaps he was one of those men who couldn't bear to have women cry around him.

"If you do go, have a look on the market cross, in the middle square. There's a sign that says, 'Here Ambrose Butler Vanished for the Last Time.' Then a date. Sometime in the 1830s, I think."

"Vanished?"

"Yes. *For the last time.*" Steady smiled to himself. "I looked it up once. Turned out that Ambrose Butler was a famous case. A blacksmith, a loner, a bit of a hermit when he wasn't working. One day he walked into the middle of the square on market day, sat down on the steps of the monument, put his cap down next to him, and vanished. For about ten seconds. Then he reappeared, put on his cap, and went away. And the next week, it happened again on market day. And every week after that, for six months."

"An old wives' tale, then."

Steady shook his head. "You'd think. But there are all sorts of accounts. It became a celebrated case. People put forward their theories. There was this German doctor, a Professor Potz, can you believe, who said the vanishing was caused by a 'void spot of universal ether' that only lasted a few seconds but vaporized anything unlucky enough to pass through it. But this didn't account for the fact that the blacksmith kept coming back, and with no apparent memory of what happened. People came from far and wide to watch on market day—the Vanishing Man of Mowbry. Then one day—a cold clear one in February—Ambrose sat down, put his cap on the steps, and disappeared. Everyone waited as usual, in a hush, but this time . . ."

"He didn't come back?"

"Right. And no one's ever been able to explain it."

I shook my head, frowning. Then nearly laughed. If this had been a way to distract me, it had certainly worked—the hot lump in my chest had dissolved. I handed Steady back his hankie.

He took it and started folding it, in half, then half again. "Sometimes I think that's what will happen with Lorna," he said, looking down at his little square of handkerchief. "One day, she'll go, just like usual. But then"—he paused as he put the hankie in his pocket—"then not come back."

I laughed nervously. "Why would you think that?"

He looked up with a rueful smile. "I have no idea. It makes no sense at all. But it's how you feel when you are in love with someone a bit magic. Like a mortal falling in love with one of the gods. Now you have them, now you don't."

I thought of the twist in my gut, the sudden stab of fear as I had said good-bye to Alec.

For a while we sat there quietly, looking out over the lake as a sudden, sharp wind stirred the tops of the trees.

Then I excused myself, thanked him for the coffee, and said I was going to call Lorna.

"I hope you feel better," he said as I left.

I smiled, and it wasn't a complete lie when I said I did already.

When I was halfway back I turned and saw him still sitting there on the grass, facing the lake. For some reason, some hunch of the shoulders, some tiny vibration his figure was giving out reminded me of my mother. Which was strange, because two less similar individuals you'll never meet.

CHAPTER 21

As soon as I left Steady, I called Lorna. There was a long pause after I dialed, the sound of air rushing around cables, and for a moment I thought it was not going to connect. But then it was ringing. She picked up on the fourth tone.

"*Jess* . . . Oh, just a sec," and there was a scratchy sound as if the microphone was being brushed against material and then Lorna's voice, reassuringly vital with that perpetual edge of amusement, as if we had just shared some private joke.

"Jess! Hello . . . I'm sitting here with my mother. Hang on, terrible reception, I'm just going out onto the balcony."

"You're still in London, then."

Anxiety must have crowded my voice because her tone shifted immediately.

"Everything okay? Is it Georgie again?"

"No, I . . ." My throat closed and for a moment I thought I wasn't going to tell her, then I took a breath and it came rushing out.

"Oh, you poor darling." The warmth in her voice made me want to cry again and I thought she was going to ask me if I would keep it and whose it was and I thought, *I can't bear it.* And then I thought, *Isn't that what I'm feeling, quite literally*, and I said it out loud as a test to myself: "I can't bear it." There was a pause down the line and when Lorna spoke again she sounded measured and practical, almost brisk. Could I make it to London tomorrow? She was staying with her mother at the moment, the carer was ill, but she'd be moving to her sister's house for the next few days—did I want to come and stay? No one else would be there, the family was away for Easter . . . (her voice cut out again here, more scratchy sounds). No, she had to stay anyway, she told her sister she would look after . . . she'd call me back later, the reception was better at . . .

I lost her voice again and suddenly I felt mad to have called her, to be entrusting myself to a person I hardly knew.

"Jess?"

My chest felt tight. "Yes?"

"Just hang in there. It's going to be okay."

Tuesday was one of those high spring days that feels like an insult to a crisis. The trees in the park frothed with pink and white blossoms, banks of daffodils so yellow and cheerful they hurt the eyes. I dragged my wheelie bag up through the dappled shade of an avenue of chestnut trees, following signs to the Japanese garden.

The meeting place had been Lorna's idea, of course. "The Japanese garden?" I'd asked her.

"Yes, by the pond with the koi carp. There's a yellow maple tree with a bench under it." It sounded so much like a rendezvous in a spy film that despite myself I gave a little snort of laughter. She must have read my mind because she said, with a smile in her voice, "Look for the tired redhead reading *The Observer*."

There were steps up to the entrance, with a bamboo handrail. I lugged my bag up into a tiny paradise: groomed lawns and ornamental trees, a pretty waterfall. A group of Chinese tourists had stopped to photograph a peacock that was wheeling slowly round, displaying a shivering fan of emerald feathers.

THIS IS A PLACE FOR QUIET AND CONTEMPLATION, read a small sign, and under it another: CHILDREN SHOULD NOT PLAY HERE. NO STROLLERS OR SCOOTERS PLEASE.

I saw the bench that Lorna meant straightaway and went and sat down, parking my bag by my feet.

The pond had a low wooden bridge leading across it. I watched people stroll round the garden, stopping on the bridge to exclaim at the size of the carp or toss in a coin. From time to time someone eyed up the free half of my bench, but no one sat down. I wondered how I looked to them. A pale, scruffy girl with a suitcase, running from something, or someone.

I sipped coffee from a takeaway cup, kept an eye on the people appearing at the top of the steps. Just when I'd stopped checking, Lorna was there, walking down the path toward me, wearing shades, her hair aflame in the bright sunshine.

When she reached the bench, I stood up, uncertain, suddenly acutely aware of my youth, of the hierarchy between us. But she didn't hesitate, stepping forward, arms open. As she hugged me I felt her heart beat beneath her crumpled linen shirt, strong and fast from walking, a faint smell of perfume in her hair.

"You poor love," she said simply, and having been more or less numb for the past two days, I felt a sudden explosion of emotion in my chest. For the first time since I'd found out, I wanted Alec so much it hurt not to cry. She took a seat on the bench and wordlessly passed me her sunglasses. She looked tired but she still had a bit of a tan, and there was a patch of dry skin on her nose where she had started to peel. For a while we sat in silence, my tears falling thick and fast behind her shades. Then she started talking softly, as if she was telling a bedtime story, about her place in Italy, where she'd been for a couple of weeks before she'd come back for her mother. "It's the best time of year. The wildflowers have come out; the sea is like ice. It feels like everything—including me—is waking from a long, drugged sleep."

After a while she stopped and I took a deep breath and, drying my cheeks, I said, "Thank you, sorry." I handed back her shades, hiccupping, and managed a bit of a smile. "I was doing so well until you were nice to me."

Lorna smiled back. "You don't need to talk about it. Not until you're ready. I can keep crapping on about the island for years."

Of course, I told her everything. Right back from when I spotted Alec having sex in the back of the hearse ("In a hearse?" said Lorna, her lips twitching. "Goodness!"). Occasionally she asked me a question—brief, unsentimental, to the point—but apart from that she just let me talk.

When I finished, there was a silence. I looked at the haze of midges above the pond.

"There's a bench like this by the lake at college," I said. "Georgie calls it the Intimacy Couch because people sitting on it are either kissing or crying."

"She's a funny girl."

There was a gruffness in Lorna's voice that made me glance over at her. "Have you spoken to her?"

"Yes. I called her from the island when Hugh told me."

I felt a pulse start in my throat. "You did? How is she?"

Lorna hesitated. "Not in great shape. But then she hasn't been for a while, as you know. I tried talking to her about it a couple of times last term. I think that's why she drifted away from me. It was obvious she was in the wrong relationship. And I've met her parents, I can see what she's running *from*. But she didn't want to hear it."

I looked down at my sneakers, in the grass. "Did she mention me?"

"Not directly, but when I asked her . . . well, it makes sense, now you've told me."

I felt another wave of tears spring up and tried to swallow the hot ball in my throat.

"I'm not sure she'll ever talk to me again."

Lorna smiled slightly. "Don't be so old-fashioned, Jess. She just needs time. When she gets stronger, Georgie, of all people, will understand what it's like to be overrun by your passions. She may be furious now, and hurting, but she didn't do what she did because her boyfriend went off with you for the weekend. It was inside her anyway, it must have been."

I nodded, thinking that Hugh had said that, too. They were such an unlikely couple on the surface. But maybe that was the trick: their inner worlds completely in sync.

"So what do you think I should do?" I paused, my hand moving involuntarily to my stomach. "Do you think it's wrong . . ." I paused, sucked in a breath, felt the tears pricking again.

But Lorna shook her head, as if I'd finished the sentence. "I think having an unwanted child is wrong. What would you do: Bring it up resenting it? Hand it over for adoption with the risk that it grows up feeling rejected?"

I thought of Alec's brother sweeping the little china horse off his mother's dressing table in fury. Smashed to smithereens on the paving below.

"You're so young, Jess," continued Lorna softly. "Everything would change. Doors would close, or at least you might not be tempted to open them. I can see you going very far with that brain of yours. In academia, too, if you wanted. It's a brutal truth for a woman, but choosing motherhood, at this stage, might change that."

I blinked away another rush of heat behind my eyes.

"Some people see it as murder."

To my surprise, Lorna laughed at this. "If there is one thing Dame Agatha taught me, it is that murder is a relative concept. 'Thou shalt not kill' seems so black and white in writing. But what if killing prevents more suffering? Having a child conceived in error can be a recipe for untold pain."

She said this with such vehemence that it occurred to me for the first time to wonder why Lorna herself had no children. I knew that she was forty-two, and that she had been with Hugh for several years. But somehow it made sense that they had no children. I found it hard to imagine her intellectual, questing spirit submerged in the milky haze of motherhood.

"Lorna."

"Yup."

"Have you ever been?"

For a long time, she didn't reply. "If I had, you can be sure I would have done the same thing."

On the bridge, a little boy of about three was having a tantrum as his mother stopped him from trying to climb into the pond with the fishes. Under a messy crop of blond curls, a string of snot hanging from his nose, little blue veins stood out on his neck as he screamed. I glanced sideways but couldn't see the direction of Lorna's gaze behind her glasses.

"It's not that I object to children at all," she said thoughtfully. "As far as I can tell, they're all little artists before they are shoved on a conveyor belt and taught to conform. It's just I don't like what they do to their mothers. All these strong, independent women who have a baby and become exactly the same: anxious, conventional, reliant on men."

"But your sister has lots of children?"

"Lots," agreed Lorna.

Then she turned to me, pushing her glasses higher on her head. "Can I ask a delicate question?"

I laughed. "Not sure there are any other types right now."

But she hesitated, still. Put a hand lightly on my arm. "Are you sure the baby is Alec's?"

I stared at her, stunned. "Yes! I mean . . ." And for the first time I realized, in a stretched second or two of shock and shame, that it could be Nick's. This hadn't even occurred to me, not just because I'd had unprotected sex with Alec, but because my relationship with

Nick had been dwindling for weeks, and the weekend in the Old Swan had completely obliterated it. But—and here my horrified mind stuttered on the thought—it wasn't out of the question.

What kind of person did that make me?

Lorna was watching my face. "I think you know all these things, deep down. I just don't want you to be blindsided by questions later." She checked her watch. "I know a clinic, near my sister's place."

CHAPTER 22

I didn't know anyone who'd had an abortion. I assumed that I would need a general anesthesia and an operation. I had been fretting about the cost, too, wondering if my almost nonexistent savings would cover it. Gav had stiffed me for my last paycheck, which I'd known he would when I walked out without notice, and ironically, Georgie, who was careless with other people's money, owed me a bunch from a few times when she had been caught short (Georgie, like the Queen, never seemed to carry cash).

So I was relieved and not a little shocked when the doctor at the clinic, a stout French woman with gray hair pulled neatly back in a clip, told me that yes, of course, it was free. Moreover, all I needed was a handful of pills taken over twenty-four hours, some antibiotics, and a few painkillers. We could do that today, after a few tests and checks, if I wanted.

"Really?" I said in disbelief. "That's it?"

"It's no picnic," she warned me, fixing me with a strict look over her specs. "But yes, that is it. If you decide to go ahead."

I'll tell you something about the waiting room in a public clinic for sexual health and contraceptive care: There's not a truckload of eye contact happening. I should know, I spent half the day in that mouse-colored place in between various checks and procedures. Lorna stuck around for an hour or so, but then, glancing at her phone, said she needed to run a few errands before meeting the GP at her mother's apartment in a few hours, "to which you are more than welcome to come. Though I warn you, it makes this place look like a holiday resort."

A holiday, it wasn't. I'm not sure I've ever been in another place so tangibly fraught with unhappiness. From my row of plastic-coated seats I watched the few other women who came and went. There was a forty-something in stone-washed jeans two sizes too small with deep grooves framing her mouth like heavy parentheses, a girl at least three years younger than me slumped in a chair staring mutinously at her phone. No one sat near the baby area, which had an ancient tangled metal structure to push colored rings around. No men came.

I'm not a mother, I thought. *I can't be. I'm nineteen. I'm not grown up yet.*

Eventually I was called back to the French doctor. There was an examination bed in the corner which she asked me to lie on and hitch up my top. The scan, she told me, was "to see how far along you are."

I stared at the tortoiseshell clip on the doctor's hair as she bent over me, the tube farting as she squeezed some cold gel on my stomach. She had just picked up a probe connected to a small monitor when a low droning noise started to my left. I swiveled my head to see. It was a warm day and the sash window was open. A big bluebottle had got itself stuck between the sliding sheets of glass and was banging about in panic, trying to get out.

The doctor rolled the probe over my stomach. I saw an image appear on the monitor, a haze of digital snow with a dark space in the middle, and there, a little misshapen lump of more snow. The lump drifted a little to the right and then the buzzing of the fly went up in pitch and I looked back at the window.

"That's right," said the doctor, "no need to look at the screen."

She was being kind in her stern French way so that I didn't want to say: *Actually, it's the fly I'm worried about. Can we just stop every-*

thing for a moment and sort the poor little fucker out? But then she had stood up, the monitor went blank, and I watched the fly driving itself crazy until in the end it lay there inert and the droning petered out and I felt tears prick the corners of my eyes and thought, *Oh no, not now . . . please don't give up now.*

"Okay, we're done," she said, wiping the gel off my stomach with a scratchy hand towel and helping me sit up. She waited until I was on the chair next to her desk before peering over her glasses at me again.

"You're about five weeks."

"Five weeks?" I echoed. My head spun as I remembered Lorna's question in the garden. I felt a rush of panic until the doctor explained that it was dated not from conception, but from the first day of my last period, and I realized, with a sag of relief, that, of course, I'd had a period anyway since I last slept with Nick. Then she was asking me whether I was sure about the decision and I said yes, I *am*, my mouth suddenly dry like someone had poured ash in it.

After that it felt like I was standing outside my own body, which was suddenly a vehicle being put through garage checks. In another, much smaller room a bosomy nurse with wrinkles in her flesh-colored tights took my blood pressure, pricked my finger, and felt my pulse, two fingers on my wrist, humming while she studied a little watch clipped onto her top pocket. Finally, after more time in the waiting room, gazing at the now-familiar leaflets in a rack on the wall (*Pregnant and Don't Know What to Do?* and the more jaunty *We Can Cure Your Gonorrhea*), I was called back into the room where I'd had the scan.

The French doctor held up a sizable white pill in a little plastic cup.

"It blocks the hormone called progesterone, which is necessary for the pregnancy to continue. You'll need to take this now with me here."

I nodded. She put the cup down on the side table and began cutting into another pack of pills with a pair of nail scissors.

"These next four can be taken anytime in the next twelve to twenty-four hours. They will cause the cervix to soften and void. Now, you can either come back here to take them or you can take them at home. But for young women like you who have not yet had children, I recommend you take them here in the clinic. There will be some bleeding and variable amounts of pain when you pass the pregnancy. You may find it distressing."

I shook my head. "I'd like to take them away."

"Your decision. The first pill you must take here with me. It is the law. But the rest"—she gave a Gallic shrug—"it is up to you. As long as you understand."

"I understand."

She turned away to put down the scissors. I looked at the pills on the table.

"Dr. Lefrère?"

She turned toward me.

"Do any women change their minds between taking the first pill and the others?"

She paused, her face suddenly watchful. "Yes," she said. "Sometimes they do. But in that case I cannot guarantee the pregnancy will"—she paused for a moment, for the first time looking a little less certain as she searched for the word—"turn out well," she said eventually. She paused again, looking at me over her glasses. "But, Jessica—if you are not absolutely sure, I recommend a second visit with our counselor."

The sound of my name brought a sudden rush of warmth to my chest. She looked at me steadily, waiting.

I picked up the plastic cup. "Do I swallow it whole?"

CHAPTER 23

I imagined Lorna's mother would be one of those marvelously glamorous older ladies, a sort of latter-day Katharine Hepburn, with a silver-gray chignon and a regal way of moving around the room. Her apartment would be, it followed, on the ground floor of a stucco house in an affluent suburb, the kind that might have molded lion statuettes to either side of the front steps and a magnolia tree outside. So I was surprised when we parked in a visitor's bay outside an ugly block of flats, a tall rectangle of stained brown brick purpose-built in the sixties. Lorna killed the engine and swiveled toward me, explaining it was a sheltered living arrangement.

"A dreadful euphemism," she added. "What they mean, of course, is sheltered dying. Sure you want to come in? There are some nice cafés down the road."

I thought about the pill dissolving in my stomach acid as we spoke, blocking whatever it was in order to stop my womb from working.

The first pill will halt proceedings. The next will soften the cervix, causing the uterus to void.

That word, "void."

"You don't mind if I come with you?"

The lift from the foyer was overlit, with handrails to both sides. There was an overwhelming smell of lavender air freshener covering something else.

"How are you feeling?" asked Lorna as we went up.

I shrugged. "Fine. A bit odd, but . . ."

"No pain?"

I shook my head. "They said I might not feel much until the next set of pills. Maybe a headache, some nausea." *But, Jessica—if you are not absolutely sure . . .* "I feel like I've swallowed a hand grenade."

"We won't stay long. Forty minutes, tops."

Perhaps it was the lighting, but her face looked drained of its usual animation. I opened my mouth to ask what was wrong with her mother exactly when the lift pinged, and we walked down a thickly carpeted corridor with framed botanical prints on the walls and identical cream doors on both sides. I thought of Stella in the old people's home in Reigate, the moment when I'd been told by the social worker that I "wasn't needed for Stella anymore. Perhaps I'd like to be paired with someone new?" Which Agatha Christie had we been in the middle of when I was told? *Sleeping Murder*, that was it. The white cover with the purple bubble-gum writing.

At one of the doors, Lorna stopped and pressed the buzzer. A woman with greasy blond hair and very long black roots opened it. Her weary face brightened a little when she saw Lorna. "She was difficul' this morning," the carer said, clearly Eastern European. "She will be happy to see you. She got used to you, this last week, don't want me back."

"That's nice of you, Vera," said Lorna, kissing her on the cheek and giving her shoulder an affectionate press. "Too bad we both know that's bullshit."

The bedroom had those lace half-curtains that meant only a pale version of the sun filtered through, giving the room a dim, underwater feeling. The air had a minty, eye-watering sharpness to it, as if someone had eaten a whole packet of cough drops. I hovered awkwardly in the doorway, but Lorna and Vera walked toward the bed in the corner, talking naturally, and so I took a few steps in behind them and peered over Lorna's shoulder, suddenly consumed with curiosity. The woman who had produced *her*.

The body lying in the bed was almost extinguished. It was clear she had once been a good-looking woman with small, even features, but now the flesh had melted away and her powdery skin was sunken back against her bones. Her eyes were open, but stared without focus at the ceiling. It took a few moments to register that the irregular rasp and click, rasp and click was her breathing. I felt a sudden wave of nausea and swallowed hard to get rid of the metallic taste in my mouth.

"I'm happy you been using these," said Vera, patting one of the metal bars that framed the bed like an infant's crib. "Your sister, she don't like them. She says is like Mrs. Clay is in prison."

Lorna snorted. "Well, of course, Grace would. But I was certainly glad of them in the nights. Especially when she started thrashing her head around."

"Tha's right," said Vera, nodding vigorously. "I think it is the pain in her hip from the fall. I am strong. I can stop her falling if I am here. Maybe you, too. But if I am asleep in the other room, and I don' hear . . . You like some tea?"

"Absolutely not. You go out now, Vera. Howard said he would be here any moment."

"I jus' pick up that prescription on the high street and come straight back. Fifteen minutes."

Lorna shook her head. "Take a break, for God's sake. Stretch your legs. You're only just back up on your feet yourself." She reached into her bag and fished out a banknote. "In fact will you pick up some brown bread from that nice deli at the top of the hill?

"That woman is a saint," said Lorna as the door closed behind her. "I've done her job for six days and I'm a wreck. Come, let's put the kettle on. The doctor will be here in a second. Howie's actually an old friend from college; we were undergrads at the same time—he's brilliant. Have a rummage in that cupboard there, will you? Vera always keeps great biscuits."

She sounded just like Lorna but there was a funny blankness to her eyes. A coping mechanism, I imagined, a way of dealing with having a mother who was both here and not. I wondered what had happened to her, exactly. A stroke maybe, or some other kind of brain hemorrhage—something that had short-circuited her system, nearly fusing it entirely. We had just finished making the tea when the buzzer rang.

Howard the doctor was a small, spry man with large ears, round spectacles, and the air of a ticking bomb. After Lorna had introduced us she steered me into the living room and suggested I take a rest while they "had a quick chat."

"You're bound to be in a mad rush," I heard her saying to him as they walked into her mother's room. "And God knows you've been patient with me these last days. But I wanted to have one last word with you, before Grace gets back . . ."

The curtains were open in the living room and the afternoon sun had soaked through, creating a little heat trap. I had barely sat down and taken a sip of tea before a mixture of the warmth of the sun and the softness of the flower-print sofa seemed to lend little weights to my eyelids. I laid my head back against the cushions to close them for a second, and there was the hum of voices next door and then just silence.

When I woke up I was looking at a square, glass coffee table with a fan of property magazines on it. *House and Home, Estate, West London Properties, Property Weekly*. My wrist ached from being pushed back the wrong way beneath my slumped head, and my tongue had a sour, tinny taste to it. My first thought was that I had fallen asleep in the waiting room at the abortion clinic—*No, I mustn't call it that,* I thought: the family-planning clinic. Then I blinked and looked round, slowly taking in the flower-print curtains that matched the sofa, the little fireplace with a brass clock on the mantel and a side table with some framed photos on it, and I remembered where we were and thought, *Well, it is a waiting room of sorts, I suppose, of the grimmest kind.* Then I refocused on the coffee table. *Wow, is that some kind of sick joke? Who on earth puts property magazines in a dying woman's flat?*

I propped myself up on my elbow and felt giddiness wash over me, like I had just stood up in a boat. My hand crept into my pocket to check that the blister pack was still there. Four little bumps. *Miso-something.* And what was the name of the pill I'd taken at the clinic? *Mifepristone.* Was it just me that was reminded of Mephistopheles, banging three times on the door, coming to claim Dr. Faustus's soul for the underworld? Or was it just my head that was banging, a piston keeping time inside my skull?

I looked at the brass clock. Just under two hours to go before I took them. More waiting. And then my scalp prickled hot and cold as it occurred to me that if this room was a waiting room, then my womb was one, too, and the appointment I'd made for its inhabitant was with death, as well. And I thought, *Oh God, Alec, I'm so sorry. I should have told you first and now it's too late.*

The hum of voices from next door had stopped, I realized. The doctor must have gone already. I walked out of the living room and stood in the open doorway to Lorna's mother's room. Lorna was sitting in the chair beside the bed, her back to me. I was about to retreat when she must have heard or sensed me because she turned and I saw her cheeks were wet with tears.

"It's okay," she said, "come in."

She was holding something I first assumed was her mother's hand, but taking a couple of steps closer, I could see it was a little ornate silver photo frame, the kind you find in old ladies' houses.

Rasp, click, rasp, click, went the body in the bed. I must have looked as awkward as I felt because Lorna said, "Don't worry. I'm fine." And brushing away the tears, she smiled and sniffed and put the photo back on the bedside table.

It was just a headshot but I could tell it was the same I'd seen in a couple of the bigger frames in the living room. Windblown chestnut hair a bit darker than Lorna's and a freckled face, laughing eyes.

"Your brother?" I asked without thinking.

Lorna gave a dry sort of laugh and stood up.

"I don't have a brother," she said. "That's my father. He didn't look like that at the end, but then my mother has always been one for rose-tinting."

"You were close, you and your dad?"

Lorna looked back down at her mother. The old woman's eyes were closed now and her mouth slackly open. The hands resting on the sheet were veiny but not very wrinkled, and it occurred to me that despite her white-gray hair and cadaverous appearance, she was probably not *that* old. Seventy-five rather than ninety, judging by her daughter.

"We were close," said Lorna softly. "Very. And then we weren't."

She glanced at the photo and then stood up and without looking at her mother turned to go. When she next spoke the spark was back in her face again and maybe it was because there was death in the air but it occurred to me that Lorna was more alive than anyone I'd ever met.

"He was a wonderful bastard, my father. For good and for bad, he made me everything I am."

CHAPTER 24

Lorna's sister's house was the kind of place you don't want to have a miscarriage. It had blond-wood floorboards that made you feel you should take off your shoes at the front door and then dry-clean your socks.

The impression I got of Grace from her house was so utterly contrasting to Lorna that it felt like whoever had parceled out the genes between the two sisters must have had a sense of humor. The stylishly bare kitchen had giant double-glazed glass doors and a tropical terrapin tank lit by a chilly blue light worth more than the entire stock combined at Pet Projects. Lorna flicked the switch on a stainless-steel kettle and then went to fetch mugs, tapping on some walls that turned out to be cupboards.

"Don't you find the whole minimalist thing so irritating?" she said, after several failed attempts to close the cupboards again. "It's for people who care most about things but want to pretend they're not there."

Ah, so that's the way the wind blows between them, I thought, remembering her comment to Howard. How interesting. It occurred to me, having seen her mother, a pristine cadaver, her hair still set, that perhaps Lorna was in flight from this kind of life every bit as much as I was from Milton View.

After our tea, Lorna led me up the stairs, past two colorful, immaculate rooms, both with bunk beds, and into one that had pale yellow wallpaper and curtains made of a heavy expensive material that pooled on the floor like a bridal gown. I looked at the bed with its dazzling white sheets in dismay.

"Is there an old towel or something I can lie on?"

"I have towels, I have painkillers, I have a large bar of milk chocolate and a trashy novel," said Lorna, turning on the lamp by the bed.

"And you're quite sure your sister won't suddenly come back from Suffolk?"

"Not before Tuesday. Grace measured out three days' worth of turtle sprinkles into separate Tupperware boxes for me."

"Gosh."

"To be fair, one did die on my watch before. If her cleaner wasn't in Brazil this week, I'd never have been entrusted with them again."

"And Hugh," I asked, pressing the springy mattress nervously before perching on the edge. "He doesn't mind you not being around?"

It wasn't an entirely innocent question, remembering his comments down by the lake. But neither was it designed to provoke the reaction it got. Lorna—whose back was turned to me as she took towels from the cupboard—seemed to tense and her hands stilled for a moment.

"Why would he mind?" she said, turning around. I could see from her shuttered expression that this was not a question she wanted me to answer. And I thought: *However intimate the space between us feels, perhaps talking about* her *private life will always be a no-go, a teacher-student transgression.* Then her face changed as she asked me how I was feeling—and what about a hot-water bottle?— her smile reaching her eyes. "What in life isn't made a little more bearable with a hot-water bottle?"

It struck me, as she went back downstairs to fill the kettle, that what she was doing for me wasn't a million miles away from what my mother would have done, except there was a compassion in the tone of Lorna's voice and a connectedness in the way she met my eyes that not only made me feel not alone but also understood and liked.

That was the thing about Lorna. She was never frightened. There was a sense that, somehow, it would all turn out okay.

I was two chapters into the trashy novel when the cramping started.

I had anticipated nasty spasms in my gut akin to food poisoning, but in fact it wasn't like that at all. It felt more like a wide metal band circling my abdomen was suddenly screwed very tight, sending a shaft of pain the whole way through me. I felt dizzy, a tingling feeling shooting through my whole nervous system right to the edges of my teeth. The first one only lasted a few seconds.

The clinic had given me a few thick sanitary pads to take away with me. They soaked through in no time, leaving me looking anxiously at the fluffy white towels that Lorna had given me. Eventually I decided that despite the pain I'd rather be sitting on the loo and so sat there for most of the night while the contractions swept through me. I had told Lorna I wanted to be alone and after looking at me hard she said okay, she'd be downstairs in the study and would stay up late so I could come and get her anytime. But when I crept down to refill my hot-water bottle, I saw she had fallen asleep in front of a late-night news program, her legs curled up on the sofa, curls of red hair splayed across her face. She looked so deeply asleep, dark shadows under her eyes, I didn't want to wake her up.

At some point during that night—it must have been nearly dawn—one of the contractions lasted longer than the others. Maybe it wasn't the baby, but I felt a terrible tearing in me, not altogether physical, and for some reason I pictured Alec on the beach in Suffolk, letting go of the kite, watching it spin off into the sky.

———

I dreamed that Georgie called to tell me about the details of Alec's funeral. In the dream, I knew she was wrong, but understanding how hurt she was, I was full of love and patience.

"You're confused," I told her, struggling to sit up, my elbow pressing into the pillow. "No wonder, you've been through so much. But he's fine, Georgie. He just had to go home for a bit. But listen, I'm so glad you called. I've been desperate to say how sorry— how very, very sorry."

"Are you stoned?" demanded Georgie. "You're not making any sense. Where are you?"

"It's okay," I whispered into the phone. "This is just a dream. None of this is actually happening. But if it were, I'd wanna say—"

"You're slurring," she snapped. "Are you on a downer of some kind? Christ, if he got to you, too . . ."

"That's right, a downer." Being a dream, this struck me as hugely funny. "Boy, can I tell you about this downer I'm having . . ." I felt my laughter spiral out of control.

Knocking on the door. Rat, tat, tat.

"Oh, that's very good," I said, tears beginning to pour down my cheeks. "Did you hear that, Georgie? Three knocks. That's Mephistopheles, come to collect my soul. You know, like in *Dr. Faustus.*"

The door banged open, everything flooding with light.

"Jess, are you all right? I was worried, I thought I heard—"

Lorna stood at the door, still in the crumpled clothes she'd been wearing when she met me in the park, hair sticking out to one side, a crease down the side of her cheek. "Oh, sorry. You're on the phone . . ."

I felt a sudden slice of pain through my abdomen and a moment later became aware of the roughness of the towel doubled up beneath me, a sensation like a bruise between my legs, the tinny sound of Georgie's voice, calling from far away in the handset. *People don't feel pain in dreams.* I looked down at my slack hand holding the phone, held it back up to my ear. Georgie was saying something now about the church, telling me to write down the address that Alec's mother had given her.

That's not right, either, I thought. Alec doesn't have a mother. She died of cancer. Perhaps he hadn't confided that to Georgie—so then I shouldn't say anything to correct her, it would only be more hurtful. I looked up at Lorna and suddenly my nervousness at talking to Georgie and the nonsensical nature of our conversation struck me as terribly funny and I couldn't help laughing again.

"Have you been smoking weed?" said Georgie suspiciously. "Where are you? Are you at home?" She gave a nasty laugh when I told her. "At *Lorna's?* Really. How perfect . . ."

I took a deep breath, sat up properly, wiping my eyes. "I'm sorry. I don't understand. What conversation? Who are you trying to tell me has died?" I tried to speak very slowly, aware that the painkillers and lack of sleep were making it hard to separate out the words.

Lorna stood in the doorway, her face very pale and strange, watching me.

"Your boyfriend Alec," said Georgie bitterly. "Piece of shit that he was."

For the next forty-eight hours—it could have been any number, time lost all shape—I was sucked into a grinding vortex of pain. The French doctor had told me I was likely to have a fever following the bleeding. But right after the call from Georgie, I vomited, knees sinking into the thick-pile carpet of the guest bedroom, tears and snot streaming down my face. Soon after that, the chills began, prickles breaking out all over my body, and I lay, curled up in a slick of sweat, hugging my lower stomach, where the cramps, stealthy and violent, were circling.

Lorna had closed the curtains to let me rest, and they stayed closed after that, as the light bothered my eyes and seemed to worsen my fever. And besides, I didn't want it to be day. That would be to admit this was real life, and not some murky half-lit horror movie I'd stumbled into. In the minutes that were lucid I would lie, numb and sealed off, staring at the geometric patterns on the heavy, satiny material of the curtains—tunnels of interlocking, receding squares that tricked the eye and that I could still sketch now, six years on, given a pencil and paper. I found that if I kept my eyes trained on the squares with absolute discipline, I could stop myself thinking about Alec—beautiful Alec, cold and dead—for several seconds in a row. But after a while I gave up on this, too; the fleeting relief was outweighed by the fresh shock of grief that followed it.

The only time I left the room was to walk, legs shaking, to the bathroom. Often when I came back I would find Lorna taking away a blood-spotted towel and stripping the drenched sheets again, smoothing on some new ones, laying down a clean towel and bringing me another jug of black-currant cordial, after which she would wait and watch, hands on hips, to make sure I drank.

She was angelic during those days. The cramps meant I barely slept, and badly, and the little I did, I tried to fight off, because when I succumbed the nightmares came: lurid ones, involving blind fetuses and mass graves and Alec's copper-stamped iris sitting in a jar on a pathologist's table, still burning with life.

I must have shouted or cried out in my sleep often because when I surfaced Lorna would be there stroking my hair, and telling me *it's okay, really it's okay, it's better this way*, and then fetching a fresh hot-water bottle and some chamomile tea sweetened with honey, sitting on the edge of the bed talking nonsense until my body became less rigid, the dizziness and teeth-chattering less pronounced.

On the second morning, she took my temperature again, grim-faced, and said, "Okay, enough of this shit, I'm calling Howard." And then the curtains were open, and Howard was sitting on the side of my bed, pressing my tender stomach gently and asking me questions in his calm, businesslike voice before scribbling on a pad and ripping off a page.

"The infection is easy to see off," he said, explaining that I'd had a relatively rare complication of a medical abortion—probably because I had thrown up the antibiotics that the French doctor had given me. "It's this I'm more worried about." He leaned forward and touched me lightly on the temple. "There are a couple of people here I can recommend you talk to, though it would be a better idea if it was someone you could see for a little while, regularly, either near your college or at home. I can put some feelers out, if you'd like. Which is best, do you think?"

I glanced over to the door but Lorna had melted off.

CHAPTER 25

After two days, once the new antibiotics kicked in, I felt restless. My legs were still weak but steady. I dressed, then went into the bathroom to splash cold water on my face—the paleness of my skin and dark shadows under my eyes made me look like a ghoul.

Halfway down the stairs to the living room, I froze.

"Listen, I can see how it looks but you're wrong . . ."

Lorna's voice, coming from the study. I peered down past the banisters. I could see her through a crack in the door, a slice of her shoulders, the phone pressed to her ear.

"Hugh, darling, that's just a fucked-up conclusion to jump to." A pause. "I'm with her now. Of course I'm being careful." She moved farther into her study and her voice became muffled.

I crept back upstairs and lay back down on the bed, fully clothed, heart thumping.

An hour or so later I heard the front door click open and then slam shut.

I was dozing in bed early that evening—book still propped between nerveless fingers—when Lorna walked into my bedroom and snapped on the bedside light.

I propped myself up on one elbow, working some moisture into my mouth.

She was wearing a pair of faded jeans with a very thin gold chain belt and a black silk, sleeveless top. Her eyes looked dramatic, rimmed with kohl. Only her hair was its usual wild, ungroomed affair.

"Are you going somewhere?" I wanted to add, *You look wonderful*, but didn't. One of the pills, I wasn't sure which, had left a metallic taste on my tongue.

"Yes. To dinner. With you."

"To dinner?" I echoed. "But I have no clean clothes. And my sneakers . . ."

"I thought about that," said Lorna. "Come on."

She was sleeping in her sister's room, at the front of the house. It had bay windows and powder blue walls, the bedside lamps throwing out cones of light. Lorna made no reference to the unmade bed, the print of her body on the sheets.

Behind the bed, there was a walk-in wardrobe hidden by sliding doors.

"Choose something," she said, rolling them back. "Grace has some nice stuff once you get past the floral prints."

I blinked at the hanging racks.

"Really?" I said. "It feels a bit weird."

Lorna considered me for a moment longer and then, before I registered what she was doing, she'd crossed her arms and whipped off her own top. She was wearing a black bra, with pale lace embroidery over the cups—I could see the ivory skin of her breasts glowing through the gauze, the faint creases on the skin of her stomach. "Come on," she demanded, holding out her top without a trace of self-consciousness. "Swap."

I felt the blood rush to my face. "What?"

"That top," she said. "It's depressing me. I'll wear it, and you can wear this one. It's mine, so you don't have to worry."

Partly because I was stuck for words, and partly because I wanted to hide my now-hot face, I struggled out of my top and handed it to her. Then without looking her in the eye, I took her sleeveless top and pulled it on—the black silk slithering down over my sides, still warm from her skin.

"Uncross your arms," said Lorna, cocking her head. "That's better. Beautiful, in fact."

I stood under the overhead lights, feeling absurdly self-conscious, as if I had just undressed, not dressed.

Suddenly, the space between us felt very small.

"Where are we going?" I asked quickly.

"Not so very far," said Lorna, smiling. "Ever shucked an oyster?"

The sink in the kitchen was filled with a glittering pile of crushed ice. Piled on top of it were what must have been twenty whole oysters, closed, with crusted bits of seaweed and barnacles on them.

"So what you do is wedge the blade in here carefully . . . then wiggle it a little until you find the hinge. They're tricky little bastards, but all of a sudden they pop. There you go." Lorna opened the shell a crack, then scooped under it with the knife. "They're attached to the top and bottom with a little strand of muscle, which is quite strong. Once you've cut through that . . . there!" She gave a sharp little twist with the knife. "Then they're dead . . . Look."

I looked dubiously at the silver-gray pulp with its wrinkled edges, sitting on the half-shell.

"And you eat it just like that?"

Perhaps it was the painkillers mixed with the wine—*Oh, a glass or two will be fine, you don't need to treat Howie's every word as gospel*—or perhaps the oysters with their cold, creamy taste of the sea that washed away the past few days, but for most of that evening, I felt giddy and surreal and a little elated. It wasn't like I was happy—I knew I wasn't, I knew I was terribly fucked—but it was like, for a couple of hours, someone had suspended the horror movie in my head.

"Helluva lot more than you bargained for," I said as I helped Lorna set the table, "when you offered to put me up for a night."

"Actually I quite enjoy being a nurse," she said. "The pragmatism of it keeps your mind off other things. You know that Christie was a volunteer nurse during the First World War, originally in a hospital before she ended up as a chemist's assistant. That's how she got all her very accurate knowledge of poisons." Lorna banged a cupboard door shut with her elbow, grimacing. "They say Martindale's *Pharmacopeia* was the most well-thumbed book on her shelves. Which is impressive, because I've read it, too, cover to cover, as an exercise in getting to know my subject. The length alone could kill you. Now, let's sit and eat. I'll make a salad in a minute."

Supper turned out to be just the oysters—the salad was much referenced, but never delivered—and a plate of crackers with some very rich, rough black olive paste that someone called "Cesco, from the island" had given her.

"You must come out there," she said, reaching for another oyster.

"Sounds amazing," I agreed, chomping down a cracker and washing it back with wine. I hadn't realized how hungry I was. The saltiness of the oysters and the olives seemed to be making me more ravenous.

"I wasn't just being rhetorical," said Lorna, resting a shell on the side of her plate and leaning forward to fix me with her smiling eyes. "I meant, come back out there with me."

I paused, glass in the air.

Hugh had said that the island was where she liked to go on her own. Now she was asking *me*. Did this mean she thought I was in dire need of help? On some level that I couldn't quite access, I registered quite how big this offer was, how deeply flattering. She, Lorna. My mentor-tutor. Me, Jess Walker. No longer just a student. Then, what? Protégée, companion, plaything? Friend?

I put down my glass and leaned forward, feeling the wine hot in my veins.

"Who was Sybil?"

Lorna's expression didn't change, but she looked away. Picking up an oyster from the side of her plate, she tipped it slightly so that some of the juices ran off. Then she reached for a wedge of lemon and squeezed it on the silvery pulp. I saw the frilly edge cringe slightly, revealing the pearly white shell.

"Sybil was a student of mine at Cambridge. Best I ever had. I'll tell you about her someday." And she tipped the oyster into her mouth. I felt an obscure rush of jealousy.

Lorna finished swallowing and wiped her mouth before saying, "The island is out of season now, so the airfares are cheap as chips. Happy to sub you, though, if that helps. Of course, you won't be able to think about anything like that until after Thursday . . . More lemon," she said suddenly, standing up, and moving back to the fridge.

After Thursday. Thursday was the funeral, another two days away. The South African police had ruled out foul play. But Alec's family, believing this to be a whitewash, wanted a second opinion. Suspicious that any autopsy performed on South African ground would be open to corruption, they'd requested his body be "repatriated" to England, where they would perform a second postmortem before burial.

This much we knew, not from Georgie, who was blocking Lorna's calls now, too—feeling betrayed, we assumed, by the fact that she was "harboring me"—but from Aunt Zanny, who Lorna had tracked down via the university database and spoken to at length ("Boy," Lorna had said, rubbing her ear as she came off the phone, "she may be sad, but she's definitely not shy").

But now the cocoon-like feeling—shock, wine, oysters—had cracked and a dark wave of thoughts and questions crowded in.

Was Alec's body in a plane at this very moment, crossing the oceans? What happened in a postmortem? Would they scoop out his organs, weigh them on little scales, then sew him back up? Did they put them back in before they sewed, or keep them out for more tests? Would they bury him without his heart?

I looked down at my hands on my lap, realized they were clenched into fists.

Impossible, I thought. *Impossible that this is actually happening.*

"Jess?" Lorna was over by the sink, slicing a lemon. She came back, dropping down on the chair beside mine. Taking both my hands in hers, she uncurled my fingers and held them. She wasn't smiling, but her face was so open it felt like an embrace.

"You're much stronger than you think," she said.

CHAPTER 26

We drove to Norfolk in Lorna's sister's car, a glossy urban SUV with pristine mudguards. Lorna lent me a navy-blue pencil skirt that was too long and a crumpled navy shirt that I'd had a brief, unsuccessful attempt at ironing. The bleeding had almost stopped now but I was still wearing panty-liners that made me feel bulky and self-conscious. Lorna was wearing a long, stretchy black crepe dress, red lipstick that clashed with her upswept hair. With her giant sixties shades, she looked like a glamorous Mafia widow. I caught sight of my white face in the passenger seat mirror. My chin had broken out in pimples, either from the hormones, lack of sleep, or stress, and there were blue-black shadows under my eyes. *At least he can't see me now*, I thought darkly, but the thought that followed: that he would never see me again—*never, never, never, never, never, never, never*—caused such a stabbing pain behind my eyes that for a second I thought I would black out.

As we got off the motorway and began to head down twisty country lanes, I had to grip the tops of my thighs to stop my hands from shaking. Less than four weeks before I had been cycling down these roads toward the Old Swan. Apart from the weather—it was a fine, dry spring day—nothing had changed. The villages: some pretty, some not, little redbrick houses with their gardens and washing lines, TV satellite dishes on their roofs. People leading ordinary lives, eyes turned away from Death, who was waiting, waiting everywhere.

"I think we've gone the wrong way."

"Little detour," said Lorna, rummaging in the packet of chocolate raisins that was sitting in the cup holder. "To pick up Aunt Zanny from the station."

My head swam. "Aunt Zanny?"

"You're right, I should have asked you," agreed Lorna, her mouth full of chocolate. "I told Alec's aunt we could scoop her up from the station. I thought that as we were technically gate-crashing it might be easier if we turned up with a relative as our rubber stamp. It's only a tiny diversion," she said, swinging the wheel as we pulled into the station forecourt. "Look. That's got to be her. In the hat."

"*Bless* you people for picking me up," said Aunt Zanny and, although I should have been prepared for it, the South African accent gave me a jolt. "Have you any idea how far it is from Norfolk to Wiltshire? Five hours, *three changes*. Of course, Divvy said she could pick me up, too, but I could tell it was the last thing she wanted to do."

I offered to jump in the backseat. Despite the fact that Aunt Zanny was half my size—most of which was hat—she accepted promptly. "Age before beauty," she said, giving me a coquettish sort of smile.

So I sat in the back and took her in from one angle: diagonally, from behind, which was basically a pair of shiny red lips moving almost continuously behind black net. The hat itself (a gauzy affair) must have been pinned into her hair because she didn't move to take it off and it rubbed against the roof of the car for the whole journey. When she occasionally swiveled round to include me (the hat rasping as she turned), I could see her red lipstick had bled onto her front teeth and there were deep wrinkles around her mouth. From smoking, perhaps. But possibly just talking. Because boy, could Aunt Zanny talk. The journey from the station to the church was twenty-five minutes, and I swear she spoke for twice that long.

"Truth is, Divvy and I are not exactly close, never really were," said Zanny, accepting a handful of chocolate raisins from Lorna, and throwing them in without pausing. "I reached out to her when she moved back to the UK—God knows I understand what it's like to make that move—but she wasn't interested. She thought I'd taken Greg's side. Which I hadn't, by the way, I knew damn well how hard my brother is to live with. Then Alec moving in with me last year . . . Hard for Divvy, too, of course, with them being barely on speaking terms. But he made everything hard for her. Oh, I *knew* that . . ." She reached for more raisins. "How did you two know him?"

Did. The word hung in the car. Lorna's eyes met mine in the rearview mirror for a moment, then she said something noncommittal about us being new university friends of Alec's.

"I would love to know how you found him at college," said Zanny, giving us no time to answer at all. "Always such an unknowable child. Such charm, and so clever. But things happening all around him. Divvy bore the brunt of it, of course . . ."

"This Divvy . . . ?" prompted Lorna, her eyes on the road.

"Davina," said Aunt Zanny with surprise. "My sister-in-law. Alexander's mother."

I must have started at this because Aunt Zanny glanced in the mirror. "Oh, he didn't talk about her? Not surprising. *Such* a complicated relationship. For years she always took his side. Like what happened with Sipho, the maid. And her daughter. What was her name? Oh, my memory, it's always *names* I forget, why is that . . . And it went both ways, of course. Divvy let him down, too. I always told her it was a bad scene, that she should have let him know earlier. Not that confidence was Alexander's problem. But we never know how these things can take root. 'Trust' is probably the best word for it. Yes, *wrecking trust*. But she was sick, she had cancer, you know. I had to move in, for a while."

She'd been talking still as she reapplied her lipstick. Now she paused at last to press a Kleenex between her lips, leaving two bloody semicircles on the tissue.

I stared at her, my head beginning to throb. None of this made sense. It was like we were talking about the same person, but reversed in a mirror: recognizable, but just a little off. Alec's mother had died, of cancer. He'd told me that. Or at least, I was sure he had, when he'd told me that story about trying to stop time as a boy. Hadn't he? I tried to recall exact sentences. But they slipped away as I reached for them. Wrecking trust? His brother, Basti— he'd been the one who'd messed with everyone's heads. The leather of the car seat was getting sticky under my grip, a sudden sharpness to the ache between my legs. *Please stop talking now*, I begged her silently. *I need to think. Please.*

"Always been a sucker for a pair of beautiful eyes on a man," rattled on Aunt Zanny. "Did you ever hear that story about the woman who bumped into Paul Newman in an ice-cream parlor? It wasn't until she walked out of the café that she realized she'd put her ice-cream cone in her handbag. In her *handbag*, can you imagine?" She delivered this on a crescendo of smoker's laughter, and then suddenly, unexpectedly, her shoulders began to shake. Strange honking sounds came from below her hat.

"It makes no sense to me that he's gone," she said, in between heaves. "Such a force of life. I didn't think you got to feel that way again, at my age. I'd forgotten, entirely. I'd just become old Zanny who talks too much. I knew he'd leave at some point. Disappear and not look back. But it makes no sense that he's gone like this. All that life and exuberance, switched off. Like a radio."

"I'm sorry," said Lorna quietly. "I'm so sorry."

I reached forward with a fresh Kleenex, unable to bear not asking.

"We don't know much," I said, "about how he died."

Aunt Zanny nodded and mopped at her nose. "It's a bit of a mystery. They found lots of hefty painkillers in his system, his kidneys shut down. But they're calling it an accident, saying that he must have slipped up, self-medicating for some minor virus—and it's quite true, you *can* buy all sorts of terrible poison over the counter there. But of course, none of the family believe it, and I tend to agree. All that wonderfully brave journalism he was in the middle of. They got to him somehow . . ."

I shook my head in disbelief. Suddenly, none of this felt remotely real. Talking of murder and political conspiracy with a garrulous old lady in a big hat. Surely Lorna was about to stop the car and tell me the whole thing had been an elaborate hoax. And then we were swinging into the church driveway, and my stomach flipped and I thought, *There you go, you see: He isn't dead, after all. There's his car.* Except the hearse looked much cleaner and there was a driver in the front seat where Alec should have been, a man in a black suit with a peaked cap over a gray face. *Death's chauffeur.* The rear compartment was empty, except for a bed of flowers. A few people wearing black were walking slowly toward the door of the church, arms linked. Silence fell in Lorna's car, broken only by the crunch of smart shoes walking over gravel.

Then Aunt Zanny unbuckled her seat belt and opened the passenger door. By the time she was out of the car, she was gabbling again, about her hat this time, about the fact that she'd stored it in the attic and moths had nibbled little holes in the netting.

CHAPTER 27

It was a small church but packed. A boy of about fifteen with carefully gelled hair and a grave expression handed me an order of service. Even in my dazed state the first thing I noticed was the nature of the congregation. There weren't quite as many black faces as white ones along the pews, but it wasn't far off, either—an unusual sight in an English country church. It was noisy, too, with the rumble of people talking. A large middle-aged woman in a bright violet headdress was blowing her nose loudly. At the front, in between the pews on a dais, lay his coffin, piled with all sorts of flowers that I've never been able to look at since: pink spider lilies, their stamens caked in pollen; dark purple tulips.

I must have been standing stupidly in the aisle, swaying even, because Lorna took hold of my elbow and steered me into one of the back pews, where Steady—looking different in a suit, his face solemn, his thatch of hair combed—had saved us places. I looked around in bewilderment. *I know no one else here*, I thought, and then with a start I saw Georgie, her cap of blond hair above a purple silk dress, a few rows ahead. Maybe Lorna saw her, too, because she took my hand and gave it a little squeeze just as the priest walked in.

"We are gathered here to mourn the untimely passing of Alexander Van Zanten," he began, his hands raised and parted as if holding an invisible box.

I couldn't see the whole of the front pew. Apart from the swell of people, many taller than me, I had a stone column partially blocking my line of sight. I flipped over the Order of Service and my stomach lurched again. On the back was a grainy black-and-white photo of Alec as a young boy, hair lifted by the wind as he crouched behind a sandcastle, squinting in the sunlight. Alexander S. Van Zanten (December 13, 1986–May 12, 2012). May 12. Dear God, the day I'd gone to the clinic with Lorna. My hands moved instinctively to the dull ache in my stomach. Had it been a boy, I wondered, that twisted piece of scar tissue inside me? A beautiful little boy? Or a girl, with a shard of alien color in her eyes? I felt so light-headed that I leaned against Lorna, hard, and she looked round at me, taking my elbow again. "Okay?" she mouthed, very pale herself.

A beautiful, elderly black man with grizzled hair and a three-piece suit was reading out a passage from the Bible in a low, lilting voice. "The virtuous man, though he die before his time, will find rest . . ." Light was streaming through the stained glass. Then we were standing for a hymn. I felt my lips move, but no sound came out. Sitting. Standing. Sitting again. Then a very thin pale girl with a set expression was walking up to the pulpit. She had long black curly hair scraped back off her angular face. I looked down at the piece of paper in my hand again.

The Eulogy . . . . Celia Van Zanten

She stood on the top step, her chin only just reaching above the pulpit. The church fell very quiet. Even from the back I could hear the rustle of the paper she was holding. "Everyone who met my brother, Alexander, would agree he was an exceptional human being." Her voice cracked and she paused to clear it. The congregation shifted a little in their seats.

"It feels so strange to use that word, 'was.' Alec, for all his complications, was the most alive person I ever knew. He had a kind of energy that dazzled. As his younger sister, I grew up in his thrall."

I glanced over at Aunt Zanny. Her chin was high, face obscured by the silly hat. Celia was telling us about when Alec and she had been kids. "My very first memory is of lying on the bottom bunk while Alec told me a story from up above in the dark. The stories usually ran as a series, sometimes for weeks and months, and I could barely wait till bedtime to hear the newest installment. The one that ran the longest was about Alfred J. Moon. Alfred J. Moon, my brother told me, was a key-cutter who had a shop in a little alley somewhere in Johannesburg. On the front of his shop was a sign that read, 'We Have the Key to Everything.'" Celia's gaze flicked up to look at the congregation, a shadow of a smile crossing her face. "Alfred was an old guy with glasses and silver hair and very clever, long fingers. The walls of the shop were silver and gold, covered with rows and rows of blank keys hanging on hooks . . . keys of every shape and size. When you walked in, the draft coming through the door made all the keys tinkle like little sleigh bells."

I felt the goosebumps rise on my arms. I had a sudden vision of Alec conjuring images as we sat together outside, of a little boy lying under a jacaranda tree, one arm thrown across the still body of his German shepherd.

"But Alfred J. Moon had a secret. A little back room to the shop, with walls also covered in keys. These were much smaller, though. Like keys to a jewelry box or a fairy garden, and they were not blanks. At the start of each of Alec's stories, someone would walk into the shop. What they thought they wanted was an extra key— to a car, or a house, or a shed. But there was always something deeper that was wrong, some locked door in their mind. Alfred would take a long look at the person who walked in, listen to their request, and then go into the back room, where he carefully selected a key. Then—don't ask me how—he would slip it into their minds. A neglectful mother, a sadistic nurse, a lonely little girl. Alfred would set to work on their minds, undoing padlocks, throwing open doors."

Celia looked up shyly, as if sure she would have lost her audience. The woman with the purple headdress blew her nose again, noisily, but otherwise everyone was silent.

"In the days leading up to the miners' strike, which Alec so bravely covered—which affected the relatives and friends of many of you here today—many of the miners, who wouldn't talk to the rest of the media, spoke only to Alec." At this there was a murmur of agreement from the pews, more handkerchiefs came out.

"On the day of the massacre he was the only journalist who managed to talk his way into the Andrew Saffy Memorial Hospital. There he spoke to some of the injured strikers, including a rock drill operator. That interview became the only comprehensive first-person account of what happened at the Small Koppie, where miners were brutally executed. But due to the cowardice at Alec's paper it was never published at the time. Today, I have an extract from it here . . ." More rustling of paper. And then she was reading, but it was Alec's voice I heard, startlingly the same as when he had told us the story that day on the drive to the Half-Hitch. The same casual but confiding tone, drawing you in, as if he were in the room. I felt the mood in the congregation shift again, become more agitated. What had Alec meant to all these people here? I wondered. I felt a wrench of loss, not only for the future, but for a past I would never know.

Celia looked up. "Alec was passionate about trying to expose what really happened on the day of the massacre. He died trying to solve one more mystery: Who had killed the miner Stevie right before he was to testify in front of the commission?" Here Celia paused, her small hands gripping the lectern. There was some color in her face now, little circles of pink on her white cheeks. "I doubt anyone here believes the official finding in South Africa that Alec's death was accidental. We, his family, intend to discover what happened to him in that hotel room in Johannesburg, what made a healthy young man of twenty-six suddenly collapse and die. For now, though, I will say this: Alec died trying to unlock the door to a room that many people in the world didn't want us to see. And, in doing so, became another martyr to South African politics."

A murmur arose from the congregation. A man in one of the front pews began to sob, his shoulders shaking silently.

"In a short while my brother's body will be put in the ground. Not the African ground that broke his heart, but a peaceful place where he chose to live these last few months. Near my mother, who always believed in him"—here Celia paused, glancing at the front row—"in the country where he was trying to make a new life."

His mother. The ground began to pitch again. So, Aunt Zanny was right and I had been mistaken. Or had I misunderstood Alec? *New life.* Dear God. I clenched my fists, felt the nails biting into my palms.

"Of the regrets I feel standing here today," Celia was saying, "and there are many . . . The biggest is that I never did manage to find the key." Here she paused and swallowed, pressing the heels of her hands into her eyes. "The key to the mystery of Alec."

She said some more words, but I don't remember them. And then she was taking her papers off the lectern and stepping down from the pulpit. Absolute silence in that packed church, just the click of her heels against the stone floor.

Glancing over, I noticed Steady was gripping Lorna's hand.

After the service ended, Lorna told me to wait outside the church while she went to find Georgie. "I take it you don't want to come with me?" she said, but the question was rhetorical, and we both knew it. It didn't matter whether *I* wanted to. Georgie had turned once in her pew during the service, seen me sitting next to Lorna, her gaze switching between the two of us, then cut her eyes away with such disgust that I knew I didn't have a chance. The apologies I'd rehearsed died on my tongue. She wouldn't hear them until she hated me a little less. Certainly not today. Today, it was probably better for her if I steered clear.

Of course, I ran into her a few moments after I'd walked out of the church.

She was standing against the outside wall, one arm crossing her body as if trying to shield it. Her face looked drawn, and she had more makeup on than usual. When she saw me, she gave a brittle laugh and took a deep drag on her cigarette.

"Should have brought Nick. It'd be like the old band back together again. Minus one, of course."

"I'm so sorry," I said in a rush. "What I did was unforgivable."

She exhaled, saying nothing.

I shook my head, searching for more words. I felt acutely conscious of the bulk of the panty-liner between my legs, the brown spots of blood that would be speckling it. The last of Alec. A breeze stirred the leaves of the oak trees. The clear, high sky was an unholy blue. Alec in the graveyard now, the coffin being lowered into the earth with his family around him. His family, who might have been part of my future, who now I'd never know. Georgie rubbed her arms. I fought the urge to step forward and hug her fiercely.

"I want you to know," I began, my voice strange and rough, like I hadn't used it for some time, "that nothing ever happened between us before that weekend."

She looked down for a moment, cigarette burning between her fingers, and I felt a stab of hope. Perhaps here, where the game had become zero-sum, she could forgive.

But when she looked up again her eyes were bright and hard with anger. "You child," she said softly. "You fucking *child*. Just how stupid are you?"

I took a step back, as if she'd slapped me.

"I thought you were so smart, so observant," she went on, each word a poisoned dart. "You noticed everything, saw through things. I thought that it was because you were better than me. Because you weren't blinded by your ego. You didn't have the vanity the rest of us do, that makes the world a mirror. But I was wrong. You're just another dumb shit who can't see past herself."

I stared at her, my eyes swimming.

I knew I should say something, explain, apologize some more. But the ball of pain in my throat was so huge and hot that it choked off the words. A few people walked past us, mourners in black, the women's heels clicking on the gravel. One of them shot us a curious glance. *Perhaps this isn't unusual*, I thought dimly. *Showdowns at funerals. Like breakups at weddings. Death and time, putting the screws on.*

"I've tried to imagine the hell this has been for you."

"Have you, Jess?" said Georgie with scorn in her voice. "Have you really? Because let me tell you—having your heart broken by the guy you love and then being shat on by someone you thought was your best friend . . . Well, that's a pretty hard thing to wrap your head around. Even when you're the one it's happening to. I lay for two days in the hospital hating him, hating you, hating myself. Then went home and did the same there, all over again. The funny thing was, my mother turned up trumps. My *mother* of all people. She sat by my bed for pretty much three days in a row, talking. Sober, too. She was the one who told me that it wasn't about Alec, what I'd done. That if anyone was to blame it was her. For being utterly selfish, for trying to be a parent without taking on any responsibility." Georgie raked her foot roughly through the gravel. "Just like that, after all these years. She said it. And that helped. It helped a lot to know that not everyone surprises you in a bad way." Georgie looked up suddenly. "She was the one who told me I should go and find him."

"Find him . . ."

"Yes. She told me to go to South Africa. Make it clear that it hadn't been about him, what I'd done—that he should neither blame nor credit himself for it. Meanwhile, I get my dignity back. Give myself a chance to move on."

I blinked at her. But she hadn't, had she? She hadn't gone.

"You bet I fucking did. I booked a ticket then and there. Booked a room in Jo'burg, too. A mother with a guilty conscience and a credit card has its upsides. I sent him a message, telling him to meet me in a bar the following evening. One of those messages you hope will flip someone's stomach, turn them inside out and then maybe, just maybe . . ." She trailed off and shook her head, her voice hard again. "Less than twenty-four hours, and I was there, sitting on a bar stool, looking damn fucking hot—overdosing does great things for your figure, I'll give it that." And she gave a ghost of a smile here, reminding me of the friends we'd been, so that my heart turned over, and I hoped, despite everything—despite the fact that it would crucify me—that she'd got what she wanted: that he'd turned up and told her he loved her and he was sorry, that I'd meant nothing.

"Did he come?" I made myself ask. Trying, even as the words came out, to shield myself from the reply.

"Yeah, he came," said Georgie flatly. I looked down, feeling something inside me twist. "Looking just fine," she continued. "Like he hadn't lost a wink of sleep. I thought we'd talk about us, or you. But we didn't. Instead he told me about why he couldn't love properly. This girlfriend from a long time ago, who'd died. A moped crash, he blamed himself . . . He wasn't over it. Not at all."

I nearly nodded, stopped myself just in time, realizing how it would sound. *Yes, I know—he poured his heart out to me, too, right before we slept together.*

Georgie dropped her cigarette, ground it slowly underfoot. And lit another one. "That was the fucking irony, Jess. It was never about you. It was never about me, either. It was only ever about this girl. The joke of it was that we thought he saw something in us. But he was just looking through us to catch a glimpse of her."

I shook my head. "That's not true," I said. "I know what he felt for you was the real thing. He told me."

Christ, what was I saying now? Trying to fill the moral vacuum by heaping in more deceit. I felt a slice of pain suddenly, across my abdomen. I glanced at the church door. Lorna would be here any moment. What would happen then? Would it come out somehow, about the pregnancy? And what then? A full-blown shouting match in mourner's garb?

Georgie's lip curled. "Waiting to be saved by Mother?" A fresh wave of anger seemed to wash through her. "Be careful of that woman, Jess. She claims to offer some poetic path to self-discovery, but the truth is far more prosaic. She's a liar, a fucking liar. Why is it that all her favorites break down or disappear? Let me tell you something for free: Lorna Clay's the biggest player of all."

"That's not right," I said, shaking my head vehemently. "I can understand why you're angry with her for helping me. But she's not to blame for anything. It's my fuckup. All mine."

"Oh, you." Georgie's lips thinned cruelly. "You're just a lamb to the slaughter."

"Please. I know I deserve all this. All of this and more. But not today. Today I can't . . ." I felt the hot ball rising in my chest and swallowed, hard. Forced the words, "Can't face losing you, too."

For a moment the glittering eyes, the brittle expression seemed to waver. I caught a glimpse of my friend. Then Georgie shook her head violently, as if I'd asked her some diabolical favor. She looked past my shoulder to where a sleek black car with tinted windows had pulled up.

"That's me," she said coolly. And without a second glance in my direction she walked away, drawing the belt of her coat tighter around her.

I had to rest my hand against the honey-colored stone of the church to steady myself. The door slammed, the car pulled away. Her pale, swollen face behind the darkened window, eyes facing forward. No wave, not even a glance.

I remember watching the taillights swinging around the corner. And I remember, very clearly, thinking: *At least it can't get any worse than this.*

CHAPTER 28

Behind Lorna's slumped head, waves skimmed past the porthole. The insistent grumble of the hydrofoil's engine should have lulled me to sleep, too. But I was by now so chronically under-slept that I felt strangely keyed up, my head fizzing with static even while my eyes stung with tiredness.

After Georgie had left me standing outside the church, I'd been in a such a state that Lorna had frog-marched me to the car while I gabbled.

"Jess," she said, interrupting. "Give your head a break. You'll drive yourself crazy with all these questions. Come to the island for a few days. Catch your breath. Then you can turn that formidable brain of yours to anything you want."

For a moment or two I'd considered going back to Milton View, sitting there in silent misery while the world went on as normal around me. All that flap and bother about tiny, inconsequential things: the twins' revision for practice exams, my father's funny-bone surgery, my mother's anxieties about the Japanese knotweed that was pulling up the drains behind the kitchen.

"No more questions," I agreed. My fingers shook, closing the buckle on my seat belt. "How soon can we go?"

Glancing now at Lorna's unconscious profile (whose beauty even in sleep still struck me—the tumbling chaos of her hair against the high cheekbones, the long, straight line of her nose), I thought of how many times I'd broken my promise over the past twenty-four hours.

Because the questions hadn't stopped. They'd continued to pile up.

How much had Alec been hiding from me? What were the things he had tried to conceal about his family, and why? Why, specifically, had he intimated his mother had died—because he *had*, thinking back, I was pretty sure of that.

Had the South Africans really killed him? Had his sister been right about that? Surely if it had been an assassination something would have shown in the autopsy, other than a natural reaction to painkillers? Hadn't the English postmortem drawn a blank, too? And even if not, would they really have killed a journalist? Who were "they" anyway? The politicians, the mine owners? And where was Basti, Alec's brother, now? Why hadn't he been at the funeral? Could I find a way to go to South Africa myself, track him down? How would I get the money? Alec'd told me that he'd been due to testify two days after leaving the Old Swan, but his sister said that he'd been killed just before he was due to testify at the Commission—and that was two weeks later. During which time, Georgie had been out there to visit him. Why had she said that, about Lorna being a liar? *A fucking liar.*

And on, and on, more and more. Gathering in number, like bats in a cave, as my eyes grew accustomed to the darkness. Sleep . . . if only I could sleep.

A few rows away a large, middle-aged woman talked in rapid Italian with two girls, both clearly her daughters. One of them, with a long, sullen face and short bob, reminded me of someone who had been at my village school and hadn't crossed my mind in years. An annoying girl called Sam Seagry, who had pale eyelashes and a loud nasal voice. I hadn't been very nice to her, it struck me as I gazed out at the choppy surface of the sea. Unkind, even. I wondered where she was now. I felt a sudden desire to apologize.

In the end I must have dropped off, because the next thing I remember was someone—a man in a blue uniform with a shiny bald head and foul breath—shaking me awake roughly, saying something quickly in Italian which I gathered, in my jumbled state, meant that this was the last stop, everyone had to disembark.

"*Dovete scendere. No si puo dormire.*"

I blinked, bewildered, and sat up. The engine idled with a hissing noise like air going out of a balloon. The cabin was nearly empty. The few remaining passengers were queuing up to walk down a metal ramp.

Lorna rolled her head toward me and opened her eyes. For a moment or two she stared at me, such a look crossing her face—bewilderment and a sort of creeping horror—that I thought I should offer to turn straight back home on the same boat. But then she blinked, her expression changing so quickly that I thought I must have imagined it.

"How are you feeling?" she asked, shaking some little mints from a box.

Like a mad person. "Very grateful to be here."

"Good," she said. "Let's go, then. Nino should be waiting."

I followed her down the ramp, dazed by the sudden brightness of the sunshine, my wheelie bag clattering behind me.

And that was my first view of the island: traumatized, drunk on sleep deprivation and grief. I remember it, though, as if I am walking onto that jetty now. The warm bank of air hitting me as I came out of the air-conditioning in the hydrofoil, the smell of the sea and engine fumes, and some kind of mineral tang that I later identified as sun striking volcanic rock.

The port itself was tiny, just a cluster of little blue and white houses strung along a paved promenade. Behind it, the slumbering bulk of the island seemed huge and empty, layers of rugged hills stretching back into hazy blue sky.

A few people had gathered to watch boxes being unloaded. Locals, I judged by the deep tans and weathered faces, waiting for supplies from the mainland. A few of them shouted greetings to Lorna. A man with a tanned bare chest, black shades, and straggly cutoff denim shorts was strolling up toward us. I assumed he, too, had come to meet a delivery until he lifted the flat of his hand toward us, a centurion's greeting, and called out, *"Ciao, Prof!"*

"Look at Nino," said Lorna with a wry smile. "My so-called caretaker. Never done an honest day's work in his life."

Close-up he was much older than he first appeared. When he flicked up his shades, I saw the spray of deep crow's-feet fanning out from the corners of his eyes and his thick black hair was graying at the temples. *"Prof."* His hands lingered a little too long on Lorna's waist as he kissed both her cheeks. *"Più bella che mai."*

Lorna wriggled out of his grasp. "Nino, don't be ridiculous, it's been two weeks. This is my friend Jess."

Nino gave me a frank once-over, his small black eyes hard and shiny, before cocking his head to one side.

"Nino Rondello," he said, putting out a hand, the singsong lilt making it sound like he was pleased with the rhyme. There were half-moons of grime under his fingernails as if he had been working on an engine. "But we have met before, I think?"

I shook my head. "This is my first time here."

Nino's eyes didn't leave my face. "But somewhere else, maybe. You think, I suppose, I am some local guy who never has left the island?"

His accent, although heavily Italian, had a noticeably American inflection.

"Basta, Nino," broke in Lorna. "The poor girl has just stepped off the boat. Stop baiting her."

Nino laughed loudly at this, showing beautifully white and even teeth. "You must be one of her favorites," he said to me. "She doesn't protect others so well."

Lorna glared at him, and he shot her a dark look back. Something seemed to pass between them. For a moment I thought they were going to argue. What did he mean? Had any other of her students been here? But the next minute Nino had taken my wheelie bag and we were all walking up the jetty and they were chattering as if nothing had happened, slipping easily in and out of English and Italian.

How was *la mamma*? Nino was asking Lorna. Still alive? Too bad. Did she know, he, Nino, had had a grandfather who had done the same? Gone on and on, sucking oxygen from the room. Everyone sitting around the hospital, wasting time on this disgusting skeleton. A good doctor would just help her on her way, *capisce*. If not, there were other ways. He, Nino, would have no problem using *un cuscino* to do the job. In fact if Lorna paid his air ticket, he could come over to London, do this favor for her—no sweat . . .

"*Un cuscino?*" I asked Lorna, a couple of steps behind.

She threw me a wry glance. "A pillow."

We stopped at the bottom of a steep slope where a battered, wine-colored jeep with an open roof was parked under a tangle of bushes. Lorna told me to get in the front passenger seat next to Nino. "You need to see the view. I've done this drive a thousand times before."

It was now around midday and the leather seat was very warm through the thin cotton of my shorts. I reached back automatically for a seat belt, but before I had found it Nino glanced over at me and laughed, gunning the engine loudly.

"*Cara*, here on the island, nobody wears the safety belt except the policeman. And then, only when he is *sbronzo*."

"*Sbronzo?*"

"Hammered," said Nino.

Lorna leaned forward. "Just let the girl wear her fucking seat belt, will you?"

Nino shrugged.

He released the handbrake and the car jumped forward.

CHAPTER 29

The road snaked up through the hills, a rocky scrubland of gorse and cacti, hemmed in by low, ancient walls that staggered up the mountainside. Abandoned and overgrown, they looked like strange, interlocking burial grounds. The air rushed in, fresh and cool, carrying with it the smell of herbs and dry grasses. I felt the sun on my face, the thrum of the wheels over potholes. *Maybe Lorna's right*, I thought. *Maybe here I can lose myself a little, forget the world.* Erase, at least temporarily, the thought of his beauty entombed underground.

Nino had switched into Italian and, glancing over his shoulder at Lorna, was asking after the health of someone. *Ragazzo* could mean "boy" or "boyfriend," I remembered. He must be talking about Steady, then—his voice had taken on an ugly, sneering tone. For a while I tried to follow, but their Italian was now too quick for me.

From time to time we passed a house—squat, with a flat roof and small windows. Several of them looked as if they had been abandoned halfway through building, their raw walls putty-colored and unfinished, as if some terrible event had chased the workers off, prevented them from ever returning.

Nino slammed the steering wheel, one-handed, into the hairpin bends, flashing me his smile as we careened past overhanging boulders, strung up with steel meshes.

"Slow down, Nino," said Lorna, her voice sharp. "You know I can't stand the way you take these corners."

I gripped the edges of my seat, switching my legs to an angle so that his hand on the gearstick was not grazing my knee. Eventually, on a bend that seemed to me just like the others, Nino pulled over by a widening in the road and killed the engine. The only house I could see was set back a little way from the road with peeling walls and sagging lines of laundry hung across a terrace.

Crickets rasped, making the silence loud.

"We're here?"

Lorna was climbing out of the backseat, hoisting her rucksack onto her freckled shoulders. "Not exactly."

By this point the bleeding had almost completely stopped. I was no longer having to wear the thick panty-liners that made it feel like I was keeping a sandwich in my knickers. The occasional twinges of pain were now no worse than a bad bout of indigestion. In physical terms, I thought I was over it. I hadn't counted on the trek to Beccafumo.

Stone steps ran down from the road and gave way to packed red earth that wound its way through gorse and the black volcanic rocks. Lorna was sure-footed and much quicker than me. In no time at all she had become a distant figure, disappearing and then reappearing behind large boulders and high bushes. Nino hung back, and I was left clumsily picking my way, spiny shrubs scratching my bare legs under my shorts. Skidding on loose stones as Lorna drew still farther ahead, I was reminded of those moments in class when her brain seemed to accelerate out of view and she'd glance around the room, surprised to find no one was keeping up with her. Except here, she didn't seem to want me to catch up; she seemed to be trying to put as much distance as possible between us.

Hurrying past a boulder a moment later, I came to an abrupt

halt, my stomach lurching. The land to my right sheered off abruptly. A shower of little stones I had dislodged bounced against the cliff face and plummeted into the sea, maybe three hundred feet below. Ahead was a winding cliff path, at times, as now, not much wider than a window ledge.

"Holy shit," I muttered under my breath.

Steadying myself with a hand against the warm rock face to my left, I peered down. The sea seemed much rougher on this side of the island, boiling over the sharp rocks that stuck up like giant teeth from the water. I gripped the side of the cliff, my vision blurring.

"You feel the urge to jump, no?" said Nino. He'd come back along the narrow path, blocking the sun. "Sometimes I have this urge, too, when I look over the edge. The island is full of ghosts, that is why." There was a soft, goading note to his voice. "It is an urge not to die but to be free."

I stared at him, pulse jumping in my throat. His face was blacked out by shadow. Why did he not put out his hand to help?

More stones shifted and skittered, ricocheting down the cliff. My fingers scrabbled for a stronger hold behind me. My legs started to shake with a clumsy, heavy feeling so that I thought: *If I try to move now, I'll have no coordination, I'll slip, I won't make it.* For a moment, frozen with my back against the rocks, I felt a wave of absolute terror. I saw myself plunging down the cliff face, bouncing like a sack against its unrelenting surface. Then a splash as I hit the sea. Nothing more.

"Please," I said, hearing the high note of panic in my voice. At this he smiled—his white teeth gleaming—and extended his hand. For a moment I hesitated before giving him mine. His grip was strong as he pulled me onto safe ground. His chest was so close to mine I could smell the sourness coming from his armpits.

"Thanks," I muttered, not meaning it at all. I felt my own sweat trickle down the back of my T-shirt, my legs still shaking so much I could barely stand.

"*Piacere*, Jess," said Nino breezily, and turning his broad brown back, he walked away.

The cliff path must have gone on for maybe a quarter of a mile; it felt like ten.

At one point I had to clamber up a sheer piece of rock, and, at another, my stomach heaved as I skirted a dead rat in the center of the path, its stiff legs pointed skyward, flies crawling over the mashed pink wound of its head.

Lorna had long since vanished out of sight and even Nino was now far ahead. Hurrying round another bend, I found myself at the bottom of a meadow of tall grasses that climbed up toward the volcano. The air was humid, alive with droning bees. Halfway up the slope, blurred by a dazzling sun, was a cluster of houses.

How was it possible that so many people lived in such a remote spot? It was only as I drew closer that I realized it was a ghost village. The houses were all abandoned and in different states of ruin: some whole shells, with ferns and wildflowers sprouting out where the floors and windows should have been, others just fragments of overgrown walls.

"Nino?" I called out. "Nino?"

A slight echo, but no answer. There was a rustling in the thickets, the sound of something scuttling over a rock. I heard my breath, quickened and loud in my ears.

"Nino?" I called out, this time with more urgency. "Lorna?"

The pain in my stomach sharpened. I stumbled around the ruins for some minutes, looking for the path, but although there were rocky clearings, they all ran into dead ends. *Where am I?* I thought wildly. *Am I really here on Lorna's island, or is this some strange dream?* Perhaps I was still asleep on the hydrofoil, and this was, in fact, my conscience that I was wandering around, abandoned and overgrown, teeming with paranoia.

A sudden movement a few feet ahead. A flash of something shiny, a streak of khaki and black moving like liquid mercury before disappearing into the long grass. A silent scream filled my throat. I spun round quickly and walked fast in the opposite direction, toward a broken arch.

"Lorna! Nino!" I shouted now, my voice breaking on a sob.

"Here." Nino's voice was so close that I jumped.

Beyond the arch, he leaned against a crumbling wall, a stiff piece of grass clamped between his teeth, his face impassive. I wondered how long he had been there. He must have heard me calling.

"Where's Lorna?" I said tightly.

"A little further up the volcano." He said something in Italian that I translated as *she doesn't scare easily* before setting off again.

I hurried to catch up with him, the grasses grazing my hips. "Is that why people left these houses? Too close to the mouth of the volcano? They were scared?"

But he didn't hear me or at least he didn't answer, disappearing behind another ruin. That's when I heard the sound of sobbing. High-pitched, like that of a child—a girl, or a very young boy. I stopped, looking round, cold fingers of unease on my neck. The sobbing stopped suddenly. No sign of anyone. No noise apart from the low whine of insects in the bushes. *The island is full of ghosts.*

"Jes-s." Nino's voice came floating back as he reappeared ahead of me. "Please move your ass . . . sorry, I forgot you're English . . . *backside*. Snakes round here. A friend of *La Prof* was bitten. If it had not been for the chemist who made Lorna keep medicine in the house"—he mimed a syringe—"it would have ended differently. Me, on the other hand, I don't mind snakes, but when I see a needle . . ." He shuddered.

Before I could tell him that I thought I had just seen one, he pointed ahead, his face changing. *"Ecco la!"*

About fifty feet above us a figure dressed in orange appeared to be floating in midair. For a moment I wondered whether sleep and grief had finally caught up with me and I was hallucinating.

Low-level cloud was obscuring a house made from raw sandstone, almost the same color as the earth. Lorna was climbing down from a flat roof terrace. She must have had a quick shower because as she came down to meet us I saw she had changed out of her travel clothes already and her damp hair was pulled back into a ponytail. If I hadn't been feeling so dazed I might have asked her if she was all right: Her eyes were pink and there were little blotches round them. But the ache in my lower stomach had become sharp and all I could think of was sitting down.

"Some walk, isn't it?" she said, taking my hand. "Come, I'll show you your room."

CHAPTER 30

After the glare of the sun, the house felt very cool and dark. There was a kitchen with uneven terra-cotta tiling, a living room with rough, plaster-colored walls. A large print of a forest, lost in fog, hung over an empty fireplace. Lorna led me down some steep stairs into an even darker room, opening the bolt on the shutter of a small window. Light streamed into a small, womb-like space. The curved walls were skimmed with the same flesh-colored plaster. The sight of the bed—a small double, with clean white sheets—nearly brought me to my knees.

"Come up when you're ready," said Lorna, leaving quickly, as if to give me space. "I'm just putting on some pasta."

For a few minutes I sat on the edge of my bed in a stupor. Then I went into the closet bathroom and splashed some cold water on my face, feeling my heart rate slow back to nearly normal. Someone had left a jam jar with a little bunch of fresh wildflowers on the ledge above the sink. There was no mirror, for which I was grateful.

I unzipped my bag on the bed and pulled out some fresh clothes. I needed a break from everyone, including myself, I decided. My nerve endings were too exposed. Nothing felt safe, least of all my mind.

Lorna was walking out of the kitchen with a large bowl of pasta when I came back up. "Take this out to the terrace, will you?" she said, handing me the bowl and a block of cheese.

A wooden table under a vine-covered pergola had been laid with two place settings.

"I've sent Nino back down to the shop to get a few things," said Lorna, uncorking a wine bottle. The smile was back on her face, but her eyes still seemed absent. "He says there's a storm coming in the next couple of days."

I looked out at flat sea and cloudless sky. "What happens here when there's a storm?"

"We get cut off. It's kind of primitive." The cork came out with a dull pop and she picked up my glass to pour. "The sea is God here."

What do I remember about that lunch? Everything and nothing. I was still taking painkillers, more out of a desire for numbness than anything else. Maybe this was the reason that the wine went straight to my head, or maybe it was still the shock, or the lack of sleep. In any case, now I see it all through a smashed lens: the sun splashing onto Lorna's red-gold hair, and behind her the sea, blue shading into darker blue. Images of Alec, like flashbulbs, periodically went off in my head—his eyes staring out of the hearse; his hands holding my face, my body. Each time it happened I made myself stare at Lorna instead, at little details about her, as if gripping on to them would stop me from falling again: the patterns of the freckles on her chest below her collarbones, the pale underside of her forearms. *Thank God*, I kept thinking. *Thank God for you.*

Her strange mood seemed to have passed. She told me how she'd come by the house. Apparently, she'd stumbled across its ruined foundations while on a walk up to the volcano's summit eight years before and decided, on the spot, that she must build a home there. That decision resulted in a two-year construction saga involving a mixture of helicopters, donkeys, students helping with the dig, and bribes. Nino had the nominal title of caretaker while she was away, although in reality most of the work was done by a lady from the village who came up to clean and maintain it.

"So what *does* Nino do?" I asked, with an edge.

"He swindles tourists," said Lorna promptly. "He patched up one of the ruins in the ghost village and has styled a 'restaurant' there, which is where he lives, too. He overcharges visitors to take them on walking trails and then, when they are exhausted and starving, routes them past his place and serves them a wildly expensive lunch. He always cooks them rabbit which he claims to have hunted that morning, but in fact brings up frozen from the little supermarket in the port."

"Do you like him?"

"Nino?" Lorna laughed. "Good question." She sat back in her chair, her laughter lines fading. "He's dishonest and, I suspect, sadistic. He takes pleasure in frightening tourists on the cliff walk. But someone once said the world would be a better place without Nino Rondello, and in the end I didn't agree." She poured me some more wine. "Come on, you're falling behind."

At some point we finished eating and I moved to a reclining chair while Lorna got into the hammock, still telling stories about the island.

The sun turned a deeper orange, like candied fruit, and slipped beneath the line of the pergola. The ropes creaked in the breeze, one of Lorna's bare feet dangling, so I could see the sandy freckles on her slim ankle.

"The person I most wish had seen this place is my father," she said suddenly.

I thought of the photo in her mother's bedroom, the handsome young man with the windswept chestnut hair. *He was a wonderful bastard, my father.*

"How did he die?" I asked, loosened by the second bottle of wine, the hypnotic light, a sense of being untethered from the rules of the world.

"Drink," said Lorna, sitting up in the hammock to reach for her glass of wine. "It was the only thing he couldn't talk his way out of, in the end."

A sudden breeze stirred the bougainvillea and the cutlery on the table tinkled. Lorna looked out to sea.

In profile her face was strong, stern, like it had been stamped on a Roman coin.

"He did everything to extremes, my father. Including love. For the first seventeen years of my life I was completely in his thrall. We went on road trips, through France and Ireland, met the clients he sold wine to, kissed the Blarney Stone. I was the favorite daughter, his best friend, his co-conspirator. My mother and sister barely had a look in. Then I got a place at Cambridge. After that, he hated me."

Cambridge. So she'd been a student there, too. "Why would that make him hate you?"

Lorna was silent for a while. When she finally spoke a gust of wind carried her voice in the wrong direction. I had to strain to hear her.

"It took me a while to work that one out. In the end I realized that for all his impulsive, romantic behavior, he didn't like women at all—not unless they were fully under his control. He wanted absolute dominion or nothing. Cambridge was a step too far toward independence, the beginning of a path away from him, the promise of treachery. The day I got the letter from college saying they'd given me a place, my friends threw a party for me in the pub. I wanted him to come. He stayed at home, drinking whisky. And when I walked back in, he stood up from the chair that was planted opposite the door, his shirt buttons undone to his chest, his hair all crazy . . ."

Lorna's lips had gone pale. Images flashed in my mind.

"What did he do to you?"

Her eyes slipped sideways again and I thought she wasn't going to tell me; I thought I might again feel the difference between us, the wall I had crashed into when I tried to ask about Hugh or Grace, motherhood or Sybil.

But she looked back at me, her eyes very bright and strange. And when she spoke, her voice was different—low and a little husky, without her usual projection.

"He went crazy. I mean, properly crazy. He pushed his chair over—it crashed on the floor—then he came over and grabbed my hand." She flexed her right hand absently as if remembering the grip. "He pushed me onto the sofa and lay on top of me, fully clothed. Of course, I fought to get away. I thrashed and pulled at him. But he was a big man, my father, and heavy, and I couldn't breathe properly for the weight of him."

She breathed through her nose, slowly, her nostrils flaring.

"He didn't try to fuck me, Jess. But I knew that he wanted to. I could feel it pressing into my thigh. He just lay there, grinding down into me, squeezing the breath out of me. And he kept saying, 'Just shut up, just shut up, just shut up.'"

I stayed silent, feeling the horror between us, like a weight in the air.

Lorna nodded. "One of the hardest things about it is that nothing very material happened. He didn't stick his hand down my knickers, or even really hurt me. But he broke my heart that day, and something else, too. My trust. Ever since then, I've always doubted whether love is anything much more than possession. Especially for men." Her face was suddenly very cold and hard. "Anyway . . . enough. We're spoiling a good view."

I hesitated, unsure whether to press her. "God, Lorna. I'm so sorry."

"Please." She shook her head. "No more. Let's talk about someone else."

"Of course," I said hurriedly. *Someone else.* She wanted to talk about someone else. I scrolled through a list of people in my head: not Hugh, not Alec, not Georgie . . .

Lorna watched my brain tick over for a few seconds, then burst out laughing. "Or maybe some*thing* else."

Somewhere near the end of the second bottle we must have dozed off. I woke to the sound of glass against china and sat upright, blinking. Under the pergola, Lorna looked up from stacking plates on the table.

"Didn't want to wake you. But the midges were coming, I thought you might get bitten."

I stood up, planting my feet carefully so as not to sway. The sun was not much deeper in the sky, but there was graininess to the light. Out at sea, more of the waves were foam-tipped. The wind had picked up, circling the terrace. A glass fell over, rolling precariously to the edge of the table.

"Let me help," I said, hurrying over.

We ferried things to and from the kitchen. "Tea?" said Lorna, clicking on the kettle.

I suddenly felt light-headed and sat down. "I'm fine, thanks."

Lorna came and sat down at the table, too. Taking out a tobacco pouch and some cigarette papers, she started to roll. My heart twisted as I gazed at her quick, fine-boned fingers while she rolled, licked the seal, tapped the end twice on her hand. It was just under a month since I'd watched Alec last make a cigarette, leaning against his hearse, outside the bike shop. I stood up quickly, sweat prickling my forehead.

"You okay?" asked Lorna, peering at me. "You look sort of green, actually. The sun and the wine together. You should go and lie down."

I felt the room sway. "I think I might," I mumbled.

"Go, please. I'm nearly done here."

Downstairs I couldn't even shower. I crawled under the sheets fully clothed. My trembling had turned into full shivering now, my brain felt like it was being squeezed. *Onset of hangover*, I told myself. *I should really drink some water.*

The day began to whirl through my mind, like a reel of badly cut film. The sea, the walk, the ghost village, Lorna's voice, her fingers rolling the cigarette. Or was that Alec? Alec's ghost walking through the room. Something was gathering at the edge of my consciousness. Paranoid thoughts, wild horses on the verge of a stampede. And then, mercifully, like someone was pressing chloroform to my nose and mouth, I felt the drag of sleep.

CHAPTER 31

S livers of gray light seeped through the cracks in the shutters. That now familiar lurch of grief as I came to, then remembered. Except something must have floated up into my subconscious while I was sleeping. Because this time, just behind it, was a fragment from my dream: Alec rolling a cigarette, testing the ends of the thin paper with his thumbs and forefingers.

Nicotine. It was one of the examples I'd used in my essay on poisons—the essay Lorna had rubbished as lumbering and pedestrian. Which Christie had it been? *Three Act Tragedy.* Three victims, each dying from nicotine poisoning. The first instance—the vicar, who drank a cocktail—went entirely undetected in the postmortem. The second victim, a heavy smoker, only diagnosed in the end because his symptoms matched exactly with the vicar's.

Christie's murderers often used poisons that could be easily disguised by their non-toxic uses—*So obvious!! What's your bigger point??* Lorna had scribbled in the margins. And I hadn't had one, really, just that Christie had been ingenious in the way she'd hidden her murderers' methods in plain sight. *Digitalis, aconite, strychnine.* Everything is poisonous, given in the right dose.

A door banged somewhere, making me start. Footsteps overhead, something heavy scraping along the floor above. I leaned over and felt for my phone in the dark. The screen lit up when I pressed it. *No Service*, 4:42 A.M. English or Italian time? I lay very still, listening, as the screen light died again. Nothing now. Just the sound of my own breathing.

They said Alec had collapsed in his hotel room, full of painkillers. No one who'd ever met him would believe it was suicide. His sister, Celia, believed the South Africans had murdered him to shut him up. But if it was murder, it had been cleverly disguised. Would whoever killed Stevie, gunning him down from a car in broad daylight, really go to such lengths? Wasn't it more likely to be someone who knew Alec, who could have come into his room without forcing entry? His brother, Basti, maybe, who wished he'd never existed? But they were estranged. How would Basti have known that Alec was there, in that hotel, waiting to give evidence?

Georgie had known where he was, had flown to see him, full of rage and pain. Pain. Her pockets were always spilling over with drugs. Legal ones mainly, hard-core painkillers from the treasure chest in her mother's bathroom. It would have been easy for her, while stinging with rejection, to spike his drink. I'd seen her palm tablets enough times in seminars, cool and subtle as a pickpocket.

Then there was Lorna, with her encyclopedic knowledge of poisons: *They say Martindale's* Pharmacopeia *was the most well-thumbed book on her shelves. Which is impressive, because I've read it, too, cover to cover.*

Lorna had money. She had bought our plane tickets to the island with a few clicks on her computer. Getting a plane to South Africa would have been easy enough for her. Alec had said not to trust her; Georgie had said she was a liar. *A fucking liar.*

Here my mind, skidding out of control again, braked sharply.

I was grasping for connections that had no basis in real life. Lorna barely knew Alec, had only met him on a few occasions. People didn't murder just because they could, or even because they were angry and heartbroken.

The square of light round the shutters was getting brighter.

Feeling a wave of claustrophobia, I pushed back the covers. Shining the flashlight on my phone, I walked upstairs. The stone was cold under my feet.

A grainy pre-dawn light filled the living room. The kitchen was empty, too, a cupboard door open, a glass of water on the table.

I walked out onto the terrace. There was Lorna, with her back to me, sitting on the low wall, looking out at the view from the side of the mountain. She didn't move a muscle as I walked toward her.

"Lorna?"

The morning mist hung like giant cobwebs over the ghost village.

"*Lorna.*"

She turned. Her face looked tired, her lips very pale. She gave a faint smile. "Sorry, *miles* away. I was just thinking about my mother."

"Your mother?"

"Why she won't let go. It was strange being with her that week before you showed up. I hadn't been with her for so many days in years. Maybe never. Almost unconscious during the daylight, but every night, the nightmares came. Thrashing her head around in her bed . . . these sounds that came from that tiny body! Fuck. I found myself drinking brandy at two A.M. just to get back to sleep. Thank God for Howie, popping his head in every day, or I might have lost my mind."

I stared at her for a few moments, then dropped down beside her on the wall. "You're amazing to have done that. And then scraping me off the floor, too."

And I'm a fucking idiot who's read too many murder mysteries. Lorna had been with her mother solidly that week before Alec died, then with me in the clinic as he lay dying.

She was looking at me now, in that forensic way she had. "How's it going in here?" she asked, tapping a finger to her temple.

I hesitated.

Lorna nodded, then looked back out to the sea.

"How quickly do you reckon you can go downhill?"

———

The path—if you could call it that—started just behind the ghost village and led down, at a frightening incline, to the pebble bay a few hundred feet below.

We slithered between the ferns and undergrowth, skidding on and scattering loose earth and stones, stopping very occasionally to catch our breath. About a third of the way down, hurrying to catch up with Lorna, I stumbled on a rock, nearly losing my balance entirely.

"Are we rushing for a reason?"

Lorna just laughed at me, her shoulders shiny with sweat.

"There's always a reason."

It took about half an hour to get down to the bay. There wasn't a breath of wind down there. The sea was a shining mirror of long, flat pink clouds and the rocks sticking up from the water were doubled by their reflections. Tiny waves lapped on the pebble beach. Lorna laid her towel out on the stones and, kicking off her shoes, started stripping off her clothes as naturally as if I wasn't there at all.

I stood a few feet away, towel round my shoulders like a cape, and began to undress.

I looked round. She was taking off her knickers. Her beauty was arresting. I couldn't help staring; the small upward slopes of her freckled breasts with their pale nipples, the auburn fuzz between her long lean legs, which were so dense with freckles she seemed to be painted sandy brown.

I think she knew I was watching her, but it was a while before she turned and, catching my gaze, smiled casually.

"I normally swim without," she said, shaking free a black swimsuit. "But I thought it might embarrass you. Would it?"

"Heavens, no," I said.

Heavens, no? Did I really say that? I sounded like my mother being offered a second slice of cheesecake. *Half an hour ago I was lying in my bed thinking you were a murderess and now here we are skinny-dipping.*

"Oh good," said Lorna, flinging the bathing suit to one side. "Let's not, then. So much nicer."

"On the other hand," I muttered, "it's probably quite cold at this time of day."

"Cold?" Lorna burst into her gravelly laugh. "It's like a bath out there." And she ran full tilt, pale buttocks flashing, the water churning up beneath her, until, with a little whoop, she threw herself in.

For a moment, I sat there, my cheeks warm, wishing I were more like Lorna—uninhibited, easy in my skin. Had there been other girls like me she had brought down to this swimming cove? Had they been braver and more daring—chasing after her naked without hesitation? Had they been her lovers? I wondered. Before Steady or during?

And then I thought, *Fuck it, Jess Walker*, and with a burst of courage I pushed away my swimsuit and, running over the pebbles, staggered into the water after her. I stopped short with a gasp as the waves swirled up to my calves, and then—knowing I was lost if I stopped to think—plunged in.

The water was so cold that it burned. At first I kept my head held high, making lots of quick little breaststrokes as if I could warm up the water around me. Then, when I thought I could bear it no longer, my toes touching the seabed to turn around, Lorna shouted, "Surrender to it!" Looking farther out to sea, I saw her head had emerged forty feet in front of me, ripples spreading out around her. "Go down!" she shouted.

I gulped some more air and dived, my arms pulling back the water like heavy curtains, and the sea sluiced up between my bare legs and I breathed out a stream of bubbles until the oxygen was gone. I don't know what happened in those seconds but when I broke the surface again, lungs burning, blood pounding under my shocked skin, I felt exultant and fresh, like a snake that had finally wriggled out of its old, derelict sheath. It must have been written across my face because Lorna said, "Told you!" and then set off out into the bay in a fluid crawl, her arms slicing through the waves. I followed her, trying to ape her swift, rhythmic stroke, and for some time we swam together in the bay as the sky changed around us, blushing a deeper pink that was almost fuchsia until the light flattened and became yellow and everything in the bay looked ordinary again. She glanced at me then, treading water, her hair slicked back like an otter, her wet, freckled face achingly lovely, and I knew without her telling me that this was what she had been chasing—the magic just before the day.

I laughed out loud then, and the sound of it shocked me—like someone who was filled with joy and life, not someone who had just lost her lover, killed the chance of a child. For a moment I felt a wash of terrible, terrible guilt at my own fickleness, and this blatant feeling of love toward Lorna rushing through me, and then I dived again and this time when I came up the guilt had gone and if the phrase were not so freighted with irony I would say that I felt newborn.

I'm bad at geography and distances. In the years since, I've looked at maps and tried to trace where we went over those three sun-bleached days, before the storm hit. I think we must have covered most of the island. Certainly, we walked for four or five hours every day, following the little mule tracks that crisscrossed through the scrub.

For the first hour or so we would still be warming up from the swim, our hair and skin cool and tight from the salty sea. But through the morning as the sun grew hotter, so did we, and when it got too hot—the sun a dazzling fireball, and our underarms and thighs were sticky with sweat—we took shelter. Under an olive tree or the shade of a wall, we'd sit and eat the packed lunches we'd bought from La Sirena, the little restaurant in the port that was open at odd hours. (Lorna refused point-blank to go to the bar next door, which was always open and seemed almost as nice. "Non-negotiable," she said in a voice like a falling guillotine, and I assumed she'd fallen out with the owner, or someone else who worked there.)

Alec didn't leave my mind for very long. I did my best to screen out the questions, knowing that Lorna was right, that until the family came back with more answers about his death, it would be better to give my head a break. But walking behind her on those single-mule tracks, sometimes it felt like each path was an avenue in my mind that I couldn't help but follow to its destination. Was it possible that he had, in fact, died from the painkillers they'd found in his system, and if so, why had he been taking so many? Georgie had said he was looking *just fine*. Could she have given them to him?

Sometimes it felt like my mind, whirring with these thoughts, had split off from me entirely. I found the only way I could bring it back was to focus on the present. The sounds of dry grass crunching underfoot. The damp curls that lay flat on the back of Lorna's neck.

One day (we were heading toward the little yellow church, if I remember, which held the fragments of Roman mosaics of galloping horses) Lorna, walking ahead of me on one of the mule tracks, swinging her arms, started talking about Sybil.

"One of the things I loved about Sybil was the way she whistled when she was stressed," she said, unprompted, as if there'd been absolutely no gap in time or place since I'd asked about her back in Grace's kitchen in London. "It was a lovely tell of hers. If she was worried about something, or someone, she'd just start whistling, really loudly, at the wrong moment. Which was rare, because not much bothered her. She was the first person I ever met who broke the rules—*and boy, did she break the rules*—from a position of strength. Of sheer life-loving exuberance, rather than a place of damage. Which is a scary statistic, when you think about it. But Sybil was a unicorn."

"What did happen with her at Cambridge? Is that why you left?" I asked, because with blue sky above and the sea wrinkled and vast in front of us, it seemed like nothing from the past could be so terribly bad.

But as soon as I'd said the word "Cambridge" out loud, all the odd, unsettling voices surfaced—those two girls outside the Ark, the warnings from Alec and Georgie. Did I really want to know?

There was a long silence. Lorna had stopped swinging her arms. But still she didn't look round, instead accelerating slightly as we reached a flatter part of the track. The patch of sweat on the back of her vest had been growing. First the shape of Germany, now France.

Lorna paused at a tumbledown stone wall, the remains of a crop terrace, and looked at me for the first time since she'd started talking. Shot through by the light, her eyes were like amber resin. "You can go looking for reasons why you lose someone," she said eventually. "I drove myself mad, trying to. But sometimes you just have to walk away."

I thought of Alec, shook my head. "Not in my case," I said. "I don't think I can."

Lorna looked at me for a moment or two. Such a look, such intensity, that time seemed to bend. For a moment, I thought she might lean forward and kiss me.

"So many similarities," she said, "between you and Sybil. Not just the way you look. That same curiosity. That wide, fresh mind that pulls people in. You don't know about your power yet, but you will."

And then she turned away.

So are the rumors true? I wanted to ask her. *Were you fucking your student? Have you had those feelings about me, too?*

But I didn't ask anything, not because I was scared, but because it felt like she had extended something to me, a little silken thread, which I didn't want to break. And so we sat down with our backs against the wall and ate our picnic lunch. Side by side, looking out at the sea, munching slowly, surrounded by the sounds of the island, the insect noises among the grasses and the drone of fat bees. And afterward, we lay back in the shade of a nearby tree, drowsy, replete, our widespread arms inches apart as we gazed up at the blue sky. Empty, except for high little wisps of clouds, like lambs' tails—or occasionally a bird of prey, winding in lazy circles on the thermals.

CHAPTER 32

—————

The day of the storm the air was so heavy that even simple actions like walking up the stairs or screwing together the stiff old metal espresso-maker sapped my strength.

Lorna, however, seemed undaunted by the stifling atmosphere and spent most of the day weeding and spraying the small vegetable patch that had been infested by greenfly. Her hair was tied up with a knotted scarf from which snakes of copper escaped, and her sleeveless top was soon darkened with sweat.

I found it hard to take my eyes off her. Her skin was now a toasted caramel color—almost the same as her hair and eyes—and she seemed fitter than usual after our walks and swims. I could see the little muscles flexing in her upper arms as she dug. When she broke for coffee we sat on wicker chairs on the terrace, eating peaches so ripe that the juices dribbled down our wrists.

I helped for a while, piling uprooted weeds into trash bags and then swinging on the hammock, idly flicking through *The Murder of Roger Ackroyd*, which I had found in the little box-room library. For the first time since I had run away with Alec I thought about my studies.

Term officially started in a few days, although classes were loose in the short gap between the long Easter break and the dissertation period. Out here, it was hard to imagine going back at all. University life seemed absurdly far away, inconceivable without Alec and

Georgie—or even Nick's friendship. Without them, I would essentially be starting again, but this time with a bruised heart and body. Alone except . . . I glanced out at the garden again where Lorna was standing, hands on hips, staring out at the gloomy clouds. With a smile, I looked back down at *The Murder of Roger Ackroyd*.

I must have dozed off because when I woke up the air held a sudden chill and the sky was darker. I felt eyes on me and jerked up, startled. Lorna was standing at the end of the hammock holding two tumblers of red wine and a blanket. "Storm's coming in," she said, just as a wind came through the terrace and ruffled the vines. "Hold these, will you, and make room for me?"

To my great surprise, she climbed into the hammock with me, but the other way around, so that we were facing each other. The hammock rocked wildly and it was a relief to laugh as I held up the wineglasses, trying not to slop them.

"Right," she said, pulling out my book from under her legs and wriggling a bit farther down, so that we were both wedged in, shins pressed together. "Tell me about this dissertation idea of yours."

Unnerved and elated by the drilling focus of her eyes, by the proximity of her, I rambled a bit about my idea: While Roger Ackroyd was the famous example of an unreliable narrator, my main focus would be *Absent in the Spring*, the tragic romance that Christie wrote under a pseudonym. "Tell me if I'm screwing this up," I asked.

"Go on," said Lorna, her face impassive.

I sat up a little straighter to make my point. When I'd read the romance, the narrator had reminded me so powerfully of my own mother that I had come out in goosebumps. This perfect middle-class housewife who has been emotionally deluding herself all her life. The slow but masterful reveal as the reader begins to see between the lines: that she is, in fact, despised by her children and only tolerated by her husband, who for a long time has been in love with another woman. Her self-deception makes her version of events unreliable.

"Good," said Lorna, sipping at her wine. "I like that a lot."

"But it's as far as I've got," I admitted, sitting back. "I need at least one more text."

"Sure," said Lorna, moving her hips to start the hammock swinging again. "And based on what you just said—there's one obvious choice."

We rocked for a few moments in silence. "Not with you, I'm afraid."

"Come on, Jess," said Lorna. "You *are* rusty . . . Unreliable narrators. What year was *Roger Ackroyd* published?"

"Um . . ."

"Nineteen twenty-six. What else happened that year?"

"Well. That was the year she disappeared."

"Right. And if you remember, some people thought her disappearance was an elaborate publicity stunt to boost sales of *Ackroyd*. Now, *Absent in the Spring*. Written twenty years later, in a white heat. It took her just three days to complete, cover to cover. Later she referred to it as the one book that satisfied her completely—the book she always wanted to write. Why? The protagonist wasn't a straight portrait of Agatha—but she did have striking similarities. She was also a woman who went missing for several days . . . and while lost, she found the truth. And like Agatha, after her disappearance—during which she saw *everything* for what it was, suddenly understood it all, her self-delusion and her emotional shortcomings—she came back to 'real life' and put the blinders on again. Plunged herself back into a life of self-deception. Just as Agatha, after Archie left, after her heart had been smashed up, became increasingly private, pathologically so."

"What you're saying," I said slowly, "is that Christie *herself* is an unreliable narrator?"

"Bingo," said Lorna, her eyes shining. "The woman who, after nineteen twenty-six, could never quite look herself in the eye. Who dodged her own heartbreak for the rest of her life. Which means that the perfect final text to put in your essay . . ." Lorna trailed off, looking at me expectantly.

"Is her autobiography?"

"Excellent." Lorna smiled, took another sip of wine, and sat back in the hammock. "I knew there was a reason you are my favorite student. A-plus-starred or whatever it is you get these days."

I grinned and drained my glass. No, I wouldn't be alone next term, nor for the rest of these three years—because beyond the sadness and regret that trailed Alec's ghost, the lost friendships, Lorna would be there.

Just then the thunder started: low, deep growls, very distant, like a beast turning in its sleep.

"We should go inside," said Lorna. "Looks like it will be quite a show."

The wind kicked up another few notches, rattling the spoons in the bowls. The ground felt strange after the hammock—like I was still swaying—and my head began to spin. How many glasses of wine had I had?

More rumbles, closer now. A glass fell over and began to roll around the table. Lorna caught it with one hand, unsmiling. "Help me clear, will you?"

I helped her gather plates. Her mood seemed to have changed, become a little edgy.

"Fine to be up here in a storm, is it?" I asked, a little nervously. "I mean, I presume there's a lightning conductor or something?"

"Sure," she said briskly. "Nothing to worry about."

We hadn't long settled in the living room—fifteen minutes, maybe, I remember we had started a game of backgammon and were arguing about whether you could stack more than five counters on one spike—when there was a loud, banging noise. At first I thought it was the storm—perhaps the wind buffeting a shutter—but then there was more banging and the sound of a voice.

"PROF . . . *PROFFFFFF*!"

"Christ, that's Nino," said Lorna, standing up quickly. "What the hell's he doing out in this?" More banging, the sound of some disgraceful swearing in Italian.

Lorna shot the bolt and Nino practically fell in the door.

"Stupid fucking *turista*," he said breathlessly. "I told him not to go off the path. Just take a piss in the sea! Who cares if anyone sees."

"What happened?" asked Lorna quickly.

Nino said something rapidly in Italian that I didn't catch. Before he'd finished speaking she was moving purposefully to the kitchen.

"How big is he?" she called out briskly. I heard the fridge door open.

"Quite heavy," said Nino. "Maybe two hundred pounds."

"When?"

Nino checked his watch. "Just under twenty minutes ago. I ran back."

"Is he panicking? If he's panicking, it will be worse."

"He's not exactly happy."

"You'll have to take me there, then run for more help."

I could hear her rummaging in the fridge, the clinking of bottles. I stared at Nino. "What's going on?"

He scowled and shook his head and called out a few more things to Lorna in Italian.

She came back into the living room with what appeared to be a medical kit. Unzipping it quickly on the coffee table, she fingered a syringe and some tiny bottles, holding each one briefly up to the light. *Vials*, I thought in astonishment.

"Can someone tell me what's going on?"

"Snakebite," said Lorna shortly. "A hiker. On the footpath. Need to get there quickly."

I felt something jump in my chest. A thrill of fear, and something else. Excitement perhaps. Purpose. "Can I help?"

"Yes, you can," said Lorna, slipping the bottles back under their elastic holdings. "Flashlights and waterproofs in the hall. If the storm breaks before the Guardia arrives, it's going to be very wet and very dark out there."

"It will break," said Nino bitterly. "And everyone will say I am a shit guide and I shouldn't take them in a storm. But we had plenty of time, I was on schedule—"

"Them?" interrupted Lorna quickly.

"Yes," said Nino. "A girl, too. *La figlia*. Maybe twelve or thirteen. *Molta bella*. But stupid. Kept wanting to stop and take photos on her phone. I was telling her, we need to move. I know the island; I know the weather. Now look. She is crying on the side of a cliff and her father has poison climbing his leg."

Lorna zipped the bag and stood up.

She turned to me. "Jess, are you in?"

I didn't hesitate. "Of course."

"Let's get a fucking move on, then."

CHAPTER 33

———

Even though it was only late afternoon the storm clouds had now almost completely blotted out any light. It could have been eight or nine o'clock at night. As we came into the ghost village, there was another rumble, directly above. A second later a jagged streak of lightning, impossibly dramatic, cracked the sky.

"We should take cover," said Nino nervously.

"We don't have time," said Lorna, not breaking stride. "Keep moving. And watch your feet, for God's sake."

More lightning, sheet this time: the world flashing on and off.

"No one should be walking in this," muttered Nino. But he didn't turn back, and in fact quickened his step. We both did. It was impossible not to obey Lorna in this mood. I wouldn't have been surprised if just then all the ghosts in the village rose up to follow her.

We were through the ruins and onto the grassy slope when there was a loud clap, an abrupt silence. Then a hissing noise, like the sound between radio channels.

A moment later I felt it on my head and shoulders. The rain had started.

At some point during that walk down—were we still on the grassy slope, or was it later when we had hit the cliff path?—I remember

Lorna turning to look at me. Her hair darkened and plastered down by her cheeks, her eyelashes spiked with rain, face serious with purpose, but alight, alight, alight and saying, "This is it, Jess. This is living. *This*."

But when I think about it, as vivid as it seems, that memory—so vivid that I could reach out and touch her cold, wet cheeks, trace the pattern the rain was making down them, trembling on the bow of her upper lip—I think it must have been a dream, because she couldn't have said that. Not the real-life Lorna.

We broke into single file as we hit the cliff path. Nino first, his head pitched low against the rain like a bull about to charge. Then Lorna. Then me.

I knew I shouldn't look down at the sea but I did: cascading rain, white-flecked waves churning far below. After that I tried not to. The path was slippery. We had drunk quite a lot of wine. *For God's sake, don't fall.*

It felt like ages, but in reality they weren't far along, not even halfway to the road. They were waiting just below the path, under a hanging rock. A middle-aged man lying on the ground, a girl crouching beside him.

He was huge, swarthy, barrel-chested, with blunt features made frightening by his grimaces of pain. To one side of him, his daughter—with a narrow, white face and one of those elongated, prepubescent bodies, her legs so skinny they looked like they could never hold her up—was alternating between sobbing and talking shrilly to him in German. To the other, Nino was struggling to cut the bottom off the man's trouser legs with the small scissors in his penknife. Someone—surely Nino, I couldn't see how the girl would have managed it—had propped the man's injured leg on a boulder.

They all looked up as we arrived, with varying shades of relief.

"Are you a doctor?" said the man in accented English. The bags under his eyes were enormous and dark.

Lorna smiled at this ("I am, as it happens") and with a few more very casual words of greeting—"Okay if I sit here?"—and a nod to Nino, who turned and headed off to fetch the Guardia, she crouched down and unzipped the medical kit. Stabbing the needle quickly into one of the vials, she loaded it with clear liquid.

The girl looked at the syringe and gave a squeal of horror. Her father started talking to her rapidly in German, his voice low and tense.

Lorna looked past him and over at the girl. "Now, you're probably thinking what terrible luck for your dad to be bitten by a snake *and* to be caught in the storm," she said conversationally. "But if you think about it, what are the chances that someone with an antidote would be round the corner, ready to help? Now, that's what I call *luck*." She held the vial down low, so it was out of the girl's eye line, but I could see she was inverting it several times as she spoke, mixing the liquid with something already in the bottle so that it went cloudy. "That's an impressive walk you've done today, by the way."

The girl sniffed and held back her tears, and I saw her father's face relax a bit. I glanced at Lorna. *Clever*, I thought.

She was still chatting away as she looked at his ankle, asking me to point the light. I could see the red swelling on his upper foot with two tiny dots in the center like someone had made marks with a purple felt-tip pen. Lorna seemed unfazed, asking if he had any allergies. "Pussycats, ponies, penicillin?" Take a moment, she was saying. There's no rush. This is important. "Nino gave you lunch in the ghost village, did he? I bet he told you he'd caught the rabbit he cooked for lunch? Actually he gets them from the freezer in the supermarket down at the port."

I was just thinking that Lorna would have made a wonderful doctor—calm without my mother's chilliness—when I was surprised to see that her hand, poised with the loaded syringe in it, had begun to tremble. Looking at her face, I saw it break—anxiety, fear. Something starker, even.

Then she stabbed the needle, depressing the syringe.

And I thought, *So you are human, after all.*

CHAPTER 34

"Use my sink. There won't be any water downstairs," said Lorna, coming out of her bedroom and tossing me a towel. She was rubbing her hair with her own. "I'll get us drinks."

Her bedroom was like mine but bigger, with the same raw walls and floors. A large bed made up with white sheets, a canary-colored dressing table with a mirror. I stumbled through into the bathroom, splashing my trembling limbs with hot water and rubbing myself dry as best as I could. The open tap gave out a long, plaintive note and my face in the mirror looked wild, my eyes bloodshot from the cold and rain, my teeth stained red from the wine we had been drinking, what seemed like an eon ago. It had taken another hour and a half for the Guardia Costeria to arrive, wearing high-vis jackets and carrying a stretcher, the beams of their headlamps slicing through the rain. Nino had left with them, still insisting on his experience as a walking guide.

I don't know what made me stop to look, but as I walked back through her bedroom I glanced at her dressing table again. Paused, took a few steps closer.

I know that object, I thought, *I really know it*. And yet I'd never seen it before. A little bone china statuette of a rearing horse, gold detailing on its mane and tail.

I stared at it, my head whirling. Familiar, and yet not. I could have sworn . . .

And then it came to me with complete clarity.

I don't know how long I stood there. Maybe only minutes but it seemed like an age. My brain felt like a pinball machine in which all the little balls had been released at once. A coincidence. It had to be a coincidence. Little china statues of rearing horses, how clichéd—there must be millions of them in the world.

But the detail, exactly as he'd described: the gold paint on the mane and eyes, the china so translucent it looked almost blue. I was back in the old estate as he told me the story of his brother sweeping everything from his mother's dresser out the window to the terrace below. I was back with Alec, the mist rolling over the grass, the drum of wings as the pigeon burst noisily out of the ruin, his laughing eyes.

I bent down in front of the figurine, picked it up with a slightly shaking hand, and held it to the lamplight, half expecting to see cracks running through it from where it had been glued back together. No cracks, although it looked old enough—flecks of the gold leaf had worn off, one of the eyes was almost blind. A coincidence, surely. A cruel one. I put it down on the dressing table and turned to go back to Lorna.

I was halfway out of the bedroom before it struck me.

The color of the dressing table.

Alec had said his mother's was painted yellow, too.

"When was he here?"

Lorna was looking through the open terrace doors at the rain. She turned, wearing a puzzled smile. "When was who here?"

"Your horse, the dressing table . . ." The words rolled from my mouth like stones.

Her face suddenly lost expression. "I'm sorry. I really don't understand."

"That way you roll cigarettes . . . Exactly as he did, those two taps at the base of the hand. I thought everything was reminding me of him, that I was seeing ghosts. But you picked it up off him, didn't you?" I said in a voice that didn't sound like mine at all. "The *ragazzo* Nino was asking you about when we arrived . . . Alec has been here to the island, hasn't he? He's been in your bed, too. Lying in your sheets, looking at that little horse . . ." My legs were trembling. I slumped down into a chair, my voice dropped to a whisper. "Hasn't he?"

I opened my mouth as if to laugh, realized that the gurgling feeling coming up through my throat was hysteria, and shut it again.

For a long while, Lorna didn't say anything. She stood staring out at the storm, her face very pale and still. *Come on*, I thought. *Come on. Say something.* Anything to stop this grotesque scenario unfolding in my head. Help me back to what life was a few minutes before, grief-stricken but orderly.

She shook her head. "I don't know what story he told you, Jess. I really don't. But yes. Alec was here. He was here with me."

And it was done. A bright knife plunged deep into my soul. People talk a lot about heartbreak. Losing Alec was that, the blood that came out between my legs was that. But soul-break? This was a different feeling altogether. More like madness. Like all those rules you took for granted, like gravity, or breathing, or the meaning of a smile, had evaporated. Everything, now, was in play.

Lorna was watching my face with concern. "Alec isn't . . . He isn't . . . who you think he is."

"Wasn't?" I said bitterly.

"Isn't," insisted Lorna. My head reeled again and for a wild, wild moment I thought: *She's going to say he's alive.* That the whole funeral had been some sick practical joke. There was no body in the coffin. That he was still here on the island, somewhere, under these stormy skies.

"Jess," she said gently. "The only Alec I care about is the one still living in your head."

"Please." Suddenly it was harder for me to breathe, like we were in very high altitude. "No clever words. Just give me the facts."

She nodded slowly. "Okay. Ask me anything you like."

More lightning, sheet this time: the blackness of the night sky stuttering. "When did it start?"

"We met at the beginning of autumn term, before I met you. A drinks party for post-grads with fellowships at Jon the Don's," said Lorna.

"Straightaway, then?" I felt my legs shaking. That strange itchiness behind my eyes.

Lorna bit her lip, looked away. "The first time . . . Jess. You saw us."

"No." I shook my head, not wanting to see. But too late. A flash of myself running, Nina Simone's voice loud and throaty in my ears. His body through the window of the hearse. A white hand clasped against the window, the pale underarm of a redhead.

"So Georgie, all along . . ." My lips felt numb, it was hard to push the words out. "That talk about triangles." *She'd been thinking about herself, not me.*

"I kept trying to call it off. Whenever I saw them together. But then that night you all turned up to the puppet show and Georgie was in a state, he told me that it had never been real with her, that it had just been his way of getting over me. But now he had got himself entangled . . . she was too unstable. He couldn't leave her. He was worried what would happen."

I thought of our hands across the table in the bar. The thickness in the air. He'd even used the same lines about Georgie. Had any of it been real?

"But you started seeing him again, anyway," I said.

"We couldn't keep away from each other."

A sudden gust of wind shook the doors. Somewhere a shutter slammed. Lorna stood up. "We better go into the kitchen."

I stood too. Something about the melodrama of the storm enraged me. I didn't want to elevate this to some kind of tragedy. Georgie had been right. Lorna was a common cheat and a liar, nothing more. Lorna must have intuited this because when we got to the kitchen she snapped on all the lights, poured us both tumblers of whisky. I sat down on a stool across from her, made myself look directly at her face. Under the overhead lights you could see the faint lines on her forehead. The crazy mess of freckles, the green in her amber eyes, her hair darkened by the rain. I hated her beauty then. It was a false alibi.

I cleared my throat. "How many times did he come here?"

"Four," she said promptly.

Four. Four times he'd flown over here, stayed with her.

"He stayed with you here in your room?"

"Yes."

"In your bed."

"Yes."

"When was the last time you were . . . together?"

"Jess . . ."

"Just tell me."

She gave a date. A week after he'd left me, with a new life inside.

"But that's impossible," I whispered. "You went to South Africa?"

She shook her head. "He came to the island."

I felt the pain in my chest spread. He'd left me, after those three sublime days. He'd left me and come straight here. My head spun.

"Did he tell you then? About me and him?"

"No." She hesitated. "No, you told me that."

"But he went to South Africa. The miner who was murdered . . . Was all that bullshit, too?"

But even as I said it, I thought: *I read those articles, I know he was there*. And for a moment, I wavered. At the Old Swan he'd told me not to trust Lorna. I thought of the girls by the steps to the Ark. Who here was the liar?

"Funnily enough, he wasn't a cheat in his work," Lorna was saying. "At least I don't think he was. He only stayed here for a few days before heading off for the trial. I found out with you about him dying. That was the first I'd heard of it, too. But, Jess, you're missing the point. The point is not that he was my lover for a while—"

I felt a swell of anger. "Really?" I asked coldly. "What the fuck is the point, then?"

Lorna played with the salt shaker in the middle of the table. "You remember the eulogy at the funeral? The stories he used to tell his sister about the key-cutter . . . what was his name?"

This time it was me who flinched when she tried to hold my gaze. "Alfred J. Moon."

Lorna nodded. "Alec liked to get into women's heads. Move things around. He liked to think he was unlocking people, releasing their potential. But he always ended up pushing them too far, breaking them. The same pattern, always: getting close, finding their weak spot, then exploiting it. Impossible to prove, though. No weapon to be found. Each woman had her own stash of poison inside. He didn't have to administer it—he just had to knock over the bottle. Which he did, time after time . . . with his sister, his mother. Georgie. You. Probably—almost definitely—others."

I thought of the girlfriend who had died in the moped crash.

"Everything I did was my choice," I said vehemently, but the words sounded hollow, even to my ears.

"He was adopted at two years old," said Lorna. "Half starved, from crack addict parents. Zanny told me the real problem was that Davina didn't tell him until he was nearly thirteen."

"You're wrong," I interrupted quickly. "That was Basti, his brother. A lot of those things . . ."

But the words died on my lips.

Lorna just looked at me then. She didn't even have to say anything.

Do we need to go into details? I don't think we do. Because if you've been listening properly you'll know that all the clues were there already, every one of them. Even if I had decided not to read any of them, to leave them unsolved, spread out before me, like the pieces of a jigsaw puzzle whose picture I didn't want to make.

Aunt Zanny had said most of it in the car on the way to the funeral. The picture she had painted was the same one Alec had offered me of his brother.

"We are here to mourn the untimely passing of Alexander S. Van Zanten."

Basti. Sebastian. The truth had been right there in my hands.

If what Lorna said was true—about the way Alec treated women— was that what had fucked him up? Had he ever told me the truth about himself, from that first time in the yard? Maybe, like many of Alec's stories, it was half true, and he had just chosen a different ending, an ending he liked better. Maybe the person walking toward him through the long shadows was not his father, but his mother coming to tell him the story of who he really was. Perhaps that was not the day she really died—but the day she died *for him*. Or was I imagining that, too, imposing a kind of order on him that had never existed?

I can't say I came to any conclusions that night as we sat there in silence on those hard kitchen stools with the rain pouring down outside. Addled as I was with wine, stoned out of my mind with shock and new, disorientating grief. Or even later, staring up at my bedroom ceiling, praying for sleep to take me.

CHAPTER 35

I woke up into a different world. The shutters in my room didn't open to a blue sky, but a flat, gray one, choked by cloud. The rain was still coming down, smearing the line between sky and sea. The one thing in my jumbled, exhausted, wired mind—and it wasn't so much a thought as a fizzing feeling in my chest—was that I needed to get out of here. Get off the island, away from Lorna. I could figure out the rest—where I was going, how I would get there— when I reached the airport in Sicily.

I pulled on some clothes, threw my things into my bag, and walked out of my room without a backward glance.

As I emerged I was aware of a distant whining noise that grew louder as I walked up the staircase—the muffled sound of rushing air, like a vacuum or a leaf blower. I walked through the living room to the kitchen, braced to see Lorna, but both rooms were empty. The sound, I realized, was coming from the library. For a moment I considered just leaving but with the rain belting down outside, something pulled my feet around: I never could resist the lure of a closed door.

I walked up three steps and pushed it open.

There was Lorna, sitting cross-legged in a long white sleeveless nightie, bed-hair tumbling round her shoulders, holding a hair dryer to a pile of wet books. She didn't hear me over the noise, and for a few moments I watched her as she peeled the pages individually to dry them, directing the blast.

It occurred to me, as I stood there, that this time yesterday I would have seen this completely differently: as funny and charming, typical of the Lorna I had got to know, that touch of eccentricity that comes with genius. Yet who *was* Lorna, really?

She looked up, switched off the dryer. The sound of falling rain filled the silence. "Hey," she said. "Did you manage to get some sleep?"

Anger swept through my chest, burning my throat.

"Not much," I said abruptly. "I'm leaving now."

She glanced at my bag and then up at the high window overhead. It had clearly been left open last night, and the rain had soaked one wall of books. Now it was closed, framing the downpour.

"There won't be any boats going in this," she said. "Besides, you'll break your neck if you try to use the cliff path."

A sarcastic reply sprang to my lips. But she was right, of course. I knew that. There was no point leaving the house when the weather was this bad. Even in clear weather, Nino was the only one who did the cliff walk solo.

"I'd better get on, before more spoil," said Lorna. "Pass me that one, will you?"

She pointed to a book a few inches from my feet. It was facedown and obviously waterlogged. *De Spijbelaars*, the cover read, with Lorna's name below it. *The Truants* in some other language.

"Dutch," said Lorna, reading my mind. "They gave me a wonderfully generous advance." Her mouth quirked. "It rather tickled me, the idea that it was first translated *out* of double Dutch, then into . . ." She looked at my face and shrugged. "But I guess you don't feel much like talking."

I don't know how long I sat in the living room, with my bag by my side, listening to the rainstorm, waiting for it to subside, while Lorna kept going with the hairdryer next door.

I stared at the drawing of the forest above the fireplace. In certain places it was impossible to tell where fog ended and treetops began.

After a while, the drumming on the roof slowed. I went outside onto the terrace and watched from under the streaming pergola. Behind the veil of rain, I could see the white tips of the waves chopping up the surface of the sea.

After a while Lorna came out and stood watching, too.

"I'm going to try a walk. Just down to the cliff path and back. Presume you don't want to come?"

I stared stonily ahead.

Lorna sighed and then went back in. A few minutes later she walked down the steps, wearing her waterproof coat, and headed through the overgrown grasses toward the ghost village.

Beneath my anger, I felt a tide of something worse coming in. A dirty feeling of shame and humiliation. Ever since the Old Swan I had been feeling guilt about Georgie. But that guilt had been trumped by the memory of what had burned between Alec and myself. *This*, he'd said to me, looking me straight in the eye, *this is pure* . . . And I had believed it. I had believed that what had been building between us for months was romantic and inevitable. When in fact it had been a minor sideshow, a detour from the main event.

And all the while it had been Lorna—my mentor, my confessor, my liberator. Lorna, who had rescued me at my lowest point. I saw her walking toward me in the Japanese garden, tanned and beautiful, the sunlight shining through her hair. It had been an illusion.

She'd let me carry all the blame for Georgie, those feelings of treachery, right from the start. That first visit to her house, that talk about triangles. When, desperate, I had reached out for her help—had she swooped in, not as guardian angel but to . . . ?

Even amidst the cascade of angry thoughts, the idea winded me.

I shook my head, as if I could dislodge the question. But already little roots had extended through my brain, curling round memories, reclaiming them. I thought of her sitting on the bench under the maple tree, quelling my anxieties about the abortion: *If there is one thing Dame Agatha taught me, it is that murder is a relative concept.* Then stirring up doubts about Nick, suggesting I go to a clinic. How much of her had wanted me to abort her lover's child?

I stood up from the chair and walked toward the edge of the terrace, my legs trembling. The anger felt unsafe, I didn't know what to do with it. I looked down into the rain, for Lorna. There she was picking her way through the ruins of the ghost village.

She'd been mad to go out walking in this, reckless and irresponsible. Of course, Lorna, author of *The Truants*, believed the rules didn't apply to her. It made sense that she'd been able to fuck Alec behind our backs—behind Georgie's, behind mine, behind Steady's—all along. It made sense that she could go through the abortion and my mourning without saying a word. How would I feel if she never came back? The feeling in my chest was like a build-up of pressure. Suddenly the air was too polluted to breathe. *Good,* I thought. *I'd feel good.*

It came then, amidst the chaos and rage. A small, clean, white space, strangely peaceful.

Could you, *if the right sort of pressure was applied, kill someone?*

For a moment—maybe a second, maybe much longer—I stood, hypnotized by the thought.

Lorna's small blurry figure on the cliff path, far below.

It would take me five minutes to jog down there, maybe ten. A well-judged shove, that's all I'd need. I saw her stumble, arms wheeling in space, then plunge down, barely a break in the surface of the choppy sea. *She never should have attempted the path in this weather.*

The edge of the wet stone wall cut into my palms.

I blinked, made myself breathe.

Get me out of here, I thought. *Someone, anyone. Just get me out.*

———

Hunched against the rain, bag in hand, I knocked on Nino's door. He looked behind me for Lorna, but asked no questions.

"There won't be any boat in this. This evening, yes."

"Is it safe to walk down?"

He shrugged. "*Si.* It is always safe, so long as you know what you are doing."

"I'd like to wait here for a bit before we go."

And we did, with the rain drumming on the corrugated iron roof above, until I was sure that Lorna had passed by on her way back and would soon be in Beccafumo.

We went very slowly along the cliff path, Nino checking behind him occasionally. This time there were no games as we passed the ledge—Nino gave me his hand, without lingering. We passed the overhanging rock where the man and his daughter had been last night. There were no marks on the ground. It was like I had imagined everything. I thought of asking him about Alec—when he had first come here, how long they had stayed, how they had seemed together. But beyond torturing myself, there didn't seem any point.

Only the small café in the port was open. The hydrofoil office was closed, as was La Sirena, the chairs on the terrace stacked on top of wet tables. I gave Nino most of the contents of my purse as we said good-bye, and his face warmed up a fraction.

"You are fine here, yes? It will be a long wait. And the food in there, unfortunately . . ." He moved his hand from side to side. I thought he would leave then, without a backward glance. Instead he hesitated, his small, restless eyes meeting mine for a second— switching like a bird from side to side.

"*La Prof.* Like all women . . . she is complicated. But she has a good heart."

If the poison hadn't surged up again in my chest, I might have laughed.

I waited in the café for five hours until the ticket office opened. Drinking bitter coffee, wondering if Lorna would turn up. Hoping she wouldn't, most of the time.

The rain slowed and then abruptly stopped. By the time the hydrofoil came carving into the bay, the late afternoon sun had started to peep through, and some of the shops were opening up and putting chairs and tables on the promenade.

Even as I arrived at the gangplank I found myself searching the length of the jetty, the sweep of the port for a speck of red-gold hair, but there was none.

As the boat pulled away, the sun burned through the last of the cloud. The island turned back into the sleeping mass I had seen on the first day. A soft evening light grazed the sensual curves of the hills, leaving pools of dark shadow in the valleys.

I looked up to where the cliff path started, saw the faint smudges of the ghost village amidst the green, just below Lorna's house.

It was so high, I thought, higher even than it had felt when I was up there. Just a few days ago, everything about the house had been part of the romance of Lorna: its remoteness, to which only the favored few were granted access. Now I saw it as a symbol of her arrogance. Perched up there, seeming so natural with its earth-colored walls. But it was just a different kind of ivory tower, after all. One from which she looked down on the rest of us mortals, choosing and then discarding us at whim.

CHAPTER 36

As soon as I got back to the mainland and turned on my phone, message alerts crowded in like a stream of Morse code. A couple from my father (*"Your mother said you left in a hurry, just checking in,"* which I knew translated as: *Your mother asked me to call, I'm not sure what I'm supposed to say*); a text from Nick (*Heard about what happened to Alec. I'm here if you want to talk*); and a string of missed calls. My heart jumped when I saw most of them were from Georgie, including two little bald texts. *R U on island?* And a couple of days later: *Let me know when back.* No sign-off (she usually filled the message box with a good inch of *gxgxg xgxgxgx*).

Standing in the forecourt of the airport, my bag at my feet, I tried calling her back.

Straight to voicemail.

With stiff thumbs, I texted. *On way back now. Can we talk? Jx.*

In Heathrow I left a bland little message on my mother's mobile (I could rely on her not picking up—the reception was still rubbish at Milton View, and besides, she saw cellphones as things you kept in the kitchen, to be checked at the end of the day, not *mobiles* as such). Then I jumped on the train.

I'd lost track of the date on the island, so I was surprised to discover that term had started again. Campus was full. The weather, although much colder than on the island, was crisp and fine and the staggered steps of the Bowl were filled with students chatting, smoking, on their phones. I walked straight past everyone. On the way through the swinging doors into Halls I passed Walt from my corridor, who stopped and said, "Hey, Jess—how was yours? Have you heard about the bee petition?"

"Hey," I muttered back, but didn't stop walking.

Georgie's room was empty. I'd had a hunch that she wasn't back, that she wouldn't be back, but the sight of the stripped mattress made me feel unutterably bleak. Like turning up to the hospital to see the vacant bed of a relative who has just died, a cleaner mopping the floor. The only sign of her having been there at all was a small stack of pictures from her wall, including the photo of Amelia Earhart, sitting on the padded topper she'd brought to soften the lumpy college mattress last term ("I know I'm being the princess with the pea here, but God, these mattresses are like lying on sacks of Jerusalem artichokes").

Did the fact that the bedding was still there mean she *was* intending to come back, or had she just forgotten it? I felt light-headed suddenly and sat down on the edge of the bed.

I should eat something, I thought. I hadn't had anything apart from a packet of very salty Italian crackers I'd bought on the journey back. Then I caught sight of something high up on top of the cupboard, a flash of red and silver—the label of a Russian vodka, Georgie's favorite. She always kept one bottle stashed up there. The cleaners must have missed it. I climbed up on the mattress to reach it.

I went back to my room. The bottle was three-quarters full. After a couple of tots from my tooth-mug, the cloud in my head seemed to lift a fraction. I drank some more. My head felt clearer still. *It's going to be okay*, I thought. *I just have to get used to being on my own again. I was pretty good at that before.*

I tried Georgie's mobile again, twice. The first time it rang several times before switching to voicemail. The second time, only one ring, before it was rejected.

A moment later, a text back.

Got message.

I waited, but nothing more came. When I tried ringing again, the phone was switched off. I drank until I passed out.

Once when I woke, teetering in the gray, foggy no-man's-land between consciousness and sleep, I heard a snatch of conversation in the jumble of voices that came and went in the corridor.

"Can you believe it about Georgie Duncan?" said a voice I vaguely recognized. That second-year historian, the guy who Georgie had snubbed during Freshers' Week. What was his name? Max.

"Actually I sort of *can*. She was so full of pills you could hear her rattle."

"No, I mean . . . her *boyfriend*." Max's voice was smug with fresh gossip. "The South African dude. He died. That's why she tried to top herself. Didn't you know?"

I felt myself clawing up through cobwebs of sleep. *No*, I wanted to say to Max. *Call yourself a historian. You've got your chronology wrong.* But something—alcohol, or the deep-bone tiredness I'd felt since I'd got on the plane home—pushed me back down under.

When the dreams came they were of flesh, living and dead: entwined bodies; a drowned corpse with foam at the nostrils and gaping mouth, crabs crawling out of the eyesockets; Lorna and Alec rocking together, her freckled sandy limbs gripping his tanned back.

———

Georgie found me up on the rooftop of the Ark. I was sitting on the wall, forcing down an egg mayonnaise sandwich (*Reduced*, said the sticker. *No shit*, I thought).

Absorbed in my thoughts, I didn't hear her approach.

"So. You're alive."

I whipped round, startled, nearly dropping my sandwich.

"Watch out." Georgie's face was cold. "You wouldn't want to fall."

"No." My voice stuck with emotion. I swallowed and tried again, "I can't tell you how—"

"Yeah, well." She looked at me. I thought I could see the shine of tears in her eyes. "It's been very fucking annoying, worrying about someone you'd quite like to kill."

My heart rose. "Listen, there's so much to—"

"I see you're here for the 'Madwoman in the Attic' convention," she interrupted.

I blinked. Then looked down. My clothes were currently churning in a washing machine in Halls, so I was wearing a coat over a long, moth-eaten Victorian nightie (which I had originally discovered in the airing cupboard in Milton View) with some rain boots underneath. "I've been a little out of it."

"Right," said Georgie bitingly. She made to turn away.

"Can we speak for a moment?" I said quickly. "Please?"

She shrugged my hand off her arm. "There's nothing to say, Jess. I just came to pick up my stuff. I thought I may as well say good-bye, too."

She walked toward the fire escape.

"Hey!" I stood up to follow her. "Why did you call me, then? You called me several times. You told me to let you know when I was back."

"Just stay away from Lorna Clay," she threw back over her shoulder. "She's not just a liar, she's dangerous."

"You know about her and Alec, then?"

Georgie paused in her descent, wheeled round slowly.

"You don't seem very surprised," I said. "Did you already know?"

We were sitting on the bed in my room—like we had done dozens of times together over the past two terms. I'd told her almost everything, but left out details that I thought might cause unnecessary pain. Alec and Lorna having sex in the hearse. My pregnancy.

"Not for sure," Georgie said, taking another pull on the vodka. "After the funeral, when I called Steady to tell him I was quitting college, we spoke a bit about Alec. I could tell from his questions that he had his suspicions."

I thought of the moment when I'd caught him in Lorna's office, rummaging through her papers. Then him holding her hand in the pew at Alec's funeral. What was it that Lorna had said about him? *It's a rare thing, being a romantic.*

"What did you mean about Lorna being dangerous?" I asked.

"Pass me the bottle back," said Georgie, and took another two pulls. I saw her mole move as she swallowed.

"Alec's old girlfriend, the one who died." She paused. "She was that student of Lorna's at Cambridge. The reason she left."

The breath caught in my chest. I stared at her as the pieces came together so naturally and easily I couldn't believe they hadn't before.

Alec, at Gideon's party: *It's just you remind me of someone. It's very striking.*

Lorna on the island: *So many similarities between you. Not just the way you look.*

"Sybil."

Georgie nodded.

"Alec came over to Cambridge for a semester as an undergrad," said Georgie. "Six years ago. He was dating her."

My brain ached. "So he must have known Lorna then?"

Georgie almost smiled. "That's why I freaked out when Steady told me you'd gone to the island. You may have fucked our friendship, Jess, but that doesn't mean I want you to be in actual danger. I'd rather you put yourself on the rack for several years instead."

My whole body went hot, then cold. "Oh God . . ." I said, knowing before she said it.

Georgie nodded. "The three of them were together, on the island. When Sybil died."

Georgie didn't know much more than that. And neither did she want to, she said, as she stood up from my bed. She was done with all of us. Alec. Lorna. Here she paused, then fixed me with cool blue eyes. "You."

The shock of it, the twist in my gut, took my breath away. I forced myself to find the words. "I know what I did was unforgivable. Technically." She looked at me unsmilingly. "If you'll just give me one chance, I'll earn you back. Please."

But she shook her head and turned away. At the door, she paused as if she was about to say something. But she didn't. For the longest time afterward, I tried to guess what it had been.

The two microfiche readers in the Cambridge Central Library were kept in the basement.

A couple of hours after Georgie left me, the cloudy feeling of shock had turned into something pointy and determined. It only took a few phone calls and a train ticket to get me where I wanted to be.

Old school, I thought, feeling, despite everything, a little thrill as I sat at the whirring terminal with its hum of static and faint smell of vinegar, twisting the dial to flick through old copies of the *Cambridge Evening News*.

Click.

Click.

I found the date that Lorna had left Cambridge and then worked backward. The article was so small I almost missed it—a couple of inches in the "News in Brief" column on the right-hand side of the page.

Sybil Waugh, aged twenty-one, an English undergraduate at Caius College, had died in a motorbike accident in Italy. A few more facts, the names of the island and her father, who was a professor of law at a different college. No mention of Lorna. No mention of Alec.

I stared at the humming screen until the print blurred.

So, Alec's version was correct, or at least seemed to be.

I thought of Lorna's confession in the storm, her pale, set face. *Ask me anything you like.*

Why had she told me that she had only met Alec last term? What else was she trying to hide?

I thought of Steady framed by the window up in Lorna's office. Digging into the frozen soil, down below in the garden. Then later, rifling through the post in her office, looking for something, perhaps, to confirm his suspicions. Lorna had been in London when Alec died, looking after her mother round the clock. It had been Easter break, easy enough for him to jump on a plane. Not a time when a professor of Philosophy would be missed for a few days.

When I got back to Norwich I sat at my desk and wrote an email to Lorna. I wanted to see her as soon as possible. There were things I needed to ask. The out-of-office reply came through immediately. But a few minutes later, a reply from the same address.

Been waiting to hear from you. In London. Back Thursday.
Come to my house at noon?

It wasn't until I was scrolling back through the emails that had come through at the beginning of term that I found one from the department's secretary.

Students of Dr. Clay are advised that she will be taking com-
passionate leave during the assessment period . . . Dr. Porter
will be taking over direct supervision of her students.

For the longest time I stared at the words on the screen until the letters became shapes, funny squiggles of code on which I hung so much meaning. Then I felt a hot burst of fury in my chest and snapped my computer shut.

CHAPTER 37

Over the next three days, I readied myself to see Lorna like I was preparing to go to war.

A war in hostile territory with an unknown enemy. Each day, I set my alarm for six A.M. and went for a long run through the empty grounds, looping round the lake, past the empty benches, through the woods. When I got back, dripping with sweat, I took a shower, so icy it burned. Then I sat at my desk with towel-dried hair and a cup of strong black coffee, and attacked my dissertation.

I read and took pages of notes, my handwriting smaller and neater than usual, as if I was working with a finite amount of paper and ink. At night, when the nightmares came, I made myself an intruder in them and forced myself awake, sitting up and switching on the overhead light, reading a book until I had chased the images out of my head.

By the time I was walking up Lorna's street, I felt, if no less nervous, then a little less ravaged—like a wound that has grown the thinnest of skins, just enough to stop it endlessly weeping.

I had braced myself to resist the propaganda of her beauty, but the Lorna who opened the orange door looked like a bad facsimile of the woman I knew. She was deathly pale apart from a raw pink upper lip, with dark shadows under her eyes. The outline of her lips was reddened and pronounced like she had a fever. I'd gotten ready with care, belting in my jeans so they didn't look baggy, pulling back my curls into a tight ponytail to give me a severe look. I'd even applied some makeup that I'd found in the bottom of my wash bag: rouge over my hollow cheeks, a little lip-gloss that my sister had given me. The scent of it, girlish and fruity, gave me a sudden ache for home.

Lorna's gaze swept me up and down. "You look like shit," she said bluntly. "What have you been doing, starving yourself? Not that I can talk. Don't know which is worse for one's looks: misery or the common cold."

I didn't smile. Over her shoulder I could see crates lining the hallway into the kitchen, where all the cupboard doors were open and piles of plates and glasses were stacked on the table.

"I saw the email about your leave," I said tautly. "I take it you're moving."

Although the sight of Lorna had hit me hard, my voice came out strong. I saw her eyes widen fractionally. Then she, too, became brisker, as if accepting the memo. *No small talk. Straight down to business.*

"We'll have to sit in here," she said, steering me past knotted black bags and through a door in the hallway. "Everywhere else is full of boxes."

Compared to the rest of the house, her front room was bizarrely old-fashioned—more drawing room than living room, despite its small size. We'd sat there a few afternoons during the Loafing Hour in the two squishy armchairs angled toward the fireplace. That intense, happy intimacy, the little flurries of euphoria as ideas and jokes spun between us. It seemed to belong to another age.

I took a seat in one of the armchairs while she went to get some coffee.

"Sorry about the fire," she said, coming back with a tray, "it smokes like hell. But they've cut the heating off a few days too early. It's playing havoc with my cold." She started to chatter about how many times she'd called up the electricity company, how there should be a law against playing Vivaldi as hold music. But my expression must have been stony, because she broke off.

"How long are you going for?" I asked.

She held my gaze. "Permanently. I'm off to the States. West Coast." Stanford, she said, had dangled a professorship. More money and spare time, too.

My stomach flipped over.

"When do you leave?"

"Monday."

Three days. I hid my shock.

"I'll take a break first," she said. "Drive around a bit, perhaps coast to coast—I've always fancied driving a green Cadillac. I'm using my compassionate leave as notice."

All the anger I'd felt over the past ten days came whooshing back up like water in a geyser. "*Compassionate* leave?" I sneered. "Really? For whom? Alec? Or you?"

"My mother died last Friday," said Lorna.

I blinked, wrong-footed, sat back in my chair. "I'm sorry."

"Don't be. A relief for everyone. And a catalyst for me. It made me realize how long I've been hanging around in limbo."

"What about . . . Professor Steadman?"

"Hugh isn't coming."

Oh, I thought, but managed not to say it. My image of her wobbled a bit—I had imagined her hypocritically playing happy house with Steady, cuckolded and deceived. I wanted to ask her whether they had broken up because she had told him about Alec—it occurred to me that the dark shadows under her eyes could be for Hugh. But that would be showing an interest in her feelings, which felt like a concession too far.

"I'm ditching my book, too," she added, filling two espresso cups. The coffee was very thick and black, like we'd had on the island.

"I'm over Christie. Trying to make a feminist revolutionary out of a woman who wasn't one. She might have been, she could have been, but she wasn't. In the end she balked. Made her life and work about restoring order on the surface. The chaos and heartbreak underneath frightened her too much."

This, too, shocked me. She'd been working on her book for over a year, I knew. Publishers and readers were expecting it. Ditch Christie, on those grounds? Really? Lorna had long since reckoned with the trade she had made as a writer; she of all people knew that detective stories in the Golden Age were about neat endings. The culprits were not wild or inspiring, they were broken. The detectives tidied up the parish, they didn't fuck with it. The trick, as she'd taught us, was to dig a little deeper . . .

"So what, then?"

She gave a wry smile, spooning in sugar. "I'll find myself a real outsider to think about. They suit me better."

I gave a short nod, felt the pull of her mind. *Don't get sucked in. They're just words.*

"But let's not talk about that." She handed me a cup, gave me a searching look. Her bloodshot eyes had lost none of their directness. "How are you?"

I held her gaze. "I'm okay."

"Really?"

"Yes."

She shifted, crossing one ankle over the other. Her bare feet were still tanned, the skin under her nails paler than the rest. *The sun must have come out after the storm*, I thought. I had a flash of her lying the way she liked to on the rocks down in the swimming cove, one elbow bent, cheek propped in her hand, watching the play of the sun on the waves.

"I'm here about Sybil," I said. I reached into my pocket and withdrew the printout from the library, a copy of the newspaper article.

She leaned forward and took it.

Then she looked up at me and for a moment I saw something flash across her face. A tiny movement at the edges of her lips, an expression I'd seen in class when I'd said something smart. *Pride*, I thought in amazement. *She's proud of me for doing good research.*

"How did you manage to keep your name out of the paper? And Alec's?" I leaned forward. "Why did he come to Norwich? Was it to be with you?"

She fiddled with the brass studs on the arm of her chair for a few moments. I had just started to get impatient, convinced that the pause was a dramatic one, when she looked up. It was obvious that the pain on her face was unsimulated, her eyes bright behind a shimmer of tears. "I was in love with him, too."

I shook my head, cutting away my eyes. My chest tightened. *Don't do this. Please, not this.*

"I'm sorry about so many things, Jess," said Lorna, brushing her eyes with the back of her hand. "How I got so tangled up in it I lost my bearings. How we had sex right here in our house, when Hugh was a stone's throw away on campus, lecturing about morality." Her voice was coming out in a curious rush. "About how one moment we would forswear each other and the next be lost in each other. How when I kissed him, it was like jumping off the top of a cliff, every time."

I gripped the edge of my seat, staring at the patches where sunlight had faded the leather on the arms, wanting to leave, wanting to stuff my fingers in my ears but gripped, too, unable to stand up and walk away. I had to see this through.

"What happened on the island?" I pressed. "With Sybil."

Lorna stood up, moved over to the drinks tray, spirits in cutglass decanters with little silver labels hanging on chains around their necks. She picked up the one marked WHISKY.

"Do you want some, too?" she said, pouring herself three fingers.

I nodded. She handed me a glass and then sat back down. The blinds on the windows were half open, striping her with light and shade.

"Jess, when you hear this . . . I think you'll understand why I didn't tell you the whole truth before. Certainly your opinion of me will plummet even lower than it is already."

I bit back a sarcastic comment. *Whatever she says,* I told myself, *is just as likely to be a lie as not.*

"When I asked Sybil if she wanted to bring Alec to the island it was in good faith," Lorna began. "She and I were very close. Much as you and I have been. Only by then we had known each other nearly three years. She was crazy about her new boyfriend. He came from a different world, he was clever and cocky and handsome. She had asked him over for drinks at my house a couple of times. This was pre-Hugh, you understand. I was thirty-six and single. I had a lot of students round those days. And I was flying high at the time. *The Truants* was just out. There was a bit of hype around me."

There's always hype around you, I thought, watching her tuck her feet up underneath her. *Surely you know that.*

"I invited them both out to the island. It was just before Sybil was about to start putting her head down for her finals. Almost exactly this time of year."

I nodded. The cutting in my pocket had said May 20.

"Things feel different on the island, as you know," she said, looking down into her glass. "And as soon as we arrived, something changed."

And she started describing how an atmosphere began to build between her and Alec. Tiny things at first. Moments when she'd turned and caught him looking at her when he shouldn't have been, over the top of a book, or when Sybil was talking. The times he offered to help Lorna go on errands, even when she hadn't really needed his help. The way the conversation flared between them when they were on their own, like there was something else being fought over, between the words, and never enough time to say it all.

Then one night, Lorna continued, about halfway through the week, when Sybil went to bed and they sat up drinking wine, Alec reached for Lorna's hand and started stroking it. Nothing *really* transgressive, you understand, but the thing was, it felt like sex.

I'd been sitting very upright as she spoke, like I was in court, receiving a sentence I was ready for, but at this I felt my body sag, like someone had taken the frame out of it. I felt a great tearing in my chest. *Really? Not even that? Do I not even get to keep that?*

The sun was slanting into Lorna's eyes but I don't think she noticed because she kept on, without changing tone, her voice speeding up a little, as if there was relief in the words spilling out.

"After that, there was a charge every time we were in a room together. I could hear our breathing change when we were close. Whenever I wasn't with him, I could dismiss it. He was a *boy*, just an attractive boy testing his powers. Sybil, I thought, was completely unaware of what was going on."

Lorna stroked a finger along the rim of her glass. "One evening the kids took their mopeds; I took a walk. We went down to the bar next to La Sirena."

"The bar we never go to?"

Lorna nodded. "I can't even look at it, at the table out there on the terrace where we sat."

And she described the argument that Alec had told me about, just the same, with him goading Sybil about being a corporate sell-out. Except that Lorna had been there, too, watching it all play out, watching the way he slowly took Sybil to pieces.

"Then she turned on me," said Lorna. Her voice was rough and dry, like the words pained her as they came out. "Started shouting that I had poisoned him with my views. Accused me of having come on to him. Of trying to steal him for myself."

"But weren't you?" My voice came out cold and hard.

Lorna's eyes filled. "No, it wasn't like that . . ." Her lips had drained of color. Her voice dropped even lower. "Yes, there was a current between Alec and me. But don't you see, Jess? I was *crazy* about Sybil. I lost my cool then. It must have been my own frustration. There were things I couldn't say to her . . . Things I felt for her. I started shouting back."

When Sybil had run out, Alec had turned to Lorna. "You *have* to make her believe there's nothing between us," he'd said, handing her the keys.

Lorna was the one who'd taken chase on the moped into the night. She was the one who had taken the corner too fast, pinning Sybil in, not giving her room. She was the one who'd caused Sybil to crash headfirst into the wall and bounce onto the road like a rag doll.

For a long time there was silence in the little room.

After the accident they agreed that Alec would say he had been on the other bike. Partly because of insurance, which wouldn't have paid out if Lorna was the driver, but also because they knew that after questioning, he could disappear back to South Africa. If her name got out somehow, linked to a student death, it would wreck her career.

"I know that sounds mercenary, it wasn't like that. I was broken-hearted and ravaged with guilt. Alec was also in pieces and wanted to help. It seemed like the best thing at the time. And"—here Lorna paused, tilting her face to look at the ceiling so that the shaded stripes of light caught her diagonally—"it suited him somehow—I could tell that, even then. There was something he liked about the drama and tragedy being linked more directly to him."

"Did you sleep with him afterwards?"

She shook her head. "Not then. He went back to South Africa.

I left Cambridge. Partly because I was scared it would come out. But also because I saw her ghost everywhere. In the quad, in my room, in every girl with long dark hair who went past on a bike. Alec and I kept in touch, loosely. A year later, he came to England to visit his aunt. I was in Norwich by then."

I took a long gulp of whisky, knowing what she was going to say.

It had been a brief fling but passionate. They both agreed that it wouldn't work out. Not just because of the age gap, but because of Sybil. Not long after he went back, Lorna had started dating Hugh. And then last summer, Alec had got in touch again, explaining about what had happened with his paper. Asking for help in getting a fellowship. Lorna had agreed on the basis that, if he got it, they would pretend not to have met before.

What she had told me about seeing him at the party, that rush of feeling, like a drug between them, had been true as far as it went. She hadn't seen him for five years. She'd failed to prepare herself for the fact that in that time he had changed from a boy to a man.

She kept trying to stay away, but the pull had been too strong. She kept making promises to herself that she broke within hours, within minutes.

Lorna stared over at the fire, and I knew she was seeing him. I felt my body prickle with cold sweat. I dug my fingers into the arms of the chair.

"Looking back, he started working on me from the day he arrived. He was too smart to talk about Hugh directly. Instead he appealed to my greatest weakness: my intellectual vanity. By using my own words against me. His point was, just as *The Truants* was true to everything I believed, my Christie book was symbolic of the compromise I had allowed my life to become."

It was only after Christmas, when Lorna saw what a state Georgie was in, that she had begun to add it up. That she saw it was the same line Alec had taken with Sybil. That, viewed from a certain angle, there was a kind of grim modus operandi to the way he approached women, claiming to liberate them, but always, somehow, undermining them.

Lorna picked up her whisky again.

"It took me a while to see it. That night . . . The way he'd wound her up, the suspicions he'd fed her. The look on his face when he threw me the keys. *You go after her.*"

Lorna chased back the last of the whisky in her glass. "The truth was I didn't want to face up to it. And so I didn't. Not until I heard Georgie had overdosed and spoke to her in the hospital. She told me about him going away with you. And I saw that it was happening again. Just the same. Deadly triangles, using one point to stab the other."

She fell silent then, cradling the empty glass in her hands, her face drawn and still.

The fire smoked, but the heat had gone out of my anger, leaving a dull, spreading pain.

"Why bother?" I said finally, in a flat voice that didn't sound like my own. "After all the lies. I don't see why you're telling me everything now."

"Do you not, Jess? Do you really not?" Lorna's voice trailed off. Her head was still bowed as she studied the stitching on the chair. For the first time, I noticed a few grays among the fiery auburn hair. When she looked up, her eyes were bright with tears.

"Because, my dear, you're still holding on to an illusion. And I'm worried you're going to fuck your life up mourning a false idol, refusing to lay it to rest. A love that had no reality and a child that should never have been born."

The image of Lorna that I had come here to battle splintered and cracked like someone had taken a hammer to a mirror. There were pieces now all over the ground.

After a couple of seconds it was too much. I couldn't look at her, so I looked down at the coffee table instead, a heavy old chunk of lacquered wood with a sheet of glass over it, to make it even. Dust had gathered under the surface of the glass, pooling in the crevices, lodging deep in the cracks of the wood.

With the dirt so ingrained, I couldn't see how you'd ever clean it.

Soon after that, I left. Lorna walked me to the door. As I crossed her threshold, I felt an ache deep in my chest. An ache that, come to think of it, hasn't really gone away since.

"You know, Jess . . ." She hesitated, her hand on the edge of the door. Her eyes searching for mine, a sudden flush to her pale cheeks that made me think—or would have made me think, if she weren't Dr. Lorna Clay—that she was nervous.

I waited for her to speak.

"We could stay in touch," she said. "Just from time to time. Apart from anything else . . . it would be one way in which he hadn't won."

For a few moments, looking away, I considered it. I imagined the next two years I'd have to scramble through, walking past her room in the Ark with the little sign telling me she was OUT, into lecture halls where I had watched her alchemy, in the seminar rooms where she had made me feel giddy with the promise of life, of being more than myself.

"I can't."

She blinked fast, turned away. "I understand."

As I reached the gate, she called out my name again.

I stopped, turned.

"One small favor?" she said. "Last thing I'll ask."

I hesitated. "Okay."

"Your family," she began, "they sound like good people."

CHAPTER 38

The bus from the station dropped me at the top of the lane that led round to Milton View. It was one of those drizzly, depressing days in late May when it should be spring and everyone in England considers emigrating. I rolled my bag round the puddles, past Farmer Roberts's cows, who didn't bother looking up from grazing as I passed. Someone would have picked me up from the station if I'd asked, I reflected. But it would have felt humiliating, somehow.

The Land Rover was in the garage, rear facing out, which meant it had been driven recently. These days it was almost never used. When we were small kids, we'd gone everywhere in it, picnicking, biking, camping. I remembered the jam of bodies in the backseat, the tussle over who got the jump seat. I walked past it to the back of the house. There was Freddie's car in the drive. Stef's, too.

Sunday lunch. God. So everyone was here.

The handle on the back door was stiff, as usual. I walked through it, chest tight, only to be greeted by silence. No skittering of Labrador claws on the flagstones, no voices coming from the TV room as I stood in the hallway, bag in hand. Silence.

"Hello?" I said, advancing, the handle of my bag falling with a clatter. "Anyone home?"

I walked into the kitchen, but it was empty, tidy, the surfaces wiped. No smell of roasting meat and potatoes coming from the oven. For a moment I was flummoxed, as if I had walked into our neighbors' house by mistake, and then it dawned on me. Of course: pub lunch. They'd have walked across the field to get there. A feeling of anticlimax settled over me. I hung up my jacket and walked slowly to the top of the house.

My room had a faint air of disuse, the bed too well-made, the smell of flies singed by the ceiling lights.

I lay down on the bed, feeling that transformation from adult to child that always happened when I came home, like a fairy tale in reverse; the swan back to an ugly duckling. Up above my bed was the highest point in the room, where the sloping, beamed walls angled into the peak of the roof. It was still painted the pale blue I'd insisted on doing myself when Stef had moved out and the room had passed to me.

"I want to feel like it's the sky above me," I'd said. Pretentious, precocious—was that the story of my childhood? Fearful of being the forgotten middle child, had I, in my clumsy way, distanced myself and made strangers of them?

For a while I dozed, until I heard noises from below, the opening and shutting of doors, the bark of a dog, faint voices coming up through the stairwell.

". . . Jess's bag?" The voice of one of the twins floated up the stairs.

"Halloooo . . . Is that the prodigal daughter?" My father's voice.

I ran down two flights and then stopped on the half-landing above the hallway, looking down at the flushed, upturned faces. Wet hair, pink noses. My heart pounded in my chest.

"Nice haircut." My brother broke the silence. "Isn't that what they're calling shabby chic these days?"

All of them looking at me. The twins, grinning like I was the punch line to some unexpected joke. My father, his eyes a little too shiny. I walked slowly down the rest of the stairs. Gladstone bounded up to meet me, tail thumping. I kneeled down to fondle his ears, grateful for the diversion, then straightened up to meet my mother's eyes. She carried on unbuttoning her coat, and for a moment we looked at each other as we always did, as if picking up outlines through a gauze screen. Then her arms opened just a fraction and I went to them. I could feel her chest bones beneath the silky material of her blouse, the little tap-tap of her heart.

"Where on earth did you spring from, then?" She pulled back and I looked into her face. It seemed a little older, a little more tired. I caught a flicker of relief in her eyes and something else, complicated and buried.

Then she turned away to hang her coat so that I only just caught the words as she moved away. "You'll stay for a bit, won't you?"

CHAPTER 39

—————

Two weeks later I walked into a hair salon in a small village on the north coast of Norfolk. There was only one customer, an elderly woman with a towel round her neck, wearing very red lipstick and with her hair divided into lots of silver foil parcels. She gave a slight start when she saw me—I saw confusion turn to recognition and then the dismayed expression of a woman who is discovered *in flagrante* at the hairdresser's.

"*Goodness,*" she said. "You're that nice, quiet friend of Alec's?"

It had been—as Freddie would put it—a piece of piss to track down Aunt Zanny. I knew roughly where she lived from my walk along the beach with Alec. And Zanny had given Lorna and me a torrent of personal information en route to the funeral. Among some of the more solid facts (including a detailed medical history of her beloved West Highland terrier—sadly, no longer with us) was the name of the next-door village where she worked in a bric-a-brac shop a couple of days a week (more of a favor than a *job*, really, the owner, Rosie, having recently lost her husband to throat cancer—which would have been quite bad enough without discovering, when they read out the will, that he had *a whole other family* living down in Ipswich).

"Sure," said Rosie when I told her who I was looking for. "You'll find her in the hairdresser's, as usual."

I sat down in the empty swivel chair next to Zanny's and watched her talk at me in the mirrored wall. On the car ride over I'd re-hearsed a speech justifying why I'd come to find her. *For the last couple of weeks I've been wondering how to get in touch with Alec's family for more details about what happened but was concerned about intruding on their grief.* But beyond the momentary sting to her vanity, Aunt Zanny didn't seem to question my having turned up unannounced, and it was she who, moments after I arrived, steered the conversa-tion to the Van Zantens.

Presumably I'd heard the news about Alec? I hadn't? Aunt Zanny looked sad, then gratified. She'd wondered whether it was only family and very close friends, *the inner sanctum as it were*, who were notified. Perhaps I should be asking direct . . .

I bit my lip. "At the funeral Celia said they were expecting more information to come to light."

Aunt Zanny nodded. "They were suspicious of the postmortem results in South Africa. Very unspecific. System shut down, that sort of thing. They asked for a second opinion. Samples taken to be tested after the burial."

The results had been crushing for the family, Aunt Zanny's re-flection explained to mine. Odd as it sounded, they'd pinned their hopes on it being a political assassination, making Alec a hero in death. Especially poor Divvy. Oh, he was a difficult boy—difficult was understating it, really—and always had been. But Davina, be-ing his mother, perhaps especially because he *was* adopted, held on to all the good, the things he did in his professional career, which were, undoubtedly, rather heroic. The *risks* he took with that awful story. A lot of people didn't want those things written about. There had been death threats to him at the newspaper. And then this thing about the miner who was murdered, which she, Zanny, hadn't quite followed. "I'm a *Daily Telegraph* reader," she went on, "and *they* never ran Alec's stories, not even in the weekend papers, but apparently his articles won awards and what-have-you, so they must have been *good*. He was always clever. Very, very clever." Her eyes swiveled as the hairdresser rolled a little trolley to one side of her chair. "Ah, is it time? Pauline is a genius at color," she said to me, as if the woman carefully beginning to unpack the silver strips from her hair was deaf and mute, "but this stuff does take an age. You'd think the process would get faster over the years, but I'm always here two hours to the dot, aren't I, Pauline?"

"What did they find out?" I prompted.

"Such a terrible anticlimax," said Aunt Zanny as Pauline pulled out more bits of tinfoil. Strands of her hair, coated in something gloopy, hung round her neck. The smell of it made my eyeballs cold. "It made me think of my friend Eloise. Her brother Harry was digging out some burned bread from a toaster one morning with a knife—and *whoosh!* That was it. Electrocuted. I *know*"—she gave me a severe look—"hard not to snigger, even though it's not funny at all. To the sink?" She stood up as her hairdresser pulled back the chair. "Just need to wash this foul stuff out and we can keep talking."

Several ice ages came and went as Aunt Zanny's hair was washed out, shampooed twice, and her scalp massaged. When she got back, her hair towel-dried and sticking out like a baby bird, she had, incredibly, lost the train of our chat and started speaking about a new terrier puppy she was viewing later that week. "I mean, no one can *replace* Crumpet, I'd never want that . . ."

It took me a few minutes to pull myself together.

"Alec," I said as patiently as I could. "You were saying . . ."

"Silly me," said Aunt Zanny. "I do worry about my concentration sometimes. They say this is how it starts. Not that I could forget Alec." Suddenly she looked stricken, her eyes filled with tears. "The idea that he could have died before me feels impossible, you know. All that *life*, and nothing left behind."

I nodded, looking away. My chest tightened. For a moment I couldn't breathe. Would I always think of it as part of him, that child I'd never had? Would it grow older with me, stay with me, a spirit, hovering just outside the frame, that only I could see?

Aunt Zanny reached forward. "I'm sorry, my dear," she said, her hand on my knee. "I don't know if you'll be relieved or saddened by what they found out. It was all very underwhelming in the end, you see," she said, wiping her eyes. "No suspicious circumstances, nothing to do with politics, in fact. He died of an allergic reaction."

I blinked at her in the mirror. My mouth suddenly felt very dry.

"Yes. You know. You hear about it with peanuts. Not sure *what* in his case . . . Just stopped his heart."

I thought of a redheaded girl at school, who, it was whispered, would die if she was stung by a bee and had to carry an injection round her neck in a pouch on a lanyard. Never took it off. The sports teacher used to hold it during netball matches.

"Oh goodness, I'm no medic," said Aunt Zanny. "But what is it . . . that *word* . . . Dear, will you just move onto the next chair, give Pauline a little room?" She looked at me then, her voice changing. "You must have been very close, to come all this way. I miss him terribly, don't you?"

And that was it. I'd been so geed up on the drive over, and this news, which should have been a relief in some respects, felt like a cruel blow. That the Alec I had known, the life force that had overwhelmed me, could be snuffed out in such a banal fashion.

I drove home along the motorway in a daze, watching the white lines slip under the wheels. Was this what it felt like to lay a loved one to rest? I wondered. This hollow feeling in my stomach, this bleak chill of loneliness.

I saw the junction coming up and switched lanes, setting the blinker ticking.

When I got home, I thought, I would call Nick.

CHAPTER 40

For a long time, I thought about Lorna every day. I wrestled with the desire to get in touch, though whether to hug her or scream at her depended on the day.

I found myself looking for her everywhere. First, and not entirely irrationally, around campus—in the Ark, around the lake, or scanning the racks of bicycles to see if there was a bottle-green one with a basket.

Love makes you superstitious, you see, and I was sure that if she had come back to the university even fleetingly, then I would be the first to run into her. Whenever I saw anyone with a similar build and coloring—which was not often—I felt both a leap in my chest and a jolt of panic, an instinctive desire to crouch and shield myself.

Georgie didn't return. I sent her regular emails, but I never heard back. Her mobile number was cut off. Her mother's personal assistant hung up when I said my name. After several months I gave up trying. In my second year, I gave up on my course, too. That summer term, after Lorna left, Dr. Porter became my supervising tutor. But he never really forgave me for being a Lorna acolyte, and I realized that I was done with stories, too. Lorna and Alec had both traded in stories. Once this had seemed magical, the spinning of new worlds. Now it felt like a flight from the truth.

I switched to a law degree, with the intention of becoming a criminal barrister. Perhaps this was inspired by Agatha Christie, but more likely, the powerful sense of injustice that sat like a stone in my chest and meant that (much to Walt's surprise and delight) I signed up for pretty much every petition and march he asked me about. Try as I might, I found law hard going. Reading textbooks on tort felt a little like eating a whole box of crackers with nothing to wash them down.

But the dryness suited, as well, in some respects, and for the rest of my degree, I worked steadily and went through the motions of having a social life. Everyone seemed to be very young, and try as I might, I couldn't get interested in the things that they talked about. Sometimes I would find myself sitting on my own on the Intimacy Couch by the lake feeling a little foolish, like I was stubbornly waiting for a blind date I already knew was not going to turn up.

Entirely to Nick's credit, he and I remained friends. He was kind and funny, above all forgiving. For several months, I couldn't manage anything more than companionship. Then one evening I went around to his house for a dinner party and discovered, to my surprise, that we were the only ones there. Afterward, we sat drinking wine on the sofa and listening to the low, husky regret in Tom Waits's voice. I felt something in me ache. Nick looked at my face and smiled. Locking his hands behind his head and lying back in the sofa cushions, looking wry and wise and a thousand years old, he started telling me about oxbow lakes.

"Do you remember when we were on mushrooms that day and I was blathering on about rivers?"

It was the closest we had come, by unspoken, mutual consent, to talking about Georgie and Alec. I felt my pulse begin to trip.

"I told you about when the water cuts into the banks over time?" He leaned forward a little and drew a light *S* on my knee. I nodded, feeling the blood start to move more quickly under the skin where he touched me. "Did I tell you about oxbow lakes?"

I shook my head, the warmth spreading through me.

"It's when the river meanders to such an extent that it cuts itself off from the main stream and creates a little separate pool of water. I find them beautiful, but a little sad, too," said Nick. "Because it's like time standing still. And a part of me, a big part of me, wants to help it start moving again."

We kissed then, and I felt my body and heart light up, and for a moment I thought it would all be okay.

Then a few minutes later I had what I suppose can be described as a panic attack.

Occasionally I would see Hugh walking around campus, and it struck me, even from a distance, that his face looked grayer and older and blanker, like someone had put the wrong filter on a camera. I always changed the line of where I was walking, made sure we never got too close. Then about halfway through my second year, I was sitting in the Bowl between classes when I saw him passing. On impulse, I jumped up and walked over to him.

I regretted it almost immediately. His face, kindly and lined, held on to its smile, but a little veil seemed to fall over his eyes.

"It's Jess, you may not remember . . ."

"Of course I remember," he said evenly.

"I just wanted to say thank you," I said, stumbling a little over the words. "You were very kind to me when I was in a bad place, and it really helped."

His expression didn't change. "How's your course going?" He paused for a second. "Are you finding it okay with Lorna gone?"

No, I wanted to say. *No, I'm not finding it okay at all. How about you?*

Instead I told him that I had swapped to do law. I saw something, almost a sparkle, come back into his eyes. "Oh dear," he said. "It's lucky she's not here, then. Lorna would kill you."

I took a breath. "Are you . . . in touch with her at all?"

Steady's eyes flickered for a moment. "No," he said, "we're not in touch. But I believe she's in the States still. I think—at least I hope—it suits her better there. She's a one-off, Lorna, and I think this place was too small for her, in the end."

I nodded, bit my lip. And then he said good-bye and wished me luck, warmly, but with a finality, and I understood that he would rather I didn't come and find him again. But it struck me later in my room, what a generous thing it was he'd said, because he had far more to forgive than I had. And I thought—*Nick forgave me, Hugh forgave Lorna. Who am I to hold on to a grudge for so long?*

I felt a massive spike of nerves when I sat down to the keyboard. Then I allowed myself to do the Internet trawl I had been avoiding with the studied discipline of a just-dry alcoholic steering clear of a bar. What shocked me, within minutes, was just how little there was. Nothing at all dated after I had last seen her, except for some press coverage about her moving to teach at Stanford, a mention in an article about "brain drains" to American universities, and a little piece in a literary magazine that said Lorna was writing a book about Angela Carter while teaching in the States. The only thing that suggested she was alive was the fact that there was no obituary.

What the hell is going on? I thought, staring at the blinking cursor.

I opened a new email and sent her one line—*Just wondering how you are?*—but within seconds, it had bounced back. *Undelivered mail.*

After that, I made some calls. First to Stanford. Lorna was no longer working there, said a voice in the English department, crisply. Apologies, but she had left no forwarding address or email. I called the literary magazine where the piece about Angela Carter had appeared—the journalist was vague, it had come on a press release, she said—no, she didn't remember where from. Then I had a flash of inspiration. Picking up my copy of *The Truants*, I flicked to the Acknowledgments and found the name of her agent.

It was easy to track down the agency, and within the hour I was calling.

"Felicity is in meetings all day. May I ask what this is regard-ing?" said a girl's voice at the end of the line.

I took a deep breath. "Lorna Clay."

There was a pause and then a few moments later, a click, and a woman's voice came onto the line: deep, cigarette-laden, urgent. "Who is this? Do you have some news about Lorna?"

I hung up.

After that, I began to look for her in earnest. I went to London to visit Grace's street with the pollarded trees, but the distracted Spanish au pair who answered, still reprimanding small children over her shoulder, told me the family hadn't been there for six months. She gave me a forwarding email for Grace. I wrote to her twice before she answered, in a short, cool two lines. No, she had no contact details for Lorna. As far as she knew, her sister had moved to the States.

I visited the home where Lorna's mother had lived. The short, bespectacled administrator in the office looked heartened at the sound of her name—had I come to settle up on that outstanding water bill?—but when she realized the purpose of my visit, shook her head, her face closing like a venetian blind. "If you track down any of the Clays, please let me know," she said snippily. "There's a whole pile of paperwork that was left unsigned."

After a brief struggle with my memory, I remembered the name of the restaurant in the fishing port on Lorna's island, La Sirena. For a couple of days it just rang out. Assuming that the wrong number had been listed, I nearly gave up. Eventually, though, I got through to a scratchy line and spoke to an Italian waiter who had no idea what I was talking about, let alone whom. The manager told me that he knew *La Prof*, of course, but he thought she hadn't visited the island for some time, maybe two years. Nino, they fur-ther revealed, had moved back to Sicily for the season. They weren't sure when or if he was coming back.

I looked for Alec, too, of course. Less so, but with more of a sense of dread, because when he did visit me, often at night, it was with a violence that was painful. With a sick rush I would find myself in the Old Swan again, on those misty mornings, as the stags stalked in the fog beyond, or lying in that bedroom with the yellow wallpaper at Lorna's sister's house with a sense that something inside me had broken—*I* had broken it—that nothing would ever repair. And the tears that came then were hot tears that seemed to come from somewhere deeper than the belly, from a bottomless part of the soul, the part we learn not to visit every day, because that would be to cross over to the other side.

Then, one spring day in my third year, walking past the Ark, I realized that I hadn't looked up to check Lorna's window as I passed for some time, and it dawned on me that both of them had left the foreground of my mind and melted, if not quite into the background, then somewhere just out of focus.

And life became ordinary again.

CHAPTER 41

Nearly six years after Georgie walked out of my room and my life, I read about her mother.

I was sitting on a park bench in North London on my coffee break, flicking through a paper, when I stopped (*I know her, who is she?*) at a small black-and-white photo of a laughing young woman.

> Lady Melinda Duncan has died, aged 64. The renowned society hostess, remembered best for "Heretic," the Bacchanalian music and ideas festival that ran in the grounds of . . .

I bolted back up to my desk and wrote Georgie an email straightaway.

It took a couple of weeks for her to reply.

Jess Walker. I wondered how it would feel if you ever got in touch. I've thought about you a lot over the years. Yes, it's been a tough few months. Thought black lace would suit me, but I was a blubbering wreck. I wailed like an Italian widow . . .

Over the next week we traded emails.

You'll be sorry you asked, I wrote back. *I'm in my second year working as a solicitor for a law firm in London. I wear a lot of navy blue and have straightened my hair. Paralegal drinks every Thursday in the crypts are surprisingly wild, but . . .* I paused, then felt my eyes prick as I carried on typing. *It feels like any moment someone's going to arrest me for being an imposter. But maybe that's what working in white-collar crime does for you.*

Her account of the intervening years was rather more shocking. After she'd dropped out of university she spent two years on a virtually back-to-back tour of rehab centers round the world.

Going cold turkey after heavy pharma abuse is a bit like having your head held down in a bucket full of water. Like drowning and being told you are inhaling air. And the therapists and nurses are the ones that are waterboarding you.

After that, she moved to the countryside, to a little mill on a stream, by a meadow.

You in a rural idyll? I typed back. *I can't see it . . .*

Yeah, I know. Quite a turnaround, isn't it? She was on the edge of what passes for a perfect English village, she told me—thatched cottages, a gastropub serving craft beers and osso buco, church services every third Sunday of the month. *At first I didn't think it was me at all. Everyone here has a certain kind of mindset. Now I'm starting to worry that I fit in.*

There, on a whim, she had invested in a potter's wheel and reconnected with her old hobby. Things had gone well. She was now putting on her second exhibition. Her first one, at a small gallery in South London, had been a surprise sellout. Her love life had been a shit-show, *I mean, a real shit-show, made out of actual shits,* until the last four months when she'd been dating the man who owned the artisanal cheese shop (it was next to the church—*Cheeses of Nazareth,* she called it). It was making her very fat and she was beginning to suspect she was lactose-intolerant. On the plus side, she thought she may be in love. Would I come visit her?

And so it was—my stomach uncomfortably light—that I found myself standing outside Georgie's place on a clean autumn day, a little shy of six years after Alec had been put in the ground.

Georgie opened the door.

It was as if she'd opened it straight into the past. I was completely unprepared for what her standing there, barefoot, three-dimensional, would do to me.

"I know," she said. "It's the cheese guy. I've put on about a stone. You look"—she scanned me up and down and then grinned suddenly—"like you're shitting yourself."

"I'm so sorry about everything," I said as we hugged. "I'm so sorry about your mother. Turns out that psychic in Kerala was full of shit."

At that, Georgie gave that laugh I loved, head back so I could see her ugly mole.

She was very much the person that I had known—still wry, funny, glamorous, self-deprecating—but she'd toned down the nervous energy that made you feel like you needed a lie-down after some time in her company, become more grounded. And something else, too, a slight distance in her eyes and tone, which I picked up on immediately and made my heart ache. She didn't seem to be holding anything against me anymore, there was real warmth and forgiveness, but there was scar tissue, too, twisted and tough, between us.

She lent me some rain boots and we took a walk down to the woods, climbing over stiles slippery green with moss.

We talked about her mother for a while. "She always had something of a death wish. It's almost like, when she knew it was actually in the cards, she could relax." Georgie breathed in sharply and I could tell she was fighting back the tears.

As we walked on, the conversation switched around a fair bit. We spoke about her upcoming exhibition, the man from the cheese shop, what had happened to a few of the people we knew about from college ("Did you hear about Walt—he became some big corporate stooge at Coca-Cola, the filthy sellout"). I tried to mask it but I could hear the strain in my voice when I asked whether she was still in touch with Nick. Vaguely, Georgie told me. She knew he had got some extremely cool and important job measuring earthquakes. "Quite literally, seismic. But he was always much cooler than the rest of us, wasn't he?" More recently she'd had a round-robin email from him about this storytelling group he had set up.

"Storytelling group?"

"Yup. Sounds quite great actually. We should go, one week. It's called the Tuesday Club."

My heart started behaving strangely then, and I had to blink and look away. *He remembered.*

"Yes," I said, feeling a warmth spread through me. "Yes, I'd really like that."

After that, the silences that fell as we skirted in single file round ruts of mud or rustled through the fallen leaves felt entirely natural. Just when I was feeling most at ease—pausing at a blackberry bush, hunting for ripe ones—she said, "You're not over them, are you?"

I knew instantly to whom she was referring but some defensive instinct made me keep my eyes on the bushes. "Who?"

"*Whom.* Lorna. Alec. You haven't moved on."

I tried to look away but the red-gold of the leaves overhead mocked me. My voice was brittle even to my own ears. "Actually I don't think about them much anymore."

"That's what I mean," said Georgie. "You've locked them away in some box in your mind where they're festering. Drowning them every week in that crypt with your paralegal drinks." She turned, offering me some blackberries on a flat palm, but I saw the challenge in her eyes.

And I thought: *Is that right?* Had I locked them up because I was scared of the memories and the pain? Or, something worse—something Georgie was driving at—because I was scared of that other version of myself? Frightened of what it trailed in its wake?

Lorna had been a doorway into another world. Alec had, as well. I had followed them, crossing lines, and the world had flared with color. But it had unleashed a landslide, too, an avalanche that had ended with Alec under the ground, my hands full of blood, Georgie betrayed, Nick brokenhearted, Lorna gone. Since then, I had shut everything down in an effort to be safe, trussed up in my new regimented life. Living in a world in which everything made sense, but meant nothing. A life in which, afraid of the fire, I had put it out altogether.

"Do you remember that very uptight man at the pub when we took mushrooms—the one with the pregnant wife and the two blond kids?" Georgie asked. "Well, a couple of weeks after that day, I got a call from him. Plummy voice, slightly shaky—he said he'd tracked down my number via a friend in the local police station."

My eyes widened. "You've got to be kidding? You never told me this."

"Claimed he hadn't slept for two weeks. That the sight of me stripped naked and throwing myself into the river with no inhibitions had rocked his world. He'd left his job, left his family, and was now considering gender reassignment surgery."

"You *are* kidding."

"Of course, it was Alec," said Georgie, grinning. "Though if he hadn't started laughing, I wouldn't have guessed. His accent was pitch-perfect, ex-army, minor public school."

I laughed.

"As twisted bastards go . . ." said Georgie.

I nodded and managed a smile, but my heart contracted. And looking at her face, I could see she felt the same. And there was a kind of bittersweetness to that, to knowing that the loss was shared.

We'd got to the woods now, and Georgie opened a little gate to let me through.

"I *did* suspect something between you two, you know," she said. "I was just so baked out of my mind I decided to ignore it. I saw the way you glowed when he spoke to you. And that time he ran after you at the puppet show. When I got to the bar, you were all lit up . . . both of you."

I blushed, oddly gratified and ashamed, all at once. "I'm so sorry."

Georgie nodded but didn't say anything. The dappled sunshine made camouflage patterns on her skin that shifted as she walked.

"In the end, though," she was saying, "however much I *see* what he did to me . . . did to you . . . to us"—she glanced at me quickly as she said this—"I'm particularly sorry that if he was going to die, it had to happen the way it did. That it wasn't political martyrdom, something romantic or dramatic. That it was so drawn out and painful."

I frowned. "I don't think it was," I said. "I was told—his aunt told me—it was an allergic reaction. Not dignified maybe, but pretty quick at least."

Georgie shook her head. "Not exactly."

And she told me how, after a spell in rehab near Cape Town, she'd gotten in touch with Alec's sister: Alec, Celia had told her, had been bitten by a snake. The second postmortem had spotted fang marks, but they'd been dismissed as cause of death: It wasn't the snakebite that had killed him. Weirdly, he'd reacted to the antidote. A rare, but not unheard-of, condition. *Serum sickness*, they called it. It took several weeks for them to work it out—Celia had to keep insisting on new tests from the samples. His death would have been staggered, apparent full recovery from the bite—then two weeks later, the organs shutting down, one after another, like some old guy in a geriatric ward.

Here Georgie broke off and kicked away a stick, watched it bounce across the ground. The canopy of leaves was a lot denser by now, only a little sunlight trickling through.

"The funny thing is—if I'd been there, I could have told them. Turns out, my dad was right. There is something fishy about someone who is allergic to horses."

She turned. I'd stopped dead a few paces behind.

"Everything okay?"

"Just a little twist," I said, leaning down to my ankle to buy

myself time. I breathed in the peaty smell of the fallen leaves, trying to ground myself. Images flashed before my eyes. *My God*, I
thought. *How did I miss it?*

We didn't talk much more about the past. There was only one fur-
ther exchange about Lorna, once we'd made it to Georgie's pot-
ting shed.

"Isn't it too strange, her vanishing like that? Do you think she'll
turn up again, somewhere odd, and pretend she's had amnesia? Or
do you think maybe she was really unhappy, and we just never saw
it? Do you think she's even alive?"

I thought of the sentence she'd written on the whiteboard in our
first seminar. *People disappear when they most want to be seen.*

"I don't know," I said slowly, my mind still whirling. "But then
again, I'm only starting to see."

Georgie had just handed over the piece she had made for me, a
stark white pen-pot, simple and fine and beautifully even except
for a small dent on one side which she had made with the edge of
her thumb pad. "You know about the Japanese concept of *wabi-sabi*?
Flawed beauty. The idea that, in accepting the imperfections in
life, you learn to appreciate its real beauty. Pretty cute, no?"

I nodded, touching the little hollow in the surface.

"Thank you," I said, and my chest filled with something bitter-
sweet that made it hard to speak and I thought: *Next time, when I
see her, I'll tell her how truly grateful I am.* To her, for her friendship.
To all of them, in a strange way. For what they had allowed me
to feel.

She didn't point out the piece of paper that was pinned on a cluttered corkboard above a desk in the corner. I had ripped it out of
my journal and given it to her when I'd left her house that Christmas. The ink was faded but there was no mistaking it. My crappy
little pen sketch of her asleep in the greenhouse.

CHAPTER 42

Nino hadn't changed in the slightest. The sight of him strolling down the pier with that same lazy, slanting walk with which he had met us six years ago was so familiar that I felt my eyes prick. As he arrived at the gangplank it struck me that if anything there was less, rather than more, salt and pepper in his thick black hair. *Ah Nino*, I thought, smiling through my blurred vision. *Vanity of vanities. You've been at the dye bottle.*

The years peeled back and I felt so connected to my raw, bruised nineteen-year-old self, so familiar with the sights and smells of the island—the ugly concrete pier, the hills rolling back behind, the slap of waves, and the tang of salt and petrol—that it took me a few moments to register that he didn't know who the hell I was.

"*Signorina*," he said, eyes flicking down to my bare ring finger before moving back up to my face, his smile intensifying. "Welcome. You have been here before, you say."

A few days after I had got back from Georgie's and made my plans, I called on the restaurant's still-scratchy line, braced for another unhelpful response. When Nino came on, sounding grumpy, I was so shocked to hear his voice that I just said that I was a friend of *La Professoressa* who was coming to visit Beccafumo again. No, no, I was arriving alone. Nino had sounded suspicious, like I was angling for a discount on one of his hikes, or perhaps not to pay at all, but he agreed to meet me with a car at the port.

I thought as soon as he saw me he would remember.

But his small dark eyes looked me over with interest, no recognition. "You are not staying long?" he said, offering to take the single piece of hand luggage I was carrying. "A pity, the house is always ready, and no one comes." He glanced at my work blouse and the jacket I had put on that morning. "A little escape from work, is it?"

"Yes." I smiled. "A little escape."

Nino opened the passenger door—different car, a nicer jeep, but he still parked it in the same spot underneath the overhanging bougainvillea. Watch out, he told me, brushing off some petals from the seat, the leather was hot.

The fact that he didn't remember me had caused my world to tilt. Of course, I'd only been there six days, I told myself. Six days, six years ago. He had taken hundreds, maybe thousands, of tourists round the island since then. The fact that those days had been during the most intense two weeks of my life, two weeks of such high definition that everything since had felt like a bad photocopy, meant nothing to him.

Nino was driving down onto the pier to do a turning circle, passing La Sirena, with the same blue tables and chairs out on the terrace, the white walls a little more battered and peeling. *Someone should buy that restaurant*, I thought. *Paint it up fresh, start spreading the word.* I could see it now, tables heaving, spilling over with the life of the island.

"*Il Professore*," said Nino casually, tooting the horn at some brainless seagulls. "He says it is okay for you to stay?"

I stared at him. "You mean *La Professoressa*?"

I had called the island a few times over the first couple of years after Lorna had vanished and always been told the same story, each time allowing another little wave of grief and loss to wash over me. Now for the first time it occurred to me that they could have been covering for her. That perhaps she had been hiding out here from the world for all this time.

"I mean *Professore* Steadman," said Nino abruptly. "I haven't heard from *La Prof* for many, many years. I used to think she saw the island as her real home." He shrugged, his face hard. "But evidently not." He glanced over at me as we climbed up the coastal road. "Please use the seat belt, *signorina*," he said sternly. "The new policeman, he has no idea. He gives fines for everything."

Like Nino, the house was unchanged, eerily so.

As I could see, he told me, unfastening the shutters, he had kept it all in very good order, just as it used to be, many years ago, when *La Prof* had come here. That had been Professore Steadman's instructions when he had last visited. Keep it exactly the same. All the gardening, all the maintenance.

Oh, Steady, I thought. *You are still waiting. I'm so sorry.*

"When was the last time he visited?" I asked, walking round the terrace in something of a trance. There was the hammock that Lorna and I had lain in together, there was the table with the blue and white tiles, where we had eaten lunch on the day of the storm. I felt the thickness in the air that day, the salty smell of the sea in the wind, the threat of the storm coming.

Nino—after a couple of *vediamo*s, eyes heavenward as he counted in his head—told me the year. I nodded numbly. The same one that I had discovered Lorna had disappeared. Steady must have been out there looking for her, too.

Nino was telling me something else now. I registered the defensive tone before I caught the meaning.

Sometimes he, Nino, got caught up here late with some of his hikers. Maybe the weather changed, or someone got tired or pulled a muscle. On these occasions, Nino had allowed them to eat and sleep here: He was sure *Il Professore* would have told him to do the same. But if they had insisted on paying him *un po' di qualcosa* for this, he had always, always, put it straight back into the house account—why, only last week he'd had to order a new water cistern, the other had rusted completely.

"Of course," I murmured, thinking, *So that explains the upgrade of the car.*

Perhaps it also explained Nino's suspicious tone when I had told him that I wanted to visit the house. Perhaps he thought *Il Professore* had sent me over to check up on him because someone in the village was telling tales.

"*Grazie*, Nino," I said, turning to him. "I'm fine now. Here, let me . . ." and I felt in my pockets for some of the euros I had picked up at the airport.

"But you do not have anything to eat," he said, staring.

"I'll be fine until the morning. Really," I said. "I know my way down to the village."

Nino shrugged, looking partly bewildered, partly resigned.

As he turned to go he cocked his head slightly to one side. When was it exactly, he asked, that I had visited the island before?

For a moment I wrestled with a strange desire to tell him everything. He would remember if I told him about the snakebitten German, the rescue in the storm.

"Oh," I said, shaking my head. "A long time ago."

As soon as he'd disappeared down the hill, I did something I'd been thinking about since sitting on the hydrofoil from Sicily, staring out the portholes at the spray over the waterline. I walked straight through the house into Lorna's room.

There it was, still sitting on her yellow dressing table. The little rearing china horse that Alec had described so well. I ran my hands over the pale, delicate china, brushing the dust off its surface and feeling the gold-painted eyes.

Did it mean anything that it was still here?

The story had been Alec's, made up for me near the Old Swan. I wasn't even sure that the horse had meant anything to Lorna. So perhaps it meant nothing that it was still here. Least of all that she would be coming back, one day, to get it.

A sudden cold feeling zipped up the back of my spine. I whipped round, the horse still in my hands. But there was no one there. Just a stripped mattress in an empty room. I sat down on the corner of the bed, my chest aching.

"So, where the fuck are you both?" I whispered out loud.

I slept that night in Lorna's bed, a deliberate act. I expected nightmares. I expected plenty of them. What I hadn't reckoned on were the waking thoughts. The images that had been circling me ever since that moment in the woods when Georgie had told me.

Nino, in the ghost village, the day I had arrived, telling me about the friend of Lorna's who had been bitten by a snake.

Lorna, in the storm, holding the syringe, asking the man who'd been bitten if he had any allergies. *Take your time*, she'd told him. *This is important.*

The reason I had ruled out any chance of Lorna's involvement in Alec's death was that she had been with me when he died on the other side of the world. It was impossible, I'd reasoned: I, myself, was her alibi. How could I have forgotten that line of Christie's that Lorna most liked to quote? *The impossible cannot have happened. Therefore the impossible must be possible in spite of appearances.*

Alec had gone straight from the Old Swan to the island, to be with Lorna. He had been the friend of hers who had been bitten by a snake. The only question was: Had she known that he would have a terrible reaction to the antidote? She had been with him at Georgie's the day he had been unable to ride out with the others.

Lorna had laughed, with Georgie, about the joke he'd made in the visitors book about his allergy. Was it possible she had put it all together? Was it possible that she *hadn't*?

I stared up at the ceiling, asking the question that had sat in my chest since my walk with Georgie.

Had Lorna, as she pushed the needle into Alec—maybe into a vein in one of those hands, those beautiful, restless hands—known very well what could happen? Had she, in that moment, devised the perfect crime, in which the murder weapon was not the poison but the antidote? After all, who was ever convicted for administering a cure?

There was something that made perfect sense about Lorna as the feminist avenger, come to wreak destruction on the man preying on women's weaknesses. And if she *had* meant to . . . how much was planned, how much opportunistic? Perhaps she had even foreseen the possibility of his being bitten—tempted fate, led him barelegged down to the ruins where she knew the snakes roamed, then packed him off on the hydrofoil a few days later, a dead man walking.

And if this was the case, maybe it was *that* she'd been confessing to me that day in her drawing room. Not the affair with Alec and Sybil, but the darker act. Alec, the perfect victim: one whose net effect on the world was negative. Lorna, the perfect killer, the academic who dreamed of breaking the rules.

Or was I just doing what I had always done? Creating a myth out of an ordinary woman.

Because, of course, she *couldn't* have done it. It made no sense, the idea of leading someone out to be bitten by a snake in the wild. And then, once that had been accomplished, just happening to have an antidote on hand to which he was fatally allergic. Moreover, even if Lorna had been wise to his allergy, there was no way that she could have foreseen the rest: the time delay, which would mean that Alec would apparently recover, leave the site of the crime, then travel to a place on the other side of the world where his life was also under threat, thus giving her the perfect alibi. *Nonsense*, I thought. Dangerous nonsense.

And for a few moments then, I thought I could see her—swimming in a cold lake on the edge of a mountain range—the Adirondacks, perhaps, or somewhere greener and softer, New Zealand, maybe. But then the image faded and was replaced by a family house on the edge of some big hot city, where she was lying, reading in a hammock away from the noise, with shorter hair, a different name . . .

What is it about an unsolved mystery, Lorna had once asked us in class, that captures us so, that makes us lean forward, looking for an answer? Is it just the challenge of cracking it ourselves or do we rather hope that it will never be solved? Because in solving something, in pinning it down, in reducing it to one reality, something of the magic is lost. Don't we all hope, even the fiercest realists among us, that there is another answer that transcends our understanding? A heaven above us, after all.

Did Lorna leave us wondering, with no clues left behind, because it made her own self into a myth? Or was it for our sake that she'd left no trace?

Darkness was already melting into dawn when it occurred to me that the reason why answers seemed to keep presenting themselves and then slipping away, disintegrating like Alec's smoke rings, was because of the nature of Lorna herself. For all the certainty she posed in her work—for all the revelations she doled out like drugs in class—there was something unknowable at her center, something that shifted and changed like a trick of the light. Something that Steady understood about her, that had always been vanishing.

That may have wanted to be mythologized and missed. But didn't, in fact, want to be found.

———

The next morning, I went down for a swim in the bay. I missed sunrise. When I woke up the sun was high and strong, the gulls cawing in the air.

I felt the relief of daylight pushing out the horrors of the night. Despite everything, I felt wide awake and fresh. A little buzzing in my veins, like the blood was announcing itself as it ran through every channel.

I was also, I realized, starving. Despite Nino's warning, some foraging in the kitchen turned up a jar of almonds, an only slightly stale loaf of bread, and even an orange, a little past its prime. (*Exactly how often do you stay the night, Nino?*)

I ate my little picnic on the wall of the terrace, trying to ignore the fermented taste of the orange, and then, tucking a bath towel under one arm, made my way down to the bay. The outlines of the rocks and bushes were so crisp and defined they hurt my eyes.

It was a little later in the year than the time I had come out with Lorna. Although the sun felt hotter, the sea seemed just as cold. I spread my towel out on a flat rock and undressed, watching the light jitter on the barely crumpled surface of the sea.

I must have managed fifteen minutes in the water, my limbs pumping to try to fend off the icy cold, before I gave in to it and swam more slowly. After this, I thought, I'd walk round the coastline to La Sirena and order myself a giant lunch. I could imagine renting a little boat, staying a few more days. *Perhaps even longer,* I thought with a smile.

I pulled myself back out of the water and, rubbing myself with the towel, lay down on the rock, wrapped up but still shivering.

Looking up at the high blue sky, I remembered a chilly day near the beginning of spring term. End of January, perhaps. We were all walking along the towpath that ran by the canal on campus. Georgie, Nick, and I were chatting, and at some point I turned to see that Alec and Lorna had fallen a little way behind us. They had paused to argue some point. She was berating him for lazy thinking, and he was shaking his head: But how do you know that, how do you *know*? One of them was testing the other, but now I can't remember which, just the sight of the two of them, their gazes fierce and bright, their breath smoke in the air.

And it occurred to me that, over the years, my feelings about Alec and Lorna had seeped into each other. Because when I remember them now, it is the same white-hot feeling. Not the twisted way that he—and perhaps she—ended up channeling it. But the searing focus and attention they both turned on things, cracking them open, boring down into a core most people don't know exists.

And always the same note in their vibrating, restless souls. An agitation that rises in me still as I go about my daily life.

That voice whispering in my ear: "This is the moment. Go. Grab it. *Now*."

ACKNOWLEDGMENTS

If you take as long as I did to finish a book, chances are there'll be an embarrassing number of people to thank along the way—both for helping me with my writing, but also for the longer, more important stretches in between.

First, to my extraordinary agent, Claire Paterson, for her confidence, support, and stamina in getting me across the line. To everyone else at the Janklow and Nesbit offices, including Allison Hunter for her brilliant work across the pond. To my smart and intuitive editors, Alexis Kirschbaum at Bloomsbury and Helen Richard at Putnam Penguin, who guided me to find more depth, mileage, and shine in my writing. I feel like I hit the jackpot with you both, as well as your incredible teams.

Thanks for more writing help along the way: in particular, Maggie Hamand and her teachers at the Complete Creative Writing course, who helped me better my craft and find that crucial rhythm needed to finish a draft; the inspiring Charlotte Mendelson, who taught me that the most important thing about writing fiction is to "put the pen in the vein"; Nicholas Casewell at the Alistair Reid Venom Unit, who was incredibly generous with his time, intelligence, and imagination; and the late Lorna Sage, who lit up my world during my master's degree at UEA, and inspired the lighter shades of the Lorna in my book.

If writing a novel is like giving birth, my sister Samantha has been its surrogate mother: From its conception on our walking holiday in Filicudi, and through the several drafts I then crawled through, she has been unconditional in her willingness to help me develop the plot, edit scenes, and pretend she wasn't bored when she had to do it all over again for the seventh time: I'm not sure there are enough jumpers in the world with which to thank you. My other sister, Joanna, also a talented and generous reader but, most important, a true emotional ballast, without whom I would probably still be driving around some ring road somewhere, having left my phone in the fridge and with no idea what day it is. For the rest of my family—Dad, Noush, and Jonathan—for keeping the faith. For Xanthe, who steadied the world for me, and Berenice, who taught me to make sense of it.

Thank you to my best friends and writing companions Lucinda and Eva, and Christianne, who always makes it feel like we are still in Rome. Free cocktails for my favorite people who turn up in their dancing shoes every year and make slightly too-short speeches: Zumbs, Sasha, Alice BB, Jonny and Julianne, Ed Havard, Ed Haddon, Mark, Rob, Benji, Jo and Rupert, Louiza and Jonny, Apples and Daniel, Mel and Ben, Ads, Tim and Dixie, Frank and Saba (in absentia). Also thanks to Ellie and Alex, my much-too-bright and special cousins for all their help, humor, and insight with later drafts. To Tods and Debs for writing solidarity, Angela and Michael for their love and encouragement. And Gaia, who let me write in Podere I Troscioni, my favorite place in the world.

A giant, neon-lit thank-you to Emma Freud, who plucked me out of writing in cafés wearing my earplugs and gave me a Room of My Own. To Ben, who makes it slightly less of a Room of My Own, but much better for it. And Natalia, who made the last two years of balancing motherhood and writing fun, as well as possible.

Most of all, thank you to Samuel and Elsie, who managed to be both patient and excited for me when I kept "finishing my book":

writing a novel always seemed like the most important thing to do with my life before you were born. Now I know better.

When I met James, he pretended he needed some help with the book he was writing. We went for several lunches that I thought were meetings, he thought were dates. Twelve years later, I often pretend that I am helping him still. But in truth, in all that he does—husband, editor, father, adventurer, champion, friend—he's the one who turns the world for me.